The Ancestral Arts
of
Sophie Wölf

BERNARD M LYONS

E Book ISBN: 978-0-6459435-0-4
Print ISBN: 978-0-6459435-1-1
First Published in 2023.
First Edition 2023.
Second Edition 2023.
Third Edition November 2023
Version 1:0.
Assassinus Publishing Pty Ltd
Developmental editor: Amy Allworden/ Proofreader: Belle
Manuel / Beta Readers: Eloise L, Emilie Knight, Bailee Taylor,
Jada Davis, Jessica Posey, Stephanie H

Contact the author at BernardMLyons@gmail.com

For Margaret Lyons

Chapter 1—Talented Ancestors

On the downside, having your dreams recorded by some machine in a *university experiment* sounded vaguely dangerous. On the upside… it paid $50.

Sophie felt an odd conflicting mix of nervousness and importance. There was that little buzz that floated around in the top of her chest she got when she was excited. Fifty dollars was better money than her Café shifts paid.

Sophie glanced up from the book she was reading, as they drove through the old town streets, on the way to her papa's work. Her papa worked at the Otto-Friedrich-Universität Bamberg, or more simply, *the University of Bamberg*. She thought about what books she could now buy… thinking about book purchases was always a good distraction.

The whole experiment was strange. For starters, she wasn't allowed to tell anyone about it, she had already signed some serious legal papers. The whole thing sounded weird. The idea of getting her dreams recorded on some computer that would allow them to be watched back again later… Sophie thought about it, but just couldn't imagine how it would all work.

From what her papa told her, the whole dream recording thing was a huge deal. He had said that she would be one of the first, and the actual dream *could* end up being shown to important professors around the world. Stressful.

Her papa's old Fiat 500 (Sophie called it cute; her papa didn't like that) turned into the University entrance and stopped before a white and red boom gate.

"Oh, damn," Ernst said, fumbling around for his ID card. Sophie peered into her papa's wallet, overfull with every business card her dad had been given in ten years, including a long since unusable video hire rental card.

"I appear to have...misplaced my identification." He hit the buzzer next to the boom gate to speak to the guard. Sophie watched her dad fumbling for his ID. She leaned over to get her head closer to the speaker.

"Papa has misplaced his identification. Can you wait?"

"Yes," the guard's voice screeched out of the speaker.

There was silence. Sophie always felt awkward when there was silence. Speaking to a disembodied voice coming out of a metal box didn't make it easier. She had a compulsion to speak anyway, even if there was no need to.

"Ah... are you having a nice day?" Sophie asked.

"Yes." The metal box grated.

Thirty seconds went by, and Sophie felt the compulsion to fill the silence "My papa is still trying to find his identification."

"Yes." The metal box repeated.

Silence. Ernst kept searching for the card, clearly flustered.

"Errrh...do you like working as a guard?" Sophie asked, more nervous conversation.

"Yes."

"Errrh." Sophie couldn't think of anything to say. The guard was silent. Awkward.

"Do you actually guard things, or do you just mainly... sit in an office?"

The metal box didn't respond.

"My papa does work here. I mean, he's not trying to sneak in. I mean, why would you..."

"Card located!" Ernst said, waving the card victoriously in the air, then peering over at Sophie.

"You can stop talking now," Ernst said, giving her an understanding nod.

"I wasn't talking," croaked the voice from the speaker box.

"Oh no, not you, sorry... I meant my daughter." He glanced at Sophie and smiled.

"Here's the card." He held it in front of the security camera. "Ernst Wölf. History Professor."

The gate raised. The car rolled forward, and two of Sophie's books fell off the dashboard. Ernst glanced at his daughter, giving her a playful stern face. They both started laughing. Sophie smiled. He was a bit hopeless, but she loved her papa.

Sophie snuggled back down into the comfy leather car seat, warming her hands near the hot air pumping out of the car's heater. She continued reading the tattered copy of *Wuthering Heights* she had picked up cheap online, every minute passing meant she was a few more pages into the exciting parts. People said she had unusual book reading habits for a fifteen-year-old, nineteenth century romance and modern fantasy. She put the book down, and wondered... When the experiment started, what if she did something embarrassing in her dreams, and it was recorded, and then shown all around the world as one of the first ever recorded dreams?

She just imagined the King of Bavaria watching recordings of her dreams, in a room full of his top scientists... What if she was doing something completely banal in her dream? What if she was picking her nose? What if she was doing something boring, like putting out the washing or fixing up her hair? All the kids at school would laugh at her. Maybe a video of a dream of her doing something embarrassing would go viral on the internet.

She concentrated, trying to think of cool stuff to do in her dreams. Surfing would be cool. Winning a martial arts tournament. Though she didn't do martial arts. Or surf.

Ernst's little car pulled up in his car spot, taking up about half the space. Sophie shifted the plastic bookmark onto the page she was at, the bright red tassel dangling out of the top of her book as she put it into her bag.

"Ok...Soph...are you nervous?" Ernst peered down over the top of his black square framed glasses, brushing his long hair away from his glasses. It was the same dark hair that Sophie had, except for her prominent red stripe. Her hair was her papa's, her pale skin her mother's.

"Nah, Papa," she lied. "Well...I have a certain level of...apprehension."

"Sophie, you've got nothing to be apprehensive about. Professor Marcus is a colleague of mine, and highly respected at the university."

"That's okay for you to say. You're not possibly going to have footage of yourself picking your nose shown to the whole world."

Ernst studied her for a moment, smiled and rustled her hair. At least *he* didn't appear worried about it, which was reassuring.

Together, they weaved their way through the archaic red brick buildings. She was glad he was with her, this older part of the University was a rabbit warren of little rooms and stairwells, some of which dated back to the 1600s. Sophie went to turn the wrong way, then corrected herself before Ernst noticed. It was easy to get lost in the corridors.

Almost like a colour coded diagram, the different eras of the university were exhibited by the different coloured layers. Yellowish sandstone, scarlet-red brick, and shiny silver glass and steel for the new buildings.

Sophie breathed in the cold air, zipped up her jacket, and walked up the stairs of the shiny new building, the blue hue of the glass reflecting the buildings around like a hall of mirrors. Through two sliding glass doors. Then into a waiting area.

Sophie initially thought no one was there, but then saw an older man sitting down, with grey hair and a goatee, a grey suit, a woolen vest, and a red *bow tie*. She remembered her papa had said people who wore bow ties were either really smart or wanted to appear like they were.

He stood up and introduced himself.

"Hello again, Ernst, thanks for coming."

"Marcus, hello!" Ernst hollered, shaking the professor's hand vigorously. "Marcus, this is my daughter Sophie. Sophie, this is Professor Marcus."

The professor shook Sophie's hand. Papa was happy. *Okay for him… he wasn't about to be an experimental test subject.*

Sophie took her mind off it and started a little mantra, repeating the same words in her mind: *Think of the $50. Think of the $50. More Books. More Books.*

"Hello, Sophie." Marcus had a faint German accent, not unlike Ernst's.

"You're fourteen, yes?" He scribbled some notes on a clipboard and then put it down.

"Fifteen," she corrected.

"We're going to see if we can record your dreams and play them back for us to observe them. We'll need to do this over a few sessions. Does that sound fun?"

"Not really," Sophie answered, then noticed her dad giving her *that look*.

Marcus clearly didn't expect the response and paused. "Well, I think you will find it *very* interesting."

Two assistants in lab coats, one a chubby Asian man with a long ponytail, the other a short girl with blonde hair and glasses appeared. The man with the ponytail was Henry, and the blonde girl, who was quiet, introduced herself in a soft voice as Frida.

Sophie laid down on the soft black leather sofa, the leather scrunching as she settled into it to get comfortable, while Professor Marcus handed her a headset. Glancing at it, it appeared pretty much like normal black headphones, two earpieces with a black band across the top. The main obvious difference was that it had a black visor that you couldn't see through.

"Let me explain quickly, nothing that happens here will hurt you, it's all completely harmless. You'll go to sleep for thirty minutes or so, and then we will wake you up, or you may wake up earlier. There'll be no permanent effects, and we've been doing this for some time now with no problems. You okay with all this?"

Marcus's reassuring checklist only started to make Sophie think of what could go wrong. "Yes, sounds fine Professor."

"Okay, after I put these on, you will drift off," Marcus nodded.

Sophie realised her nervousness had disappeared, replaced by a little feeling of excitement in her chest.

She squelched down into the black leather of the long sofa, the sofa squeaking as she did. It was a little cold, but soft and comfortable. The sofa was relaxing at least. She wondered how long it would take her to fall asleep.

Professor Marcus put the headset on her, adjusting it slightly. She stared into the black visor in front of her eyes. She could hear a slight humming sound, and very quickly, she felt herself being tugged into a deep slumber. As she drifted off, she heard the Professor say:

"Go to the house on the hill. Ask to be an apprentice."

Then Sophie woke up.

No.

She hadn't woken up.

She *knew* it was a dream, but otherwise she felt like it was quite real, and that she was awake. She scanned her surroundings.

She was in a traditional style house… old. Medieval old… it was so real, she wondered if she had been relocated to another location after she had fallen asleep with the headset on.

The room had ornate timber carvings in the dark oak beams supports, contrasting the walls of white plaster. Two large rich tapestries of court scenes covered the walls.

Sophie glanced down at what she wore. Medieval version of pajamas, an ugly off-white nightgown. She ran her hand down the material, it was rough cotton. As she took in the surroundings around her, she was filled with a sense of wonder.

It was incredible.

Next to her, on a wooden bench, on two chairs were two sets of clothes. There was a shirt with some hose, and a beautiful, blue dress of the style worn at the time. She hopped out of bed, and picked up the dress, bringing it close to her eyes. It appeared hand sewn.

Popping her head around the door to investigate the main room, she could see no one was there. There was some wonderful old furniture, and some period clothes in a chest.

Sophie stared at the dress; pretty, but not practical. She went to get changed, but then remembered the dream was being recorded. Closing her eyes, in the hope that would stop the dream recording her getting undressed, she awkwardly put on the woolen tights and a shirt, almost falling over. Gazing around, there were some old-fashioned styled kitchen implements. It was like she had stepped into a medieval era movie set.

Sophie inspected the shuttered windows, pushing them open after unlatching the ornate brass latch. Cautiously, she peeked out, not quite knowing what to expect. She was immediately grasped by the vision of what she saw, it completely grabbed her attention in a vice-like grip. All she could do was just stare.

A cold, clear fresh air hit her face, and she took in a deep breath. Clearly, she was in the top story of an old house and had a marvelous view of a 500-year-old town. It was like her hometown of Bamberg, but without any modernity, at all. No electric cables, no cars, no mobile towers. Odd shaped little chimneys stuck out of the brightly coloured houses, with smoke curling up from each. There was an obvious hill off to the west, a house on it in the distance, located strangely apart from the town. The overall vista took her breath away.

Sophie stood there, trying to take it all in. If she squinted her eyes, it was almost like the spectacular images on incredibly expensive high-definition televisions she had seen in some shops. Except, it appeared completely real.

Peering down at the street below, she could see a smattering of medieval dressed people. Just like some of the old perfectly preserved pretty little German villages she had adored on tourist trips with her papa.

She breathed in the air. It was fresh and clear, like you got in the mountains.

Normally, this would have surprised her. However, Sophie realised she felt quite comfortable about all this, like *she was supposed to be here.*

Sophie went cautiously down the stairs, through the bottom room, and then stepped out into the street. Opening the door, she walked out onto an amazing, lovely village street, with cobblestones, lovely medieval shuttered houses, people bustling about, all wearing medieval clothes. It was a sunny day, a warm breeze hit her cheeks, and she rolled up her sleeves a little. The town was quiet, more so than modern Bamberg, as people happily went about their business. She walked past a little tinker's wagon, with pots and pans on display, the tinker stood in front of it, clearly ready to pounce on anyone walking within five metres of it.

"Good morning to you, young sir. A pot or pan for your mother to cook with? Your mother would love one of these." The tinker waved a pot in front of her.

"I don't have a mother," She uttered.

The tinker went quiet, squinting at Sophie, as she sped up, scurrying past him.

It suddenly dawned on her; Sophie realised he had assumed she was a boy! With short hair, and not wearing a dress…she must appear like a boy to them.

The village was small, smaller than Bamberg. There was nothing she recognised. She guessed there were about thirty houses; they were beautiful, each one was painted a different colour… blue, yellow, green. Thin columns of smoke arose, grey twists rising and eventually blending into the sky. They came from red and brown brick chimneys, jutting out of dull grey/brown thatched roofs. Brooms, barrels, firewood, and various things were piled out the front of each house, but everything was neat and tidy. And colourful. Apart from the tinker, there were a few people wandering up and down the street. A man struggling to carry a wooden box, a couple walking slowly, chatting. An old man slowly led a horse with a rope bridle.

No one paid her any attention.

She studied it all, the tinker, the people, the buildings. Her head swiveled this way, and that, eager to take it all in. An element of awe crept over her, but she was comfortable, not frightened.

Sophie stood gazing at it all in wonder for a while, not quite sure what to do. She then thought about what someone...Marcus? had said as she was drifting off. About *going to the House on the hill.* She then remembered she had seen one obvious hill from the window of the house she had woken up in. Still taking in the sights, she reached up to touch a lantern on a house, running her hand down the plastered wall and feeling the rough texture. Her roaming gaze caught sight of a beautiful building in the distance.

This must be the house, she thought.

She left the village and headed in that direction. Walking down a dirty road, which turned into a dirt path, ambling up to the lone house.

She took a deep breath, letting the chill air beset with a hint of pine fill her lungs, and slowly headed in that direction.

As she headed towards it, she realised that the house on the hill was big. It was like it was built to face off against the village. Its size screamed out that it was important, or whoever lived there was. It immediately made her wonder who lived in it.

The instruction stuck in her mind. *But...how did Marcus know what was going to be in her dream?*

The only thing she knew about this place was that she had to go to the house, so she reluctantly kept walking. When she finally got there, she slowly knocked on the door.

The door opened, and a man answered. The man was dressed in a white loose shirt, a red vest, and red/brown woolen hose and he held a dark grey floppy woolen hat, a feather stuck in it. Sophie thought he was handsome, with big blue eyes, a tanned face, and copper hair. His chin was finished with a red-brown beard neatly trimmed into two points, sticking down. He tilted his head so that the points of his beard both thrust forward towards Sophie almost like little hairy daggers.

The ornate, carved door opened wide, and he stood in the middle of the door frame. Whilst raising an eyebrow, he studied his visitor, up and down. The muffled noise of dogs barking and the high pitch of a pig squealing loudly came from *within* the house.

"Good day to you, young gentlewoman. Can I help you?"

Sophie gazed momentarily at the twin pointed beard, then realised she was staring. Did a twin pointed beard make some sort of statement? Was it like...*medieval punk?*

She quickly realized what an odd situation it was. All she knew was that as she was dozing off, someone had said to ask for lessons... or an apprenticeship... or something. She really had no idea what she was doing here.

Sophie considered her situation. She was in a dream, instructed to go to a particular house. Why? What was the point of all of this? Then again, she considered the money she was getting paid, for basically sleeping. In any case, it was only a dream after all, what could go wrong?

So, she improvised.

"Um...hello... I've come here for lessons," Sophie said.

"Have you?" The man assessed her, frowning. "Are you from the village?"

"No." Sophie shook her head slightly.

"Okay, well, that's a good start. Come back later." He made a vague sort of sound that was a cross between a laugh and a scoff and closed the door.

Sophie squinted at the closed door, her teeth grating. She wondered if he would get angry at her for knocking again... then reminded herself it was *her* dream. She knocked on the door once more.

The man answered, casually eating an apple.

"Errhh... hello, again. You're still here."

"Yes... and what do you mean come back later? I'm here to speak to you about an apprenticeship... I think. I have no idea what in though," Sophie said, getting slightly terse.

He closed the door in her face.

Again, she knocked. The door opened.

"You again." The man studied her, now taking more note.

"Yes. Clearly you have some sort of issue with making people wait or testing them. I guess you see it as funny, or it's part of a character test. I don't know. But I want to talk to you. I'd like to talk to you about lessons, or an apprenticeship or both," Sophie said.

The man's head and shoulders shifted back from Sophie. As he was assessing her, his teeth loudly gnashed through an apple. He swallowed and coughed to clear his throat.

"Lessons, apprenticeship. Well, what exactly do you want the lessons to cover?"

It was improvisation time; some flattery may help.

"I don't know. The main thing is... I heard you are the best at what you do in your profession, and many people have told me to come here for an apprenticeship. I've heard you are honest and treat your apprentices well. You sound like the ideal teacher." The fast talk felt like it might actually work. She was getting curious now, and hunched her shoulders, slightly frustrated.

Talking him up, and being creative couldn't hurt the situation, but now she wasn't sure what would happen if she *didn't* get an apprenticeship. The experiment seemed to depend on it. Sophie reminded herself, this was only a dream. If she didn't get it, fine.

The man raised an eyebrow.

"Where are you from, lad?"

"Bamberg. And I'm not a lad. Have they invented glasses yet? If they have, you need to be an early adopter," she replied quickly, but caught herself before finishing her little attack off with an eye roll. She then considered if medieval people even knew what an eyeroll was.

He stared at her oddly for a second.

"Bamberg? Never heard of it. So, you want an apprenticeship then lad?"

Sophie went to correct him again about being a girl and thought it may be best to just leave it.

"Yes, please." An apprenticeship? She had come this far, and she was starting to get curious as to what he did. What was he teaching? His house was nice, but the whole place resembled a farmhouse. She wasn't interested in learning farm skills. Sophie started to wonder what it was he did, he didn't appear to be a full-time farmer.

"Well... for starters, sweep the floor, get the eggs from the chickens, and bring in the wood from outside." He thought for a second. "Midday. You can make my lunch, clean up the yard, and tend to the animals. If you do that well, we'll see."

He handed her a broom, a very old one, with bristles made from twigs.

"Am I flying this somewhere?"

His gaze met hers, then he pointed to the floor, and made a sweeping motion. Sophie went outside and wondered what witch was missing a broom. She swept. She then found where the chickens were and got the eggs. Then brought in the wood.

When she finally came in, the man was sitting on a chair in the middle of the room. Sophie stopped abruptly, as her eyes focused on what she saw, her brain trying to make sense of it.

Five apples were floating in mid-air, slowly moving in a circle. Floating in the middle of the circle of apples was a small fire. Sophie froze, just staring.

It was magic.

No one had done real magic in the German states for decades; she'd seen videos of people doing magic in the war. Seeing it in her dream shocked her. Instead of her normal nervous talking, her mouth opened slightly, silently agape.

"My name is…" He hesitated. "Well, that doesn't matter for the moment. By the way, you'll be my apprentice. I need an apprentice, and you have the essential quality; you're not one of the annoying villagers. Plus, the red stripe is outstanding. I will teach you to do… this…" His hand swished through the air at the floating apples, flamboyantly.

"…come back here at noon, tomorrow."

Chapter 2 - The Harlan Experience

When she woke up, her papa had left. Professor Marcus drilled her with questions, interested in every detail. He took copious notes, writing everything down in an old navy-blue notebook with "Sophie" scrawled on the front with big black marker. The book was full of different coloured post it notes, sticking out at the side, with more colours than a tropical bird. Sophie noted he used different coloured pen notations, which made the book resemble children's homework more so than scientific note taking.

She wasn't quite sure what to think about someone having a notebook all about *her.*

Sophie wondered why he had to take notes, when he just could have watched her dream recording, but decided against raising it. Plus, she was getting paid by the hour, the longer anything took, the better.

"You have a whole book on me, and we've only just met. Is that acceptable?" Sophie said.

Marcus blushed a touch, looking at the ground momentarily.

"Well, it's a complex process, and I... we need to plan out the whole thing. The dreamcast sessions take a lot of computations," he said, slightly quickly, Sophie noted unsteadiness in his voice.

Marcus was clearly keen to hear about the dream, Sophie mentioned that she was supposed to go back to the man in the dream there at midday tomorrow. Her papa had implied there was going to be a few sessions, but she wasn't sure how often they happened. The professor glanced at her, and went quiet, his face frozen momentarily in thought. He then asked her to return during school lunchtime tomorrow.

Sophie put the few odd occurrences to the back of her mind and let herself be happy about the situation. She would have more money to go into her largely empty bank account, which meant more books. She thought about a reprint of Wuthering Heights, her favourite nineteenth century romance novel, and a new Brandon Sanderson fantasy series that was coming out. She then thought of her room and realised she needed another bookshelf.

She had so many questions, so many thoughts about the whole process. The whole thing was very exciting.

But... the floating apples. The memory of them still stunned her.

Was the apprenticeship for magic tricks? As far as she knew, with all the negative history of the summoners, and the other mages, there were very few people in the world that could still do serious *actual* magic. Well, at a high level. Some countries even had laws banning magic. Some of the German countries who were generally pretty laidback and not strict *generally*... had laws about magic. So, if there were any mages that could still do high level magic, they kept it to themselves for their own safety. She'd never seen anyone do a spell, that is never seen anyone do *proper* magic.

Sophie started to think about the whole process while it was just a dream, the way Marcus spoke about the apprenticeship ... How could she learn from someone in her dreams? Can you do that? Was there more to be learnt? Sophie sat thinking about the concept.

But the dream was so uncannily real. She imagined, what if she could learn magic? She could help people, protect Bamberg if needed, maybe help her papa somehow. Her thoughts ran away as she started to think of all the possibilities. Images played through her mind, forming a little movie of grand adventures, with her as the heroic star.

Lately Sophie had thought about her life and had been feeling down about a lack of direction. She didn't have a significant hobby, apart from reading, and had no idea what sort of job she was going to do, or what she would study at university.

Constant questioning from her papa about what she would study at university, but she was scared to tell him she wasn't even sure if she wanted to go. A fantasy of thought struck her, could being a great mage be... *her thing?*

She then thought of the anger and fear people had of mages. Could that hurt her papa and Hisako? She felt a knot of apprehension well up in her chest...just for a moment, it quickly disappeared like melting ice and took the fear with it. If she could learn magic, this was an opportunity to bring magic back to the world. An unbelievable rare opportunity that no one else had, not in decades. And it was hers. Maybe?

Sophie shook her head and realised she was getting carried away. It was a dream. Of course. You can't learn anything new from a dream because your brain creates the dream. Your brain only knows what you already know.

Ernst had now gone to work, Sophie left Marcus's office, to head out to the tram stop. Leaving the building, she immediately pulled her jacket collar up tight around her neck, trying to keep warm in the brisk Bamberg chill. It was a ten-minute walk to the tram stop to go to school. On the way out of the University, she saw something that gave her a big smile.

It was a white Honda scooter, with a white sticker. *"I Heart Jazz"* stuck on it.

She could have picked it out of 100 white scooters. It belonged to her school buddy, Harlan Lupin. She hadn't seen it here before. Odd.

***

The old retro 1960's tram rattled along its rails through the town. Slowly. Sophie would have usually allocated the twelve minutes to reading, but instead, stared vacantly out the window. But this day, the daily pattern was broken. Her mind drifted off with thoughts of the mysterious dreamscape mage, Medieval towns, long colourful dresses and floppy hats.

Her recollection of it was clear, exactly like a normal memory, rather than the vague way she remembered dreams. Normally, Sophie couldn't remember her dreams that well, or at best, parts of them. But with this... she could smell the smells, remember the feel of the cold brass window latch on her fingers. However, she had felt safe...and the whole experience was so intriguing. She had this compulsion to really want to go back. Straight away.

The floating apples stuck in her mind. They reminded her of an anime she had been watching. Maybe she was watching *too much* anime.

The little tram stopped near her school, *St Ignatius, International School for Seniors*. It was a sort of big white box of a School with little square blue framed windows. An old building from the 1950s, it was one of two schools in Bamberg. Bamberg was generally so old, with much of it appearing like it was straight out of the Middle Ages; 1950s buildings were practically new in comparison.

There were a few students milling around the black ornate metal gates, like bees busy around the entrance to a hive, excitedly chatting to each other, buzzing from group to group. Then the students headed in as class was starting. Having been to a few different schools because her papa's job required moving, so far, this was her favorite school. It was not just the school, but the students. Sophie *actually liked* coming to this school.

As an international school, many of the students were from different countries. It was like a little United Nations for kids. Talking to the different students and hearing about their backgrounds was almost like having a collection of embassies sharing the same courtyard. She had Harlan and some other good buddies here.

She, of course, was just happy to be at a school where she didn't have to relocate and once again make new friends. Well, she *hoped* she didn't have to. She hoped she didn't hear another apologetic announcement from her papa. *"Sophie, I'm sorry, I have a new job and we have to move…again."*

The rest of the morning was pretty much ruined for study. Sophie's mind wandered off to the medieval setting she had just encountered, thinking about the town, the boys, the man with the floating apples. She realised she didn't even know his name. Then, with a shock she realised half the class had gone by without her paying attention: the whiteboard was full of mathematical formulas she didn't understand. She started scribbling "mysterious formula" into her notebook. She could YouTube it later or ask Harlan.

The class finished and Sophie had a free session, so she headed off to the library to prepare for her next class, more maths. Entering the quiet and almost empty library, she was just sitting down in her seat when she saw Harlan walking in, with a slight swagger. He plonked down in the seat next to her and gave her a slow-motion punch to her shoulder.

Harlan was a tall boy from the United States. His long brown hair sat on his shoulders, he had dark blue eyes, was a year older than her, and wore black denim. He once made the mistake of wearing cowboy boots, predictably, everyone called him cowboy. He hated it, and never wore the boots ever again.

Harlan was from a farming and rural part of the US, and while there were other Americans in the school, both his accent and his height in a school in Bavaria, sort of made him a novelty.

He was a generally carefree easy-going guy, which was why Sophie got on well with him. Though at times lately he was preoccupied with some family issues he wouldn't talk about. In any case, Sophie always felt comfortable and at ease around him. He was always there to listen to her, and... she for him. They had been best friends for four years or so. Another reason why she hoped she didn't have to change schools with her papa's job.

Harlan flopped down on the chair.

"Hey, Soph, how you doing?" He playfully whacked her on the arm.

"Hey, Harls." Sophie playfully whacked him back on the shoulder, trying to hit him slightly harder so she could get the upper hand. He was a tiny bit taken aback at her hitting him with a little force. "How was your weekend?"

"Oh yeah. Had a big chat with my dad. Working out some family stuff. Things I gotta do while I'm over here."

"What *you* been doing lately?" He gave her a curious expression. Did he know she had done a dreamscape session? She wasn't allowed to talk about it, so dodged the question.

"Oh, you know, *Wuthering Heights*," Sophie responded, knowing Harlan had little knowledge and even less interest in nineteenth century literature.

"Ah." He nodded. "That old song." He pursed his lips like he was considering something and then pulled a book out of his bag and handed it to her.

"Well... er... this is that book you asked for. Helpful?" He gave her a rare, serious face. Odd, she thought, she hadn't asked for a book.

"Thanks, Harls, er..." She took the book, confused. "Thanks."

Sophie examined the book, *Dreams and interpreting them by A J Mittinksy*. She glanced at Harlan, and then at the book again.

Harlan nodded, winked... and quickly left.

She spent the rest of the afternoon *completely* distracted. Clearly Harlan had given her the book to show her he knew about the dreamscape sessions. Possibly he was there doing it as well and may have seen *her* when she saw *his* scooter. The fact he didn't want to talk about it directly gave her food for thought.

***

Next day, Sophie went to school, making progress on her old tattered copy of *Wuthering Heights* on the tram. However, it was hard to concentrate on the adventures of Heathcliff and Cathy; all she could think about was the dreamscape. She wanted to catch up with Harlan, but her class with him wasn't until the afternoon. Constantly glancing at the clock on the wall, time progressed ever so slowly. Painfully.

It was lunchtime, and she had to restrain herself from physically running through the school to catch the tram to the university. It was still cold, but the heating on the old tram was working quite well, and she got a seat up the front where it emanated warmth. The tram trundled along the street. Sophie vaguely peered out the window but was mostly thinking about her upcoming second session of the dreamscape. That excited feeling inside that had been a knot of nerves two days ago, was now an excited energy spreading through her body.

Once again, she hopped off the tram with a few of the university students, to go back to Professor Marcus for the midday "dreamcast" sessions, as he called them.

Walking into the Professor's office, she noticed Henry standing there, constantly adjusting his weight from one foot to another like he was uncomfortable and pulled his collar to loosen it. Frida was also there, fidgeting, before putting her hands behind her back. They both held notepads, and Henry a laptop.

"Hello, Henry. Hello, Frida. You both seem odd and a little nervous."

They both mumbled a barely audible "hello" and shuffled themselves quickly out of the office.

Turning the corner to where the sofa was, and expecting to see Professor Marcus, she was instead confronted by two tall, burly men in suits, standing each to the side of it.

Sophie took a deep breath and froze.

"Hello, Sophie, we're from the police. We'd like a word with you if we could. Please, sit down."

Chapter 3 - MI 21

Sophie glanced at the men, judged the distance to the door, and realised she could have sprinted out before they got her. She fought the panicky urge to run out of the door and rationalised the situation… she'd done nothing wrong. In fact, part of her was curious about what they wanted. Glancing at the seat they had been pointing at, she sat down, still slightly nervous.

"You two both have cheap matching suits. Am I going to be arrested?" Sophie said.

"Sophie—" The taller man, with a short beard raised his voice slightly. "…okay… please, you're not going to be arrested."

The other man was shorter, however stocky, and bald, with a particular blank expression. Clearly unimpressed with Sophie's comment, he glanced at his suit, reassessing it.

The two men went to grab two chairs themselves. Their matching dark suits, similar business shirts and no ties, made them an odd pair. Slightly menacing police twins.

At this point, a third decidedly more interesting man entered the room, from the back office. Sophie was taken aback. Visually, he was very different to the other men. The way he walked gave him an air of importance, though the two other men didn't particularly regard him as such. In contrast to the other two, he was wearing a fitted pinstripe black suit, dark purple tie, vest, and dark floppy hair, short at the sides and a moustache. He reached over for a stool that one of the men was going to sit on. Sophie was impressed by his suit and struggled against the compulsion to tell him so.

"Oh, can I?" he grabbed the stool from one of the initial two men before he could sit on it, and sat behind them. The bald man grunted, scanned the room, and sat in the chair with a back and arms. The two men in the identical black suits then both leaned forward. Sophie glanced at them, they appeared slightly serious, but not particularly threatening.

The bearded man spoke.

"Sophie, my name is Hans, and this is Heinrich." Sophie peered at the third man expecting an introduction for him. It didn't happen. He sat watching intently.

Hans continued, "We'd like to ask you some questions about Professor Marcus. He's disappeared." Hans spoke in perfect British English, while Heinrich sat listening.

Hang on. Marcus…disappeared…no more dreamscaping? Suddenly Sophie's heart sank. She was aware of this sudden rush of heat up the nape of neck…it always did that when she was going to be in trouble. She involuntarily shifted back in her seat.

"What do you mean… disappeared? I was enjoying all the…er, *things,*" Sophie said.

"SLEEP!!!"

The word surprised her. She stared at the man in the pinstripe suit who had just shouted it out. Then at the two burly men. They dramatically closed their eyes and slowly, their heads slumped forward onto their chests.

Suddenly, the pinstriped suit man behind them with the floppy hair had jumped forward and grabbed both the men by the shoulders to stop them from falling off their chairs. It happened quickly, Hans and Heinrich were now asleep… the pinstripe suit man adjusting one, then the other, so they didn't fall out onto the floor. He stood up and offered a very polite handshake to Sophie.

"Rupert. Pleased to meet you," he said pleasantly, his accent was hard to place, it seemed to be an obvious formal old world British accent… *with a touch of German?* He pulled up his stool, so it was closer to her.

"We *very much* need to talk."

Chapter 4 Rupert

"I'm Rupert Morton-Smythe... Her Majesty's Mage." He handed a card to Sophie.

```
┌─────────────────────────────────────────────────┐
│                 By appointment                    │
│                                                   │
│                                                   │
│   Rupert Morton-Smythe MBE                        │
│   Royal Mage to HRH Queen Elizabeth II            │
│                                                   │
│                                                   │
│           Phone 0414 567 34567                    │
│           email: RoyalM@HRHOffice.Gov.uk          │
└─────────────────────────────────────────────────┘
```

Sophie jumped back from him, her hand involuntarily going to cover her mouth.

He had made the men sleep but seeing the word *mage* actually on the card shocked her.

"You're a mage," she whispered.

Most people's reactions to a real mage was fear. They immediately thought of the *summoners*, conjuring up huge demons from who knows where, like the ones that were used to destroy cities in the war in England back seventy years.

Summoners...summon. Even though normal mages couldn't summon a cup of tea, let alone giant demons, many people just fear all mages, unless on the rare occasion, they had one in the family.

It struck Sophie; she had lost her fear of mages... possibly after meeting the mage in the dreamscape?

Sophie read the card. This was either some elaborate practical joke, or this man was the Queen's appointed mage.

"Oh, be a sport and don't go showing that card to people. It won't do you much good in any case." Rupert patted one of the sleeping men on the head. "Malcolm and Angus here work for MI21. Her Majesty's department for the investigation of the stuff people with limited imagination find hard to understand."

Sophie was puzzled. "Aren't they...*Hans* and *Heinrich?*"

"No. Malcolm and Angus. I don't know why they insist on using *Hans* and *Heinreich*. They don't sound the least bit German."

He rocked the stool back on its two back legs, studying Sophie for a few seconds in silence, then continued.

"While best to be subtle about it, forget what they said about not studying magic. You *had* a rare opportunity to learn from a master mage, one of the best. Unfortunately, it like that opportunity is gone." He shrugged. Rupert had a pipe in his hands, but it wasn't lit; he twirled it around his fingers as he spoke, for a while as he spoke, then put it in his pocket.

"So, you're wondering what in the blazes is going on, I should imagine?"

"Well, yeah, sort of." Sophie relaxed, a quizzical expression on her face.

"Professor Marcus is what we call a *Magicist.*"

"Magicist...er...that's not a word."

Rupert ignored her observation.

"He's part scientist, part mage. Specifically, an *Illusionist* mage. When science doesn't get him so far, he gets magic to do the rest." Rupert glanced back at Hans/Heinrich—Angus/Michael. Hans was sliding out of his chair, and Rupert pushed him back up, narrowly preventing him from falling on the floor.

"Damn, I think he's starting to drool."

"Oh, hang on, I want to ask..." Sophie had so much to ask him, Marcus was gone, and Rupert appeared to now be the one source of information.

He put his hand up to silence her.

"Sophie, old girl. Professor Marcus, as you may or may not know, is not recording anyone's dreams. He's putting you in contact with your ancestors, through a process called *dreamscaping,*" Rupert continued. "Do you know where Marcus is?"

Sophie shook her head.

"His wife?"

"No. Not sure I would tell you anyway. I don't trust you, and you talk strangely," Sophie said.

"Oh," he muttered, squinting at her, under a furrowed brow.

"Well, trust issues aside old girl, we came here to get him, and as Malcom said, when we got here, he'd left." Rupert paused, glancing at both the sleeping men once more.

"Rupert, why did Marcus leave?" Sophie asked.

Rupert paused, looking at Sophie silently, without movement. It was that moment, just for a second, something about him made her afraid of him. He seemed to be considering whether to speak.

"He left because he is afraid. He's created a monster. One of his mages has got too much power from the dreamscape. He left because he fears that she will destroy herself and all of Bamberg."

Sophie sat there silently. This sounded bad. Clearly the ancestral arts were powerful, and in the right hands they could help. But of course, in the wrong hands…

"Do you know anything about this person, the reason he fled?" Rupert asked.

Sophie just shook her head, enough times to indicate she really didn't.

Rupert looked at her, studying her face, like he was trying to tell if she knew the truth? He then nodded his head, turned and checked the two men, before glancing around the room and uttering a frustrated sigh.

"I could *really* do with a cup of tea. Anyway, the thing you need to know is, keep your skills to yourself. You've got access to spells that the other mages don't have."

Had access to, she thought.

He paused and glanced at her earnestly.

"Other mages?" Sophie said, tilting her head.

Rupert glanced over at Sophie quietly, pausing for a second.

"Damn. You actually don't know a whole lot here, do you?" He glanced at the two men again, then back at her again.

"There's practitioners of the six paths of magic we know of… the more common Illusionists, like Marcus's notes say you are,

Court Magicians." He pointed at himself. "Druids, elementalists, *summoners,*" he said this oddly, like he was uncomfortable even saying it "…and blood magic. As you know, we assume there are few summoners now left, and we all know the blood magic path disappeared hundreds of years ago. Thank God." He paused for a second and continued.

"The rest keep to themselves after all the prejudice against mages following the 1950 Civil War in England. To be honest, all the mages are a bit rubbish, knowledge of magic has diminished to its present sorry state. There are non-mages who do sleight of hand and card tricks that are more impressive than some *actual* mages."

"So, the… er …old mages that have been around, their magic ability has died off? Or something?" Sophie asked.

"Yes. It is the access you and the rest of jolly old Marcus's mages and the dreamscape that is the potential. The potential to bring magic back."

Sophie glanced at Rupert as he robotically twirled his pipe quickly around his fingers. He went momentarily quiet, considering something, then appeared concerned.

It gave her pause to think. So quickly she had been introduced to the incredible world of dreamscaping, and it was gone. Her heart sank.

"Oh, well. Get ready." He shifted back to his chair. "…ahh, before the other two wake up, I need to give you these. I got them out of Marcus's office, had your name on them. So, you can keep learning."

Sophie's heart jumped. It was her headset. She grabbed them and held them tight in her hands. It had a sticker on it simply saying, *Sophie.*

"Oh… thank you!" Sophie beamed. She could have hugged him, even though he was a stranger. Now she could continue with the dreamscape sessions.

"You're welcome. Put them away before the others wake up."

Sophie put them in her bag quickly.

Rupert muttered something under his breath and clapped his hands. Suddenly, the men woke up, Sophie was surprised to see they were fully awake, like they had never been to sleep at all.

"So, when did you see him last?" Hans/Malcolm asked Sophie, continuing exactly from the second he was put into a state of slumber. He glanced back at Rupert.

"Oh, sorry, we didn't introduce you. This is Rupert. He never says much."

Sophie turned subtly to Rupert with a raised eyebrow. He waved the hair out of his eyes, peeking at her under his brow.

Malcolm continued talking to Sophie about the dangers of magic. He mainly was interested in wanting to know about Professor Marcus. Sophie told them she had only met him once and hadn't spoken to him that much, which was technically true. They rapidly started losing interest in her when they realised how little she knew.

They said she could go.

Sophie realised for a moment; she had thought the dreamscape sessions were over. It shocked her how hurt and unhappy she had felt. She was so relieved to get the headset from Rupert; though mixed with the relief was a feeling of concern that there were five other mages about. Disturbingly, one of them was a summoner.

She reached into her pocket to read the card Rupert had given her. The details had now changed to those of a German plumber in Hannover.

"Great," she sighed.

Chapter 5 - SpellBox

After going back to school for an uneventful afternoon of trigonometry and physics, her most hated subjects, Sophie headed home again. She had to explain the recent news to her papa. He was going to wonder what was going on.

Maybe he knew where Marcus was?

Also, no Marcus, no money. She would also have to get her job at the café back… if they would take her back.

Then there was the mention of the errant mage, that had caused Marcus to flee. Someone with talented arts that were too much power. The comment had troubled her, but she really had no idea what to do about it. But if Marcus had fled because of it…

As Sophie came through the door, her Papa was standing in the kitchen, making a pot of tea, next to Hisako as she prepared dinner. Hisako was the long serving nanny/cleaner/cook. With her own mother gone, Sophie sometimes felt Hisako was like a *sort-of-mama*. She'd been with them for so long, she was part of the family.

Sophie smiled just hearing her voice, and for the moment, she put the troubled thoughts out of her mind.

Hisako was cooking on the stove, the smell of some Japanese meatballs—Sophie's favourite dish—and steamed vegetables wafted through the apartment. The house was warm, and the sound of her papa and Hisako's chirpy conversation escaped the kitchen. Sophie always felt brighter when the two were chatting, and her papa was always in good spirits when she was around. The two had got on well, over the years.

"Hi, Papa, Hisako chan. I'm home."

"Oh, hi, Sophie. There is a box there for you, *mein schatzi*. More books." Momentarily, Sophie's spirits lifted, she had books on order, and they had arrived early. The buzz of new purchases.

Ernst spoke without glancing up at her, keeping his eyes on some boiling water.

"How was school today? How was your dreamscape session?" Ernst asked. Sophie remembered she hadn't spoken to him yet about it.

"Well, interesting you bring that up." She paused for a second, thinking about the real story, and how much she should tell her father.

"It seems like the dreamscape sessions are over. Professor Marcus has disappeared." Sophie said.

"He...what? Disappeared?" Her papa glanced up, momentarily pausing his tea making.

"I went for my session. These odd men were there, they explained that he had left. It's probably for the better."

"Marcus gone? Odd men?" Ernst seemed serious suddenly. "What?"

"Well, yes, he's gone. Sorry, Papa." Sophie realised her papa was quite taken aback.

Ernst face was puzzled and concerned. "Marcus mentioned to me he had a problem student that he said he had 'lost control of'. He had come across as...troubled lately." Ernst sat down.

"Would he have left because one of his own students was causing him trouble?" Ernst was clearly worried, he appeared to be asking the question more to himself, than anyone else. He turned to Sophie.

"Who were the men, Sophie? What did they say to you?"

"They were police. Well, British Police. They had warned me about magic."

"Magic?" Ernst bristled. He suddenly turned to Sophie, an almost frightful, serious expression now dominating his face. It was completely unlike him. Sophie took a slight breath in when she saw his reaction, stepping back.

"I don't understand, what does magic have to do with it?" Ernst stepped out of the kitchen and came over to Sophie.

Sophie realised he had completely ignored the fact that police were mentioned.

"Well in the dream... I met a man, and he was going to teach me magic."

Ernst crossed his arms, still serious.

"MAGIC!" Ernst stared at her intently. He never got this upset. He was the most easy-going father out of all her friends' papas. She was shocked.

"Marcus told me nothing about magic!" Ernst realised that both Sophie and Hisako were staring silently at his reaction. He took a second to compose himself.

"Oh...sorry. Look, Sophie, I don't want you playing with that stuff, no good will come of it."

Hisako nodded, slowly. "Yes, Sophie, no good will come of magic. You should stay away from it."

Sophie was surprised, even the usually quiet Hisako had something to say. She instantly thought of the headset in her bag. Her papa would not be happy. He put his hand on Sophie's arm, now more relaxed.

"However, you can't learn magic from a dream. In any case, Marcus is gone, and the sessions are over."

Except they weren't, Sophie thought.

Ernst went back to the kitchen, and the little episode finished. Sophie noticed Hisako cheekily stole a biscuit from a pack her papa had bought. They both laughed and started chatting in the comfortable way they always did. Sophie's shoulders relaxed.

Some people reacted badly to magic, mainly through fear of things that happened decades ago, but her papa reacting like this was even worse, and completely out of character. Sophie walked over and sat down in her favourite chair in the lounge room, slightly dismayed.

She wanted to continue the dreamscapes. The headset was in her bag. Ernst would be furious if he knew. The last few days have been some crazy highs, and now... a low. So much had happened. Sophie had gotten such a kick from the first dreamscape, the realistic visual world, the potential to do magic, the history...she couldn't imagine not doing another.

***

Sophie popped up, grabbed the box, and went into her room. She double checked the bolt on her door, then sat cross legged on the floor of her room, squashing down into a plush purple mat with her back up against the bed, checking the headset.

Pulling the headset out of her bag she spun it around in her hand, observing the detail. Such a little object that so completely changed her world. It was much like a normal headset to listen to music with, except it had a flat black eyepiece that adjusted and came down over the eyes, like a visor. She held it hesitantly, like it was a powerful magic relic. In a way it was.

She began to wonder if she would indeed go through the same dream, or something completely different. Could she *will* herself to go to the same medieval setting, and meet the same man again?

The headset didn't have a switch, it was just always on, which was odd. Where did it get its power? It didn't have a plug or any type of connector. She thought momentarily, was it some sort of prank? Maybe she would put it on, and nothing would happen? Sophie laid down on the bed, put the headset on over her ears and the little visor over the eyes.

She waited for something to happen, hoping it would work.

It wasn't a prank.

The visor started to hum, steady rhythmic sounds, and she drifted into the dreamverse state. Once again, she appeared in the same house, shunned the same dress and put on what she now realised, in this time period ... were *boy's* clothes, the tights and the loose linen shirt.

She went downstairs, didn't see the two boys, though other village people politely greeted her, and she proceeded out of the village, down the path, to the house on the hill.

Once again, she knocked on the door of the big house, but this time the reception was more cordial.

"Ah... Good Morning to you. What name shall I call you? I am Johannes."

"Oh hello, I am Sophie. Thank you for teaching me. Taking me on as an apprentice, for your... magic...floating apple fire... thing." *Awkward.*

"Ah, Sophie... but that's a girl's name?" He appeared confused.

"I am a girl!" Sophie frowned. This was getting ridiculous. People were programmed at this time to think that all girls wore dresses and had flowing long hair.

His serious face broke as he smiled. "I know."

It started to dawn on Sophie that the dream characters, like Johannes, were completely realistic, to the point where they would joke with you. Sophie knew this was her dream, but she couldn't help but treat Johannes like he was a real person.

"So why the short hair?" He was curious.

"Well—" She didn't realise her modern hair cut would be causing so many issues. "It's just practical."

"You think differently to the other peasants in the village. I mean, some of the villagers don't think at all, so you're ahead of them." He nodded and smiled. "I like that. First things, first. Come this way." He led her through the quaint house. A new cat, Ginger with big white tipped ears, hopped off the table and followed them as they went out the back door and into a yard.

"Pick up all these twigs and put them near the back for kindling. Then you'll peel this barrel of apples, pull out twenty turnips from the garden over there," he pointed to it, while eating his own apple. "Please, do it as quickly as possible."

After about two hours of work, which actually went quickly, she finally finished everything he had asked. However, instead of teaching her anything, he asked her to do more. Cutting fish heads, chopping apples, picking mushrooms. When she was finished, Johannes sat her down.

"So, you're originally from Bamberg?"

"No, Stuttgart originally. We relocated to Bamberg."

"Ah Stuttgart. Count Ulrich IV, eats too much, wears a big floppy hat, has a big floppy head. Or... is it Ulrich V now?"

"Ah, yes." Sophie had no idea what he was talking about.

"And you'd heard of me and wanted me to teach you."

"Yes. I'm very eager to learn. I've heard you do the most amazing things and I've heard all about ..." She thought for a second. "...what you do with apples..."

"Well, good gentle lady, let's not focus on the apples so much. I would not normally show someone something so quick. In fact, I would normally have them doing work for me for weeks before I would even show them something. But, well... you know... I haven't had an apprentice for some years, and Sophie—I am indeed impressed that you are so persistent." Sophie noticed his tone had just become more serious.

He grabbed another apple, and took Sophie out to the backyard, where two cats were sitting: a big, slow-moving black cat and a skinnier grey cat. The ginger cat had been following Sophie around, while the other two lazily slept in what was turning out to be a warm day.

"Sophie, pick a cat."

"Okay, the ginger cat."

Johannes gave her an odd expression, checked where her gaze was—then pointed at the two cats in front of her.

"Er, there is no ginger cat option. Just these two."

"The ginger cat is right there!"

Johannes still appeared confused. "No ginger cat. Ginger cat, no. Pick another colour cat."

"Okay." Sophie didn't understand why Johannes couldn't see the cat, but ignored it and pointed to the grey cat, which followed her finger as she pointed.

"Sophie... Sophie... Sophie. I'm going to get you to try to put this cat to sleep. Not everyone can do spellcasting. This is a test to see if you can. Concentrate on the grey cat. Concentrate on your arm and your hand." He quickly tapped her forearm, and then her knuckles.

"Imagine the cat going to sleep."

Sophie picked up at his mention of the word *spellcasting*, but then focused on the task at hand. "I'm doing spellcasting?"

"Yes... Do you understand what that means?"

"Yes, of course!" She had no idea.

"Next, make these patterns with your hands." Johannes traced a symbol in the air, almost like a little picture. It was a cross combined with a circle, and then he drew three flowing lines on the top of it. He did the symbols slowly first, then faster, and faster, repeating them over and over. There was a final thrust of his fingers through the symbol, towards the cat. Sophie watched him and started practicing the hand motion.

"Good. Now be a good apprentice and keep practicing it many times. Practice it 200 times. And at the end of the casting, use the command word, *leggen.*"

Sophie continued the process.

The grey cat didn't sleep. It sneezed twice. The big black cat wandered off slowly, uttering a low growl as it went. The ginger cat sat there, staring intently at Sophie's hands as they went through the motions.

Sophie felt stupid, things had started off exciting. In the end she could achieve nothing.

Johannes, however, didn't come across as disappointed, saying that some people get it quicker than others. She woke up once again in her bedroom, momentarily confused about where she was. Sophie decided that this dream was even weirder than the last. Now frustrated, she took the headset off, and scribbled a few notes from how to do magic into a notebook she kept next to her bed.

She still wasn't entirely tired, checked her watch, and decided to open her box of books that had come in the mail. It might make up for the frustration.

She refocused her thoughts to the new books, always a pleasant buzz. There was nothing like the thrill of a new box of books to open. Picking up the light tan cardboard parcel, she noticed it wasn't from her normal London book supplier.

She shook it. It was light, too light for books. She shook it; something rattled inside.

"Papa, this box, it's not a book." She realised Ernst probably didn't hear her through her door.

Sophie opened it.

Inside was a strange pair of old wooden glasses. And a headset. A dreamcast headset. *Another* dreamcast headset.

Chapter 6—The letter

She now had *two* headsets. The one she had just used, from Rupert, and one sitting in a newly opened box on her lap. What was going on?

The glasses appeared to be extremely old, carved out of wood, with round frames, and tiny ornate metal hinges. She put them on, but they were normal glass, they didn't make anything appear bigger, or even blurred.

Pulling the headset out, she spun it around in her fingers, her gaze scanning its features. It was identical to the one Rupert gave her. As she pulled it out of the box, she noticed a folded piece of A4 paper came out with it. There was writing scrawled on it in green pen.

She warily picked it out of the box, holding it at arm's length, like it was going to jump at her like a spider.

> *Stop Adeline. Stop the Rising. Get help from Rupert.*
> *Use this headset to continue your lessons*
> *Marcus.*

Marcus! He must have sent it before he left. Who was Adeline? What was *the Rising*? At least she knew who Rupert was... but what... What was going on? She sat staring at the two headsets, before she realised how late it was getting and she needed to get to sleep.

Confused thoughts and questions buzzed around in her head, like bees around a hive, before she finally succumbed to sleep. However, this time, she didn't dream about Johannes at all.

Chapter 7 - Harlan's Explanation

Sophie needed to talk to someone about all this.

Harlan.

The next day, Sophie headed straight back to school to find Harlan. She had *lots* of questions to ask him. She shared one subject with Harlan, History, and she found him in the classroom.

As soon as the class finished, Sophie grabbed Harlan by the jacket, and hurried him off to lunch.

"Harlan. Marcus is gone," Sophie said.

His hand rubbed behind his neck, a slightly pained expression on his face. "Er, who?"

"Harls, don't pretend you don't know what I'm talking about. I saw your scooter at the University. You handed me the dream interpretation book, as a hint, right? I know you do dreamscaping with Marcus. He's gone," Sophie said, quickly getting to the point.

"Errrh, uhm." He adjusted himself in his seat awkwardly, like a student lying about not having done their homework. "You know Soph, we aren't supposed to talk about it..."

"Forget that rubbish. He's gone now, so it doesn't matter. More things have happened."

Sophie sat with him and told him the entire story of Rupert. He sat and listened, eating a more than average number of Turkey sandwiches. At the end, he folded his arms, and seemed disturbed.

"Dayum. Well, I can't believe Marcus is gone. How am I going to do my sessions?"

"Maybe you will get a parcel as well?" Sophie empathized.

Harlan shook his head, as he spoke. "I was fixing to do so much more. Still a lot to learn."

"Okay, now I've told you the story... you need to see this. It's a note from him, it was in the box." She energetically shoved the note in his face, watching as he read it.

"A note?" Harlan read it and scrunched up his face. "Who... who is Adeline? What's the Rising? Is it about cooking?"

"I think it means rising, like... *uprising*." Sophie stifled a chuckle.

Harlan still appeared confused. "Then, well, who is... uprising? And what are they uprising against?"

"No idea. It's sleepy Bamberg. Everyone is always pretty happy here," Sophie said.

"So, Marcus, he is running away from these guys?" Harlan asked.

"Papa and Rupert said Marcus left because he had trouble with another student. The way Rupert spoke about them scared me. He was talking about danger to all of Bamberg. Though I thought Marcus may be just running from the police."

"Another student," Harlan said. "Maybe that's who Adeline is?"

Sophie shrugged again. "Maybe."

"Yeah, so this Rupert guy you mentioned. I'm not sure I trust him." Harlan frowned. "You need to be careful of this guy, Soph."

"Well, he made those guys go to sleep with magic, so he's a mage at least. That's interesting," Sophie argued. It was slightly cold, and Sophie shivered, as she ate part of a sandwich her papa had made.

"Could have been hypnotism for all we know." Harlan was unimpressed. "Ya know, Soph—" He grabbed her shoulder and regarded her earnestly. "—you're *too* trusting sometimes." Sophie glanced back at him and just shook her head.

"But still, another reason to be down. I'm already a bit down about the search for my bio mom.. I'm getting nowhere."

Sophie knew Harlan, while generally upbeat, occasionally would be pensive or thoughtful. She wondered how he had been going trying to find his biological mother, but it often made him down to talk about it so she had decided not to bring it up.

Just then, they heard some students running, the squeak of running shoes on the school hallway linoleum, and the hubbub of raised voices. It was normally the tell-tale sign of something happening, someone getting in trouble, or a new student arriving. The voices, the reactions, were high pitched, and loud.

The two popped up with their lunches and headed upstairs. Following the running kids, they approached a classroom. A small, excited mob of students were peering into the class, from outside through the window. They shuffled around to find a window that was free, and peeked in.

"They're all asleep!" Sophie peered in. The room was full of students, asleep at their desks, like children having a mid-afternoon nap. "Why are they all asleep?"

"Rupert?" Harlan peered at Sophie.

The two of them watched as teachers walked in and started waking the students, who eventually roused, a little groggy.

School went faster than usual. There was the excitement of the sleeping classroom, some police attended, and it was put down to a gas leak. None of the students were hurt. Sophie considered if it was connected to anything but couldn't work out how. It stuck in her mind, and she continued wondering if it was somehow related to her own recent developments. Somehow.

***

Leaving school, she remembered the art markets in Bamberg were on, so instead of taking the tram home, she sacrificed another chapter of *Wuthering Heights* (having unsuccessfully tried to walk and read in the past) and walked past them. The traditional art markets were a tourist attraction in the middle of Bamberg.

People had set up little stalls; a lot of the locals did it because it was an easy way to make money. The Bambergians all had a huge sense of pride in the markets, which had a long tradition going back 100 years or more. Walking along the markets was always amazing, so many distractions, with each stall cramming in their goods to the allocated space, it was hard to take it all in.

She watched someone at a stall selling small, framed, stained glass windows. Someone else was selling swords, another stall had little copper metal lanterns, of a medieval design. The beautiful objects reminded her of the various things from her dreamscape sessions, from Johannes' house and the village. To her an ornate medieval style lantern, or a mug with calligraphy lettering fired into the band at the top, or a simple medieval style chair was beautiful and artistic. Immensely more interesting than their modern counterparts. However, she thought that to Johannes these would be everyday things, nothing special.

Sophie recognised a few of the students from school at the stall, and said hi to Hans, one of the younger ones she knew who was selling wonderful lanterns. She chatted to him about how they were made, the details of how he put them together were amazing.

She took a minute to glance around her, a slow twirl, taking it all in. The stalls, the beautiful old buildings. The clock on the town square. Bamberg was a wonderful place, the beautiful old medieval houses. So often she considered how magnificent it was and tried not to take it for granted. A slice of the 1500s tossed into the modern world. She thought of all the places she had lived in her life; how many were there? Fourteen or fifteen? …Bamberg was the most amazing.

As she walked among the markets, out of the corner of her eye, she noticed two large men also observing the crowd, like they were looking for someone. While she weaved through the crowd, half peering at the stalls, half trying to dodge between distracted meandering tourists she noticed, the two men seemed to be walking *with* her. She changed direction in an odd way, and they changed direction too. She tried not to meet their gaze directly, but as she strolled along the markets, they were definitely keeping pace with her.

She stopped at a stall, pretending to examine some beer steins. Instead, she pulled out her phone and sent a text to Harlan. He responded straight away.

Sophie: Are you near the markets? Can you come and find me quick? 2 weird men

Harlan: Yes. 2 mins away.
Sophie: Near the beer stein stall
Harlan: C U soon. Stay in the open with people

Hovering around the beer stein stall, awkwardly, Sophie finally saw Harlan arrive, concern sprawled across his face. She gave a huge sigh of relief.

"You okay?" he said.

"Yes, can you see them?" Sophie said.

"What do they look like?"

"Two weird men. Big guys," she said. Sophie could feel her heart thumping fast.

"No, can't see anyone like that. Are you sure?" he asked.

"I think so."

Sophie glanced up and cautiously scanned around. There were lots of people, but not two men. She had a sinking feeling, like she was starting to imagine things, and then started to chuckle to herself.

"I think your imagination may be getting carried away, but hey, I'll walk you home anyway," Harlan said.

They both dawdled at the markets a little more and left the market area. Sophie was conscious she was keeping Harlan from whatever it was he was doing, so she decided to take the shortest route home.

They were chatting and walking at the same time. Sophie breathed in the crisp air, and with the sounds of the market in the background, they turned into a narrow laneway. About halfway down the laneway, Sophie heard footsteps behind her. She felt the hairs on her neck rise. She turned to see the two men walking behind them.

She stopped.

They kept walking towards her. Harlan turned and saw them and gasped. He grabbed Sophie by the arm, pulling her back from them.

"Sophie Wolf?"

Sophie didn't answer.

"Sophie Wolf. We know it's you. Your spellbook. Give it to us and we'll leave you alone. *We need it.*"

Sophie went to run but one of them reached out and grabbed Sophie's bag, pulling it out of her grasp. He started rummaging through it.

"Hey, leave her alone!" Harlan shouted. Harlan stepped back, crouched, and did a mighty jump, kicking the man in the chest. The man was shocked, and stumbled back, letting go of Sophie's bag which fell to the ground. Sophie immediately tried the sleep spell on him, her hand flashing a symbol. The man reacted with surprised at her, backing away from her hands as they scribbled the symbol in the air.

It didn't work. She tried it again.

He went to grab her again, but out of the corner of her eye, she saw Harlan' arm raised and jerked hard towards the ground. There was a flurry of movement, a flash, a bang, and all of a sudden, there was smoke everywhere. She immediately reached down and felt where her bag was.

She could barely see in front of her, she didn't know which direction to go. She felt her bag and grabbed it. As she got up, she could see a figure in front of her. It was dark, but the figure was tall, a tall dark silhouetted figure with horns, stag like horns.

She screamed, and then felt a hand on her wrist, grabbing her. She glanced down, and to her relief, she recognised Harlan's hand, pulling her through the smoke. The men were calling out to each other. They scampered away from their voices, keeping quiet.

Harlan pulled her away from the men, down the alleyway, through the smoke. She put her hand over her mouth, suppressing a violent urge to cough.

They sprinted out of the smoke, through the alleyways, until they were back at the markets, with people. Sophie went straight to Hans's table.

"Hans, can we hide under here? We are being chased!" she pleaded.

"What?" Hans stammered, appearing confused.

They didn't wait for permission, and got under the table, the tablecloth covering them. Sophie peered at the feet going past, under the table, and saw the two men's legs and feet stomping by, pausing, then continuing. They waited for a few minutes, thanked Hans, and ran the other way. Harlan saw a Taxi and they ran to it, getting safely inside and directing it back to Sophie's house.

***

"Soph, what is going on? Yer know, this is not normal being chased around by two weird guys."

"No idea." As the adrenaline started to wear off, she felt her heart pumping fast, but starting to slow. "Something to do with the Adeline girl, I guess?"

"They said they wanted your spellbook?" Harlan was calmer than her. Maybe the fact he'd been doing all this for longer, he was used to it, even if his adventures had only been in the dreamcast.

"Yes, I have a notebook that I write my spell creation notes in. I guess it's a spellbook. I don't know what use it would be to them, they only work in the dreamcast." Sophie put her hands under her arms to keep them warm.

The taxi arrived at Sophie's house. At her door, she fumbled with her keys. Her hands were shaking still from the encounter. Harlan saw her to the door, gave her a hug, and then took the taxi home. She was safely in the house, an immediate sense of relief gratifying her.

"I'm home."

There were noises coming from the kitchen, and the faint sound of 80's music.

"Hi, Sophie," her papa called. "I'm just finishing making dinner."

Sophie sat down at the table and her papa brought out sandwiches.

"Oh, sandwiches. Splendid." She smiled. Ernst made them appearing simple, but inside was an array of surprising elements, and he never said what it was as a sort of surprise.

The sandwiches were tasty, but Sophie was still thinking of the encounter. The two men. She would have to be more careful about where she went, and make sure she was with people. She thought about how it may affect school, and her life, as she hungrily chewed through the sandwiches.

"How's school, Sophie? Get up to anything interesting?"

"Nah, just a normal day," she said, distracted. A classroom of kids mysteriously falling asleep was *not* a normal day. Being chased by two weird men was not a normal day. But she didn't want to tell Hisako or her papa. Sophie had decided to keep her magic a secret from Ernst, it was best not to worry him about this stuff.

"Papa." Sophie shuffled in her seat, picked up her sandwich. She tried to put the images of the two men out of her head. "Now that the dream recording sessions are finished. I'm going to have to go back to my old job at the cafe."

"Oh, yes." Ernst glanced up from his computer. "Well, I know you don't like working there, but better you work there than be dabbling with stuff you shouldn't be." And he was back at his computer.

Sophie felt jealous of that computer, it got all his time.

She checked the time on her pink wristwatch. An obvious pink girl's watch from when she was younger, and she was overdue for something more adult—that didn't seem like it— came with a Barbie doll. She noticed her dad's phone and picked it up to make sure her time was correct.

When she picked it up, she stared at the phone. It had a missed call from her history teacher, Mr Freidrickson on it. *Errrh… why was Freidrickson calling her papa?* She felt very weird. A flush of heat up the back of her head… The feeling she got when something odd was happening.

"Dad, I just checked your phone." She took a bite, talking with her mouth half full.

"Mr Freidrickson from school called."

Sophie's dad peeked up from his computer and was quiet for a second. "Oh, yes, he called about your marks. He just wanted to say they were very good."

Sophie was puzzled at hearing this and stopped eating. Her marks were okay. She didn't think they were that great. The last thing she needed, with the recent drama, was teachers making a fuss about schoolwork.

***

Next day at school, Sophie had last period free, so she left early to go and meet Harlan, catching a tram to that part of Bamberg where the café they were meeting was. It was an old Café from the 1960s, that Harlan liked. By the time Sophie finally got there, he was there already. She was just about bursting to talk to him.

"Who were those men?" Harlan said.

"No idea. All I know is they wanted my spellbook," Sophie said, somewhat worried.

"Did you tell your dad? Harlan said.

"No. I can't. I told Papa I'm not doing the dreamcast anymore," Sophie said.

"Sophie, we need to keep you safe. Don't go near the markets. Call me if you have any problems," Harlan said.

Sophie shook her head. "No, I need to learn magic quickly. I could defend myself against this sort of thing."

Harlan just watched her silently, for what seemed longer than it was. "Soph, they didn't want to harm you, they just wanted the spellbook. At least that's something. I guess having knowledge of magic is a valuable commodity these days. May be worth a lot of money to the right person."

Sophie considered this, but it didn't really make matters better for her.

"Hey, look to change the topic, Soph. I have news… got my headset in the mail as well. Sent by Marcus."

"Ah, well some good news at least." She knew Harlan would have been anxious, as she certainly had been.

"Presumably, Marcus sent these out to people he wanted to continue with the program?"

"Guess so." Harlan shrugged. "Anyway, It's a relief. And these, I got some glasses as well."

Harlan pulled out a pair of glasses, very similar, but not the same as the ones Sophie had got in the box. Like Sophie's they were round glasses, made of wood, old and ornate. They appeared rather crusty, and very old. Ancient. Sophie felt her head physically shift back from them, almost in revulsion.

Sophie was still thinking about the men, but the glasses appeared bizarre enough to distract her. "Oh, they're like mine. Do you know what they do?"

"His letter said *Glasses of True sight. Those with no sight can see. Those with sight can see the unseen.*" He put them on, peered around and shrugged. "He said only I'm allowed to wear them."

Sophie glanced at the glasses momentarily and shook her head. Well, at least Harlan knew something about his; it was more than she did.

"Anyway, I really need to ask you about all this." She was eager. "But before I do I need to do something."

Sophie went through the hand motions she had practiced so many times in her dream. She glanced at him, and cast the spell, saying the command word "Schlafen".

He stared at her blankly for a few seconds.

"Well, I dunno what that was, but Sophie, I'd be careful about waving my hands about like that. You know what the locals are like. And you know, we aren't supposed to be talking about this, we've both signed contracts."

"Marcus is gone, so who cares about the contracts," Sophie said, sitting down and peering directly at Harlan. "What else do you know about these sessions? Have you told me everything you know? I'm dying to find out."

"Okay… okay, hold your horses Soph." Harlan thought for a while, appearing serious,

then sighed.

"I'll tell you all I know. But you must promise not to tell anyone I told you all this. We could *both* get in a lot of trouble with this confidentiality agreement thing."

He scanned the café. It was largely empty.

"Professor Marcus was likely to tell you some of this anyway, so really, I'm just telling you this because he is gone. The sessions are all about connecting people with their ancestors, you know…via genetic recorded memory."

"*Genetic DNA recorded memory?*" Sophie squinted.

Harlan nodded. "Yeah. You know, some people say their ancestor's memories are recorded in their own DNA. You're born with your ancestor's memories… you know… in your cells, yeah, sort of thing."

Sophie had read some blogs on the internet about people believing that, but she thought it was weird, fringy sort of science.

"How many sessions have you had already?" Harlan said, without explaining it.

"Only two so far," Sophie replied.

Harlan nodded. "So, you have met the same person twice, and he or she is in an historical type of dream, right? That's the difference with a dream. In the dreamscape, you will always meet the same person. Marcus calls them your TA. That stands for *Talented Ancestor.*"

"Yes. His...he... my TA's name is Johannes..." Sophie said. "...he's like a medieval era guy in a house on a hill. He's got like... a really annoying sense of humour."

"Annoying? Dayum." Harlan frowned. "So, Johannes *is* your ancestor." Harlan smiled. "So, you know, Johannes, as your TA, he would be like your great, great, great, great, like a million times great grandfather. He's your ancestor from 500 or something years ago. The headset connects your dream state to the stored memory of your ancestors in your body... well, in your DNA."

Sophie nodded, thinking about it all as it sank in.

Harlan kept going.

"I've done about forty, so I'm a fair way along compared to you."

"Forty!" Sophie was surprised.

"Yep. About a year. My ancestor is French."

"I didn't know you were French?" Sophie thought Harlan was about as American as you could be.

"I'm not, er...I mean, well, way back, so a tiny bit yer know. Anyway, he... Arsène... lives in a House in London, about 200 years ago. He teaches me stealth techniques, climbing, hiding, running on rooftops. In the night. In London. It's very athletic and skillful."

Sophie was puzzled.

"So, what does he do? Is he like a rooftop athlete?" She smirked.

"No." He rolled his eyes and waved his hands in front of him for emphasis. "It's...well you know, all about stealth."

Sophie raised an eyebrow.

"Is he teaching you to be a spy?"

Harlan fidgeted. "Well, er, yes and no."

Sophie's eyes widened.

"Harlan... he's teaching you to be a thief!"

Harlan grimaces, and tilted his head, trying to introduce subtlety into the conversation.

"Er, you know, you don't need to emphasize the whole thief part. It's thief skills. I don't do anything bad with it. It's more about the skills... it's an art, you know."

Sophie was smiling from ear to ear at Harlan. She loved it when she had something over him, and he was uncomfortable. He adjusted awkwardly in his chair, strategically changing the conversation.

"But… Harlan, you love money… you are the most business-oriented person I know."

Harlan shook his head.

"Yeah, but I can earn it by being honest. I don't want to steal it. Anyway." Sophie noticed him changing the topic. "So, tell me more about your talented ancestor."

Sophie went quiet. She realised; she would be telling someone that she was doing magic. Or trying to tell them. She certainly trusted Harlan more than most.

"Well—" She paused. "Johannes… does magic. That's what the hand motions were, and that's what the spellbook is for."

Harlan went quiet. Sophie sensed the concern that usually came with using the word *magic*.

"Like on stage?" Harlan asked, caution in his voice.

"Well, no, like they used to…like casting spells."

"Like a summoner?" His voice conveyed his concern.

"No… NO… NO… just a normal mage …actually he was making some apples float around—" She drew a round shape in the air. "—in a circle."

Harlan regarded her, his head askew, silently. Sophie also went quiet. People reacted oddly when talking about mages.

"So, don't tell me, I guess you can't do them in real life? So that's why I didn't fall asleep."

"Well, no. Actually…I can't do them in my dream, either. He wants to teach me magic spells. But he is making me do all this *farmwork* first." Sophie could hear the frustration in her voice.

Harlan laughed and whacked her on the arm.

"Can he teach you a spell you can actually do?"

"At the moment I'm trying to put a cat to sleep." She frowned slightly.

"So, you can specialise in working with sleep deprived cats. What else does he teach you?"

Sophie thought for a second.

"Well, he's a farmer."

Harlan laughed out loud.

"You could learn to be a medieval farmer. How exciting! You could specialise with turnips." He whacked her on the shoulder, and picked up her bag on the table, mimicking someone pulling turnips out of the ground, inspecting them, and putting them in a bag.

Harlan laughed. Sophie started laughing as well. There had been a certain amount of tension in the air, but Sophie started to feel some relief. Sophie was relieved to be able to talk about the dreamcasts to *someone.*

"Okay, so this is a real historical person doing spells. Why aren't they in history books?"

"Well... I don't know." Sophie lowered her voice, peering around. "The spells work in-dream—they appear *so* real. Harls. I have watched him cast them; I can do the hand motions perfectly."

Sophie continued chatting to Harlan about the whole process. She realised, talking about it made her come to life. She felt sort of proud, and excited.

The idea of learning magic that would work in this dream state was amazing, exciting, and interesting. But what was the point of it all? Part of her felt a bit hollow inside, like she was wasting her time, particularly as Harlan apparently was getting real skills.

Peering at Harlan she noticed he was regarding her oddly. Then she realised he was peering past her at something. She turned her head to see directly behind her was the man that ran the café. A chubby, bald man with tufts of brown hair on the sides of his head and a red apron.

He had his arms crossed, his teeth gritted, his jaw set firm.

"Okay, you can leave. Now!"

"Er, what? We haven't finished." Harlan said.

"I don't want you here. Time to go. Don't come back!" He was very firm. His hands dropped from being folded, to being at his side, his fists clenching and unclenching, the words almost hissed out of his mouth.

Sophie got up to go, and Harlan, not moving fast enough, was helped out by the man who grabbed his arm.

"Hey!" Harlan wrenched it free. "Okay, ahh, hang on buddy, we're going!"

He pushed them out of the door and then went back inside.

Harlan shook his head. "What was that about?"

Sophie was stunned. "It's because he heard us talking about magic. People hate it. Because they are scared."

"Wow. I mean, yeah, just wow. What an idiot. Well, at least we didn't have to pay."

They started walking back to school, both a bit shocked about being kicked out.

"Oh, Harlan, I had forgotten to tell you, apparently there are five other people at school in the program. No idea who they are. But I think the first thing we should do is try to find out!" Sophie said.

"Five others? Okay, sounds like a plan." Harlan glanced at the watch on his wrist. "Oh, two p.m., we should get a move on, or we'll be late for our next class." He started walking faster.

Sophie glanced at the pink watch he had on. It was the same as hers. Then noticed her naked wrist. "Hey... my watch!"

Chapter 8—History 4B with Mr Freidrickson

Next day, Sophie made a point of sitting next to Harlan in History. With her trips to medieval Europe in her dreams, History classes were like travel briefings. She may get some good marks in *one* subject.

Her history teacher was a quirky sort of character. He was an Australian man called Mr Freidrickson. He stood out because not only did he have an artificial hand, but he had an eyepatch. The stories behind how he had acquired these were a mystery to the students. No one knew the actual reason, which meant there was a variety of stories in circulation, some of them believable, and others not. It was generally presumed he'd been in an accident.

What he said was also often a mystery. Sophie and the rest of the students at times, couldn't understand his "Aussie" English.

In any case, Mr Freidrickson was a really nice teacher, popular with the students, and regularly told funny anecdotes in his history lessons. A particular good one was the story of King Ludwig I of Bavaria; killed when he unfortunately happened to be in the toilet in his castle, and a great rock from a siege catapult crushed him in there.

"Okay, today we will be studying seventeenth century history, in particular the English civil war."

Freidrickson started.

"Sir, can I ask a question about the medieval period?" Sophie asked.

"Yes, Sophie, of course you can, the medieval period is very close to the seventeenth century in many ways. What's up matey?" Mr Freidrickson called people mate, matey, or little Matey. No other teacher did this. Sophie wasn't even sure other Australians did.

"Well... what I want to ask... people had apprenticeships in those times," Sophie said.

Mr Fredrikson smiled. "Yes, much like today, with some differences."

"If you were an apprentice, would you be expected to do all the housework, before you were taught your apprenticeship classes, including, like, for example..." She paused. "All the cooking, cleaning yards, and food preparation?"

Mr Freidrickson appeared puzzled. "Sophie, I think yes, they could be expected to do other duties... I guess you could say they didn't have as many rules back then." His face expressed curiosity. "Why do you want to know?"

"Shut up, Soph," Harlan muttered, and gave her a slight kick under the table.

Sophie ignored him. "I think the apprentices were worked sort of hard back then. Apprentices these days have it easy."

Harlan gave her a second kick under the desk, hoping she would stop.

She gripped her leg, grimacing. Mr Freidrickson peered at them both for a second blankly, and then continued his class.

After school, Sophie headed off for coffee again, with Harlan. There was still lots to discuss.

Three coffees and two donuts later, she had worked out most of the details of how the dreamscape worked, well as far as Harlan knew.

She thought about getting homework done quickly, so she could dreamscape again tonight. Heading home on the cute little blue Stuttgart bus, Sophie arrived home to find Ernst there.

Ernst stuck his head around the corner of his little work area.

"Hi, Sophie, seems like I'm home before you for a change. How are you? How's school?"

"Hi, Papa." She gave him a quick hug. "Good, history is really interesting."

Ernst smiled, flicking his long hair out of his eyes. "Ahh, good to see. You'll need good marks if you want to be a history professor like your papa." He smiled.

Sophie glanced up at him.

"Heh, maybe. They may get confused with two Professor Wolfs."

Her papa smiled, clearly happy about the thought.

Sophie had a warm feeling after talking with her dad, he was happy that the dreamscape sessions were finished. Seeing he got her involved with them in the first place, it was a little unusual.

She walked into her room and stopped.

Her room was messy. But this wasn't its usual mess of books and the odd bit of clothing lying about. All the drawers to her dresser were open and her clothes were dumped onto the floor. A clock on her bed table was lying on the floor broken. Her room had been turned completely upside down.

She felt that strange flush of heat that came up the back of her neck when something was wrong.

Sophie examined the room in disbelief. *Why would Hisako or Ernst make a mess of her room?*

Sophie then realised the window was open. She hadn't opened the window when she left.

Then she noticed the hole.

In the brick, next to the window, near the window latch, was a fist sized hole. Completely through the brick. Sophie had to check it twice. She walked over to it, slowly staring. It was a hole. Completely through the brick wall.

There was nothing on the ground, from the hole being cut or drilled. The hole was smooth, like it had been *melted* through the brick. It didn't make any sense.

Sophie knew very little about breaking and entering, but surely it would be easier to break the window, or jimmy it open with a metal lever or something, than make a hole through the brick.

A feeling of panic set in, and she staved off the fear and tried to concentrate on what she was going to do. She felt her hands shaking and clasped her palms together to calm herself.

"Papa?" She yelled loud enough for her papa to hear. She could hear a slight quiver in her voice. "Have you been in my room?"

"No, Soph. You know I don't go in your room. Why?" Ernst called out from the kitchen.

"Has Hisako been in here?" Sophie was getting a sickening feeling in her stomach.

"No, I don't think so," Ernst yelled.

Sophie went back into her room and closed the door. She didn't want Ernst walking in and seeing this. Then it struck her.

Her notebook was missing. Her notebook/spellbook, which normally sat on her dresser. She had a black notebook that had spells written in it. Well, one spell.

She had gotten it recently and had used it to take notes after her two sessions. As soon as she came out of her dreamscape state, she would write everything down. Including the all-important symbol.

And it was gone.

She took a deep breath in as she realised what they may have wanted.

The headset.

In a panic, she vaulted across the bed in one leap, and ran to where she had hidden it. The device was stuck in the top of the cupboard, mainly to keep it away from Hisako who came into her room sometimes while cleaning. She felt herself panicking, reaching for the box, her hand grabbing around, and then her fingers found the cardboard, feeling the shape of the box and the lid … and she was flooded with instant relief.

The box was still there, untouched.

The lid quickly came off in her hands, and both headsets sat there. Sophie picked up the phone and immediately called Harlan.

"Soph? What's up? Everything okay?"

Sophie sat down on her bed. "Not really. Someone broke into my house."

She started crying.

"SOMEONE... BROKE INTO YOUR HOUSE! Frigging hell! What! Are you okay? Did they steal anything?"

Sophie walked over to the window and put her hand through the hole. It fitted completely through, so she could put her hand outside, right through the wall. She fought against the immediate compulsion to tell her papa. He wouldn't react well, and it could be the end of any dreamscaping.

"Yes, they made a hole in the wall and got my spell notebook. Don't worry about it, it had hardly anything in it yet, and I can remember most of it. Harlan, I feel weird. It's an awful feeling," Sophie said, starting to tidy up, with the phone on her ear.

"Yeah, had a bike stolen in the US…it was awful," Harlan muttered, sounding deflated. "But I'm glad to hear you're okay. And it's good that there wasn't a lot in that spellbook. You should be able to recreate it pretty easily, right?" Then suddenly he yelled, "OH… the headset!"

"They're okay, Harls. Both of them. I'd hidden them from Ernst."

"Oh, thank God." Harlan's voice came over the phone again. Hearing his voice was reassuring.

"Don't stress, lock the window. They have what they wanted, so they won't come back. Lock the window properly, don't think about it, and get some rest. We'll chat tomorrow. I'll help you fix the hole," Harlan said.

He was trying to be reassuring, but Sophie could hear a slight waiver of worry in his normally confident voice.

Sophie tried to finish off her history work for Mr Freidrickson, but it was useless. It was her favourite homework, but she couldn't concentrate on it. Thoughts about the break-in were smashing around in her head like bumper cars. She'd have to wake up early and do it in the school library before school started.

She had a distinct urge to dreamscape, but her brain was fried, and she felt a little bit shaky. She fell asleep with the headset in her hands, and woke up in the morning with a start, kicking herself she hadn't gone to see Johannes. He would have known what to do.

Chapter 9—Cats and Spells

The next couple of days continued for Sophie, but largely, the break-in plagued her.

She spoke at length to Harlan about it, who as always, tried to cheer her up. She eventually tried to focus back on her school, and on the note that Marcus had sent her. The fact that Marcus lied annoyed her, but he no doubt he had reasons; some international people were chasing after him, and he was potentially concerned about creating a monster out of some child.

Thinking about Marcus's position, he had several kids doing the dreamscape sessions. She didn't know how many exactly, but the more there were, the more something was likely to go wrong.

They sorted through what was going on and agreed, they should focus on finding Adeline, see if they could find any more of Marcus's dreamscapers that could help, and stop whatever the *rising* was.

Once again, the end of a school day. She returned home, quickly tossed down some of her papa's bacon and eggs sandwiches and went off to her room.

She glanced over to where the hole in the wall was. She had put a poster of her favourite fantasy TV show in the spot to hide it. She had no idea how to fix it, and she knew trying to explain it to her papa would probably not end well.

Grabbing the headphones and her new notebook, she noticed her pre-session nerves were all gone, replaced now with a buzzy feeling of excitement, even if it meant the session involved doing Johannes's household chores. There was a vague feeling of responsibility about finding Adeline, but for the moment, she put it aside. Sophie locked her bedroom door, put the headset on, and quickly drifted off to sleep.

Once again, Sophie was on her way to the path to see Johannes. Same routine. Waking up. The Village, walking to Johannes's house. Knocking on the door.

This time Johannes was a lot happier to see her. He got her to do about an hour's worth of work first (this time chopping some meat, and milking a cow, which he had to show her how to do).

Then on to the sleeping spell practice, with Johannes's grey cat once again "volunteering". Johannes, Sophie, and the cat were all sitting outside, the warm sun-dappled spots of light on the ground through the leaves of a big oak tree. Sophie had to put the break in out of her mind and concentrate. Johannes sat down and watched.

"Sophie. Soooo… how many times have you tried this now?"

"About 300"

"You know, I'm surprised my cats haven't just fallen asleep through boredom." He chuckled to himself. "Sophie, you know the difference between when a friend asks you to do something, and a parent does?"

"I think so…" Sophie said.

"When your parents want you to do something, you respond because there is power. You need to speak with power and instruction in your voice. That's how you get things done. Also, the hand casting, do them properly, you're not doing some sort of weird dance." He gave a disgusted expression. "… and you need to make the symbol exactly."

Sophie had been making the symbols *exactly* as they were supposed to be. It wasn't her fault; Johannes was starting to annoy her now. After so many failures, she was getting very frustrated, but was determined to get this right and wasn't going to stop until she did. She focused on the cat.

She focused on her voice, trying to imbue power, trying to speak with the heart. She drew the symbol perfectly in the air and willed the cat to be asleep.

"Sleep!" she commanded.

The cat, which had been cleaning its fur, froze and peered at her for a second, then dropped to the grass flat, instantly asleep.

Johannes did a little clap, then gave her a ludicrously deep bow, till he was right down on the floor. He then flailed his arms around like they had the bones removed, in a rather over dramatic exposition of relief.

"Well, you either bored it to death, or your spell did work!" He said, raising his voice excitedly. He grabbed an apple and tossed it to her.

"I'm sorry about the sarcasm, Sophie, you have done really well. Congratulations, you are now an Illusionist apprentice in the arts of charms, spellcasting, and incantation. My first apprentice in three years. However, now you've done your first spell, the cow has made a mess near my back stairs."

He handed her a shovel. Sophie didn't care, she went off happy to clean up after the cow. It was just a dream, but after the 300 frustrating attempts at casting her first spell, she finally felt like she had accomplished something.

***

When she finally woke up, she sat on the edge of her bed. It was ten p.m., but she was all excited, and wondered what to do now that she didn't feel the vaguest like sleep. Her brow furrowed as she considered this probably meant falling asleep in the middle of a school lesson, or at an extreme, sleeping on the desk and drooling on her books.

She realised she was enjoying the dreamscape sessions. The sessions gave her the thrill of being in a beautiful cinematic movie, being in full control of what happens, and being able to remember everything that happened afterwards, clearly.

She smiled and nodded to herself. She had cast her first spell. It was a basic, not very useful spell. A spell that put a cat to sleep. It was in a dream, so had no actual use or consequence in the real world, whatsoever. At all.

But she had a *massive* sense of achievement. *I can't wait to tell Harlan.*

It took three glasses of hot milk and two hours before Sophie calmed down enough to get to sleep. She was still abuzz when she woke, quickly getting dressed. Sophie could get to school at the normal time. She hunted down Harlan, who was with some friends, talking about some movie they had just seen.

She pulled him aside.

"Sophie, what's happened?" Harlan was excited for her; he knew something was up.

"It's important, I've got to talk to you."

"I put a cat to sleep," Sophie said.

"Oh, I'm sorry, was it your pet?" Harlan with a sympathetic voice.

"No... in my dream. I've done my first spell! A sleep spell, I put it on my cat."

A dawning of recognition came over Harlan's face. His face instantly changed to a big smile.

"Well, Soph... Well done!" He slapped her on the shoulder and almost knocked her off balance.

Sophie went through the story, almost as a relief. In explaining it, she quickly showed the casting hand signs to Harlan, trying not to be obvious.

Momentarily Sophie glanced up and noticed one of the rare Asian students at the school, one she didn't recognise. She had raised her head from her phone and was studying the flourish of Sophie's hands. When she noticed Sophie watching her, her gaze quickly dropped back down.

Sophie checked her hands, and realised she was being a little obvious. She glanced back at the girl that had been observing her. She was gone.

A slight chill came over Sophie. She didn't know why, but she instantly felt she should be more discrete.

Chapter 10—Tomoko, Harlan and Sophie at the *Electric Light Kafe*

After being kicked out of two cafés, and being given decidedly unwelcome vibes from other baristas, they had decided to find another café and try to not talk so loudly. That is, before they ran out of them; Bamberg only had ten. Harlan had spotted a new one, and he'd let them know it sounded promising. Harlan had said it was, "Old, weird, sort of cool and quiet."

It sounded perfect.

They had decided to meet up early before school for a change. Sophie considered Harlan would be late, and probably half asleep... but it was worth trying, and there was lots to discuss.

Sophie crossed the cobblestone streets, as some University students rode past on their bicycles. She slowed down to let them pass. The damp was in the air, and when she stopped to adjust her scarf, she could feel it settling on her scarf, making it moist. The chill was a nice refreshing feeling.

Sophie liked the rain, she liked the cold, and she liked Bamberg. The whole package. She scanned the shopfronts, trying to find the new café.

Sophie had been trying to read street numbers, but then realized she didn't need to... she could see two scooters parked up ahead.

For a café, it was a traditional old building, she tried to guess, it was probably from the 1600s, like all the others on the street. Red window frames, and a traditional wooden sign hanging out the front, on an ornate metal wrought iron frame that was newer but meant to appear antique. Painted on a wooden board that sat within the ironwork, it said, in slightly fancy lettering:

Electric Light Kafe

The café was a bigger building, taking up two shop fronts. This was a quieter part of Bamberg, with houses and a few businesses around the area. *Easy to park, and away from the tourists,* Sophie considered.

In the front was a vinyl turntable, and a bunch of records in a box next to it. A black Vinyl record spun around on it. Sophie recognized the song; it was a song by an 80's band, *the Human League.* Her father always played them and loved them. Sophie didn't.

At least the volume was turned down, Sophie thought. She checked out the café. The architecture was fashionably antiquated, with a few retro posters on the walls of 70s rock bands. About forty vinyl LP covers lined the walls, to the ceiling. Sophie took thirty seconds to take it all in.

"Table for yourself love? Just grab one." Sophie hadn't noticed the waiter (owner?) come over. He had an English accent, was an older man, with an amazing head of reddish-brown curly hair, a beard to match, and he wore aviator style sunglasses. It was hard to tell how old he was under all the hair, but he must have been in his fifties at least.

"Were you a rock star in the 70s?" Sophie said.

The man peered at her strangely.

"Oh, she's with us," Harlan called out, heading off Sophie's conversation before it got more awkward.

"All right then, grab yourself a seat then, love, I'll be right over," the man said, studying Sophie momentarily, then turned back to help some other customers.

Sophie sat down and got a round of greetings. She noticed Harlan was in a better mood than he was yesterday.

"Yeah, that's Jeff. I think he's ok. So far so good," Harlan said, pointing at Jeff.

"Good. We are running out of Cafes," Sophie said, a slight frown emphasizing her concern.

"Yeah, he has cool hair. He always wears... er, aviator glasses," Harlan said, ignoring Sophie's comment. "What's with his 70s fashion choices, he's a musician?"

"He looks like he is." Sophie nodded, reading a well-used, slightly coffee stained menu. It seemed like it was designed by a rock musician, who may have been better at music than menus layout.

"Whatever. Let's just buy lots of food so it will be expensive for him to kick us out," Sophie said. She was somewhat nervous about café's now.

Jeff came out and took their orders, apparently in good spirits. They each ordered three donuts, and Harlan ordered strudel.

Sophie had told Harlan what her story was, now Sophie wanted to hear about *his* story. Into the second coffee, the slightly cautious Harlan opened up. Harlan told Sophie that when he dreamscaped, he generally traversed the rooftops of London, under the dubious tutelage of the master thief, *Arsène*. He had encounters with rival thieves on the rooftops. He learned how to pick locks, pick pockets, throw objects to distract, and walk quietly.

Harlan explained that he *sort of* had a problem. He could learn things in the dream... but in real life, his natural dexterity and his height and weight sometimes let him down. Frequently he would go to hide in a corner, and his leg would stick out. He had twice put his foot through someone's tiled roof while practicing in Bamberg. He could learn the skills in the dream, but, physically, he was sort of clumsy. Still some things, like lockpicking, he could do quite well.

Sophie suddenly noticed Harlan acting a little peculiar. Suddenly, and awkwardly, he put his coffee up to his lips, and said, behind it, "Sophie, don't look up, but there is a girl from our school over there. The student from Japan. Tomoko, I think."

Sophie left it a while, then had a quick peak. "Harlan... at the school, I think I saw her watching my handcasting yesterday."

Harlan shook his head, frowning, his lips still behind his cup of coffee.

"Soph... yeah, you know, you need to stop doing that in public... you'll have a mob of pitchfork wielding Bambergians after us. Does she know something?" Harlan wondered, sounding concerned.

Sophie pondered, "So what if she does?"

"Oh damn, *she's coming over!*" Harlan whispered under his breath, his gaze in his coffee cup.

The girl crossed the room, pulled up a chair and sat with the two of them, giving them a broad smile. Sophie felt the heat rise on her neck, from the awkward interaction. Harlan pretended he hadn't noticed her walk over, with an awkward reaction at the last minute.

"Oh, hello, Tomoko," they both said in unison. The faux innocence was nauseating.

"Halloo, you two." Tomoko had a thick Japanese accent. She'd been at the school for a year or so, and had a reputation for being one of the more intelligent students, but also consistently happy and positive, despite the situation. Whenever Sophie saw her, she was always smiling. Sophie couldn't work out where she got all the energy from to be constantly happy.

"I heard you in class talking about the apprenticeship, in History class and all the work, and I think it is wonderful," Tomoko said, a big smile on her face.

"I don't think all the work is wonderful... sometimes all the work you...er apprentices need to do goes for hours, and then... the apprentice only had a short time to actually learn something," Sophie said. Harlan threw Sophie a dirty look.

"It's wonderful you too are learning magic. I've been dying to talk to someone!" Tomoko smiled.

"What? No... How do you?" Harlan was surprised.

"Magic..." Sophie went to speak, but decided it was better not to confirm anything, and let Tomoko herself speak first. Tomoko appeared to be quite happy to do so. "Well, I heard you talking all about medieval apprenticeships in history class, which sounded unusual." Tomoko started.

"See, Sophie?" Harlan screwed up his face in mild pain, muttering under his breath. "Told you... you shouldn't have said that."

Tomoko continued. "...and then I saw you at school talking to Harlan, waving your hands around, like a *majutsu-shi*."

"Mar joot so...?" Harlan asked.

"You say..." Tomoko thought for a second. "...ahh, I mean, wizard. Mage. You were talking and doing the casting signs with your hands. I recognised them."

"Sophie, you gotta be more discreet about this. You're going to get us both in trouble," Harlan said, clearly exasperated.

Harlan appeared serious. Sophie remembered they both had signed contracts with the University and considering the recent memory of the break in and the encounter with the men, she was unsure about talking to someone she didn't know.

The table went quiet. Tomoko could see they were hesitant, and clearly wanted to have a conversation about the dreamcasting.

"Oh, Sophie. Harlan… Do not worry about it, I am studying magic in the dreams as well. I am here by myself in Bamberg. I cannot tell my family; they would worry and may bring me back to Japan. Plus, with Professor Marcus gone, I do not really think the secrecy agreement has to be followed anymore."

"Tomoko, I'm not sure what it's like in Japan, but here in Bavaria, you can't just walk around doing magic," Sophie said.

Tomoko nodded, though her expression questioned the advice.

Sophie continued, "They got rid of the old laws here. It's like most countries, everyone there knows about the summoners in England in the 1950 Civil War."

Tomoko nodded. "Yes, in Japan too. Everyone knows of the summoners, but we don't dislike the other mages."

Sophie had always realised there were differences in how some countries saw magic, but it had never struck her *exactly* how different they were. There were some terrible things that mages did in England during their civil war. Sophie remembered the old black and white photos of buildings turned to ash and towns to rubble, and knew the countless lives lost were often just families cowering in their homes. After you saw the images, they were burnt into your memory. Sophie had no intention of doing anything like that. Not that it mattered, she couldn't do spells anyway.

"Magic…it is not illegal here, is it?" Tomoko glanced at Sophie, then Harlan.

"Not in Bavaria now, but it was forty years ago. Not just Summoners, but all mages were made illegal and chased out of towns. Female mages were put in the *Drudenhauses* here in Bamberg and in Hallstadt. Even before the English Civil War, a thousand mages were killed in the 1600s in Wurzburg. We all know the stories," Sophie said.

"It is still illegal in some of the Other German countries. Württemberg, Hannover. The Hanseatic League hate mages and magic, they'll toss you in jail, or worse," Harlan said. Sophie shivered at the mention of the Hansa. Now that she was a mage, it was not a place she would be able to go.

"Anyway, Tomoko, you should be careful." Sophie glanced over at her directly to make sure she understood. It was a strange conversation, they were having a serious discussion with someone they just met and didn't know, but Sophie felt she could trust her. Sophie realised there was an instant bond with magic. It was interesting, people who just met, but both did magic... It brought them together.

Tomoko glanced at them both, noting the serious faces.

"Oh, disappointing. I liked doing magic in public. No wonder people stared at me." Sophie began to imagine the horrific reactions the locals would have had from Tomoko walking around practicing magic.

"Yeah, well we were at the University doing the dreamcast recordin' sessions as well. We were both sent headsets in the mail," Harlan changed the topic, Sophie suspected because he was bothered by talk of the summoners and the dark events of the British Civil War.

"Yes, Marcus...well I think it must have been him...he sent me one also. What type of magic do you both learn?" Tomoko asked.

"Actually... er, I don't learn magic. I study stealth and acquisition," Harlan said.

Tomoko raised an eyebrow, clearly impressed.

"He's actually learning to be a thief," Sophie said, with a smile.

"Errrh..." Tomoko mumbled. The impressed expression melted away to be replaced by concern. Harlan frowned. Tomoko noticed and turned to Sophie.

"I am so happy to be able to talk to someone about this. I haven't been able to talk to anyone. I have been keeping it inside me for ages, it is such a relief." Tomoko was happy and abuzz, Sophie noticed that she was getting louder as she talked.

"You know, this is embarrassing, but I have my special code names for you, TTO and TRS. Do you mind if I call you this?"

Sophie squinted. "Special names?"

"TTO is short for The Thin One, that is Harlan, and TRS is short for The Red Stripe, that is you Sophie, for your hair. I was watching you and taking notes, and I did not know you. I feel like confessing that now."

"Okay, the naming thing is weird, Tomoko," Sophie said, bluntly.

"Weird?" Tomoko's cheeks flushed, as she glanced at both.

"Well, er," Harlan said, stepping in to cover Sophie's bluntness, amidst a slight awkward silence. "Yeah. We're glad we made you happy anyway," Harlan said, now smiling.

Sophie felt sympathy for poor Tomoko. She knew how hard it had been for her before she could start talking to Harlan about the dreamcasting. Keeping it all bottled to herself must have been very hard.

"Tomoko, how long have you been doing the sessions for?" Sophie said.

"About…" Tomoko counted. "About a year. I know about ten spells. I love it so much, I am *so* glad I came to Bavaria." She smiled broadly and raised an eyebrow.

"Ah, you must have started at the same time as me," Harlan said.

Sophie decided to chip in with her experience. "I'm in a medieval setting. I did my first spell."

Tomoko glanced over at her, tilting her head. "You mean your first spell in the dream, or in the real world?"

The table went quiet.

Harlan had just been taking a sip of coffee, and slowly lowered the coffee back down to the saucer. Sophie froze and just glanced at Tomoko silently.

After about ten seconds, Sophie quietly spoke, "Tomoko…can you…"

"…Can you…" Harlan repeated.

"Er… can you do spells… *outside* the dreams?"

Tomoko nodded, smiling. "Yes, of course. You cannot do that?"

Sophie and Harlan's eyes both widened in unison. After about twenty seconds, Sophie remembered the need to breathe. They both glanced at Tomoko. Tomoko was declaring to them that she could do ten spells *in real life*. Sophie had been hoping that one day, she would be able to do the spells she learnt in real life, but a nagging doubt had nearly totally convinced herself that she would only ever be able to do it in the dreamcast.

Here, right in front of her, was someone that could. *The dreams were just too realistic. Johannes was just too real. The spells had to be real too. It made sense now.*

"So, you can do spells... like actual mages spells... outside the dreamcast," Sophie asked.

"Yes... spells. You mean, you can only do them in your dreams?" Tomoko appeared confused.

"Yes. Only in dreams," Sophie said.

"Hmmm...what is the point of that?" Tomoko said.

"Tomoko? Can you do a spell for us?" Sophie asked, her voice lowering, a minor tremble of excitement becoming obvious.

"Yes, of course." She smiled. "I would very much like to do a spell for you."

Before Sophie had a chance to do anything, Tomoko drew a complex glyph in the air, a flurry of lines, crisscrossed. It wasn't a symbol Sophie recognised.

"*Uitemasu,*" she said, simply.

The old fashion salt and pepper shaker slid slowly, completely of its own accord, across the table.

It left the table, slowly rising vertically, and stayed suspended in mid-air for a second, before Tomoko grabbed it right out of the air and put it back on the table.

Sophie and Harlan stared at her, with their mouths open.

"MORE!" Sophie said.

"Yeah, please," Harlan said.

As they went to pay, Sophie noticed Jeff standing behind the counter. He had his arms crossed, a serious expression on his face, deep in thought.

Sophie's heart sank as she saw him walking over. She knew it. He'd overheard them, or worse seen something.

"Now you lot... it's clear you are talkin' about magic. Which some people would take umbrage with."

"Not again," Harlan said under his breath.

"Don't get me wrong, I like mages, right? I see you lot as special 'ere. But I have to think of what everyone else thinks too. That said, this place here... it's tradition." He nodded.

"Tradition?" Sophie said.

"This is a cafe *now*, but traditionally it was a tavern, and mages came here. Mages and people with certain skills, adventuring types."

"What? You used to see them?" Sophie asked.

"Nah not me, I'm a barista, not a mage talent agency. But the owner before me, an old German bloke, told me all about it. You can see it all upstairs."

"Upstairs?" the three of them said together.

"Okay, I was considering kicking you out, but if you're going to come here, just use upstairs. All right? Away from prying eyes 'n all. It's where the other mages used to hang out apparently, so it's a fine Bavarian tradition. Come here, I'll show you." He motioned for them to follow him.

After quickly taking the stairs in the café, Sophie walked into a large sized room, old with dark wood paneled walls contrasting a white plaster ceiling. It had eight tables and wooden seats at each, and a few things stored in the corner. Sophie could see the dust on the table, but the upstairs room was roomy and had a great rustic feel to it.

"Ok, no casting spells. All right? any magic that goes on here, I could be in big trouble."

"I guess fireball spells would be bad for your corporate brand," Harlan said, waving his hand in the air generally.

"My what?" Jeff glanced at him, confused.

Sophie ignored Harlan's comment.

"Allright, I personally don't have a problem with mages, it's the townspeople that may not *appreciate* you," Jeff said.

"I would say the town's people not appreciating us is an understatement," Sophie said.

Jeff nodded. "Okay, I was being polite. They hate mages, some of them will want to chase you out of town. The others are worried what you may do... reality is, they vary between fearing you lot, and... wanting to completely drive mages out of the town with bits of burning wood and various rusty sharp gardening tools."

"I'm not a mage... they shouldn't treat me like that," Harlan said to Jeff, leaning on the table.

Jeff turned and stared at him.

"You're not? What are you?"

"I'm a thief," Harlan said.

"Well…" Jeff rolled his eyes. "That's all right then," he said, sarcastically.

"Anyways… as I said, I don't mind you mages. I'm from England, and we suffered in the Civil War from Summoners. But *unlike* most people, I know there's a difference between Summoners and Illusionists, and Druids and what not."

Sophie raised her eyebrow and flashed a quick glance at Tomoko, who returned the same look. It was odd to hear a non dreamcaster talk about mages like this, so openly.

"The thing is… it's all about this place," Jeff said, sitting down. As he said *this place*, he waved his arms around in the air. Harlan scanned the room, trying to identify exactly what was special about this place.

"When this was a tavern, and when mages were legally active in Bamberg, before the civil war, they met here. Groups of them would meet, like your party, and talk. Sometimes exchange relics or information. People would get jobs." Jeff appraised each of them, trying to size them up. "By the way, what's the name of your party?"

Tomoko frowned. "Party?"

"Yeah, you know. Your group. Like, you are clearly a mission party. You know, quests and what not. You have all your specific roles, and you are working taking on jobs. Are you on some sort of quest now?"

Sophie realised with surprise, Jeff's assumption of them was pretty well correct. It actually was what they were. Sort of.

"Yes, of course. We have assigned roles. If you have some sort of task for us, or any information, let us know." Sophie blurted out, without really thinking.

"We don't have a party name. How about the Illustrious Talented Adepts, Incorporated," Tomoko said.

"Too long," Harlan shot it down.

"I've not got the imagination or the energy for making up names." Sophie shook her head.

Harlan chipped in, "…Ok, how about *Circle 66*. And for any quests or jobs, we'll be happy to negotiate a price."

Tomoko and Sophie shrugged and nodded in broad agreeance.

Jeff smirked momentarily. "Circle 66? Okay, well clearly you are winging it and have no idea, but that's okay. You're welcome to come here but sit upstairs. I'm a foreigner, so who am I to stop you from using it? The fact that mages met here previously… and you lot have shown up here must mean something."

"Actually, we showed up here because we got kicked out of the other cafes and this was one of the few left," Harlan said.

A smirk appeared on Jeff's face, just for an instant, quickly replaced by a frown.

"Oh. I see. You're serious. All right, well you're good here with me. Just remember, any furniture you burn, or melt, or turn into stone, you pay for." He walked over to the door frame of the room.

"And here's something that will interest you." His hand wavered over some arcane looking symbols bordering the wood around the door frame.

"What are those?" Sophie asked.

"I don't know, I'm a barista, not a magical symbol interpreter. I was going to ask you." Jeff glanced at them. "Owlright, see what you make of this, then pay me on the way out."

They nodded to Jeff, and then went over to examine the symbols on the wall. Sophie felt stunned that suddenly, she was in a room that had been used by mages for may be decades or longer, in the past.

"Hang on Harlan, *you* named our group. Why Circle 66?" Sophie said, a suggestion of indignation apparent.

"It's a ranch name. I always liked it." He shrugged "Anyway, well, pretty cool, we ended up in the café in Bamberg used by Mages," Harlan noted.

"Not surprising seeing we were almost kicked out of most of the rest," Sophie said, her attention largely affixed to the door frame and the symbols.

"Oh, they're glowing," Harlan said. Sophie looked up to see Harlan studying the symbols, with his *glasses of true sight* on. There were six symbols there. The door frame was an arch, and evenly spaced out in the archway, the symbols were carved into it.

"Glowing!" Tomoko said, excited evident in her voice.

"This one… this one here. It split into four elements: Wind, Earth, Water and Fire. Is this an elementalist?" Sophie asked.

"OH! Hang on. Yeah, this symbol here, it's the symbol of the thief's guild. I saw it once on a card that was delivered to Arsène," Harlan said, touching the wood.

"That's a sword, oh a warrior?" Tomoko reached forward, touching another symbol on the wood, and took a selfie with her smiling in front of it.

Sophie walked over to examine them all. There were clearly various symbols carved expertly into the door for the different paths of magic. A drop of blood for blood magic, the head of a devil with horns presumably for summoners, two identical profiles, mirroring each other for illusionists and a triangle.

"Each of these symbols, these are all classes. They are all paths you can learn. The magical paths, and thievery and swordcraft."

"What's this one here?" Tomoko pointed. It was a hammer and a brush.

Sophie shook her head. "Not sure."

Harlan walked over and touched the blood symbol. "This one isn't glowing."

"I wonder what that means? Blood magic is long gone, so maybe it relates to that?"

"Oh, and this one's not glowing too. A triangle?" Harlan touched it, tracing his fingers in the equal three-sided triangle carved into the wood.

Tomoko wandered over and touched the sword symbol. "So, with your glasses, you can see this glowing? The glasses see magic?"

"Yep, sure can," Harlan said.

"Oh, very cool," Tomoko nodded.

After spending a minute or two investigating the symbols, and unsuccessfully trying to convince Harlan to let them use his glasses, they eagerly reminded Tomoko she was going to show them some of her magic.

***

Tomoko, in the end, had invited them to her house for a magic *show and tell*. Sophie thought Tomoko was almost as keen as she. Sophie and Harlan arrived at Tomoko's house after school, a quaint 200-year-old little white house with its own garden. The house seemed big for one person to live in, in a nice part of Bamberg.

As they arrived at the front door, Sophie's phone rang. She picked it up. Strangely, there was no one talking. All she could hear was some background noise.

"Who was that?" Harlan asked, just as they approached the door.

"No one. Must have been a pocket dial, I think. It was just background noise."

They kept walking up to the garden path. Sophie checked the door number, before rapping politely on the door. The sound of walking and clutter came from inside, clearly Tomoko was running around getting ready.

But there was no answer. Strange.

"She's taking a while to answer. Maybe she is in a cleaning frenzy and can't hear."

Harlan knocked louder, and as he did, there was the sound of something falling, smashing on the ground...

Harlan turned to Sophie, his face questioning it.

"Tomoko, are you in there?" Sophie called to her. She turned to Harlan "Maybe you can bust the door down?"

"Yeah, er, Sophie, I'm a trained thief. I can pick the lock." He pulled out a little rolled up case with some tools in it, knelt on one knee, and started stabbing the sharp thin tools into the key hole, gingerly.

Suddenly the door opened, and standing in front of them was a lady and a young girl.

"Guten Tag. Seid ihr Fruende von Tomoko?"

"Ah, yes, we are her friends. Who are you?" Sophie replied.

"Please come in." the lady said, effortlessly switching to English. She was standing next to a young girl, with platinum blonde hair, and a serious expression.

Sophie noticed the young girl subtly glanced at her mother as she spoke.

Harlan and Sophie stepped into the house and as they did, they noticed two large men in the house, a bald man in a black T-shirt, and another man with a short, trimmed beard and long brown hair.

As soon as Harlan and Sophie crossed the threshold, one of the men stepped behind them and closed the door.

Sophie noticed the young girl had a book clutched to her chest. She glanced panicky at Harlan, who had concern on his face and was backing away from them.

"Deal with them. Quickly. Quietly. I have what I need," the lady said. The man opened the door and let the lady and the young girl through the door. Sophie tried to follow them, but the bald man quickly stood in the way, then stepped in closer to Sophie.

Sophie could see out of the corner of her eye, the other man moving towards Harlan, who was going into a fighting pose, his hands raised, his leg back. Then suddenly, she glanced down to see that the man had quickly reached forward and grabbed her wrists, tight. She couldn't cast a spell.

He reached down and grabbed her by the torso, lifting her in the air. The room spun around, and her vision was filled with ceiling tiles, as she felt herself flying through the air. There was a blunt pain in her back and ribs as she bounced against the wall, she felt the air pushed out of her lungs, as she crashed down to the ground.

She shook her head, to regain her focus. She quickly glanced at Harlan, who was struggling with the other man. He had a bloody nose, courtesy of Harlan, but the other man was winning, restraining Harlan.

Suddenly, there was a loud crashing sound, as a cupboard door went flying across the room. It was the top cupboard, and someone was squashed into the cupboard space.

Sophie realised it was Tomoko. Tomoko dropped down but as she dropped her hand flicked through the air. Mid drop, her outfit changed to a pure white costume, lace and frills suspended in air, glowing white. She dropped mid-way to the ground, out of the cupboard, but then sat suspended in the air, her feet not touching the floor. Parts of her dress and her long black hair floated in the air, suspended like they were underwater.

"Leave my friends alone!" Tomoko screamed. Sophie heard the strength in her voice, inflected with the slightest waver.

The two men stopped what they were doing, stunned. The bald man, who had been moving towards Sophie, simply stopped and froze, his mouth partially open but saying nothing. The other man, holding Harlan, also had concern across his face.

"Max, grab her hands, quick," he said to the bald man.

Max, the bald man, went to attack Tomoko, still floating in the air, in her glowing white outfit. Tomoko's hand flicked through some quick hand motions. In an instant a symbol appeared.

"*Inazuma*," she said the command, and there was a bright arc of electricity, and a cracking sound. What appeared to be a bolt of lightning seared across the room and smashed into the bald man, who fell to the ground. Part of his shirt was black and singed, smoke rising from it.

He sat there stunned, staring at the floor.

The man with the ponytail ran out of the room, not turning back.

Max saw the other man exit through the door, panic crossed his face, and he sprang to his feet. He scuttled quickly out of the room, hampered by a limping damaged leg, the smell of burnt clothing lingering in the air.

Sophie stood up, holding her rib cage, crouching over, letting out a groan. She gazed at Tomoko, who was suspended in the air. The adrenaline was still coursing through Sophie's veins, helping to suppress the pain and the fear, though had to breathe hard to get her breath back.

Harlan ran over to Sophie grabbing her shoulders. "Sophie, dang, you okay?"

"Yes, thanks I think so. Just had the wind knocked out of me and my rib hurts. Tomoko, thanks for saving us, but…why did you wait?"

"Sophie, I'm sorry I was scared. I was hiding, hoping they would just leave. They took my spellbook, I thought that is what they wanted."

"Was that girl Adeline? Who were those guys?" Harlan said.

"I don't know, maybe? She came here searching for the spellbook, she must have taken mine." Tomoko said, clearly exasperated. She flicked her hand quickly in the air and dropped to the floor abruptly.

There was a noise at the door, and Sophie turned to see a chubby balding man in his mid-forties standing in the doorway.

"Tomoko, are you okay? We heard some noise from next door."

"Oh, yes, sorry, Mr Krupp." She grabbed Harlan and pulled him next to her.

"My boyfriend is here. He was practicing his martial arts. He is very enthusiastic." She patted Harlan on the stomach. "Oh, he has a flat stomach." Her voice lifted in tone.

"Harlan, show Mr Krupp your flat stomach."

"What?" Harlan appeared confused.

The man's head poked further into the room around the door, which was ajar, and then appraised Harlan, Sophie and finally Tomoko. He quickly left, muttering something to himself.

They all sat down. Sophie felt stunned.

"Well, I guess we *were* coming here for a demonstration of magic. Yeah?" Harland scratched his head, picking up an upturned chair.

"I had a lot of notes in that spellbook, I was still working on three new spells." Tomoko's voice was downcast.

"All your spells are in there? They can use it to cast your spells!" Sophie said.

Tomoko crossed her arms. "They have my spellbook, and yes they could use it to learn and cast my spells." She smiled. "That is… if they can read Japanese." She started laughing, her laughter was loud, and vaguely maniacal, in the cutest way possible. Harlan gazed at her, smiling.

Chapter 11 - Tomoko and Kentaro

Tomoko pulled out noodles, egg and pork, and quickly made some Ramen. *Shio Ramen, with pork*—her favourite. She liked living in Bavaria but having a few Japanese things in her house made her feel at home. She missed Japan. Her apartment had a little *Kamiza*, a couple of Japanese lanterns, a framed Ogasawara crest, and a photo of Kyushu, her home prefecture. Japanese food made her feel comfortable, and Ramen was the number one comfort food for her.

Living by herself meant she didn't have to worry about people knowing she was learning magic, or people knowing about the dreamscape technology, which she hadn't thought much about, until discussing it with Sophie. Tomoko had travelled to the German states with her father and mother when she was thirteen, her dad was teaching Management at Bamberg University. When she was fifteen, he told her that he and his mother were going back to Japan, and gave her a choice, she could stay and he would pay her to remain, or she could go back to Japan. She had decided to stay, and so far, it had been going okay. Apart from needing an occasional signature from her uncle Hiroshi in Würzburg.

Tomoko went over to her window and peered out over the picturesque medieval street below. The tourists were milling about, a couple of them almost getting run over by a car as they tried to take selfies with their smartphones. Her chopsticks deftly targeted the tasty broth-soaked meat first, then she noisily slurped up the Ramen noodles.

Normally her life was solitary, she had never really made friends and her family were back in Japan. Her regular habit of sitting at the window, watching the tourists clogging the footpaths below, made her feel like she was around people. Today, she felt a cheery feeling in her chest. She checked her phone, and flicked her finger across the screen, moving Harlan and Sophie's phone numbers into her "friends" category. The two new names on her friends list made her smile: all the other names in her friends list were back in Japan.

Lying on her small sofa, she put on the dreamscape headset, and snuggled back into the soft leather to get comfortable.

***

Tomoko was in a busy marketplace. For a second, she felt like she was in the insanely busy part of Kyoto, full of traditional shops, people wearing traditional outfits, … and tourists in rented Kimonos for a day's experience as a geisha or samurai.

Despite having been here before, and the whole thing being part of the dreamscape, she still found visiting the markets and the castle exciting. The same thrilling feeling built up in her chest that she got while visiting a real market in Japan. Except here, there were no tourists. She listened to the chatter, people speaking the formal Japanese she normally saw in Samurai movies… then… *actual* Samurai. Three of them pushed their way through the crowd in the shopping marketplace. Other people bowed out of their way respectfully, if they didn't their armoured retainers in the front would shift anyone out of the way that didn't do so or didn't react quick enough.

Tomoko watched on, an involuntary sense of fear growing in her stomach, even though she knew this was her dreamscape, and in it she was perfectly safe. Tomoko had seen the markets before, but she still was awed by the work of the artisans, their wares, and how everything appeared.

It all appeared so real.

"Irashaimase! Please, some excellent quality chopsticks for you!" The chopsticks were glossy, a deep dark purple, with tiny roses painted on the sides, ornate gold leaf capped the edges. A merchant was waving chopsticks at her, turning them around so she could see their splendor from all sides. He started rudely pushing them into her face.

"These are excellent chopsticks, but I cannot buy them from you," Tomoko said.

The merchant raised an eyebrow. "But why not?"

Tomoko considered. He wasn't an important character in the dreamscape. "You are just a memory of a character from 500 years ago and this is just the dreamscape. That's why."

The merchant stepped back physically from her in surprise. He seemed uneasy. Tomoko laughed at being able to mock a medieval merchant, with no repercussions. The dreamscapes were a lot of fun. It was a shame Kentaro was so serious, the lessons, so serious.

She glanced around at the pretty objects for sale, and still felt the impulse to buy things, even though she knew she couldn't take them with her out of the dream. It was weird. Everything was so real, so marvelous. She picked up a lacquered ceramic teapot, her mouth agape and its intricate carvings and tiny portraits painted on the side.

Gazing at everything, and not being able to take it home was annoying. She kept bowing at the merchants and told one he was attractive and should be an actor. She asked another merchant if she could work for him to see what he would say. All the conversations were realistic, and she covered her face to stifle a laugh.

The continuous bowing though, as was Japanese custom, however, was sometimes too much. In any case, she was here to see Kentaro Oda, the Court mage. Her talented ancestor.

She scanned around to see where she was and spotted the roof of the Lord's castle. GKS. Grumpy Kentaro Sensei. He lived in Osaka castle, which she had visited in modern Japan to compare it to how it was in its historical dreamscape. The castle itself was still very similar, but the surroundings were somewhat different, and the gardens and tree line had changed, so it was a little disorientating. Some things were in the place she expected to be, but others weren't.

She wandered up to the initial gate. There were a few beggars around, and a girl wearing a red satin dress, with an ornate hat. She had a monkey with a rope around its neck doing tricks, trying to get a few coins off people who were there to see the castle or the market. The Monkey pulled at the collar around its neck, squeaking. *Next time I am here I will steal that monkey and let him free.*

Handing over a script to the guard, she bowed even lower than the appropriate depth to the guard on the door. The guard reacted to the inappropriateness with a single raised eyebrow.

"I'm Tomoko, I have travelled far—from Edo. I'm here to see Kentaro san, my lord."

She glanced momentarily at the big spear he carried, a long blade at the end of a wooden spear. She shuddered unconsciously. It couldn't really hurt her, but the dream was so real there was a compulsion to treat weapons and danger like she did in reality. The guards were scary.

He could say no to her, blocking her entry, though people in the dreamscape tended to make things go smoothly... Tomoko had concluded it was something to do with her subconscious guiding the dream, trying to make it work.

She had spent a lot of time studying how the dreamscape all worked, it had certain rules it followed every session. Once you worked out the rules of what could happen, and what couldn't, it made the whole dreamscape experience a lot easier. It was a marvelous thing. The dreamscape generally worked to help you learn, but you could still make mistakes. You could die in the dreamscape, but you would just wake up back in reality, wherever you were lying down, with your headset on.

The retainer on the left side of the gate eyed her up and down, stepped back from her, clutching his long spear and holding it between him and her. The retainer standing on the right side of the gate read the message, stared at her, and then respectfully bowed. The initial retainer then bowed as well. It was a deep bow, which said more about how they felt about Kentaro, than Tomoko.

"This way." He opened the gate. Tomoko cleared two more gatehouses, the gates, by design, getting smaller as she went. Then she entered the actual main castle proper, taking the staircase to the upper level. She knelt respectfully in front of Kentaro's room, but before she could say anything, he called out.

"Tomoko san." Kentaro smiled. "I can *always* tell it's you. Your footsteps are heavier than some of the samurai." His voice was dark and disapproving. *Not in a good mood,* Tomoko thought.

"I will try to be more graceful, apologies, Kentaro sensei."

"Come in," he said directly. "I have much to teach you today." Tomoko had been learning magic from Kentaro for some time. She could do a range of spells in her dreamscape, all up about ten different ones. She knew she was good at them.

"Grab your things, Tomoko, we are going to the markets. I want you to do a live demonstration of some of your skills."

"Sensei, doing magic in the market?" She felt her hand drift up to her face, something she always did when nervous.

"Yes. It is one thing doing magic in a room. Another completely different thing doing magic in a real-life situation." He turned to her with a smile. "Plus, I might get to see you do it incorrectly and have the whole marketplace angry with you. That is good *motivation*."

"Yes, sensei." Tomoko fought the urge to roll her eyes, instead just nodded politely.

He was a serious teacher, but had always been nice to her, and the lessons were detailed, and she loved doing them. She thought about doing magic in the market. She thought of doing magic and getting it wrong in front of people. Her hands played nervously, touching the Obi belt of her Kimono behind her back.

Chapter 12—The Mystery of Mr Freidrickson

As Sophie reluctantly shifted the blanket off, to get out of bed, she could hear Hisako in the kitchen. Hisako was singing in Japanese while making breakfast. Sitting on the edge of her bed, she put the palm of her hand on her ribcage, pressing slightly to feel the damage from the brief battle at Tomoko's. The pain was lessened after a night's sleep. Sophie wondered if the men, and the girl who she suspected was Adeline, would leave them alone now they had the spell books. It reinforced in her the need to learn spells to defend herself and be able to use them in the real world. It was frustrating, and she thought about her day ahead, thinking of where she would be, and if they were public places where she would be safe.

Radio music came from the kitchen, accompanying Hisako's singing. As far as Sophie could tell, Hisako had everything sorted out in her life. She had money, she had friends. She loved living in Bavaria and liked working for her papa. She could leave and visit Japan whenever she wanted.

The only time she appeared even vaguely unhappy was when her papa's girlfriends were around. Ernst was relatively handsome and fit, compared to her friend's fathers, who all got somewhat chubby around thirty-something. His girlfriends were seemingly getting younger every year. But they never stayed around for long.

Now, her dad's girlfriend, Annika, was about twenty years younger than him.

This Annika had been around for about six months, she was in fact Annika number two. Annika number one was around about two years ago. She was a shorter Annika, into history, movies… cool music. She had been one that Sophie liked. Every so often there would be a new girlfriend. A new name to learn, some new introductions. Sometimes they were nice. Sometimes they were a little rude.

It was often easier for Sophie to just disappear into her room when they were around.

Sophie got up out of bed. The image of Tomoko floating in the air was still in her mind. She considered the threat of the two men, and the girl, who was possibly Adeline. Then she reassured herself that they had Tomoko on their side now. She was so happy to know that magic could be done in the real world and so impressed by Tomoko. Hearing Tomoko say she could do magic, had given her such a sense of relief.

She enjoyed chatting with Hisako, so hopped off the bed to catch up with her. She had heard her papa leave earlier, and she always enjoyed a chat about him when he wasn't about. She was curious to see if Hisako knew about why her dad got so angry about the mention of magic.

"Good morning, Hisako." Sophie stumbled out of her bedroom, pulling a purple fluffy jumper on.

"Ohayo!" Hisako said, pointing at a black bento lunchbox. "I made lunch for you; how do you like this?" Hisako opened the Japanese lunch box and showed Sophie what was inside. It was filled with sushi and gyoza dumplings. Hisako smiled at her tasty creations.

"Okay, now I have your attention. I want to talk to you about something." Sophie's heart jumped a beat, and she slowed her pace. Hisako had been in Sophie's life for so long that the woman had earned the same level of authority and respect as a parent. That usually wasn't a problem with Sophie, but Hisako sounded serious, which was rare.

"I want to ask you. Why is there a hole in your wall?" Hisako stopped cooking and gazed at Sophie directly.

"How did you know?" Sophie thought she had covered it.

"You put a picture in a frame over it, to cover it. But it is on the edge of the window frame, covering part of the window. Picture frames…are normally in the middle of the wall… not on the edge of a window frame."

"Oh. Yeah, I guess that is weird." Harlan had put up the framed picture, as the poster had not been convincing. That was the last time she asked him to cover up a magical break-in. Hisako pointed to the sofa, and Sophie sat down. She gave her a cup of green tea and took one herself.

"Tell me," Hisako said.

Sophie knew at this point she didn't have much of an option but to confess. But Hisako was someone she trusted, she felt okay about it.

"Okay, well you can't tell Papa. He's *really* not happy about this topic now," Sophie said.

Hisako's eyes widened. "Sophie what is going on?"

"I'm… I'm… learning spellcasting. I put a hole in the wall when practicing a spell," Sophie lied. Sort of.

"Oh… Sophie No… what? Why are you doing that?" Hisako frowned and sat back in her chair. She appeared concerned but took it better than Sophie expected.

"I didn't choose it. It was the dreamcasting. Papa took me there, it's his fault."

Hisako sat there quietly, her hand over her face. Her eyes darted left and right, clearly considering what all this meant. But Sophie was relieved, at least she hadn't flipped out or got as angry as her papa. In telling her, she felt a weight lifted off her chest.

"What sort of magic is it? It's not summoning?" Hisako put the tea down on the table, obviously not able to drink it.

"No, it's not. It's a path called *Illusionist,*" Sophie said, not that Hisako would know what it meant, but any detail that verified you weren't being a summoner made people more comfortable.

"Hisako, *please* don't tell Papa. You saw how he acted. I…really like doing it. I learn stuff. I feel important. And…we are rare. Mages—people who cast spells, there's very few of us around anymore. It's really important to me."

"Is Harlan… he is one as well?"

"No, he's a thief."

"What?" Hisako seemed taken aback. "*A thief?*"

"Well, yeah he would say he is a master of stealth or something."

Hisako paused. "This is really difficult for me." Concern dogged her face, but just as quickly, it disappeared. "Okay, I won't tell your papa, it's just going to create more drama. I can see this is important to you, but it does worry me. He's not going to be happy if he finds out. He gets angry about magic, not sure why. Really angry."

Sophie sat there, contemplating. "Yes, I don't know why either," she responded, wracking her brain to come up with why he responded like he did.

"Magic… I don't really mind, here in Europe people get all upset about mages and spells, because of the Summoners, but for my people, the Japanese, it was something that happened far away from us."

"Well, funny you bring that up. We met another mage, she is Japanese. Her name is Tomoko."

"Tomoko? Japanese mage? She is not a ninja?"

"Ninja… that's a racial stereotype, isn't it?"

Hisako shrugged. "I'm Japanese. It's not racism if it's about your own people."

Sophie shook her head, smiling.

"No, she's a mage too. She's… pretty good."

"Really!" Hisako raised her eyebrows and smiled, clearly impressed.

Sophie checked the time. "Oh damn, I'm going to be late. Please don't tell Papa. He will go crazy."

"I know, I know, for the sake of both of us, I won't tell him. But be careful and let me know the moment there is any trouble." Hisako nodded.

Chapter 13 - Spells of Blocking

Sophie came home again, a quick hello to Ernst, an excuse about homework, and then a scurry to her bedroom. She pulled out the headset, put it on, and was quickly walking along a now familiar dirt path, heading towards the house of a mage in fifteenth century Bavaria.

This time, Johannes was waiting at the front of the house, fixing a wooden window shutter.

"Sophie, I haven't seen you for a while!"

"Hello, Johannes." She glanced at him, realising that he could sense the time in the real world that she hadn't seen him. Her thoughts turned to what likely farm chores he would have for her to do.

"Sophie, I have two fields for you to plough." He looked her up and down. "You can strap yourself into this harness attached to the plough if that makes it easier."

Sophie stared at him. She didn't know much about ploughing, but it sounded like really hard work. Johannes glanced at her, waited a few seconds, appeared disappointed she didn't react, and started laughing.

"Ahah! I was joking with you. That would have been incredibly hard work, and you may have died." He pulled an apple out of his pocket and started eating it, and with a flourish of his hand whisked Sophie through the doorway.

"Let's teach you some more spells, eh? Today... one of the most pivotal spells... the blocking spells." Johannes leaned on the edge of the table, crossing his arms.

"Blocking spell... for blocking... the effects of other Mage's spells?" Sophie responded.

"No… for blocking *theengs*."

He bent over and swept his arm across the table, making space amongst the fruit, papers, quills, and books that were strewn across it. A few objects fell onto the dirt floor. He dipped his finger in some water, and started drawing a picture, the water left from his finger darkening the musty dry oak tabletop, like ink to paper.

"This is you. This is a small circle around your heart. This is a slightly bigger circle around your body. This is a larger circle around you and three friends." He drew four other symbols Sophie didn't recognise.

"These four symbols, balance, resistance, fortitude and depth. Understand the nature of these perfectly… and you will cast a great shield spell." Johannes grabbed Sophie's arms and pushed her into the centre of the room. She noticed the skinny grey cat (whose name she had worked out was Julius) had come in to watch, almost like it knew this was going to be entertaining. The ginger cat quickly appeared and stared at her, almost to the point where it was distracting.

Johannes stood in front of her.

"Now, Sophie, this hand swings this way. This hand swings the other way." His hands flowed slowly through the air, one circling over, one circling under.

"Now concentrate on building up the energy in the space between the two hands." Sophie gazed on, staring at him blankly. He noticed and quickly smiled.

"It is all right." He sat down on the table edge. "How about I show you. Here, throw this apple at me." He picked up an apple, started eating it, realised he had meant to give it to Sophie, and then gave her a whole one. "Now throw this at me." He stepped away from her, judging the distance as he did.

Sophie gazed at him, then at the apple, and said, "You mean throw this… ap…" she threw it at him mid-sentence, trying to catch him off guard. However, in a beautiful swirl of arm movements, Johannes instantaneously curved his hands through the air, he mumbled the command word, and without touching it, it deflected off, out the window into the backyard, probably to be eaten by the goats.

He smiled. "Sophie…sneaky apple throw!"

"Okay, Johannes I'm impressed."

"Four apples!" He reached over and gave her four apples. Sophie took the hint, she smiled a cheeky smile, clearly intent on hitting him with at least one.

This time, Johannes stood in front of her, one hand behind his back the other in front, in a sort of two fingered peace sign, but with the fingers together. Sophie checked that he was ready, and then threw them in quick succession. Johannes just slightly flicked his hand, without touching them, mumbled the command word under his breath, and the apples went off in various directions.

Sophie leaned back on the table, crossed her arms, clearly impressed.

"Wow... okay, you need to show me that!"

Johannes put Sophie in the middle of the room. "Okay, one hand up here, one hand down here. Feet planted on the ground. You ready?"

"I'm ready."

Johannes tossed four apples at her. They all hit her in the head.

"Ow." Sophie held her nose, her eyes watering.

"Oh, I forgot to tell you the spell command word. Ooops!" Johannes' cheeky smile curled up one side of his face.

"Yes, sure you forgot," she said, still holding her nose.

"Oh, I'm serious now, Sophie. Try it again, the spell command is *Weren.*"

This time she planted her feet again. Johannes deliberately stepped away from her to give her more time to react. He curled his arm and then made a slow deliberate toss at her. She swung both arms, in a similar way to Johannes, and commanded the spell with a strong voice.

"Weren."

The apple flew through the air, entered the space between her hands, and completely changed path, diverting out the window and on to the front part of the house. Johannes appeared very pleased.

"Well done, Sophie... well done!" He whacked her on the shoulder enthusiastically, causing her to step forward to avoid falling over. Johannes crossed his arms, picked up an apple, and started eating it. He appeared thoughtful. "Shame it only works on apples. No idea what to do if people are throwing rocks or knives at you."

Sophie squinted at him. "It only works on apples?"

As he walked away, Johannes then pointed at a woven wicker basket on the ground, then pointed outside.

"Basket. Pick twenty apples, please, young gentlewoman!"

Sophie smiled and went off to grab the basket. It took her longer than it should have, but Sophie found the twenty best apples and brought them back for Johannes. These little tasks were annoying, but they came with the lessons, so she had become resigned to doing them.

"Well, at this stage in your education, we need to discuss curses." Johannes crossed his arms, rather dramatically. "You know, in case you end up with a withered arm or an extra leg and are wondering why." He chewed on the apple for about a minute. "Well, do you want to know about curses?

"Ah." She rolled her eyes. "You just said we needed to discuss them," Sophie said. Curses did sound a little interesting, and slightly darker than the other magic she had been dabbling in.

"Okay, in that case, it's good you asked. Let me tell you all about them." He took another bite.

"I'm not sure why you asked me, you were going to tell me anyway." Johannes's quirks could be annoying.

"Sophie, you need to be more respectful of an archmage that knows ten times the spells you know and has lived to the grand old age of forty-two. Anyway... curses. Sit down."

Sophie sat down and went to take an apple out of a wicker basket, only to have her hand slapped away.

"Curses are not good things. I don't like them. I prefer doing something in the moment, not leaving something hanging around, where you can't be responsible for it," he said.

"What do you mean?" Sophie sat down on a wooden stool.

"Well, you put a curse on someone, and it stays with them forever, until it is removed by a mage who is more powerful. And, well... knows how to remove curses."

"Curses are serious things, like withered hands, or not bearing children, right?" Sophie asked.

Johannes shuddered, and appeared taken aback, momentarily giving Sophie a strange look.

"Well, you used to have all sorts of evil curses. The curse of the droopy eye; That made one of your eyes droop lower than the other. Curse of the yellow river nose...well." He seemed awkward. "I won't go into detail about that."

"The Curse of the noxious slightly green toes. The curse of the bulbous pulsing nose. The curse of the uncle that always wants to stay over for more than two weeks. The curse of the annoying bard that always appears at bars when you are drinking and keeps playing the songs you really hate. They were the lightweight ones."

"Lightweight?" Sophie watched on, starting to regret that she had asked.

"There are nasty ones. They were used in the past, maybe back hundreds of years ago. The heavy, more serious ones." He frowned and shook his head. "Blight on a whole village. Insect plague. Making a woman barren. Cursing a lake to keep it dry. Nasty stuff. People stopped using those, and no one knows how to do them anymore. Thank the Sun. They were wiped out of my...well *our* path of magic. I don't know how to do them, and I'm glad of it."

Sophie imagined a world where people were cursing each other with terrible curses that affected whole communities. It was crazy.

"You can put a curse on an object as well. Like, for instance, one of these chairs is cursed to give hairy legs to the person that sits on it for longer than a minute. I always forget which one, because I have wonderfully hairy legs anyway. Actually—" He squinted at the stool that Sophie was sitting on. "Does your chair have a cross carved on the leg?"

Sophie screamed and hopped off the chair, horrified.

"It's got an X on it!"

"Sophie, Sophie. I jest." He reached over and whacked her on the shoulder, reminding her of Harlan who was a regular shoulder-whacker.

"No cursed chairs here today." He smiled. "I can teach you some curses, but just some vague ones. More cantrips really."

Cantrips, Sophie thought. *Another word I don't know.*

Johannes pointed out the door and they both wandered outside. Sophie got lessons on curses and learnt how to do the curse of the runny nose, and four varieties of vomiting curses that incorporated various musical chords.

She could sense the natural finish of the dreamscape session, so had to get in a question before it finished.

"Johannes, can I ask you something?" Sophie peered at the apple, just out of reach.

"Certainly, my good gentlewoman apprentice. Perchance, I may answer," Johannes responded, more aloof than usual.

"Okay, the symbols we cast magic with. I have seen them painted on the front of your house.

"Why are they there?" Sophie enquired, wondering if she would get a straight answer.

"Ah, symbology. You know symbols are essential to our path of magic, we always draw a symbol in the air when we cast." He seemed sort of serious.

"Of course. It's part of every spell." She glanced up at him, to see the point he was making.

"If you want to make a spell's effect permanent... Well of a longer duration, you must cast a second symbol that makes a spell of permanence with the initial spell." His hand drew a triangle with two lines through the middle, in the air. Sophie copied it as he did it. "In addition, you must paint the symbol on the object or thing, or person. The symbol on my house, in truth, is the symbol for the fortress, *Heuten*. So, this glyph protects the house."

"From attack?" Sophie asked.

"From magic my dear apprentice, and to an extent normal attack, like from a pitchfork or, anything really. A knife. A frying pan. Depending on how strong the attack is."

Sophie felt that little thrill in her chest when she learnt something exciting, this could be very useful to keep them safe. She could use this magic to protect her house from someone else breaking in. She quickly learnt the spell, trying to get a good grip on the symbol drawing and casting before her dreamscape time ran out.

She woke up seriously wondering whether she would ever actually be able to use spells, or if the whole experience, while fun, was ultimately a waste of time.

Chapter 14 - Raffaella Cuppertino

Arriving at school somewhat early, Sophie, Tomoko and Harlan stood quietly at the front of the school, after the previous day's incident. They leaned on the gate, watching the students as they were walking in. Three worried faces.

"What do we do about the men? The men at Tomoko's house." Harlan broke the silence, a slight unsteady waiver in his voice.

Sophie shook her head, glancing at both of them.

"It was scary…" Tomoko, said an expression of concern on her face.

"We need to be more careful. I think we need to get to Adeline before she gets to us, and I need to learn how to do magic so I can defend myself. Maybe they have your spellbook." She nodded towards Tomoko. "Our spell books are what they wanted. Now they have them, they may leave us alone," Sophie said. They were all quiet for a few seconds.

"Could it be anyone else in Bamberg?" Harlan asked.

"No, I do not think so. Mages are super rare. Marcus would be the only one in Bamberg, apart from younger ones that Marcus has created with his dreamcasting. I don't think the London Illusionists are capable of it."

Harlan glanced at Tomoko. "You've met these Illusionists?"

"Could they be summoners?" Sophie said, almost thinking aloud.

"Summoners!" Tomoko frowned. "*Sukide wanai,* I do not like them. No, they would be a lot older than him now. They would be ninety years old, in a mage's nursing home watching old war movies like my ojisan," Tomoko said.

Sophie noted that even though the trouble the summoners caused was seventy years ago, and it took place in the UK... Tomoko was from Japan and was still wary of them. Clearly the fear for Summoners was universal, even if the fear of *all* mages was not.

***

Once again in Mr Freidrickson' s history class, Tomoko and Sophie were sitting together. Harlan came in and peered at them. He was smiling, with a spring in his step. For all of them, history was their favourite class.

"Ahh... mages sitting together!" Harlan gave them a large smile.

"Mages together, for the win!" She laughed in her slightly maniacal way, while raising her fist in an enthusiastic salute.

"You two...Shhh," Sophie hissed.

"Oh, yes," Harlan smiled, guilt evident in his voice. "Sorry, Sophie. Forgot."

Sophie patted him on the shoulder, and he sat down behind them.

Mr Freidrickson glanced at them all.

"Okay, today, listen up you tin lids, we're gonna talk about life in Renaissance Italy." He walked past one student and whacked him on the shoulder. The student almost fell out of the chair, and he pushed him back on.

"Sir." Tomoko put up her hand. "Were there mages in renaissance Italy?"

Sophie shuddered at the comment. She'd have to talk to Tomoko about being more discreet.

Mr Freidrickson smiled. "Well yes Tomoko, mate, is the Pope a Catholic?"

"I do not know, sir," Tomoko said.

"Yep, there certainly were, er *summoners* and other mages," Freidrickson said, smiling.

Sophie noticed he said the word quickly. Like most, he wasn't comfortable saying it.

"Errhh...but history doesn't record much about 'em, or what they did. Secretive bunch of blokes and sheilas I guess."

"Mr Freidrickson, is a mage... is he also a wizard?"

It was Raffaella, the school's foremost heavy metal fan, who spoke. She was dressed in her usual obscure heavy metal T-shirt, eyes just barely visible through her fringe, her long black hair that went down past her shoulders. Sophie studied her properly for the first time. She was somewhere between plain and pretty.

Raffaella was from the Duchy of Savoy, giving her English a taste of an Italian accent, imparted through her standard spoken emotionless monotones. Sophie had never seen her sound or appear emotional. None of the three knew her that well. As far as Sophie knew, she may have been the life of the party at home, and it was school that made her look like she had the emotional range of a two-ton solid block of granite. Like Harlan, she was tall for her age, and rode a scooter to School. Sophie had always been wary of her, though she had done nothing that was alarming.

"Yes, Raffaella. Same thing…I think," he said.

"Sir, did football start in the Medieval period?" she continued.

Mr Freidrickson smiled. "Well, actually Raffaella, yes and as a history teacher, I am qualified to say throughout *all* history… the best football team is *Manchester United*. Sorry, and I won't be accepting arguments against that. Historical fact."

Raffaella started saying something about *Roma FC*. A quarter of the class erupted in support, a quarter started booing, individuals started calling out that their teams were the best…and the rest had no idea what they were talking about.

"Are they talking about soccer?" Harlan asked Sophie, who nodded.

Sophie observed the chaos, shaking her head…and Tomoko just peered around at everyone, smiling at what was turning into a near riot.

Mr Freidrickson, with an expression of regret for starting a near brawl, regained control of the class after a minute or two, surprisingly without the need for police riot equipment. He deftly switched topics to talk about the Medici family, a famous family in Medieval Italy that killed a lot of people in very evil ways.

While this fuss was going on, Sophie noticed a boy called Marco dropping a note to Tomoko on her desk, subtly as he walked by to go to the bathroom. Tomoko checked out the boy curiously, sizing him up, wrote something on the note, and then put it in her bag.

***

It was the lunch break immediately after the class, the three sat out the front of the classroom, talking about medieval Rome on the balcony, overlooking the playground.

"I wish I could travel back to the medieval period," Harlan said, eating an apple he had just grabbed from his bag. "He rummaged in his bag, tossed an apple to Sophie. She instinctively had to stop herself from casting the shield spell and caught it and started eating it. He offered one to Tomoko, who took it and put it in her bag.

"You don't travel back to the medieval period?" Sophie said.

"No, er, not quite. Eighteenth century London. But my TA is not English, he's French." Harlan was talking while eating, still observing all the students running around below.

"Hang on, you said his name before... Arsène. France. You don't speak French though?" Sophie asked.

"Well, no, but...you know I dream in French." He stopped eating, glancing over at Sophie. "I dream in French and can understand what he is saying. We are in London, but at times, he speaks in French. I can speak French in my dreams. But nah...not in real life..." He thought for a second. "...Yeah...it *is* weird."

Tomoko shook her head, slightly in awe. "Sagoi! Can you understand any French language, in the real world?"

"Actually, I can understand a lot. Not all." He took a bite of a second sandwich. Sophie peered up at his tall frame, hunched over slightly to lean on the balcony rail. Tall people seemed to always eat a lot and never put on weight.

"It's probably accessing the memories of French in your French ancestor's DNA in your body, I guess'. Sophie gave him a glance, Harlan nodded.

The three went quiet for five seconds, contemplating language and their dreamscapes.

"I wish Mr Freidrickson would talk about Japan in the Meiji era, that would help me. I have to read about it in reality to work out what is going on when I dreamscape. You know, who is a Shogun, who is the emperor, how not to make Samurai angry, et cetera. It is very hard work," Tomoko said. She was momentarily frustrated.

Sophie switched subjects.

"Tomoko, what was that note Marco dropped on the desk?"

"You can read it if you want." She flipped over the square piece of paper to reveal some polite blue pen handwritten German.

"Oh, Tomoko, you have an admirer. Why did you write SPCH on the note?"

"Short. Pimples. Cool hair," she said, matter of factly.

Harlan rested his arm on Sophie's shoulder, and being tall, read it over the top of her.

"Well, yeah, if you don't try, you don't get... I guess. Though, in this case...hmmm...not the best try." He chuckled, clearly amused at the effort.

"So, are you going to respond to the note?" Sophie said, intently interested.

Tomoko shrugged.

"Well, I get lots." She reached into her bag and pulled out about twenty notes, fastened together with a pink cat shaped bulldog clip. She added the note to the collection, the clip snapping shut on it.

"Twenty-one notes so far. I do not like any of *them* though." She glanced at Harlan and Sophie smiled broadly, then laughed. Sophie stared at her, was Tomoko interested in Harlan?

Chapter 15 - Complications, limitations and the dangers associated with Fireballs.

Sophie managed to sneak in yet another session with Johannes.

She was starting to get used to the whole routine, and wearing the clothes now seemed pretty normal. The Medieval men's clothes were free fitting, and lightweight; comfortable. They didn't have pockets, but that didn't matter: she didn't have anything to put in them. She always chose the men's clothes, which still caused people (except for Johannes) to assume she was a boy. Still better than wearing a dress.

Throwing on the clothes, she ran down the stairs and opened the door. This time, instead of the town being empty, there were several armoured men standing around, talking to local town women; some of the women avidly chatting, some hanging back in groups, apparently shy. All their uniforms were clean, and the armour polished, much more than the knight she had seen previously. Maybe they were on some sort of guard duty or preparing for some special occasion. She wasn't sure.

As Sophie came out of the house, she walked between them. Their armour, different points on the angles of the chest and armour reflecting the light, like upright silver shiny beetles. The men leaned on the wall, one sat down, a smile appearing on his face from the welcome relief from of the weight of the armour. A slightly older woman, sweating, came out of a house holding two ceramic pitchers of water. The men thanked her and poured it into ceramic tumblers.

Sophie stood watching them, mesmerized for a while, until they all turned to face her. She realized she was staring, so she strode on, heading down the dirt streets once again, she encountered the two boys who always jeered, which they promptly did once again.

"Oi nonce! Be off with you, for you know little and your mother knows less."

Sophie listened to the two boys, noting that people had been making fun of each other's mothers for a long time. The two boys were annoying, but never seemed to physically touch her. They stared at her as she walked past.

Sophie trod along the dirt path, walking in the patterns of wheel ruts until they disappeared. Once again, she came upon the little farmhouse where Johannes lived.

She called out his name at the front door.

He didn't answer.

Walking around the side of the house, Sophie found him feeding his ducks.

"Ahhhh, my apprentice has come! I have missed you, good gentle Sophie. Plus, I've had to do the farm work myself and, *gods hooks,* that is depressing."

"Hello, Johannes." Sophie plonked herself down on a medieval stool that rocked awkwardly as she sat on it. The *detail* in the dreamscape sessions was incredible, she stared at the wooden stool, and she could see the grain in the wood, the slightly rusty nails holding it together, the marks it made on the floor. Everything was medieval to her, authentic, and exactly as it should have been. Sophie knew nothing about carpentry, but it appeared real.

He went inside for a minute and grabbed a broad brimmed hat.

"Johannes, what do the people here... I mean people in the village and around here... think of your magic?"

Johannes scowled. "I think the villagers think mainly about eating and drinking... their life revolves around ale, turnips and perhaps the occasional potato they think looks like Jesus. They think more about my money than my magic. If I didn't have money, they would be tying rocks around me and dunking me in a river to see if I float or tying me to a wagon wheel and rolling it off a cliff or something. Villagers are stupid. Some of them think they have gnomes in their attic..."

"Do they?" Sophie studied him, curiously.

"No, gnomes don't exist. Fae, Stag men, wood nymphs, dark spirits… that's what they need to worry about."

"In the attic?

"No, they aren't all in the attic. Too noisy. Well maybe a dark spirit. Hmmm, let's change the topic from gnome talk. Stop asking about gnomes." He shrugged. "Anyway, villagers… can't live with them. Can't burn them."

Sophie tried to make sense of all this, the main lesson she got was that beer may be more important than she initially thought. While Johannes was annoying, he was a funny guy, intelligent, sort of charismatic, she could see him handling the villagers pretty well.

He grabbed a water skin, put it over his shoulder, and examined Sophie's boots. "Good you have good solid boots on, I see. Today we go walking. Some magic belongs inside, some belongs outside. If you do outside magic inside, your house can quickly turn into the outside."

"Can't we do the spell around here?" Sophie asked.

"I don't want to burn the village. I mean, I sort of do want to burn the village. But you burn the village, then more villagers come, then you burn the village, more of them come. It's an awful cycle involving more and more villagers," he spoke, as he stepped out of the house, and patted a random goat on its head.

"Hello there, Ruprecht," he said, nimbly jumping a rickety wooden fence. Sophie also patted Ruprecht the goat and followed.

As they walked Johannes picked a longish blade of grass, putting it between his teeth.

They continued walking for about half an hour, following a meandering path down into the forest near the town. Johannes sang as they went, some old German folk songs about tasty floating apples, strange goats and a nasty witch that died from flying her broomstick into a cliff. Sophie didn't really understand them. He continued to explain magical theory, interrupted by a random verse.

Sophie got in the mood and started singing it as well. Finally, they came to a large rock, sitting upright in the middle of a clearing in the forest. Sophie examined it closely, it had old carvings in it, strange inscriptions. They weren't magic symbols; they appeared older, more primitive.

"Stand here. We're going on a little trip." He glanced at the ground, just in front of the obelisk, stroking his beard. "I need to dig that box up. Emergency items." Johannes pointed at a spot just in front of the obelisk, and before Sophie could ask him what the box was, Johannes started casting a spell. Sophie tried to listen to it, to memorise the words and the handcasting element. It was longer than the usual ones he had cast. Sophie listened to the rhythm of the spell, trying to commit the words to memory.

A misty blue blur seeped out of the ether, all around them. Normally when Sophie was casting a spell, she could feel the magic energy just in her hands, but it felt like that energy enveloped them.

Johannes finished the casting, and as he did, the blur diminished, fading to nothing.

Sophie was stunned. The dark lush green of the forest had disappeared, to be replaced by crisp, dry, brown, countryside. It was flat except for some low hills in the distance, warm, and arid.

It clearly wasn't Europe. The spell, and the Obelisk had transported them somewhere else in the world.

"Johannes, where are we?" Sophie asked, scanning her surroundings.

"It's a strange place. It's incredibly hot, and it seems to have strange animals. I suspect it could be hell."

Sophie heard a rustling in the bush. A creature hopped into view, stopped in its tracks, and stared at the both of them.

"Johannes, it's not hell, but it's sorta close. We're in Australia."

Chapter 16 The Big Club

"Austria?" Johannes shook his head. "This is not Austria. It's too hot, and the rats here are huge and they jump around a lot. One kicked me once."

"It's a kangaroo," Sophie said, smiling. The concept of fifteenth century people travelling to Australia via a magic portal, and thinking it was hell was actually pretty funny. Johannes stopped and squinted at her. Sophie realized it would make little sense to him that she would know the name of this creature.

Johannes went over to give it a pat.

"Ah, I wouldn't go near it," Sophie said.

As he gave it a pat, it used its claws to latch on to him, and then kicked him to the ground, and hopped out of his reach. Sophie laughed as he slowly got to his feet, holding his hip and groaning.

"Are there people here?" Sophie said, still chuckling.

"Yes, but they leave me alone and I leave them alone. I think they think I'm weird." Sophie could only agree with them. They continued walking through the dry grass, which brushed softly at her legs. The Kangaroo stood still, watching them leave.

"My young apprentice, how many spells have I taught you now?"

"Uhm... six," she responded.

"Okay, so something I want to teach you. If you are fighting six men, but you have a big club, when do you show it?"

"At the beginning... er... to scare them off?" Sophie answered, wondering about the analogy, and slyly glanced around it to see if there was a big club sitting somewhere.

"No. Showing the club at the beginning gives the six men time to plan what to do. Maybe one of them will go get their own big club. Maybe they will all go to the club merchant, and all get clubs. Maybe they will join the club club... No. You show it when you are going to use it. Then it's too late for them to do anything...except get clubbed."

Sophie cringed at the analogy.

"I have shown you some spells. What I'm going to show you is the big club spell. As a sorcerer, you may *want* to attract attention. Walk in the crowd, don't stand out, but have the big club ready if you need it. Do you understand the lesson here?"

"Yes," she said. It sounded daunting. She stood back a little bit from him, trying to not show the concern on her face.

He scanned around and muttered something mostly to himself. "...need somewhere... mostly rock...hmmm...last time... poor giant rat... tasty though."

He pointed into a little clearing more. It was all rock.

"Stand behind me." Sophie stood behind him but backed quite away. She hadn't seen Johannes behave quite like this. He was a lot more serious than normal. Though Johannes's "normal" still wasn't very serious.

Johannes did a complex hand motion, his fingers making a magic symbol through the air, using his fingers to paint on an invisible canvas. Expertly and quickly, he drew a symbol. While Sophia used one finger to make her symbols, she noticed Johannes used three or four at the same time, one finger drawing the horizontal lines, and the other two drawing the verticals.

As he drew the symbol in the air, she recognized an element of the fire symbol as part of the overall pattern... but didn't recognize the rest. She then noticed what was happening to his hands.

"Brinnen," he commanded.

His palms were starting to glow.

Now, on both of his hands, there was a small ball of flame, sitting in the centre of his palms. The flame quickly grew, and he suddenly thrust his hands out.

Sophie's mouth jaw gaped open in surprise, and she involuntarily stepped back as the heat and light radiated powerfully from Johannes's hands, the two small fires from each hand combined into one. She could smell sulfur. A ball of flame formed in Johannes's hands.

Johannes finished the spell, and immediately the ball of fire flew out of his hands. It sailed through the air, even so, Johannes concentrated on it, shaping it, guiding it, moving his fingers in the air. It spirited through the air, its path guided like a fiery ball controlled by strings.

Johannes was now sweating, and his face transfixed in concentration. The ball of fire landed thirty metres away from them or so, with a huge explosion. The heat made her step back.

Sophia realized now why he needed such a big space. Using this inside a house, or underground in a confined area, the fire ball would expand and fill up the room, burning the mage that cast it to ash.

Johannes addressed her, slowly. "This... is your big club."

Sophie was aghast and felt her body shaking, a damp sweat on her face and neck. It was less like a spell and more like a small nuclear weapon.

Johannes sat down on a rock, clearly tired from the spell. An excited feeling flitted through her stomach, and there was a faint quiver in her knees.

"It's time for you to do some cooking, my apprentice."

He stood next to her and went through the hand motions. Once, twice, thrice. Having spent some time learning spells, after three or four times, she felt she knew it.

His recitation of the spell, an arcane out of place German mantra, filled the desolate bush void. Sophie chanted the words with him.

"Okay, Johannes." She glanced at him. "I'm ready."

She went quickly through the hand movements. Then the recitation.

Her hands felt hot, but she resisted the temptation to stop the spell. Once again, she felt the energy build up in her chest, her shoulders... But this time, there was a corresponding energy in her hands.

A ball of fire slowly appeared in her hands. Small at first, it grew bigger.

"Concentrate, girl... concentrate. Use your hands to control it."

She did. Her hands flicked through the air, drew the symbol, and she commanded the spell to bring forth something bright from the magical aether. The ball of fire appeared in her hands.

At first it was a shock and she had to resist the urge to pull her hands away, for fear of being burnt. She managed to steady herself, then pushed it forward away from her body. The ball of flame flew straight through the air, arcing over some buch and landing on the rocks.

There was a loud explosion, bits of dirt rock, and fire landed at her feet, and all around. Sophie could feel the heat on her face, even though it was far away.

Johannes patted her on the back.

"Well, done. Now… just don't cast that in your bedroom."

Sophie sat down on the rock, panting for breath, feeling immensely happy. She had cast a number of spells now, but this was the most powerful of all so far.

Something in her mind also gave her a positive feeling. She thought briefly about what it was. She realized… it was that Johannes trusted her, even with a seriously dangerous spell. She woke up from the session feeling amazing, a rush of excitement pulsing through her veins.

Casting spells was damn cool.

Chapter 17 - The Vault

Sophie turned up to school on yet another brisk Bamberg morning. It felt like it was going to snow, and Sophie adjusted her scarf to cover her chin, shivering. Harlan was patiently waiting for her at the front gates. Harlan was excited. It was a popular meeting spot, and so many students were milling about, it took a minute for Sophie to work her way through the crowd to get to him.

"Harlan, why are you out front…waiting for me?"

Sophie could hear jazz music coming out of his headphones as soon as he lifted them off his ears.

"Oh, Jazz. Dig those crazy jazz beats." Sophie closed her eyes and adopted a trance-like expression, mimicking a person dancing to Jazz. Harlan's love for Jazz was something she knew she could harass him about and it would guarantee a good reaction.

Harlan was offended. "Forget the Jazz insults Soph, did you hear about the bank?"

"No…which bank? The bank in town?" Sophie always remembered the bank in the centre of town because it was in an old medieval building from the outside, but inside was a modern bank. The staff were always very polite.

"Yeah, well, it was robbed." Harlan paused.

Sophie crossed her arms slowly, frowning. *Nothing* like this ever happened in polite, orderly, beautiful Bamberg. It was weird. Bamberg was a little place, and lots of tourists everywhere would always mean there were lots of witnesses to any illegal behaviour.

"Was anyone hurt?"

"Well, er no, but you know, the thing is, it happened last night...it's pretty spectacular, and everyone is wondering how it happened with no one noticing."

Sophie glanced at Harlan's scooter. "Harlan, let's go have a peek."

Harlan stared at her for a moment, glanced over at the school, and smiled. "Well...Okay!"

Sophie hopped on the back of Harlan's scooter, and he took off past the students pouring into the school.

***

By the time they got to the bank, and quickly parked the scooter on the footpath, there were people gathering about. There was a hole in the wall that a person could walk through. The bricks were black, with some scattered on the ground. Sophie and Harlan tried to peer inside, but a tall, bald, serious police officer was keeping people from getting too close.

"Um, well, it doesn't appear that the wall exploded or was smashed open with a machine. You know..." Harlan stroked his jaw, trying to contemplate exactly how it was done. "Yeah. It appears a hell of a lot like the bricks were, er, melted," Harlan said.

"Yes, see the edges." Sophie pointed at the edges, they were smooth, bits of light twinkled off them like the reflections off glass. It was like someone had cut through them with intense heat. Sophie realised she had seen it before, and momentarily got a mild flashback with the jolt of realisation. They were melted like the bricks had been in her room, during the break in. At the time she had felt scared, but now seeing the same signs, she felt her nails push into her palms, and suppressed rising anger. She needed to concentrate.

"Well... yeah, that's something you don't see every day." Harlan tried to peer in the hole into the wall. It was dark inside, Sophie peered in, squinting. She could see a door was hanging off its hinges.

People were gathering around a police officer, a few journalists, trying to get information for their newspapers or TV channels. She nudged Harlan, pointing at the police officer. "Harlan, let's see what he is saying."

The police officer was chubby... he had a round face, with serious features and showed a bland straight expression. Sophie could see twinges of nervousness around his eyes and face, clearly under stress. May be just nerves talking to the press? He was talking like he was reading off a script; he was probably not used to talking to Journalists. He apparently didn't notice two kids amongst the collection of journalists, or he did notice and wasn't bothered.

"At 2:53 last night, precisely, the Deutsch Bavarian bank was broken into, via a hole in the East wall on Hepburn St. At this stage, no money was taken, and no one was hurt."

Sophie glanced over at the journalists. They went silent.

"I think the journalists are unhappy... They haven't got a typical bank story to tell."

One of the journalists put up his hand. "Excuse me officer, what do you mean nothing was stolen?"

"No money was stolen. Sorry, that's all I can tell you. Any other questions?"

Someone in what Sophie guessed was an American accent, asked in English. "Why do the bricks in the wall seem all glazed? Like they have been melted by heat?"

The officer clearly didn't have an answer for this.

"We're not 100% sure of that, but we'll be conducting forensic tests and releasing a report later in the week." Sophie wondered what the police investigators would make of it.

At this point, Sophie's phone rang. Everyone turned to her. The officer was about to speak, and he just stared at her instead. Embarrassed, Sophie apologised and backed away from the crowd as they continued asking the officer questions. She left Harlan to keep listening.

Pulling the phone out of her pocket and glancing at it, she didn't recognise the number.

"Sophie Wolf? This is Rupert Morton-Smyth, I'm a friend of Marcus. I have some awfully important business to discuss."

Sophie was stunned, held the phone away from her, before putting it back to her head. Rupert's voice sounded unusual, like something wasn't right, but at the same time, he was somehow familiar.

"Errhh hello... Rupert?" she said, feeling awkward. "Errhh... how are you? How did you get my number?"

"Good thanks, well spiffy. And, well, how I got your number is a long story. I've got some important business to discuss with you. You lot over in Bamberg are giving me a bit of a bother. There's been a break in at the Deutsch Bavarian Bundesbank."

Sophie assessed the hole in the wall, in front of her. "Yes, we know, we are there now."

"Good work old girl. I don't suppose there's any chance you can get in and have a bit of a look around?"

Sophie quickly examined the taped off area, and the serious look on the face of the police officer.

"No, I don't think they would let us in."

"Hmm disappointing. It would have been good to report that to the boss."

"Your boss?" Sophie tried to remember if he had mentioned who his boss was.

"Yes, her majesty. My contact there tells me *something* was stolen from the vault. Can you see anything at all?"

Sophie craned her neck to see through the people "Not really. There's a hole in the wall, it's dark."

"Can you see the edges of the hole, are they rough or smooth... the edges?"

Sophie peered in. "They are smooth, like the bricks were melted."

Harlan glanced over her shoulder, curious about who she was talking to.

"Yer know Soph, you can put him on video so he can see for himself."

Sophie nodded and swiped an option on the phone for the video.

"Ah." She put the phone back up to her ear. "Rupert, I'll put my camera on so you can see for yourself."

Rupert's voice came from the phone, "Good idea, old girl, hang on. I'll just switch mine on."

Rupert switched his camera on, and Harlan and Sophie both peered at it to greet him. A man's face appeared on the phone.

It wasn't Rupert.

The man on Sophie's phone appeared to be in his forties, spoke with the same accent...he was visually similar to Rupert. But it clearly was a different man.

"Hang on—wait—you're not Rupert. Er, where is he?"

Harlan and Sophie peered at the man, and the man squinted back at her. The man seemed surprised.

"I *am* Rupert Morton-Smythe. Why wouldn't I be?"

Sophie shook her head. "You're not him. You're a different man."

Harlan squinted at her. "Are you sure?"

Sophie glanced at Harlan and pointed at the phone. "See, this isn't Rupert."

"I am Rupert. What do you want me to do, get the queen here to confirm it?"

"Could you do that?" Harlan seemed excited.

"No! In God's name… I am not getting the queen to talk to you! That was a rhetorical question." Rupert squinted at the screen; his brow furrowed.

"Look here old girl, when was it you saw me? I mean this other person?"

"Real Rupert?" Sophie said.

"Yes. Er No. I mean when did you see the other man?" he responded.

"I met him here in Bamberg, nearly a month ago."

"Well, it wasn't me. I haven't been to Bamberg in ages. Perhaps six months. It was some dubious individual pretending to be me. Did you tell them much?"

Sophie wasn't sure whether she should feel guilty for talking to a possibly fake Rupert at the University, or if this was the fake Rupert and she shouldn't talk to him.

"A little bit."

Rupert still sounded confused.

"Well, if you go around talking to everyone about your business, you'll end up getting killed. This is very serious business." Rupert's tone was marginal anger laced with some legitimate sounding concerned. "Who the dickens is going around pretending to be me? Oh. You know that Marcus is missing, don't you? Did this imposter tell you that?"

"Yes. You told… er, Rupert told us that."

"Sophie, you need to trust me. Look, I'm going to give you a tad more information. Maybe this will let you trust me. It's…a warning. Marcus's assistants contacted us with the information, they knew about it and were concerned. Apparently, the professor was in trouble with one of the children in the program.

Because this child was acting dangerously with the magic they had learnt, he was going to stop the whole dreamscaping sessions. The professor's wife..."

"The professor's wife?" Sophie interrupted.

"Yes, she researches the family trees of the kids, and the Talented Ancestor..."

"Their family trees?" Sophie asked.

"Yes, before she puts them into the program... but it appears in this case her research should have shown that the talented ancestor was someone that the child shouldn't have been matched up with, possibly a sandwich short of a picnic basket. In any case, the child is out of control and not acting normally, and we aren't sure what's happening. Marcus stopped most of the program because of it and has disappeared."

Sophie realised that Rupert didn't know they had been sent the headsets and they were still continuing with the sessions. She decided to keep it to herself for the moment. She wondered why Marcus had stopped the program but sent them the headsets. *Maybe he thinks we are more trusted? Maybe he thinks what we are learning is important, for some reason?*

Rupert continued, "Yes, someone in Bamberg appears to have access to an odd mix of spells that doesn't match up to the various normal paths of magic, which I don't really have an explanation for. And I am daring to suppose that they may have had something to do with the bank event. Keep your ear to the ground, would you? Please take care of yourself, be careful. I need to go, chat later. Oh, and you have my number, old girl?"

"Yes." Sophie saved the number he had called on, entering him under the name *New Rupert*. She had no idea why he kept calling her *old girl*, when she was fifteen. Clearly not old.

Sophie hung up the phone, stunned.

She considered what was going on. Tomoko was doing magic. Someone at school was using magic to break into banks... Sophie didn't even know how to do magic herself. And now, there was a fake Rupert and a real Rupert.

Sophie sort of felt excited, and a tad concerned. Rupert had finally given her some information. If this was all real, *phone Rupert* was the Queen of England's personal mage, and was asking her to investigate some young mage who was up to no good. He also sounded like he was concerned about their wellbeing. When she couldn't tell her father, or Hisako, it felt good to have an adult that cared about them.

Sophie wondered. Rupert obviously trusted her and wanted to speak to her. Why? Why not Tomoko? Sophie had no magic... well yet. She was young and had no experience of any of this sort of thing. However, she had a talented little group. Harlan and Tomoko.

There was the loud sound of a siren as a police car arrived, she shuddered at the pitch as it drove past her, as Harlan came over.

"Looks like we need to do some investigating Harlan. The troublesome mage in Bamberg..." She pointed at the bank. "This is their work."

Chapter 18 - The Unknown Raffaella Factor

At school, Sophie, Tomoko, and Harlan were constantly on the lookout for anyone that could be a mage. Sophie's neck was getting sore from turning and twisting, looking over her shoulder looking for any tell-tale signs of students that could do magic.

There were several schools in Bamberg, but the International School was the main one from which Marcus had been getting his students. The other mage was most likely here.

They had all discussed… *How do you spot someone, at a school, who may be a magic user?* The International School didn't wear uniforms, so the students could wear anything. *What does a mage wear?* Sophie thought of famous mages in history, despite the stereotyped view of mages and wizards, there wasn't a mage uniform. It wasn't as simple as looking for someone wearing a pointy hat or a t-shirt with *Bamberg Druids Association.* The boys weren't old enough to be sporting long grey beards, and it's not like you could check out the local school spellcaster's club for likely suspects.

Harlan, being the maths person, had done the sums. The school had 1200 students, and there were about 200 or so fifteen- or sixteen-year-olds in the school. A lot of people to work through.

Harlan quickly and efficiently put his lunch into his mouth. The cafeteria was a good place to see a lot of the students at once.

Tomoko held her food in front of her face, scowling. "I Forgot my bento at home today. Wonderful homemade sushi sitting in the fridge. I had to buy these cheap noodles."

"Do you cook at home Tomoko?" Harlan asked.

"Hai… Yes, mostly. I cook a lot. Food and cooking…is really important to me."

"Errhh… can you cook for me, sometime?" Harlan perked up. Sophie glanced at him, with a raised eyebrow, as he put way too much school special spaghetti and meatballs into his mouth.

"Ah. Yes, *mochiron*." A big smile lit up her face. "I can cook for all of us. I would love to ask you both over to my house for food," Tomoko declared, looking at Sophie and jiggling slightly in her chair.

"Oh…great!" Harlan smiled.

"What do we do with our mage when we find him? I mean, he can blow up walls, apparently. Well, he could know all sorts of dark magic," Harlan said, with his mouth partially full so his words were garbled.

Sophie was indignant. "He?"

"Oh, yeah, er, sorry." Harlan grimaced. "He or she."

Tomoko shook her head. "*They* can put holes in walls. But I am fairly sure it is not dark magic."

"Ok. Let's get serious, how the hell do we find someone who was in the professor's sessions, that is learning magic, "Sophie said.

Tomoko scrunched up her face considering the problem, while contemplating her noodles. "I have to say, I do not know, at all. The only thing I can think of is *history*."

Harlan and Sophie glanced at her. "History?"

"The History class. What did we all do after we started the sessions?"

"*You two* switched into the history class," Sophie corrected her. "I was already studying it."

"Hai… yes, so it is. We started the class to help with understanding what to do in a dreamscaping. So, someone else dreamscaping may do that as well," Tomoko added.

History class, which Sophie enjoyed now that she was dreamscaping back to the fifteenth century, was later in the afternoon. In the meantime, the three of them spent two hours scanning for any tell-tale sign of a mage.

Problem was, Sophie had no idea what the tell-tale signs of mages were.

***

"And so that was the end of the first English Civil war. A tyrant replacing a man he thought was a tyrant. Tyrants are nasty blokes." Mr Freidrickson scanned the classroom with his one visible eye and then paused dramatically. His artificial hand dropped the pen he had been writing with, onto the table. The room was quiet for a second.

Eloise, a fidgety student with long brown hair, shot her hand up. "Sir, whose side were the demons on?'

Freidrickson shook his head. "No, Eloise. This was the old English Civil, as I said, in 1650. You're getting mixed up with the 1950 English civil war. That was the one with the demons, and it was a very sad thing, but that's not today's lesson."

There was a slurping sound from someone drinking water, and everyone turned to Tomoko. "Sumimas... Oh, sorry." She bowed her head to the teacher, and then the class.

"Any Questions?"

Harlan's hand shot up. "Sir in 1450, did any girls have short hair?" Freidrickson glanced at Harlan oddly, his expression changing to disapproval.

"Sophie Wolf, I have banned you from asking detailed questions about the medieval period, because I have a class to teach. If I answered all your questions, I wouldn't have time to actually do anything else."

"Sir, Harlan asked it," Sophie responded.

"Yes, because you asked him to," Freidrickson replied.

Sophie and Harlan both peered down at their desks, she shuffled in her seat, a little disgruntled.

"Okay, does anyone else have a question?"

"Me, sir. I have one please."

Harlan, Tomoko, and Sophie all turned around to see Raffaella ask a question.

"Sir. If someone was in the sixteenth century, and they were a girl, what would happen if they wore boys' clothing?"

It was the same sort of question that Sophie repeatedly asked. Mr Freidrickson raised both eyebrows and appeared confused. He glanced accusingly at Sophie, trying to work out if the specifically detailed questions were something to do with her. Sophie peered back at him, and gave him a polite shrug. He glanced back, clearly suspicious of Raffaella.

"Errrh... why do you ask Raffaella?"

"Ahh…" Raffaella scratched her face slightly awkwardly. "I saw it in a movie and wondered."

Freidrickson crossed his arms. "Well, little matey. It would probably be seen as abnormal back then. Medieval people weren't adventurous with clothes, blokes work bloke's clothing, and the ladies wore a dress. Except for the odd lady pirate. Androgenous clothing is really a modern concept."

Harlan scribbled a note to Sophie and passed it along the table, carefully so Freidrickson couldn't see it. Sophie subtly flipped it over so she could read it… it was a simple question mark. She froze, as it dawned on her, Raffaella was asking pointed questions about history, like what she herself had done. Was she a dreamscaper as well?

***

Outside the class, Sophie felt vaguely excited. Harlan seemed thoughtful and Tomoko seemed like she was considering some sort of plan.

"Well, err, so what do we do now?" Harlan said. "You know… she sort of scares me."

"Me, too," Tomoko whispered.

"She scares me as well. But maybe she is just an introvert. Maybe she just wears scary black clothes to keep people away, and her life is harmlessly writing bad poetry."

Sophie glanced at Tomoko, not sure what to say about her insight into Raffaella's *Meyers Briggs personality profile*.

"We need to confront her," Sophie said. "…we'll go up and ask her if she is a mage. We'll be able to see from her reaction if she is. That's how you tell if people are lying—confront them with it and see their reaction."

"She does sports," Tomoko added. "I have seen her go into the basketball courts around this time."

Sophie thought for a second. "Okay, so we wait till she's finished her sport stuff. Then we go up and ask her when she comes out of the gym. Okay?"

"Errhh, what do we ask her? *Are you a wizard, Raphaella?*" Harlan said, with more than a hint of sarcasm.

"I don't like the word *Wizard*," Tomoko said.

"Are you a *Sorceress*, Raphaella?" Harlan asked.

"I've always liked *spellmaster*," Tomoko said, beaming at the word.

Harlan frowned. "Sorceress sounds evil. She's not going to say yes to that. Wizard...hmm...Mage is a lot better. More sophisticated."

Sophie frowned at them both. "C'mon you two. Let's get down to the gym."

***

They went down to the Gymnasium, as some people were coming out of the exit door wearing volleyball gear. A couple of younger, tall boys were waiting around, basketballs under their arms, chatting. Sophie wrinkled her nose, the place smelt of teenagers who probably wore the same pair of socks for two weeks.

The sound of sneakers squeaking escaped the basketball court. They waited for about fifteen minutes, and a gaggle of basketballers came out. Sophie went to talk to them... but then noticed Raffaella wasn't with them.

Sophie returned to the other two, who were waiting on the bench. They were still talking about the correct term for people who use magic.

"*Spellcaster* is okay." Harlan seemed thoughtful.

Tomoko screwed up her face. "Nande? *Spell master?*"

"Erhh, nah, *Caster*. You know, to *cast* a spell."

"Wakarimasen." Tomoko shook her head. "I think I like mage after all. It is short."

"She's still inside." Sophie plopped down on the bench.

The lights in the basketball gym started to flick off.

"They must be finishing," Harlan said, glancing at the others.

At that point, the doors opened and about ten people came through, all at once. They were all dressed in black, in what seemed like padded clothing, carrying bags over their shoulders as they left the basketball court. They were mostly guys, and Raffaella was the shortest.

Sophie was taken aback. What they were wearing certainly wasn't basketball gear. Unusually, Raffaella was giving them instructions, and pointers, and all the people were listening to her carefully. Raffaella, stopped and started to put something in her bag.

Three of the men went up to her.

"Thanks once again. Great class, I learnt a lot." Sophie heard one of them say.

Sophie thought...*they were talking to her like she was running the class?* But she, like them, was only about fifteen. Weird.

"No problem, Dietrich." She shot the taller boy a quick smile, before turning to the boy beside him. "Piotr... your reverse torresso, practice it before next class." Raffaella gave him a disapproving look.

"Will do," Dietrich replied, before giving her a wave and leaving.

Sophie noticed there were adults in the class, and young people. While taken aback by all this, Sophie thought now was a good time to approach her.

"Raffaella!" Sophie finally called out.

Raffaella glanced up. She was wiping her brow. "Yes... um..." Raffaella frowned, trying to remember Sophie's name. They were only in the one class together.

"I'm Sophie. This is Harlan and Tomoko. We're all in Freidrickson's History class together."

"Ah." Raffaella glanced at the three of them in turn, waiting for them to say something.

"Oh...I just wanted to ask you something," Sophie said.

Raffaella glanced blankly at the three of them. "Okay?"

Sophie took a breath, turned to face Raffaella directly, walked up close to her, and stared her straight in the eye.

"Raffaella, we know you do MAGIC," Sophie said, loudly and dramatically. Sophie met her gaze, waiting for a reaction.

Raffaella stared back at her blankly, without a shred of emotion in her face. She didn't even blink. There was no immediate sign of guilt or acknowledgement. Raffaella turned, facing each of them in turn, waited for another five seconds, shifted slightly backwards, opened her mouth a little. Closed it. Then stared at Sophie.

"Sophie... I don't," Raffaella said.

"We know you do. We know you do the dreamcasting sessions. We know you are going back to learn lost arts." Sophie knew it was time for her bluff... She had nothing to lose. She glanced directly at Raffaella's face to see her reaction. Sophie could see a slight reaction to the word *dreamcasting*, Raffaella clearly knew what the dreamcasting was.

"The three of us saw you at the University, leaving a session with Marcus. A couple of weeks back." It was a bluff; no one had seen her.

Raffaella peered at her, then at the others.

"Yes, you did see me there." Raffaella went into her bag to pull something out.

It was a dagger.

Sophie took a step back. But then checked the dagger and noticed it had a rubber stopper on the end. Raffaella put down the dagger, reached into her bag and pulled out a huge sword.

"I've been learning this. The art of the longsword, sometimes I do Italian dagger in the hand with reverso grip." She flipped the dagger around, acrobatically. "I learned from Artessimo Bianco himself. In 1543. He is my master."

Sophie realised she had assumed they were close to solving the mystery of the mage at large but had now failed miserably. The fact that Raffaella knew about them now was a concern, they didn't really know if they could trust her.

Raffaella gazed up at Harlan, craning her neck back slightly to look   up   at   him. "Harlan. You should come to class. Eh? You may be good, you are tall, you will have good reach. As long as you aren't stupid."

"Raffaella, you… *teach* this.?" Sophie asked, pointing at the big sword.

"Raffaella was in the dreamscape program as well, learning longsword?" Harlan asked no one in particular. Tomoko nodded, starting to understand, and turned to Raffaella.

"What do you mean, longsword?"

"Longsword… is this." Raffaella held up the sword from her bag.

"Oh…you could kill people with that!" Tomoko took a step back.

Raffaella nodded. "That is what they did with it."

"Sophie, why did you ask if I did magic? You mean… card tricks, right? Why would I be doing that?"

Then a sudden look of realisation came across Raffaella's face, and she took a step back, reappraising them." Are you three in the program as well?"

Sophie nodded. "Yes. We're trying to find someone else, who is in the program."

Raffaella seemed intrigued. The people in her fencing class had been milling about packing things, but had slowly all drifted off, so just the four of them were left.

"What are you learning? Oh," Raffaella's eyes widened, as she realised what was going on. "You are using the dreamcasting sessions to learn magic. Spellcasting magic, like from before...?"

"Yeah." Sophie nodded. "Spellcasting, but please keep it to yourself."

Sophie noticed Raffaella subtly take a little step back from them all.

"She's a wizard. So am I," Tomoko explained. Sophie raised an eyebrow at being called a wizard.

"Not summoners?" Raffaella said.

"No. Mage," Harlan said.

Tomoko tilted her head slightly. "Spell Master."

"Yeah. Spell*caster,*" Harlan said.

Raffaella examined all three of them, obviously, trying to take all of this in. She turned to face Harlan.

"Harlan... you're not learning magic. What's your ancestor's art?"

He appeared earnest and straightened his posture. "Well, er, yeah, I study stealth techniques. Climbing observation. Retrieval of objects. Yeah."

Raffaella raised an eyebrow.

"He's a thief," Sophie said, in a flat tone.

Rafaella squinted at the three of them. Raffaella's face was *always* expressionless, so it was hard to read her, but Sophie gathered she was trying to assess if they were to be believed.

"I turned up for a session, and they said Marcus was gone, but then he sent me a headset in the mail," Raffaella said.

Harlan nodded. "Yep, we know. Yeah ...as he had arranged to send them to all of us, he must have been planning on leaving in order."

"Raffaella, you need to promise us, don't tell anyone we are mages. We could get in a lot of trouble." Sophie gazed at her directly, indicating the seriousness of it all.

Raffaella shook her head. "A lot of people get scared of magic. People do stupid things because of fear." She shook her head. "But promise me one thing?"

"What's that?" Harlan said.

"I won't tell anyone about your magic, if you show me some," Raffaella said, starting to put her various weapons back in her bag.

"Okay, it's a deal," Sophie said.

Chapter 19 - Churches and Dreams

Sophie leaned on the brickwork veranda outside her classroom, looking down into the courtyard, waiting to meet up with Harlan and Tomoko before History class again. The students milled about below, groups here and there, mostly split into boys and girls, chatting, a group gathered around a smartphone watching something…and then laughing together.

She spotted the nerd group, identifiable by the books and tablets in their hands, and a higher proportion of spectacles than the average student population. Mr Freidrickson walked through the middle of the school, reading his phone, and somehow managed to still navigate through the crowd without falling over or walking into someone.

Sophie gazed up from her vantage point and noticed that it had started to rain. The first drops came down, darkening the faded porous brickwork of the veranda with little splotches. A cold, icy gust of wind came in from the playground, and icily brushed Sophia's cheeks, making her shiver. Sophie grabbed part of her scarf hanging down, pulled it up and wrapped it around her neck.

Sophie started to think about all that was going on now. They weren't solving any of their problems. She had tried to do magic in her bedroom several times, but her spells just didn't work in the real world. Her papa would probably completely freak out if he knew she was dabbling in magic. There were unknown people who apparently could do magic, let loose on Bamberg, doing strange things that didn't really make sense. The break-ins and thefts of the spellbooks from both her and Tomoko were still lingering in her mind.

Rupert gave them small bits of information, but frustratingly, hadn't been able to help them. Despite all this, and even despite the frustration of not being able to do magic in reality, it was a lot of fun, and she got to share it with her buddy, Harlan. They had picked up a new friend, Tomoko as well.

"Sophie, how are you?" It was Tomoko, with a broad smile. She walked up and stood next to her, glancing down the veranda, at all the students below.

"Ahh… just thinking about recent events. Where we are at." Sophie noticed the rain was slowing down and getting lighter.

"Yes. The rising. Are we really going to be able to stop it?" Tomoko said.

"Well, if you like living here, we had better. Apparently, Adeline is a potent force, and we all have people we like in Bamberg. I love this little town," Sophie remarked, peering down at the students, happily engaged in their break.

"Bamberg, yes, well, to be honest, I was thinking of moving away. But I won't now," Tomoko said.

"Yeah? Leaving?" Sophie said.

"I did not really know anyone here; the dreamscape was the main thing keeping me here. But meeting you guys. Well, it's changed things." Tomoko grinned and chuckled in a slightly awkward way.

"Oh, well good. Glad to hear it." Sophie nodded, trying not to show surprise. She was glad Tomoko was apparently now happy when she hadn't been.

"Hey, Sophie. Tomoko." Raffaella had appeared. "You know, I'm happy I met you three." She put her bag down. Sophie looked at her, realising both of them were happy to be made part of the group. Raffaella continued "I now have people in History class I know, people to sit with. I only took it because I was dreamcasting and was trying to work out what to do in the sixteenth century at Ronaldo's Salle in Florence…" There was a pause that could have been a hint of displeasure. "…and if I had to wear those big stupid dresses."

Sophie smiled. "Oh yeah, I *hate* those dresses. Tomoko and Harlan both swapped into History after they were dreamscaping. I was already in the class. My dad is a history lecturer at the

University, I really had no choice. But to be honest, I love history."

"Really?" Raffaella squinted at her, her head askew.

"Yes, I mean when I dreamcast, I love to learn the magic. It's a real test. And the thrill of getting a spell right. It's such a buzz. But I also like taking in all the historical aspects. The town, the people, the clothes. It's all beautiful, unspoilt by the modern world."

Tomoko observed. "I was interested in history, but my parents wanted me to study Maths and Science. I took chemistry so they let me do History. I hate chemistry." She involuntarily frowned, then touched two fingers to the side of her head as if she was getting a headache just thinking about it.

"You three, I wondered where you were. Class in five." Harlan popped around the corner. "Let's hope something good happens today, and not more bad news." Harlan grabbed Sophie and pushed her towards the classroom. Sophie noticed Raffaella changed when he showed, she thought for a second Raffaella didn't like Harlan. She thought Raffaella didn't really like anyone.

#

Mr Freidrickson was a couple of minutes late, and the class grew unruly. This was a class on *The Fall of Constantinople*—which Sophie had already read about. Harlan was first to ask a question. Freidrickson narrowed his eyes peering at him, Sophie thought he was trying to will Harlan to put his hand down. Harlan didn't.

"Yes Harlan, you have a question?"

"Sir, if you are in 1450, and you were a girl, could you run fast in the shoes they wore at the time, if you hitched your dress up to here." (Harlan stood up and pretended to hitch his dress up to mid-thigh). Sophie was not impressed; this was going to appear like she had asked Harlan to ask another question.

Mr Freidrickson squinted at Harlan disapprovingly.

"Harlan, you are asking the same sorts of questions that Sophie always asks, which indicates that you are in fact asking on her behalf. Which is what you did yesterday." He paused. "However, I know Sophie is smart enough to not obviously use you again for that, so I'm guessing mate, that you are in fact trying to frame her. So, for that, you get a 1000-word assignment on the Turkish battle plan for Constantinople... *Not Istanbul.*"

"Sir..." Harlan appeared shocked, but then thought it better to just be quiet. Sophie's eyes met Tomoko's and they both smiled.

"By tonight, *mate.*" Freidrickson emphasized *mate* in that typical Australian way, that made it sound like he was serious.

Sophie glanced around the room to see who was in the class today, and noticed that the noticeboard, which seemed like it generally hadn't been touched since the 1980s, had something new on it that caught her eye. There were normally old anti-smoking adverts up there; these had now been replaced with pictures of medieval churches on it. They were colourful, and quite pretty. Presumably Freidrickson had put them up as the class was going to start talking about historical architecture next week.

Sophie noticed one of the particular churches and there was instant recognition, and mild shock. One of the churches in the photo...*she had seen it... In her dreamscape.*

Up until now, she had felt like her dreams had been in a place that was not reality. This was the first time she had recognised a building or location from her dream. Had she found the actual location where her dreams were taking place, 500 years ago?

***

With the class finished, Sophie ran over to the pictures on the wall.

"Mr Freidrickson."

"Yes, Sophie." He wandered over, adjusting his eye patch.

"These are great pictures."

"Yes... they are." He started peering at them. Sophie thought he was acting like he hadn't seen them before.

"Do you know what church this is?" She pointed at the one she thought was from her dream.

"Saint Augsburgs," he replied. "It's still there, over in Dexheim, about 250 kilometres from here."

"Ah, well yes we were thinking about going and seeing it." *Saint Augsburgs in Dexheim,* she repeated in her head. Sophie felt an excited feeling appear in her chest. She had to shake her head to clear it.

Was this the church from Johannes's time? A church she may have   walked   past   in   her   dreamscape?

Chapter 20—Scooters and unusual coffins

As soon as school finished, Sophie and Harlan rode down to Raffaella's house in the North of Bamberg, Sophie on the back of Harlan's little scooter. The wind was cold on Sophie's face, so she held onto Harlan's jacket, turning her head to the side, shielding her helmet behind his to block some of the icy air.

They had agreed to meet at Raffaella's house, where they could all ride on to the old church in Dexheim, two hours outside Bamberg.

They arrived, took their helmets off, and as they knocked on the front door, they heard the rattling of the garage door at the front. It was an old-style wooden door that swung out, rather than a metal roller that would roll up, like on most new garages.

Raffaella appeared.

She wore a black metal band T shirt and black (of course) overalls, with the shoulder straps and the front bib hanging down. She had grease smudged on her face, and eyeliner smudged, more ornately, around her eyes. The grease seemed like it was smudged by accident, the eyeliner was smudged on purpose.

"Sophie, Harlan, come in. Thank you for coming. Tomoko is already here." As per usual, her tone was flat, perhaps contradicting the expression of thanks.

It was warm inside. Tomoko was sitting there, drinking a hot chocolate, and humming to herself. She smiled at them as they came in. Seeing her, it struck Sophie that Tomoko was generally, just about always smiling, and happy.

Raffaella had two big heaters turned on, big round glowing things on stands, like bright orange sunflowers, pointing down to them, radiating warmth. Sophie and Harlan both stopped to take in the visual splendour of Raffaella's garage. All around the garage was kitsch Italian things. A plastic relief map of Italy. A picture of some football team Sophie didn't recognise. A little picture of the Madonna and child. Family Photos. Pictures of scooters.

But the most obvious things in the garage were scooters. There were headlights, tyres, frames, engines, piles of bits, Sophie had no idea what they were. There were at least six complete scooters as well, all squashed in the back half of the garage. Sophie and Harlan both walked in slowly, their heads rotating slowly trying to take in everything, at the same time as not tripping on something.

Raffaella had a scooter, half pulled apart sitting on a rubber mat. It had a metal band logo on it, and a number of winged creatures painted on the frame.

"Oh. A *theme scooter*. It matches your T-shirts," Sophie said.

Harlan stared at her, with his typical raised "you're being overly blunt" eyebrow.

"Dragons." Raffaella pointed at the scooter. "*Wyvern.*" She pointed at one of them which was apparently not a dragon, but a Wyvern. Sophie didn't know the difference but decided not to ask.

"Harlan, Bella. Bring your scooter in for a second, let's check it."

Harlan took it off its stand, wheeled it into the garage from outside, next to the scooters parked in a row.

"Harlan, I will swap you this scooter here for yours. I want you to have it." Raffaella pointed to a shiny scooter.

Everyone went silent.

Raffaella was pointing to a classic old Italian scooter. It was spotless and appeared to be in immaculate condition.

He gazed at it, slight confusion evident on his face.

"Well… er, you're kidding me, aren't you? It…looks like… its worth a lot of money."

"It works fine. It's a GS 160." It's yours if you want to swap. It's faster than your Honda, but more importantly…" She paused. "…*Italiano.*"

Harlan paused, glanced Raffaella up and down, then immediately pulled out his mobile phone. He typed something, then his head jutted back ever so slightly from the phone in apparent surprise. Sophie knew him too well; he had checked how much it was worth.

"Yep. It's a deal!"

Rafaella pulled out a piece of paper from a notepad, scribbled something on it, signed it, then got Harlan to sign it as well.

"Here you are." She wheeled Harlan's new scooter over to him and gave him the key. Harlan appeared happy, he studied the paper momentarily, scanned the key to the new scooter, and then handed over his keys to her. Raffaella then grabbed him by the shoulders, and politely shifted Harlan away from the Honda.

She then stepped back, picked up a sledgehammer from her tools, and started smashing the Honda to pieces.

Everyone stood back, wide eyed as she walked around smashing it. As it collapsed onto the ground, Raffaella stood over it, smashing it some more, like a caveman, killing some prey she had brought down in the hunt. Bits of Honda flew everywhere.

Raffaella's dad came out to see what the noise was.

"RAFFAELLA! What are you doing?"

"Papa, Honda." She glanced at him, sledgehammer poised above her, ready for a destructive descent.

"Honda? Ah." He went back inside.

After the Scooter was destroyed, Raffaella rested the head of the sledgehammer on the ground, lent on the end of the long wooden handle, and caught her breath.

"I am happy," she said. She pulled a piece of Honda out of her hair. "I hate Japanese scooters."

Tomoko stood rather awkwardly, clearly confused about what just happened. Sophie scanned around the mess and wondered momentarily why there were so many dangerous people in her life suddenly, and some of them were her friends.

***

Rafaella passed around some spare helmets and Sophie and Tomoko hopped on the back of Harlan and Rafaella's scooters. Harlan gazed down at his now crushed Honda scooter on the ground.

"Well, goodbye old friend. Yah served me well."

***

The two scooters made the trip quickly, leaving Bamberg behind them, traversing the valley road, up the mountain, Sophie was on the back of Harlan's. As he sped along, she gazed over at the pine trees as they flew past. A blur of trees, identical, conical in their hundreds. She leant in with him as he took the corner, left lean, right lean. As they were coming up the mountain road, Sophie tapped Harlan on the shoulder, and pointed at a turnoff, He nodded. She then pointed to Raffaella behind them.

It was a turnoff, to a little church.

Harlan rode up and stopped his scooter and got off while Sophie walked over to the little church. She walked through a little graveyard next to it. Tomoko took her helmet off and peered at the church.

"Is this it? Tomoko asked, peering at the building. "The Church in the photo."

"No. It's another church." Sophie shook her head.

Tomoko's head swiveled from Sophie to the church, and back to Sophie. "This isn't the church in the photo? What is this Church?"

Sophie pointed to the church, and then to a gravestone. They all walked over and read it:

Anastasia Wolf

1980—2009

Loved by family

Mother to Sophie.

And Harlan started laughing.

Tomoko and Raffaella, both spun around at Harlan, confused. Sophie stood with a thousand-yard stare, not reacting to Harlan's laughter.

"I know you all probably wondered about my mama. I generally don't want to talk about it to most people."

Tomoko was listening to Sophie, but her eyes kept wandering over to Harlan laughing.

"It's an empty coffin. Buried, empty." Sophie glanced up at Tomoko and Raffaella, and then at Harlan, shaking her head.

"Empty?" Tomoko said, confusion in her voice.

"About four years ago, momma went on a ski trip with some friends. She went missing from the resort. There had been a heavy snowfall. They found her jacket and gloves. That's the only thing that is inside the coffin, the jacket and gloves."

Raffaella squinted at the coffin, then an expression of realisation came across her face.

"She was killed in an avalanche? They couldn't find her body?" Tomoko asked.

"No. She got drunk on schnapps. Went for a walk, lost her gloves out of her pocket... and then left the resort with another man. We didn't hear from her for ages. We thought she was dead," Sophie said. She sounded blank.

"Oh." Raffaella glanced at Tomoko. They both appeared surprised.

"It's embarrassing. I've only told Harlan. He thinks it's hilarious. We thought she was dead, so after a search, we buried her a month later. She called me from England a month after to say hi, she had no idea we thought she was dead. I couldn't believe it. I was so angry."

Tomoko started to smile, and then started laughing, her high-pitched laugh surprised Sophie. Sophie just shook her head, and half smiled, mostly at Harlan.

Raffaella watched their reactions, with a slightly confused expression.

"Okay. I just wanted to show you that. It's one of my dark secrets I only tell a few people. We were going past it anyway."

Sophie put her helmet back on and hopped on Harlan's scooter. He hopped on and started up, as Raffaella and Tomoko ran over and put their helmets on.

***

It was about a two-hour drive along the motorway and through the cold mountain air to their destination. And then they were pulling into the little town of Dexheim. The historical town was much like Bamberg, with lots of medieval buildings, however, it had a mix of modern structures as well. They pulled up at the location where it was supposed to be. The location was right, but it wasn't an old Church. Sophie took her helmet off and just stared.

It was a sparkling *new* church, with shiny glass windows. Sophie hopped off the scooter and walked over to the sign on the front of the building.

"It says… this Church is St Augsburg's…we are in Dexheim." Sophie shook her head for a moment. "I think I know what is going on." Tomoko ran around the church for a minute, then went back on her phone.

"Ah… Listen to this: 'The new church was built in 1980, replacing the 1950's era church. That replaced the original medieval St Augsburgs, which burnt down in accidental fire in 1942.'"

Sophie pouted. She realised, there have been *Churches* here. The photo on the wall in the history class was old. It must have been from then.

Sophie scanned the town, the buildings all here were new. She tried to match up the buildings with what she remembered from the dreamscape. It was bewildering… she had this vague sense that some of it was familiar, but she couldn't work out what. Her heart was starting to sink… she didn't properly recognise *anything*.

"Rafaella, can we go down this street?" Sophie, stepping slowly as she peered at the old house suddenly screamed, "STOP!" She froze, gazing at one particular old medieval house.

It was painted blue instead of green, but it was the house she had first appeared in in her dreamscape sessions. She stood there in front, just staring. Hardly believing it was real. 500 years or so later, still standing.

She stared at the rest of the team, who were staring at her, wondering what was going on.

"I know this one!!! This is crazy. This is the house in my dream. Same house. I started my dreamscape in this house." She stared at it, taking it all in.

Glancing around, disoriented, she tried to pick the spot where the armoured knight stood in front of her, with his two attendants. It had been the very first time she dreamscaped. She called out, excitement in her voice. "I know this one!!!" The others smiled.

Sophie pointed ahead, her fingers jabbing into the air frenetically. "This way."

The scooters sped up, the tyres making rhythmic bumping sounds as they crossed quickly over the stonework of the cobbled streets, twisting left and right down the narrow streets.

They were now in the older part of town and moving out into the country. There were less trees, the road was paved now instead of dirt, but she recognised the way.

They quickly went up the hill.

Sophie yelled out so the others could hear her through their helmets.

"This is where Johannes's house would have been. I think." Sophie examined the area, peering into the forest, but it was gone. Sophie got off the scooter and stood there. She realised, perhaps it was stupid of her to expect it to still be there... it may have burnt down 400 years ago for all she knew. For a moment, she felt wistful. She would have liked to have just walked in and seen the house exactly as it was, with Johannes's weird decorations, the swords on the wall, the chairs... animals coming through the window into the kitchen. The cats walking about. She felt a little flat... but realised, it had been 500 years.

She wondered if something bad had happened to Johannes in this house, and there was a momentary feeling for someone that she actually felt close to, but now, was no longer around.

Harlan hopped off his scooter. Tomoko was walking around, taking in the sights, still the tourist even though she had been living in Bamberg for a little while. Sophie sat down, rustling her hair while thinking. Then it dawned on her.

The obelisk!

Sophie gazed up at the trees, the rises in the land, trying to get her bearings. "This way."

With an excited yelp, she left them and ran off on foot. The others put their scooters back on their stands, and scampered after her, Harlan briefly struggling with his new/old scooter.

"Wait, Sophie." He called out.

Sophie darted into the forest. The scale of the forest had changed, but she noticed a small creek. It was bigger, but it was the same creek from the forest in her dreamscape. She ambled about the huge pine trees, trying to get her bearings, but the forest was really overgrown and hard to walk through.

The others caught up to her, bent over, breathing hard to catch their breath.

"What is it we are looking for?"

"The obelisk. It enables travel to another place, where a similar obelisk is. Like a…" She thought. "…like a gate, I guess?" Or maybe not.

Tomoko nodded her head "I know of these things. They are not a gate; they are an artifact that enhances magic to allow travel spells, along magic energy paths around the world. There is one in Japan."

Raffaella peered at the forest, then back at the three, with a blank expression.

Sophie recognised some of the forest terrain but could not see the obelisk.

Harlan pointed to a rock. "Is this it?"

It was a huge rock, but not the same height as the obelisk, and covered in moss and grass. Sophie stopped, examined it, and realised it wasn't tall enough, but it was the only big rock they could find. Sophie's head tilted, perceiving it from different angles, then walked over and ran her hand along its moss covered facing.

It was the obelisk, but *lying on its side*. It had somehow been knocked over. It was covered in mud and dirt, moss, and grass had started growing up on one side of it.

"Harlan, give me your water container." Sophie grabbed it off him, and poured some water onto the obelisk, scrubbing off the dirt. She scrubbed hard with her hand and could just make out part of the inscription. It was practically impossible to match any of the forest with her memories from 500 years ago, as the forest had grown, there were more trees. However, the lay of the land was the same, and the position of the creek hadn't changed, so it was the right distance from that.

"Okay, let me test this out." Sophie asked everyone to stand back. She cleared the grass and a little area directly in front of the stone. Harlan and Tomoko stepped back respectfully, Raffaella observed with the slightest hint of bemusement.

Remembering back to the spell that Johannes taught her, she spoke the spell words, and then drew the essential symbol in the air to open the gate. Her fingers curved, forming the shapes for the hand cast sequence.

Nothing happened. She tried a second time, still nothing.

Finally, she tried emphasizing the words, exactly as Johannes did.

Nothing.

Sophie started to doubt herself. Everyone else was learning these arts they could use. She had spent weeks learning to cast magic in her dreamscape. Tomoko could do it. Her happiness from finding the Town and the obelisk quickly disappeared, and her spirits sunk. She felt a lead feeling in her stomach, she felt her shoulders slump. It just felt hopeless. All this effort, learning spells, nothing she did could make it work in real life.

Chapter 21 - The Box in the Ground

With the spell not working, there wasn't anything they could do with the large stone.

However, it had been there for 400 years... it wasn't going anywhere. Sophie gave up for the moment and decided to come back to it. Not being able to cast spells was getting to her. Was all this effort worth it, if all she could do was live out some mage fantasy in her dreamscape? Sophie climbed on to the squishy leather scooter seat behind Raffaella, grabbing her waist, while Tomoko hopped on behind Harlan. Their scooters took to the road, the little engines putting out way more noise than it seemed they should be making and headed down towards Dexheim.

Sophie patted Harlan on the arm. "Wait, I just remembered. The box!"

Harlan cried out, "What, a box?"

"There is a box buried at the base of the obelisk. I saw it in one of my dreamscapes."

"What is in it?" Tomoko glanced over from behind Harlan, holding on to the passenger strap to keep on the seat.

"I don't know. But Johannes put it there for himself, he called it an 'emergency box'. I have no idea what's in it but could be useful. If it's still there. Plus, I'm curious." Sophie considered, if they found the box, it would be at least something gained from all the time spent.

"We need something to dig with. Hardware store?"

They all drove around till they found a brightly coloured orange hardware store called *Hornbach*. Sophie chatted to the staff in German and got a shovel and some gardening gloves. Raffaella grabbed them and paid before anyone had a chance. Apparently, Raffaella had money, her dad was a very successful executive with an Italian company.

The two scooters took off from the store, taking to the cobbled streets, once again, turning left and right before they got back out onto the road.

Harlan smiled as his hand twisted on the accelerator, and the surge in power momentarily lifted the scooter's wheel off the road. Raffaella raced ahead, cutting in front of Harlan. Sophie noticed the smiles on both their faces as both machines noisily raced up the highway. They pulled off the road and parked in the same spot in the trees, their scooters out of sight of the road. They made their way to the Obelisk once more, Sophie cursing to herself that she hadn't remembered about the buried little box before.

Harlan, as per usual, disappeared ahead into the bushes, jumping initially, moving fast, and then stealthily blending into the leafy foliage.

He was obviously affected by her excitement, Sophie thought. Harlan's tall frame dodging amongst the trees. Suddenly, Sophie noticed Harlan had disappeared. She turned to tell Tomoko, but she was gone as well. A moment of panic set in for Sophie, as she spun around, not able to see any of her friends. Harlan's hands re-appeared out of the bush, and pulled Sophie into them, she fell abruptly on her butt.

Raffaella, Tomoko and Sophie gazed at each other blankly, then noticed Harlan was frantically motioning for them to be quiet and pointing off into the distance towards the obelisk. Harlan then stepped over to a more secluded vantage point and signaled for them to come up closer. Tomoko turned to Sophie and put her index finger to her mouth. Tomoko's face expressed concern.

Sophie pushed her way through the bush, closer to the obelisk, gingerly parting some branches to see what they were all staring at. There were two adults, a man and a woman, sitting to the side of the obelisk. In front of it, was a little blonde girl, doing the exact same spells that Sophie had done forty minutes before.

Except, this time, the spell appeared to be actually working.

Chapter 22 - Adeline

The little blonde girl stood in front of the obelisk, muttering what sounded like the same spell that Johannes had said to make the obelisk work.

Sophie peeked at her; it was clearly the same girl from Tomoko's.

It had to be Adeline.

Sophie concentrated on the rhythmic chant…the casting. It was *like* the spell she had learnt from Johannes to use for the Obelisk … but some of the words were different to the spell she used. However, unlike Sophie's efforts to activate the obelisk, the spell… was definitely doing something. *Confusing*

Sophie tried to estimate the girl's age, but guessing age wasn't something she was good at. She could have been twelve or so. The blonde girl waved her hands, Sophie watched on. She recognised the hand movements; it felt odd that instead of her doing the spell here, it was this strange little girl.

Harlan bobbed up and started trying to record it with his phone, Tomoko pushed him down, and they both peered at the girl curiously.

Suddenly, there was a blue hue of shimmering light before the obelisk. For a very brief second, a black silhouette appeared. It was an ominous figure, a tall, bulky masculine figure; its grand, dangerous stag horns radiating out from its head. Sophie tried to focus, but she could barely make out his details, the creature was mostly in silhouette. It was there just for seconds, and then was gone. The girl appeared to be using the obelisk for something different to what Johannes used it for. Trying to bring someone in or summon someone.

"Adeline," one of the adults called out to the little blonde girl.

She turned, and Sophie could see she had white, blonde hair, blue eyes and luminous pale skin. When Sophie saw her face, she realised she was probably younger than she initially thought, maybe she was 10? A jacket with a big black fur collar was pure contrast to the rest of her pale form and platinum blonde tresses. A black hood was revealed hanging down her back as she turned.

Adeline gazed at the woman... and put her hand up to indicate for the lady, Sophie assumed it was her mother, to stop. She was the lady from Tomoko's.

"Birgit," the man next to her said. Sophie could see it was the same man with the short beard that had been with Adeline and left with her mother. He had a black cap on, his long brown hair flowing out from it underneath. He was slightly shorter than the woman, who was tall and skinny. He put his arm on the woman and pulled her back to the ground.

Sophie noticed Raffaella, who had the least exposure to magic of all of them, was now watching this, completely wide eyed.

Adeline turned back and cast the spell again. There was once again a flash of blue light and the creature appeared again, this time for two seconds. Getting a better glimpse of him, Sophie could make out a tall, muscular human shaped figure with what appeared to be a stag's head and face. Strangely, she could make out in the blur, that he was wearing a suit.

This time Sophie noticed that as he appeared, he too was casting a spell. He to be casting the same spell, but from his side of the gate. Wherever that was.

The figure disappeared and Adeline immediately fell to the ground. Sophie guessed she was exhausted from the spell, apparently it took a lot of effort.

Birgit, the woman next to Adeline, addressed the man, "Lars, carry her please." Lars picked her up, holding her in both arms. As he carried her, she was motionless, almost like a floppy rag doll.

Lars started walking through the foliage, carrying the young mage. Momentarily, Sophie froze in fear. If the man had come towards them, they would have to hide quickly, and they were so close that any movement would be seen. Fortunately, he stepped off in the opposite direction and walked off.

"Where's Harlan?" Sophie noticed he had disappeared as soon as the man had picked up Adeline.

Raffaella shook her head. "Run off as per usual."

After about five minutes, Harlan reappeared out of the bushes, surprising everyone. Sophie put her hand on her chest.

"Kowaii! You scared me!" Tomoko said, her eyes widened,

"Sorry… I'm back. I followed them to their car. They drove off." Sophie noted a hint of apology in his voice, then she noticed he had pulled out his phone and was watching some video being played back.

"If you recorded all that, and sold it to someone to put online… As soon as I can do magic, I am going to turn you into something with four legs that doesn't wear clothes." Sophie sounded serious and meant it. Harlan glanced at her, a moment of horror on his face, and he quickly put the phone in his pocket. Sophie noticed Raffaella, watching quietly and calmly. Sophie wondered *exactly* what would have to happen for her to show any emotion.

After they were gone, Sophie went back and grabbed the shovel she had dropped when the commotion had started.

"What was that all about?" Harlan seemed confused.

"She was summoning some… creature. I have no idea who the horned creature is. But glad whatever it is, she can't bring him in at least." Sophie tried to remember if Johannes had ever mentioned such a creature, but couldn't remember that he had.

Raffaella crossed her arms. "That creature was interesting. I wonder what it was?"

"What if they come back?" Tomoko said, distracted.

"Don't worry, I'll hear the car," Harlan said, patting her on the shoulder, he bent down and grabbed a shovel as well, and walked over to the Obelisk with a slightly blank expression on his face—clearly not sure what was going to happen next. Sophie glanced around at the three of them.

"Okay, I'll start digging, Johannes told me there was an emergency box he buried here.

"Johannes?" Raffaella asked.

"Yes, I'm his apprentice," Sophie said, glancing down at the turf where she was about to dig.

Sophie started to dig, and everyone sat down. After a while, she needed a break. She handed the shovel to Raffaella, and said, "Your turn."

Raffaella put the shovel down, rolled her sleeves up, and started digging with enthusiasm. Sophie noticed her lofty physique, and her big biceps. Working on scooters, and all that playing about with swords clearly made her fit.

"Dang, look at those biceps Raffy," Harlan said, clearly impressed.

Raffaella ignored him.

"Guys I don't know how long this is going to take, but we need to keep going." After a while, Sophie took over from Raffaella digging, trying to guess where it could be. The Obelisk was on its side now, so she started digging at the base of it. Eventually she got tired and handed the shovel to Harlan.

Before Harlan could take it, Raffaella grabbed it again instead. She dug furiously, moving twice as much earth and soil as anyone else, sweat dripping down her face, her hair shiny black from it as it stuck to her face. Sophie noticed her biceps, now glistening from sweat, looked bigger than Harlan's.

It took a while, but eventually Raffaella got tired. Then Tomoko. Then Harlan. All of them sat down, trying to get their breath back. It went back to Sophie. She scanned the other faces, faces sapped of energy and covered in dirt.

"Guys...I know it's here. Trust me, I know it's here," Sophie said. There was a nagging doubt, and a tiny fear of appearing incredibly stupid if it wasn't.

Sophie kept digging.

"AH!"

The shovel went into the soil and there was a *thud* as it hit something hard. She tapped a couple of times gingerly. Kneeling in the hole she started removing the wet soil around the object. Sophie let out a little squeal of excitement, and everyone rushed over and peeked in. It was a metal and ivory box. It was vaguely familiar. Maybe she had seen it in her dreamscape somewhere, somewhere in Johannes's house.

"The... box..." Sophie uttered, the breathiness of her words showing her surprise. Johannes had told her he had buried this for emergencies, and Sophie was relieved to find it. The earth had piled on top of it for many years, making it appear deeper. Sophie momentarily noticed how muddy her hands were, and then noticed exactly how much mud covered *everyone*. Everyone stood back, quite surprised.

"If it's money, well, we could invest it. I can check the current value of gold," Harlan said, taking immediate interest. Sophie glanced at him, a raised eyebrow stopping him from talking anymore.

The box had been bound in cloth, and some hemp rope, which had largely deteriorated. The box itself was a renaissance style box, embossed with symbols carved into the ivory. Brass fittings were oxidized green and covered in brown mud. Sophie examined the figures carved into the box, and at first thought they were pictures of kings and Queens. She then realized they were farm animals but wearing clothes and crowns. Sophie sniggered; it was a Johannes joke. Tomoko rushed over.

"Oh, how exciting, it is a box from the past. Is this what you were expecting Sophie?"

"Well, I expected a box. I didn't see Johannes bury it, but he said he had. Just in front of the obelisk, about two paces. It's made of ivory and metal; it certainly seems medieval." Raffaella was hurriedly pulling the soil away. She grabbed the box and lifted it out...as she did, the rope binds and the cloth coverings deteriorated and fell apart, fully revealing the ivory and metal. She put the box carefully on the ground in front of Sophie.

"If this is magic, I think you had best open it," Raffaella said, taking her cue and moving backwards from it. Sophie smirked at the others moving away, like she was defusing a bomb.

She investigated the decorations on the box. It had carved inlay of some medieval animal figures, sort of like the fantastic creatures you see in medieval calligraphy. They were farm animals, of course. Farm animals were nothing special for the average person, but rated highly in Johannes's world, his animals being more like pets, and he had names for them all.

Raffaella produced a leather pouch from her back pocket and pulled a little set of pliers she from it.

"Here, use these. Pry it apart." She handed them to Sophie, and then returned to her safer position.

Sophie tried the pliers, then went for the blade in the pocketknife. The box was filthy, covered in mud. The hinges were rusted tight, but she could get some leverage on the box. It was a beautiful box; she didn't want to destroy it. She could have imagined what Ernst would have said about using a pocketknife to open a 500-year-old box. But she was eager to see what was inside.

The box opened and she felt the familiar rush of energy that came with casting. The box was booby trapped with a spell. She dropped the box in horror and froze, holding her breath. Raffaella stepped back even further, and Tomoko and Harlan both stumbled over each other to get behind the obelisk.

Sophie scanned her surroundings, then stepped away from the box. A spell had gone off, but she couldn't feel any effect. She padded herself down. She was ok.

"Are you okay?" Harlan called out, concern all over his face.

"Yes. A spell went off. I don't know what happened. Maybe it didn't work." Sophie was gawking at the box.

Tomoko called out from behind the obelisk, her head poking around. "You don't have anything extra. Like extra limbs? Maybe you are strong enough to resist it."

Sophie had heard Johannes talk about resistance. If a mage was powerful, a simple spell wouldn't work on them, their spirit *resisted* it.

"Maybe? I guess so. I'm okay."

"Yeah...you seem like your normal average self." Harlan checked her up and down, wearing his glasses of true sight.

"Average... thanks, Harls, nice of you to say." Sophie frowned.

Now to open the box. Sophie knelt, opened it fully and peered inside. There was nothing in it.

"It's empty!" Sophie couldn't believe it. Johannes's stupid sense of humour? Burying an empty box? He was so annoying at times! The box was dry inside. The walls of the box were Ivory, but faded a slight brown colour, probably from the water and dirt. She examined the box more carefully. The bottom of the inside of the box was actually wood. It was dry, and as she peered at it more carefully, she could see... *writing*. It was German.

"There's writing...Johannes's." It was carved into the wood, the letters painted red. The paint had faded, but she could still read the indentations of the carved letters.

Der Grund ist die Antwort. Schauen Sie hier und Sie werden finden, was Sie sehen.

The bottom is the answer. Look here and you will find what you see.
Sophie translated for Harlan and Tomoko, who didn't speak
great German. Raffaella and Harlan cautiously came over to have
a closer look, Tomoko stayed behind the obelisk. Sophie flipped
it over and examined the bottom of *the outside* of the box. There
was more writing, just one word.

Dummkopf

"It says," Sophie began, with a vague shake of her head biting
her lower lip in frustration, "in English…er… *fool.*"
Raffaella glanced at it. "What does that mean?" Harlan and
Sophie peered at the box.
"I don't know, I don't understand it," Sophie said, shaking
her head.
"Great. Johannes playing jokes on me 500 years later." Sophie
considered dreamscaping to ask Johannes about the box, but the
headset was at home.
Tomoko came over, leaving the safety of the obelisk. She
opened her mouth, making a short, excited exclamation.
"Ah! The bottom is the answer… the bottom of the *inside of
the box*. The box is made from Ivory, but the bottom is made
from wood."
"Yep, It's a false bottom box. I should have realized, let me
prize it open," Harlan added.
Sophie got the pliers, trying to pull the bottom of it off. The
pliers gripped the edge of the wood inside the box, and she
levered the false bottom out.
"Ahhhh!" Sophie screamed again. There was another rush of
energy. Another spell!
Everyone threw themselves onto the ground away from
Sophie, who was left standing with the box, and her eyes closed
in anticipation of some offensive spell going off.
"Again, another spell." Once again, she checked herself. The
others gathered around her.
"Soph, are you okay?" Sophie could see the concern in
Harlan's eyes. "You look okay." He spoke. Tomoko walked
around her, patting her tentatively, like she might explode.

"I'm okay, I feel normal. Like the other spell, nothing happened. Hey, look at this." Sophie pulled out the wooden panel that was acting as a false bottom in the box, and indeed, there was a smaller box inside.

Sophie investigated what was a smaller flat version of the big box, also made of ivory. It had a sliding lid, which she tentatively slid off, a slight grimace on her face.

They all peered inside, Harlan particularly looking excited.

Inside the small box were four tiny metal swords, and four tiny arrows. They were made of what appeared to be silver to Sophie. Sophie shook them around in the box, watching them jumble together like a tiny box of weaponized matchsticks. Didn't appear to be any spell trap on them. The swords had a tiny ring on the end of each. Raffaella tilted her head askew, looking curiously.

Harlan shook his head. "I was expecting diamonds or gold or something." He sounded unimpressed.

"They look like jewellery. I have double headed axe earrings at home, they are smaller than that. Can I have a look at one?" Raffaella said.

Sophie took one out and gave it to her.

"You did most of the digging, keep it. You're our sword person. It seems to make sense that you should have one."

Raffaella nodded in thanks. She squinted at the little sword, shrugged, and put it on her earring. Harlan took a photo of Raffaella, and Tomoko tried to get a photo of Sophie with the shovel, but she refused.

"Okay, the least I can do is just do a search on them and see what they are worth. You know, they may be worth something to a museum," Harlan said, trying to sound casual, but Sophie could hear the vague excitement in his voice. As per usual, Harlan often was looking at the money side of things.

Raffaella picked up the box off the ground, which was now probably more interesting than its contents. She examined the inside of the box. Her face screwed up in confusion.

"Sophie, how come you can read this? I can read German, but this is not...German."

"Yeah, I wondered that, I can't read it." Harlan glanced over.

"You can't read German anyway," Raffaella said.

Harlan smiled at what *may* have been a rare joke from Raffaella.

Sophie shrugged. "It's German." She spelt out the words in the sentence.

"Schauen—Sie-hier-und. Sie werden—finden."

"Sophie, that's not German," Raffaella said, as the three of them all shook their heads,

Sophie glanced at her friends, and then at Tomoko. Her jaw dropped open a centimetre or two. She stared at them silently for five seconds; the stunned expression of someone just realising the solution to a complex puzzle.

"IT's... THE LANGUAGE!" Sophie called out, almost shouting. "That's the key."

Tomoko gawked at her; her eyes widened as it dawned on her as well.

"Adeline and Johannes are speaking an *older* version of German," Tomoko said.

"Yes... the words Johannes says to me in the dreamscape aren't the same as what we use. They aren't modern German. They are an older version, it's fifteenth century German. It's very different from modern German, it uses different words. We can only understand half of it. It's what Adeline was using."

Sophie could hardly contain the excitement in her voice.

"Er, what? I don't understand. That's why we can't read the writing on the box?" Harlan appeared confused. "... you speak to Johannes in German in your dreamscape?"

"Well, I thought it was German, but now... reading the box, and thinking about what language Adeline was using, I realised it's the older version."

Tomoko nodded. "Mochiron...er... of course. It is the same with the Japanese I am using in my dreamscape. It is a slightly older language. But only a little different from modern Japanese. This older type of German seems very different though."

"The only thing is the word for the location in the incantation is different. Johannes used *Lochac* which indicates where he wanted to go. But Adeline uses *Heiliger Olave.*

Sophie put the box carefully down on the ground.

"Okay, stand back. I'm going to try something." She walked over to stand where Adeline had been standing. Sophie started her spell ritual again. She remembered the pronunciation of the old German language that Johannes uses. Concentrating on the difference. It was flatter, and more guttural, and he used different words. She tried to think of how *he* would have said it.

She tried the spell again, but this time trying to say the German words the different way that Adeline had said them. Some words were different, and some were the same. She started casting the spell, she felt her fingertips start to feel tingly. Little tingles of energy. The others watched on, Raffaella particularly bewildered. Tomoko watched on with a smile, while Harlan face showed trepidation.

The first part of the ritual was complete, and Sophie spoke the words for the second part with the hand movement.

There was a blue flash, everything was dark for half a second.

They were no longer in a forest.

Standing next to them was a different obelisk, and they were in the cellar of a building.

Chapter 23—Obelisks and Gentleman

"Doko… where are we?" Tomoko held her head, looking confused and a little scared. Raffaella was still stunned by it all, carefully looking around.

"Where are we, Toto?" Harlan glanced around.

"Toto…the old band?" Raffaella glanced at her, confused.

"The old *movie*." Sophie smiled and went over to Tomoko and gave her a big hug.

Tomoko's arms froze at her side, as Sophie's wrapped around her. She relented, giving Sophie a little smile, and a vague awkward pat on the back. Then, an expression of sudden realisation.

"Sophie…Sagoi! You can do magic now! I mean in real life you can do magic!"

Sophie felt the power of the spell still dissipating, flushing her skin with warmth. It trickled away, like the feeling of warm water running off you. She couldn't remember the last time she felt this happy, this accomplished.

"Finally! It's been so frustrating. Thank the sun." She was silent for a few seconds, looking around and taking it all in. All this work, the dreamscapes… She could finally do magic. A huge sense of accomplishment, but also relief.

Harlan ran over and gave her a hug. Sophie smiled.

She glanced around the room, realising she didn't know where they were, and they could be in danger. Another obelisk sat in the middle of the room they were now in. It was different from the other and standing up. They were all in a cellar, obviously used for storage, with various boxes roughly stored here and there.

The group examined the cellar, the air was stale, and Sophie noticed the walls were wet from water seeping through the grey stone walls. Sophie thought it seemed odd that an obelisk would sit in the middle of a cellar of a building. Had it been relocated to this spot? The obelisk was obviously from the medieval period at least, could the cellar and the building have been built around it? She wondered if the magic would still work if the obelisk was changed from its original spot.

Harlan checked through the boxes, his thief training helping him to quickly assess if they were open or closed and what was inside them. He took out his glasses, scanned around, then put them back in his shirt. He then went over to the door, listened to it first, and then tried the lock.

"Doko...where are we?" Tomoko said, scanning around her.

Harlan glanced at her. "We're not in Germany, or the US. I think we are in England."

"England? What?" Raffaella raised an eyebrow.

"Listen," Harlan said. The three went quiet. They could hear, in the dim distance, a police siren.

"What part of your thieves training tells us we are in England?" Sophie stared at him directly.

"No... My dad used to watch British Police shows on *BBC America*...the siren sound has stuck in my head. This door... it's got an old lock, and tight." Harlan glanced at her, working on the door.

Sophie checked her phone, it wasn't working, presumably because it was in another country's phone network.

"We are in England! My phone won't work here." Sophie put the phone, now useless, in her pocket.

"Is it locked?" Tomoko glanced over at Harlan as he worked his tools in the lock. There was a slight click, and then a slightly louder one, followed by a broad smile on Harlan's face.

"It *was* locked." Harlan smiled. "Yer know, older locks are easier to pick, this one looks like it's way old, back from the 1800s I reckon. Dayum, way easier than new ones."

Harlan tested his shoes, black rubber soled lightweight slipper things. He padded them on the ground to see what sound they made, then nodded when the sound was minimal. He then peered out the door.

"Okay, I'll go first, you guys follow... er, yeah." he said quietly.

"I reckon I'll lock this after we go, otherwise people will know someone has come through."

The three followed him carefully out of the door, and he locked it. He then walked up a staircase, the others followed behind. They were heading up, Sophie assumed, to the street level, but she couldn't really tell. Clearly the building was old. Sophie ran her hand along the brickwork, she could see some of them were wet from where the water sunk in. It was dark in the old stairwell, and she had to be careful with her footing.

Harlan had gone on ahead of them, so their noise wouldn't give away them coming before he spotted someone. Sophie led them up the stairs.

"Why are we doing this?" Raffaella said.

"I need to at least know where we are. If that was Adeline, when she was casting the spell, the horned silhouetted creature..." Sophie said.

"Kowai," Tomoko added.

"...it seemed like it was trying to cast a spell to get through." Sophie said.

"So, it may be here?" Tomoko said.

Sophie shrugged. "Well, it's not here now."

They went up the stairs and came to a door at the top. It was closed. Harlan listened at it, indicated he couldn't hear anything, gingerly opened it and peered out.

The door opened into a corridor, with paintings on either side of it. It was a very refined building and apparently quite old. Harlan slinked off ahead of them, moving quietly.

"Seems like an English building," Sophie said, in a quiet voice.

Tomoko peaked out.

"Do you think we should go out there? Couldn't we get arrested for trespassing?"

"We still don't know where we are." Sophie said, her head swiveling, scanning for any clues.

They came out into the corridor, and carefully closed the door. As they walked down the hallway, they were about to turn a corner, and Harlan appeared suddenly, giving them a fright.

"Harlan, you are always appearing quietly." Sophie held her beating chest.

"Well, it's sort of my job." He smiled at Sophie. "From what I can see, we seem to be in some old established club in London. I have no idea why there is an obelisk in the cellar."

"Let's have a peak around more and get back before we get caught," Sophie said, pointing down the corridor.

Harlan had a small mirror in his hand and pointed it around the corner. He motioned to them that the next corridor was clear. They crept along and there was a window outside on one side, with a view of a London Street. It appeared to be an affluent part of London.

They creeped further along the corridor, until they came to an open room. Harlan used the mirror to peer around the corner. He indicated to them, with hand signals, there were three people. They crept up, and Sophie could briefly see the room in his mirror. There were several men sitting in lounge chairs, drinking and chatting politely, and occasional boisterous laugh. It had all the settings of what Sophie imagined was a traditional English Gentleman's club. The four took another corridor on the right, avoiding the men, until they came to another door.

This door led into a room with several artifacts on podiums. There were bits of armour on shelves, full suits of armour on stands, swords, an old mysterious jacket in a glass case.

They walked around, peering inside. Harlan motioned for Tomoko to stand near the door. Harlan put the glasses on and immediately called out excitedly. He reached out to touch a gauntlet.

"This is glowing." He lifted the glasses off his face, then back on again. "What does that mean, is it magical?" He spun around, examining various objects. "So is this shield." Raffaella took a few photos with her phone.

Sophie fumbled around for her glasses.

"I keep forgetting to use these." She glanced over to where Harlan had his gaze set. "These are pointless. Nothing. I can't see anything with them. Not sure why Rupert gave them to me." She stared, her face showing frustration, at Harlan's glasses. *Why do the ones Marcus sent to Harlan work and mine don't?*

They all went over to an old door, which had strange painted symbols on it. The details were tiny. Harlan put his glasses on, and got up close to the oddly painted door, trying to see the writing.

"I can't read it. Maybe we can magnify it?"

Rafaella pulled out her phone, changed some settings, and handed it to Harlan.

As Harlan was pointing the phone at the door, it opened inwards and an older gentleman with a red beard, smoking a pipe, walked straight out of the door, into Harlan. He saw them all and stepped back, obviously taken aback.

"Who are you? Wha... what are you doing here?"

The four stared at him, frozen. Harlan still had the phone in the same position, now pointing at the older man's chest.

The room was quiet for a second. Sophie stepped forward, she knew she had to try something, anything.

"I'm a niece of Smith's," she said quickly, picking a common surname. "I know it's against the rules but... but he let us in to have a look around."

The man for a second was taken aback. He perceived the four of them, each in turn.

Harlan stepped forward.

"Well, hello there ... I'm... Peter. I'm... American. Great club. Heard a lot about it. I'm hoping to join when I am a lot older and need somewhere for pipe smoking."

Sophie noticed Tomoko was trying to suppress a smile: *If they catch you smiling, you'll blow this*. The man stared at Harlan incredulously, before anger slowly appeared across his face.

"Smith... Reginald?" the man said, addressing Sophie.

"Yes, Reginald Smith. Uncle Reg." Sophie nodded.

"Reginald Smith hasn't been here for two years."

Sophie continued with her bluff "He told me last week he was planning to come back though. That's why he arranged to let us into the club."

The man glared at her.

"Reginald Smith hasn't been here for two years, because he died   two   years   ago."
Sophie tried to think of something to say. Anything.

"No one told me he died! He was my favorite Uncle. Er..." It was a stupid response. The man was now furious.

Sophie bounded out of the door, closely followed by the other three.

They only got out the corridor and around one bend before they came to an abrupt stop, facing four burly men in suits. The men stood in front of them, imposingly, blocking their passage.

As they stared at them, wondering what to do, two men came up behind them as well, surrounding them.

The four large men in front reached into their pockets, and pulled out what Sophie realized, alarmingly, were tasers.

A different older man appeared, with a serious and somewhat superior/indignant look, came and stood between the men facing them. Sophie was pleased he was there, she didn't want anyone trying to taze her, it seemed painful. With some indignant murmuring, the men who had been socializing in the room appeared, trying to see what was happening. The indignant man was balding, overweight, what was left of his hair was grown long and tied back in a long thin grey ponytail. He had big black glasses, and a short, pointed grey beard.

He cast his eye over them, assessing each of them, and then fixed on Harlan, still wearing the glasses.

"Bring them in here." He motioned to a door. The four burly men, who appeared to be security types, motioned for them to go in. Harlan peered at Sophie, who returned her expression. Sophie nodded towards the room. Once inside two of the men left.

"So, what are you doing here? How did you get in? The men on the door reported nothing. Who are you?"

Sophie once again decided to take the lead.

"Sorry sir. We just snuck in through the front door. We thought no one was looking. It's such an amazing place, we wanted to have a peak. We're all tourists," she said, trying to emphasize her Bavarian accent.

"I'm American," Harlan added.

The man regarded Harlan, rather dubiously, then at Sophie, then the others.

"Okay, well no harm has been done. John—" He nodded to one of the burly men. "Please escort them out."

John, a tall, generally large guard with brown curly hair started shuffling them out. Sophie knew she needed to get back to the obelisk in the basement, but she mainly felt an immediate sense of relief just to get away from them.

"WAIT," the older man said. He went over to Harlan, still wearing his glasses of true sight. His hand reached out and quickly grabbed them off Harlan, took his own glasses off, and put them on his own face, adjusting them. Harlan instantly reached up to grab them back, but the guards gave him a threatening look and he stopped.

"These...glasses... are... an artifact." His words stuttered in surprise. He peered around the room with them, then spun and examined Harlan, then Tomoko and then Sophie, turning to face them somewhat aggressively. He looked around at them all, stopping at Harlan. "My God, what are you?" His voice seemed surprised.

He took Harlan's glasses off and put his own back on, then peered at them again. There were two burly men still in the room, so they couldn't run out. Sophie started realizing that this man may be working out; they weren't just curious tourists from Europe.

"These are too important for you *people*; I'll have to keep them." He took them off his face. "I am James Toal-Smythe, the seventh generation archmage Illusionist for the London Illusionists. He muttered a spell under his breath, and he quickly fashioned the symbol for *dark* with his fingers.

"BEHOLD."

The lights went out. They were in local darkness, with some light coming in from the next room. Sophie heard him cast the spell again, and the lights came back on.

The archmage stood there looking defiant, waiting for a reaction. It was a simple minor spell, but Sophie gathered that from the way he was acting, he regarded it as an impressive feat of magic and was waiting for them to be impressed. He was met with silence.

From someone in charge of such a grand place, who called himself an *Archmage Illusionist,* Sophie expected more than this.

"Is that all? You turned out the lights...can you do anything else?" Sophie asked. Harlan smiled and nudged her in the ribs with his elbow. James Toal-Smythe, Archmage Illusionist, appeared very surprised. The Archmage nodded, proudly.

"A *number* of spells." He waved his hand over his tie. It changed colour, from red to green. He then spoke another spell and glanced over at a painting on the wall. He made the symbol for *move.*

The painting trembled a little, and after ten seconds or so, it fell off the wall.

Tomoko started laughing, politely, putting her hand over her mouth. Sophie ran the sleep spell through her head, but now in the old German.

"*Schlafrig,*" she spoke out loud, and with a quick flurry of her hands Sophie signed the symbol for sleep in the air, followed with a slight flick of the hand that sent it towards the two men.

The two burly men crumpled to the ground, leaving the Archmage standing by himself, facing Sophie and the others.

The archmage eyes opened wide, and he stared at the men on the ground, to either side of him. Visibly frightened, he took a step back. His head swiveled quickly, staring at all of them, reappraising, then back at Sophie. He backed away from her further, almost stumbling over the men on the ground.

"How did you do that? What... who are you?" His eyes showed fear, but he was now glancing down at Sophie's hands. Harlan reached out dramatically, and took the glasses off him.

"Yep... I'll take those back. You know...that's bad...stealing a man's glasses."

Harlan backed out of the room slowly. Tomoko and Sophie kept their hands in front of them, threatening the archmage with a potential spell, Raffaella scanned the room, guardedly. He just stared at them in shock, focusing on their hands.

As soon as they were out of the room, they started moving at a brisk pace, trying to get away.

They sprinted down the corridor, as they ran past the artifacts room, Harlan ran in and grabbed some of the arms and gauntlets off a suit of armour propped up on a stand.

"Harlan, hurry!" Sophie called out. Harlan grunted and they sprinted down the stairs. They finally ran to the cellar. The door was open... and Harlan sprinted into it to find two new burly men standing there, clearly guards. The four faced off against the two men.

Sophie maneuvered around them slightly and started her spellcasting.

The men, upon seeing this, reached into their pockets and each pulled out a taser.

Exactly as they raised them, Sophie did a flurry of hand movements, and quickly said the spell.

There was a slight blue blur, and all six of them appeared back in the forest in Dexheim. The two men stood there, still in front of them, frozen and wide eyed. In an instant they had switched their immediate surroundings from a basement in an old building in London, to a German Pine Forest.

One of them dropped his taser in surprise.

Sophie smiled at them, nodded, bowed with a flourish, and turned and walked back to where the scooters were. Tomoko stood looking at them slightly concerned, Raffaella followed Sophie. Harlan walked up to the two men.

"The road to Stuttgart airport is that way. Bus comes along every two hours or so. Have a nice flight." He turned to follow the others.

The men stood there quietly in silence, not moving, just gazing around them at the forest.

***

It was a long ride home, the adrenaline slowly wore off as they rode through the chill. Sophie was now sure she could try casting the other spells she knew, just using the correct older German language would make them work.

Parked out the front of the house, she hopped off the scooter.

Harlan touched her on the arm to get her attention.

"That was sort of exciting." Tomoko smiled.

"So, what do we do next?" Harlan asked.

Sophie shook her head. "I'm not worried about those guys. They have rubbish spellcasting ability; it seems they can't use their own obelisk. We need to focus on Adeline. Find her and stop the rising from happening and affecting the people of Bamberg." She paused. "I think."

They bid their farewells and Sophie went inside.

***

Thinking about it on her bed, she laid down. Next thing she knew, it was morning.

Coming out of her room, she was on a little buzz from the most successful events of the previous night. The visit to the Gentlemen's club was amazing, but what dominated her thoughts was that now, all the magic she learnt, she could probably use in the real world simply by using the older German magic commands. She had a real chance to stop this rising, and to head off Adeline some apparent violent attack on poor sleepy Bamberg.

Ernst was talking to Annika, the girlfriend. Annika was wandering around, chatting back to Ernst in her slightly high-pitched girly voice. Sophie found her voice annoying and tried to put her out of mind, as she had to do; she had come to realise her father's ever-changing girlfriends were always going to be around. It was best to largely ignore them.

Ernst was making breakfast.

"Sophie, Breakfast?" He pulled a cheese and egg grilled sandwich out of a sandwich grill and flipped it over. The brown cross hatched marks of the grill plate were seared into the white bread, and she could see the steam rise off the warm, toasted bread. Yet another of Ernst's variations on the sandwich. Sophie was hungry and her mouth watered looking at them.

She packed her bags, eager to get to school to discuss the various issues with the other three. She realized she was counting three... Raffaella now seemed to have been included in the group. You bonded quickly with people when you shared strange adventures together.

***

On the way to school, Sophie sat on the bus. It was a good chance to think. There was a sense of relief at being able to cast the spells, coupled with guilt about not doing schoolwork.

Sophie knew that Harlan and Tomoko were both gifted students. Some people may have written Harlan off as a country hick, because of his accent, but his parent's farm was a big complex operation that was worth a lot of money. Harlan himself was a lot smarter than people realized. *You can't judge Harlan by his mediocre expression,* she thought.

Tomoko, while coming across as quirky at times, was clearly like her parents who were both academics. Very intelligent.

Sophie always felt a little stupid compared to them. Her phone beeped, indicating she had a text message.

It was Harlan.

Meet me at Jeff's Café after school.

Sophie wondered what was up. She wouldn't have minded a day off from their investigation, after the previous evening's adventures.

Most of all, she wanted to hop on a bus, head out to the forest, and try out some of the magic. She had warmed to Tomoko as a good partner in all this, another mage she could talk to. Sophie hadn't really thought about what all this meant for Tomoko. Tomoko had quickly warmed to them; Sophie suspected she didn't have many friends at the school... or maybe in Bamberg at all and was probably glad for their company.

The day passed quickly, the four agreed to meet up after school. Sophie had very little thought given to schoolwork. Magic, not maths, physics, or English, dominated her thoughts. History was the only one that got her attention. She considered it something strange, but sort of uplifting. She had visited a strange club in London, a center for mages, and her own spellwork was way better than someone who was supposed to be an *archmage*. Sophie realized that Rupert was right, the existing adult mages were bad at magic. Somehow, the mages that still practiced magic had gradually lost their abilities over time.

Was it because society had oppressed mages, or in some cases, made them illegal, and the mages had slowly lost their abilities? As Rupert had said, Sophie and Tomoko, and a few unknown people that Professor Marcus had connected to their ancestors, were bringing more powerful magic back to the world.

After school, Sophie caught the tram to meet Harlan, Tomoko and Raffaella at the Electric Light Kafe. Sophie stepped off the tram, her cheek immediately stung from the bitter bite of the cold. The clunky old trams had modern heating, but Bamberg itself was *desperately* cold today. The high-pitched squealing sound of partially working brakes faded as the tram trundled off down the street. Sophie adjusted her scarf, pulling it upwards, covering the last centimetre of her exposed neck.

This was the part of Bamberg where the buildings were from the 1700s. That is, the *new* part. She stepped up from the cobblestoned street and onto the footpath, momentarily getting her bearings, before spotting her landmark.

Two things were outside the front of the café she was looking for. The usual blue Trabant, an old soviet era car always parked out the front by the owner as a decoration, and next to it, Harlan's new/old scooter.

Sophie peered over at Harlan's scooter and momentarily wondered if a protection glyph, like they used on houses, would work on a scooter. Would a glyph keep it safe from accidents? Not sure. She thought of Raffaella's scooter, there were so many stickers and symbols on it already, a glyph would hardly be noticed.

There were a few people downstairs, drinking coffees and eating pastries in the Electric Light Kafe. Jeff was sitting in the middle of the cafe, playing an acoustic guitar, with a coffee, having a break.

"Oh, 'ullo Sophie. All right?" Jeff said, the grin appearing within his face, otherwise all sunglasses, long hair and beard.

"It's a little chilly, jeff." Sophie decided to leave her jacket on until she warmed up.

"Your buddy's upstairs, talking to someone."

Sophie walked up the stairs, wondering who Harlan would be talking to. He was sitting at a table, looking at a laptop, and then talking to it. He seemed unhappy and managed a forced, awkward smile when he saw Sophie.

"Oh, you're early. Uhm, er." He pointed at the screen. "This is my dad and my mom."

Sophie glanced at the laptop screen and got a little surprise to see Harlan's parents, there in a little box, staring back at her. Sophie had met the German family that Harlan stayed with, but of course never his parents who lived in the states.

There was a frame on the laptop with his father, a good looking, thick set man with short cropped blonde hair, and his mother. His mother was a beautiful latino woman, with long black hair, wearing a black T shirt.

"Oh, pleased to meet you. I'm Sophie." She awkwardly bent over to get her head in view of the laptop camera.

Oh, Sophie, hi, I'm Jim, Harlan's dad and this is his mother, Juanita. We've heard a lot about you. Thanks for looking after Harlan for us." He turned to look at Harlan. "Well considering the er, well what we were discussing, maybe we should stop here and continue later."

Harlan went quiet for a second, thinking. "Er, dad, Sophie is a good buddy. I'm fine with her hearing it."

His Dad appeared surprised. "Well, if you want to. What I was saying is, you know, your mother is somewhere there, and you only have limited time. You know, you may never be back there."

Sophie could see Harlan's expression, his brow furrowed, he was clearly troubled. He had told her some things about this, but not much. He had said he knew his father had been keeping things from him about his mother, but it annoyed her that Harlan's father seemed to be keeping something back from him.

"James. You obviously met his biological mother. I can tell Harlan is troubled by all this. He needs to find his mother, but he's got nothing to go on. For Harlan's own sake, tell him everything you know, would you?"

James and Juanita both appeared shocked. Harlan's gaze slowly turned to Sophie, but then back to his father to see the reaction.

"Well, er. Sophie. Well Harlan. Okay. So, I met your bio mother when I was in the military. We had a brief time together. Then she returned after about a year and gave me a baby and disappeared. I had to leave the service to bring you back. Really, that's all I know. She was beautiful, pale with blonde hair. Her name was Aderyn. That's the whole story, seriously."

Harlan nodded. "And I already know all that."

"That's really hard on Harlan. He's got nothing to go on." Sophie could hear the angsty timbre in her voice.

"Soph. It's okay, drop it. Dad can't help it. It's, yeah, like he says, it's all he knows." He put his hand on her shoulder, and she sat down.

"Look Harlan, we better go. Nice meeting you Sophie," James said.

"Stay safe and stay warm Harlan. Love you," Juanita said, she had a sympathetic look on her face, like she wanted to say or do something, but couldn't. Sophie realised it must be hard being separated from family like this.

"Love you Mom, dad. Bye y'all," Harlan said and waved. They disappeared off the screen and Harland closed the lid of the laptop, slumping forward. And sighed.

He peered at Sophie and shrugged. "I dunno. I'm not going to find my German heritage here. Don't suppose it matters. Yeah, it's still been an amazing time... particularly the last little while."

"Don't go back, Harlan. Stay here!" Sophie shook her head.

There was sadness in his voice "I don't want to go Soph. I want to stay here with you, and I sort of like our whole Circle 66 thing. I gotta work on the farm business. Anyway—" Harlan stopped, looking at the top of the stairs.

At that point, Raffaella walked in. Sophie noticed his expression changed into a warm smile when he saw her. She picked the chair next to him and sat down.

The music Jeff had been playing changed to Jazz, and Sophie noticed the tiniest squint of Raffaella's eyes, for the shortest of moments.

"This…" Harlan paused, dramatically waving his hand. "Is *really* good music."

Raffaella just shook her head and sighed.

"Okay, we met here for a reason. Let's have a detailed critical analysis about Jazz some other time." Sophie could hear the annoyance creeping into the tone of her voice.

At this point Tomoko appeared, coming over to the table and sitting down.

"I agree with Sophie, we've got more to talk about. Oh, and hi everyone." She waved a cheery hand and smiled.

It was quiet for a second.

"Oh, Jazz. Isn't this music really bad?" Tomoko said, oblivious to the previous discussion.

"Hey!" Harlan said, genuine offence on his face.

"Guys. I have big news." Sophie sat upright, slightly dramatically. "I cracked another one I think."

"Another spell?" Harlan had been rocking his chair on the back two legs but put it forward on its four feet.

"Sh. Harlan." Even though they were upstairs in the cafe, Harlan talking about spells in a loud way made Sophie twitchy.

Tomoko, being the other mage in the group, immediately came to life at the mention of *spellwork*. "What can you do? Can you show us?

Now that she could cast, Sophie had been repeatedly practicing getting the spell right and was happy to talk about it.

"I can cast with multiple fingers." Sophie took her bag off her shoulder and put it on the table. "Before, I was casting… just painting the symbol with one finger."

She waved her finger in the air to demonstrate.

"Oh, sagoi. I only use just one finger." Tomoko frowned.

"I had seen Johannes use multiple fingers. It looks impressive, and it's quicker."

"Multiple fingers," Harlan said, in German. He mispronounced it, reminding Sophie just how bad his German was.

"Yes...watch, I used to do it with one finger. Like this." Sophie's hand used one finger to draw a symbol. "But watch it with multiple fingers." She quickly drew the symbol for sleep in the air, skillfully using all the fingers on her hand (except for her thumb) quickly, she finished with a flick, and the command word. "*Slãfen.*"

Harlan and Raphaella watched her blankly for a second.

Then both lurched forward onto the table. Raffaella fell forward, into a full plate of pasta.

Tomoko noted them both, and then Sophie, smiling.

"Looks like it doesn't affect me because I'm also a..." Then she also lurched forward onto the table, instantly snoring loudly, almost cartoon like.

Sophie peered at each of them.

They weren't moving.

"Awesome." she said, addressing the table of three sleeping friends.   They   didn't   reply. She felt the grin on her face, from cheek to cheek. After not being able to do spells, and being frustrated, she was chuffed. She shook her head to clear her mind.

"Ok. Reverse spell. Reverse spell. How do I do that?" Sophie realised she was talking to herself; it helped her think. She checked no one was coming up the stairs, and once again, her hands flickered through the gestures, fingers interacting, crossing to make little symbols. This time in reverse order: Person. Night. Moon.

"Verwundung," she said, finishing off the spell.

All three woke up. They appeared stunned. Just at that point, an odd scent of roasted coffee and bacon wafted into her face, from behind. She had a feeling someone was looking over her shoulder, turned around, and Jeff was standing right behind her, he'd come up the stairs. He put a coffee down in front of a still groggy Harlan. Harlan smiled uncomfortably, and Jeff quickly left.

"Sorry about that, guys."

Tomoko, still waking up properly but groggy and confused, grabbed Sophie on the shoulder and smiled. "Can you do it again, please!?"

"NO." Harland and Raffaella both said at the same time.

"Okay, moving on, what do we do about Adeline? What is the story with the London Illusionists? Sophie said.

"Well, we need to find her. If we are going to stop her," Harlan said.

"At least we have the Obelisks to transport us now. Saves on plane tickets!" Sophie noted, as per usual, Tomoko brought up the positive in the situation.

"There's Rupert. We could ask him," Tomoko said.

"Second Rupert? The one that rang me? I don't know..." Sophie considered the two Ruperts. She somehow felt better about the second one.

"Yeah, well, he's the only one who we know who can help." Harlan crossed his arms.

"I can keep an eye on him," Raffaella said, slightly ominously, still pulling bits of cake out of her hair.

"Okay, compromise. We go ahead ourselves, and if we get stuck, I contact Rupert on his number. It's in my phone."

"Okay," Tomoko and Harlan both said in unison. Raffaella nodded.

Sophie was happy they could all agree on this. She was hoping they could work it out themselves. Though there was something about second Rupert that made her feel like she trusted him.

Chapter 24 - The Spell Off

Sophie had suggested they do some training, to prepare for when they find Adeline. The four hopped on the two scooters, with Sophie on the back of Raffaella's and once again, took off to the forest. Pulling the scooters over to a thick clump of pine trees, Tomoko and Sophie briskly walked into the forest. Sophie kept wanting to stop, but the ever-cautious Tomoko insisted on them getting far away from the line of sight from the road so no one could see them casting.

Harlan and Raffaella rolled their scooters off the road, struggling to push them on the rough ground of the forest, but managed to hide them with some bushes. Sophie caught something moving, but it was just a cute pine marten scurrying across the ground.

"Tomoko, is this far enough?" Raffaella sounded vaguely frustrated. Clearly, she was still taking in all the revelations of the return of magic to Bamberg.

"Okay." Sophie stopped and started to remember how to make the symbol for the fire spell. "I'll try this."

She focused her mind first on the spell, then used the correct movement of her fingers to make the symbols that would prepare the spell energy. Her fingers quickly made the symbols for sun, wood, fire. Harlan and Raffaella watched on, Sophie knew to them, it was just a blur of weird hand movements.

"Moyasu," Sophie uttered. This time a small fire started in front of them. Exactly as she had been able to do with Johannes.

Sophie cried out in excitement. The rest of the group smiled, before Tomoko noticed the fire was catching hold of a tree and she ran to put it out.

"My turn now." Tomoko started her own series of hand gestures. They were very similar to Sophies. She spoke the casting commands in Japanese, and at first nothing happened. Raffaella appeared vaguely disappointed.

"Try again, Tomoko," Harlan said, trying to be encouraging.

But Tomoko wasn't listening, she was still focusing on the spell she cast. Sophie watched. Tomoko's body drifted upward, until she was standing on the tips of her toes. It seemed like she was impossibly supporting her complete body weight, just on the ends of her feet. Then not even her toes touched the ground, and she was floating slowly, perfectly in a straight line upward. Every time Sophie saw Tomoko do it, she stopped to admire it. It was wondrous, and while she knew Tomoko knew a variety of spells Sophie didn't know, because she was Eastern Path, the levitation spell was the one she thought most about trying to learn from Tomoko.

Johannes had mentioned once that learning spells from another path was generally forbidden, but Illusionists were connected to the Eastern path, and some of the spells were the same. They both used a lot of *Kunst Magick*—head magic, magic that affects the mind.

Harlan, Sophie and Raffaella all watched on silently, each staring at Tomoko with the same stunned look on their face. Making people sleep, and making fire was magical, and impressive, but people did sleep, and you could make fire with a cigarette lighter, so you weren't making something people couldn't normally see.

However, people *never* flew by themselves.

After a full minute, Harlan was the first to speak, as Tomoko levitated above them.

"You did this before, but it's still cool to watch you fly." Harlan eyes widened; a huge grin appeared on his face.

"Hah! It is not really flying." She raised her voice excitedly, as she was now above them.

"I can only go up in the air, I don't have a spell for flying. I can *will* myself to move forward, I can run when I cast the spell, which makes me go in that direction, but I wouldn't call it flying."

"Damn it, I can't fly. Tomoko… you get the cool spells," Sophie said.

Harlan stared at her, blinking. "I love my thief stuff, it's my thing, and I don't want to do magic. But, dang. Flying…that would be awesome."

Tomoko slowly reduced her altitude, till she landed back on the ground. "That's always fun. Flying spells are the best, I get to be Superman. I need to practice though, in the dreamscape, when I did this, I kept bashing into the castle wall in Osaka. At least here I don't have to dodge arrows."

"Okay, I have one more. It is not that amazing, but it is a little cute."

Tomoko once again drew a quick symbol in the air in front of her, followed by the spell incantation. Her outfit changed to a black gothic lolitta outfit. It was shapely, coming in at the waste, but then the skirt flowered out, the edges trimmed with lace.

"Oh… *fashion* magic!" Harlan watched on; he said it with a smile on his face. "Hey… that's a little bit of a stereotype, isn't it? A Japanese person…conjuring up a cosplay outfit."

"Harlan, it's not a cosplay mage character outfit if you *are actually* a mage. Besides, I love it, it, er, makes a statement."

"Hey, Tomoko, where did your old clothes go?" Sophie asked.

"Ah, thank you for asking! My old clothes go into my cupboard at home, which is where this outfit was. I just have to concentrate on my memory of the clothes on the coat hangers and make sure they are actually there in the cupboard. If I'm not concentrating, I'll end up magically changing into my pajamas or my underwear."

Tomoko glanced at her watch. "Time to go home. I am cooking my karage chicken tonight."

Raffaella grinned at Sophie. "Hop on the back."

The two scooters parted ways, Tomoko, and Sophie both feeling impressed with each other's efforts.

***

School finished early. Sophie waited for the tram, and Tomoko decided to wait with her.

Sophie realised it was the first time she had spent time alone with Tomoko.

"Sophie... I wanted to say thank you." Tomoko peered at Sophie earnestly.

Sophie glanced at her. "Why... I mean... What for, Tomoko? I haven't done anything?"

"Well for letting me be part of your group." Tomoko gave her a tiny bow.

"Oh, Tomoko." Sophie shook her head. "You don't have to thank me. Besides, it wasn't really a group before you came along. It was me and Harlan trying to work out what the hell was going on. You, and then Raffaella made us a group."

"Well... before I met you, I was pretty much by myself," Tomoko said. Sophie detected something in the tone of her voice, fleetingly. Was it sadness?

"Well...I teach Ikebana. I study hard. The magic is of course amazing. But apart from that..."

Sophie thought for a second. "Ikebana. What sort of martial art is that?"

"Flower arranging." Tomoko laughed again, slightly maniacally.

"Our Housekeeper does that. She's Japanese too. Her name is Hisako."

"Oh, Hisako. Yes, she is in the class I teach at the University club. Is your dad the History Professor?"

Sophie nodded.

"Ah. She's in love with him," Tomoko continued.

Sophie's eyes widened in surprise. "SHE'S WHAT?"

Tomoko's eyes darted to either side and she went quiet for a second.

"Oh. Er, maybe I wasn't supposed to say that."

Sophie thought about Hisako's history with them, and a few things started to fit together. She remembered many times they would be in the kitchen, laughing and chatting. Occasionally he would touch her on the shoulder, and she would smile. They always seemed to get on really well. Hisako never complained about Ernst's girlfriends, but she also never spoke to them or had anything to do with them.

"Well... that would explain a few things," Sophie said, still contemplating the news.

"You should get them together, then they will be happy." Tomoko nodded enthusiastically.

Sophie avoided answering directly, it wasn't something she thought particularly likely to happen.

As they sat there, Sophie momentarily quietly, taking in this revelation, Tomoko's phone beeped.

"Oh, another break in!" Tomoko said, looking at her phone to read it.

"What?" Sophie tried to see what was on the phone, but it was in Japanese.

"I have a news alert set up on my phone browser. I have used keywords like *break in, robbery, Bamberg*. There was a break in at the library... at the University!" Tomoko sounded surprised, and alarmed.

"Let go and talk to the boys," Sophie said.

"Er, no, what? Is it safe to go there?" Tomoko appeared wary.

"If it's in the news the police will have already been there. We need to see what was stolen and see how this matches up with the other break ins," Sophie said.

***

At the library, the three goth librarians were there, arguing about something to do with history. They were arguing in German, and Sophie heard them talking about "Assyrian" and "Seleucid Empire" ... which seemed suitably esoteric for them.

"Sophie. Ladies." Sophie knew the goth librarians through picking up the occasional rare history book for her papa. They were slightly eccentric, but her papa always praised them for knowing so much and the rare books and being so helpful to his research and teaching.

Akshay addressed them, friendly, but dramatically, holding his hands out wide as a gesture of welcome. He wore his long hair in ponytails, but had a trim beard, and was clearly of Indian background. The others were so deep in their argument, they kept arguing for a time, before stopping.

Thomas had long blonde hair, pale skin and almost appeared to have albinism. As soon as he saw the girls, he went quiet. Erwin half glanced up from the computer, peering over the top of his computer to look at the girls, clearly interested in what he was typing, but trying to do both things at once.

"Come here for something for Ernst, Sophie?" Akshay said, smiling pleasantly.

"No. We heard about the break in…" Sophie put on her concerned face. She could see they were obviously not harmed so she didn't ask. "…and just wanted to come down and check everything was okay."

As soon as she said break in, they all went still.

"Ah that's nice," Akshay responded.

There was an awkward silence.

Sophie and Tomoko glanced over at the three librarians.

They stared back, until Akshay broke the silent standoff.

"Well, I'm not sure we are supposed to talk about it." Thomas leaned into Akshay, his hand keeping his long platinum blonde streaks of his face. He lowered his voice slightly. "Yes, but can we show them?"

"Why not?" said Akshay.

"Show us what?" Sophie said.

"Okay. Just come through." Thomas opened a door and Tomoko and Sophie followed them through. "Here." He pointed at a cabinet that was open.

"It was in this." He stood back and examined it. "I don't know what happened, but it was in here. The front door was locked, the main door to the library was locked. Now it's gone."

Akshay said, the frustration was palpable, and he even sounded a touch upset.

"What was it? What book did they take?" Tomoko asked.

Akshay stared at her, with a vague look of curiosity.

"It was a medieval book of poems. From the sixteenth century. It's really rare, and otherwise not available. There is only one other print, in the US. Now there's only one in the world."

"What was it called?"

"It's called *Die Sonnete der Himmlisschen Rose* in German. In English, that is *The Sonnets of the Celestial Rose.*"

"Oh, thank you." Sophie had translated it in her head a little differently, but Akshay's translation was better. She had no idea what this was all about, but knew it had something to do with the other things that were happening.

This all seemed to point towards a certain two parents and their little girl, Adeline.

Chapter 25 - McBurgers and unlikely events

"For the fourth time, I asked you, stop putting on those glasses." Sophie growled.

"You're just jealous yours, cos yours don't work," Harlan said, smirking.

Harlan was regularly, every ten minutes, trying on *the glasses of true sight*. Sophie thought he seemed pretty much obsessed with them. He would always hold them gingerly, putting them carefully in his pocket, and would not allow anyone to touch them.

It also highlighted to Sophie that hers didn't seem to do anything. She had initially been putting them on here and there, to see if she could see anything, but never could, so had given up. Sophie wondered if Harlan was having some sort of magic artifact addiction.

Sophie scanned the interior of McBurgers. Tomoko and Harlan had a burger craving, there was no burger place in Bamberg, so they'd gone to the nearby town of Lauscha. *Why was the most satisfying food also the unhealthiest?* Tomoko usually ate healthy, and Raffaella was fussy about Italian food, but they all still occasionally ate junk food. Sophie's dad always worried about dieting and calories, but that was something adults had to worry about. Sophie could eat all sorts of food and never really put on weight.

Harlan went to put on his glasses.

Sophie shook her head. "Harls, you don't have to put them on in every shop we go to."

"I can't help it. What if I miss a magic item?"

He went to pick up his food from the counter but didn't have a hand free so put the glasses on his head. However, as he was picking up the food, they fell down and he was looking directly at the man serving him.

Sophie noticed Harlan looking strangely at the man.

"Err...Thank you," Harlan said. He grabbed the bag, awkwardly scrunching up the top of the paper to get a better grip.

Sophie could tell something was wrong.

As he turned around, Harlan started giving out the things in the bag to the three at the table.

"Burger for you...chips for you...and one *antler horned half man half deer creature behind the counter* for you."

"Harlan Wha..."

"Sh... there's a half man, half deer...creature behind the counter serving people."

Sophie pulled out *her* glasses and stared at him. *Nothing. Useless.*

Tomoko's eyes widened, and she quickly glanced up.

"Are you sure it is?" Tomoko asked, looking incredulous.

"Trust me, it's hard to get something like that mixed up with something else," Harlan said, looking incredulous.

Raffaella nodded. "Half man half deer? Cool."

"If it is a half *man*, I think that it is probably a half man, *half stag*," Tomoko said.

"Sh. Stop..." Harlan appeared concerned. "Don't everyone look at once."

Sophie had a peak, pretending to look through her hamburger.

Harlan shook his head. "Yes, that's very natural," he said, his comment laced with sarcasm.

The half man/half stag food server didn't seem too bothered by them looking at him.

Clearly, he wasn't expecting the customers to be mages, or for them to have *glasses of true sight*. He kept serving. He seemed good at it. To Sophie, he seemed like any of the other servers.

Harlan kept looking at him, with his brow down, so it wasn't obvious.

"Yeah, well, whatever spell he was using, or magic, or artifact, his actual body size was about the same size as his human size. It didn't shrink him. However, it did change his head."

Sophie glanced at them both. "Well, what do we do?"

"We should leave, he could be dangerous," Tomoko said.

Sophie ignored her. "Let's follow him when he leaves."

"Ie... no. we can't do that, he is dangerous. He could kill us," Tomoko said.

"Yes, he could be dangerous, so we need to be careful. Oh! I just thought of something, remember when Adeline was at the obelisk? We could see the horned figure in the blue haze! This guy here looks like him."

"Er, yeah?" Harlan said.

"Maybe he came through the portal after I broke the seal by using it?" Sophie glanced sideways at Tomoko, eating a burger. "This could be my fault."

Tomoko shook her head. "Ie, err no. This creature could have been living here before, maybe the glasses revealed what we could never see?"

Sophie shook her head. "His horns, the profile, they are the same sort of creature."

Tomoko appeared serious. "Freidrickson had those pictures in our history class, they looked like him."

Sophie realized Tomoko was right. "Are there creatures like this all over town... that we've just never seen before?"

They agreed to watch him for a while. Leaving the burger place, they went outside, got on their scooters, and drove around for a while, returning every so often to check. Eventually getting bored, they went and parked them across the road and sat on their scooters for an hour.

"This stag man is taking ages," Harlan grumbled, his head resting on his arms, on the front of the scooter. Finally, they noticed the half stag half man left his serving duties and disappeared into the kitchen area.

"Look, he's gone out the back." Tomoko pointed.

They waited five minutes. He eventually appeared and went out to a small yellow car. He hopped in, scanned around nonchalantly, and then drove off.

"We following him?" Harlan asked, motorcycle helmet in hand.

"Of course, we are following him, he's clearly some magical creature, and maybe something to do with Adeline. She was summoning some sort of horned creature. He could be up to all manner of strange things.

The four got on the two scooters and followed the creature. They had to drive slowly behind him so that they weren't too obvious.

Suddenly, he stopped up ahead. They stopped. Sophie peeked up ahead and could see he was talking to someone on his phone. They waited patiently, trying to stay out of sight. His car lights came on and he continued driving.

They followed the little yellow car, as it drove between the old houses and narrow cobblestoned streets. Eventually it pulled up at a convenience store. Sophie motioned for them to stop their scooters, they were still far away enough, that she was pretty sure he hadn't noticed them. Sophie felt butterflies in her stomach, she could see Harlan grinning, clearly in his element. Tomoko looked on, gritting her teeth.

They parked their scooters, and Sophie decided they should follow him into the convenience store to see what he was doing. They fanned out, trying to look as natural as possible, looking at various things in the convenience store. Chocolates. Car fresheners. Energy drinks.

Harlan had on the glasses and was pointing at the man behind the counter. He appeared like a normal human guy, brown hair and red beard, wearing a band T-shirt and a black baseball cap. Harlan nodded. He apparently was a stag-man as well.

The Mcburger stag-man was buying something at the front of the store and talking to the redbeard stag-man behind the counter. Sophie tried to remain unobvious, frowning as much as possible, as she read the ingredients and application instructions on some roll-on deodorant.

Tomoko shook her head. "I miss Japanese convenience stores, they have everything." She had collected a range of products in her arms.

Sophie muttered under breath. "I think you are forgetting why we are here."

"Oh...yes..." Tomoko seemed embarrassed and put the things down.

As they waited for the McBurger half beast to leave, the door opened, and four rather large men came into the store. They wore bulky jackets, flannel shirts and big boots.

Sophie grinned, and stepped over to Harlan, pretending to show him some toothpaste. She peered at Harlan. He had gone white as a sheet, and he was wearing the glasses. The four men milled about, getting chocolate and energy drinks out of the fridge.

"Is one of them half stag?" Sophie muttered under her breath.

Harlan appeared grim. "All..." He whispered through gritted teeth; she noticed the quiver in his voice.

Sophie quickly glanced at them all to see where they were and felt the overwhelming desire to get away from them as quickly as possible. She grabbed Tomoko, who wasn't watching, by the jacket. "Let's go." As they left, she noticed the red bearded man at the till was looking at them oddly under his hat, like he was studying them, then kept talking to his friend.

Harlan, Tomoko and Raffaella got out of the convenience store, into the car park, and walked as fast as they could without running. Sophie came after them, reciting the sleep spell preparation in her head, going over the hand casting sequence. She couldn't risk fire balling the crowd and possibly blowing up the petrol bowser out the front of the convenience store.

The four hopped on the scooters and drove over across the street, waiting in a dark alley. The men came out after about two or three minutes or so, and all crammed into an old white Russian jeep with one door painted red. The car drove off.

The two scooters followed. Turning left on the cobblestones then right.

"It's going the same way the other one went."

The car turned left again. The three scooters sped up, turned left and had to brake hard. The car stopped in the middle of the road. The five creatures were all getting out of the car and coming towards them, three of them were holding tyre levers and one a baseball bat. They had all changed their appearance. They now appeared like their original, half man, half stag form.

Sophie was stunned by their appearance. Their human forms weren't pretty, but their half beast forms were plain scary. Hairy faces, large obvious teeth, their hairy muzzles wet with Stag spit. The huge horns. Sophie felt words coming out of her mouth, as a response, even before she knew she had spoken.

"Halb ermann, halb tier," Sophie muttered.

Harlan jumped off his scooter, and Sophie jumped off as well as his scooter fell to the ground. He dashed to the fence line and jumped and was gone.

Tomoko was on the back of Raffaella's scooter, which now stopped as well. Tomoko lifted off the scooter, and into the air. Raffaella turned and watched her float up, stunned.

She took a deep breath. At that moment, she heard a scream, and someone pushed past her, charging towards them. It was Raffaella screaming at the top of her lungs, running, with a longsword, evidently it had been strapped to the back of her scooter backrest.

Sophie also hopped off; Harlan's scooter fell with a crash. The stag-man had stopped. They all wore big fleece jackets, and flannelette checkered shirts. The bigger main one had a red bandana around his neck.

However, they were looking up at Tomoko. As she rose, she cast another spell that changed her appearance. Her clothes changed into a white lacy outfit, with white gloves. Sophie peeked at it. It appeared impressive, but a little ridiculous considering what was going on.

One of them threw a car jack from the car up at Tomoko, Tomoko awkwardly dodged to the side just in time as it sailed past.

Two of them were moving towards Raffaella. Despite her screaming and the big longsword, they did not seem concerned.

The remaining big stag-man started moving towards Sophie. Sophie thought quickly, breathing in the cool Bamburg air, she quickly ran the sleep spell through her mind, and drew the symbol, casting the sleep spell. The big one stopped momentarily, shook his head momentarily dazed... and then kept coming. *It didn't work. He shook it off.*

Sophie suppressed her panic as the creature came on towards her. She kept running back, and then cast another. He had long legs and Sophie could see he was gaining on her, she kept increasing her pace, she couldn't turn round to see him as she was worried that would slow her but could hear him growling and his steps.

She stopped once more and cast her spell for the third time.

This time he stopped for longer, closed his eyes and stood still for fifteen seconds. Sophie watched him wondering what he was doing. He then opened his eyes, shook his head, and then kept moving towards her, slower, but then picked up a pace.

Desperate now, Sophie cast one more, concentrating, trying to put all her energy into it. This time she stared straight into his eyes. The spell hit him hard this time... he kept moving towards her for a second, the momentum carrying him forward. but then crumpled, falling to his knees and collapsing at her feet.

Sophie felt a mix of accomplishment, but mostly relief, letting out a huge breath as she realized she had been holding her breath for the last thirty seconds.

There was a clatter sound.

Something was falling out of the sky, a stick?

She glanced up. Tomoko was floating above her, with a huge longbow, shooting arrows down at the stag men. She was moving awkwardly as she was floating. Apparently, she was having trouble shooting and levitating at the same time.

Glancing around, but keeping tabs on the smaller stag man, she grinned as she saw Raffaella was successfully attacking one of them and driving him back to the car. He was looking panicky.

Sophie noted one of the creatures was charging at her. She started running back and cast a sleep spell on him. He stopped, and it appeared he was going to doze off for a second, shook his head, and was awake.

"Tomoko. The roof! Land on the roof."

Tomoko nodded and landed on the roof. As soon as she landed, she planted her feet firmly on the roof, arched her back and spread out her chest. She then fired three quick shots in succession, all hits, hitting one in the arm, one in the leg, and a third in the thigh.

At that point, the car of its own accord started moving down the street. The remaining stag man cursed, ran towards it, grabbing one of their sleeping friends from the ground. Sophie watched as they got in the car and drove off.

Sophie stopped to catch her breath. The combat had been frightening, and she was still shaking from it. She realised the enormity of it all. These creatures were dangerous, if things had gone wrong, they could have been killed. May be all of them.

Raffaella ran over to Sophie. "Two wounded. They are not very good with weapons, street brawling. No art." She didn't even seem to be out of breath. While Sophie had been contemplating the threat and the fact they could have died, Raffaella seemed completely cool about the whole thing.

Tomoko floated gracefully down and landed next to them. There was a fearful waver in her voice. "I…we could have died. They were huge."

"Yes, I know. You shooting from up there was great." Sophie was still trying to get her breath.

"I couldn't shoot while I was flying. I had to have my feet on something firm," she said, speaking slowly, like she was still in shock.

Harlan came out of the bushes on the opposite side of the road.

"Ah. Thanks for your help, Harlan." The slightest element of sarcasm in her voice. Raffaella glanced at him, as she put her sword back on her scooter.

He grinned. "You should thank me. I hopped the fence, ran down there—" He pointed to the wall on the side of the road. "—hopped back over the fence and took the handbrake off the car. When they saw their car rolling down the street, they all started running away."

Raffaella raised an eyebrow. Sophie, while still shaky from fear and adrenaline, suddenly sensed the humour of his statement and laughed out loud. She went over and gave Harlan a big hug.

"Our first big combat, eh? Everyone ok?" Harlan said, checking out everyone, to make sure they seemed ok, then smiling and patted Sophie on the head. Suddenly he turned, his eyes widened, looking back down the road.

"Helmets on. They are coming back."

They all spun around, grabbing their helmets. Sophie ran over to Harlan, and hopped on the back of his scooter, as Tomoko got on the back of hers. "Let's go, quick!" She turned to Raffaella. "How fast can we go?"

"Fast enough, but I don't think any of us will outrun that car."

They took off quickly, Raffaella's scooter front wheel left the ground as it sped ahead.

As they took off down the street towards Bamberg, Sophie glanced back in her rear mirror. It *was* the Stag men, who were now chasing them in their car. They were in trouble. She wasn't sure if she could cast a spell while they were riding. If she stopped, she wasn't sure what spell would stop a car. She had the fireball spell, but it may not stop a car, and may destroy them and the houses around them.

Harlan accelerated, and took a corner too close to a wall, having to adjust. Raffaella was the fastest rider, she was up ahead, and taking twisting corners around the town which would make it hard for the car, which was faster on the straight, but not as maneuverable in the town.

Raffaella turned into a little alleyway, too narrow for the car. They all followed. It seemed like they had lost them. Sophie felt relieved, but still scared.

Sophie pointed to a sign on the main road out of Lauscha, and back to Bamberg. They turned onto it, and all floored their scooters. Sophie hadn't ridden as fast before.

The scooters roared down the highway when Sophie glanced back in her mirror.

The car was behind them again.

Sophie took in a deep breath of the cold air, her eyes watering. She tried not to think of the car. The image of the car smashing into the scooters popped into her head, it could easily knock them over. She could feel her heart beating fast, and she noticed how fast she was breathing. She glanced in the mirror and could see Harlan's face. He was concentrating on keeping the scooter on the road at speed, but she could see the fear in his eyes.

Both scooters were revving their engines, and flying down the road, but they were now on the straight and the car was likely to catch them. The car could knock them off the road into the trees, or even drive over them.

"Tomoko, Your bow!" Sophie screamed out.

Tomoko nodded, and turned back. She was awkwardly leaning on the backrest, but could shoot backwards, by leaning out from the scooter. She nocked an arrow, and tilted the huge bow, pointing it behind them at the car. Sophie turned her head back to see her aiming, and then peered in the mirror. The car was closing on them, the engine noise was revving fast now drowning out the sound of the scooters as it neared them.

It kept gaining, closing the distance. It was close enough Sophie could see the faces of the stag men in the rear vision mirror on the scooter.

They were angry faces.

They momentarily appeared alarmed, as an arrow sailed through the air, hitting the windscreen, but bounced off.

They were too far away, the angle of the glass on the car must be deflecting it. The arrows won't do any good

Tomoko knocked another arrow and fired. It hit the roof of the car and bounced off. Tomoko shook her head. Her arrows were not doing anything.

Sophie watched as Tomoko strangely fired an arrow that appeared to go around the windscreen and through the passengers' open window, into the car. The men appeared startled, but then laughed.

Raffaella took her sword out of the backrest scabbard, and had it in her right hand, her other hand on the scooter throttle. Sophie couldn't work out what she was doing, but Raffaella kept looking back and trying to gauge where the car was. She had a vexed look of determination on her face, pure focus. The car with the stag men was closing now. Sophie clenched her teeth and gripped the backrest tightly.

Raffaella threw the sword behind her. It headed towards the car windscreen; Sophie peaked at her rear vision mirror to look back at the result. It was a perfect shot, but the Stag men saw it coming. They swerved the car out of the way, and the sword hit the side of the car, bounced off and clattered down the road disappearing into the blackness. They almost lost control of the car, but then swerved back onto the road and kept driving.

Sophie could see Raffaella frown slightly, for a second. Raffaella then focused back on her driving and turned to call out to Tomoko on the back of Raffaella's scooter.

"TOMOKO. THE RADIATOR!" Raffaella screamed.

Tomoko obviously couldn't hear the words disappearing into the wind and the night. Her face screwed up in confusion. "What?"

Raffaella yelled at the top of her voice "SHOOT BETWEEN THE HEADLIGHTS."

Tomoko quickly knocked one arrow in her hand, and put three arrows between her fingers, to have them ready to fire in quick succession. She did a quick chant of the spell for accuracy, and then fired a shot to judge the distance. It fell just in front of the car.

She then fired two shots in quick succession. Both arrows went into the car, between the headlights. Tomoko held up her hand showing two fingers. "Two more," she screamed.

Sophie checked her mirror again. Two more arrows sailed through the air in quick succession. She could see the arrows sticking into the grill, but it made no difference, the car was still gaining on them.

"Okay, ride flat out!"

Sophie leaned in, as did Tomoko and Harlan and Raffaella both floored their scooters.

She could see the car was still gaining on them. She couldn't cast a spell now. The car was within about eighty metres. She could clearly see the faces of the drivers. One of them was baring his teeth, filled with rage.

Then she noticed the expressions on their faces change.

There was steam coming out of the front of the car, where the arrows were.

"TOMOKO! You got them!"

The car now was revving hard, and Sophie could hear it struggling. It was starting to slow down.

The scooters started to gain on the car. A huge sense of relief came across Sophie, she realized how still her body had become with fear. Her hands were gripping the backrest like a vice. She slowly started to relax and let out a long deep breath.

Then she saw police sirens. The Thuringian Free State Police. Sophie checked the map on Harlan's smartphone on the headset of his scooter, which he was using for navigating, and then peered over her shoulder, behind her. The Thuringian police were catching up to the car. But the car turned off the right and down a side road.

Sophie noticed that *instead* of following the car at the turnoff, the police continued on the highway to follow the scooters. The car had slowed and limped off down the side road, and the police ignored it.

"Tomoko, toss your bow!" Sophie yelled out.

"NO! I love my bow!" Tomoko screamed.

"We'll go back for it. You want to end up in jail?"

Tomoko grimaced and flung it away from her. It flipped through the air, disappearing into a bush.

Sophie checked where they were on her phone and motioned for them to keep going. Raffaella turned back confused, and Sophie just pointed ahead. Finally, after about five minutes, Sophie pulled over and stopped, waving to the police.

A big white BMW police car pulled over behind Sophie and Tomoko, with lights flashing and the siren going. They both hopped off the scooter.

Sophie once again checked where they were, called someone on her phone, and then handed it to Tomoko.

The police officer turned the lights and siren off, got out of the car, then stretched to get a little computer from his dashboard. He was a big burly man in his 30s, bald, officious looking, with a blonde moustache. A smaller officer, her blonde hair pulled back into a short ponytail, followed him out of the car, typing something into a handheld computer.

"Guten arben," he said, examining the scooter oddly.

"Hello, officer," Sophie said. "Were you after us or that car?"

The officer regarded both of them, in a somewhat suspicious fashion, and then switched to English.

"I had my lights on, and you didn't stop," he said. He was reading the license plate of the scooter, and apparently typing it into his little handheld computer.

The German police are so efficient Sophie thought.

"We thought you were chasing that car behind us. It was behaving strangely, so we were trying to keep ahead of it. I think there was something wrong with it. Errrh... as soon as it turned off, and you kept after us, it worked out you were actually chasing *us,* so I stopped for you. And here we are."

The officer shook his head slighting, saying nothing.

"That doesn't matter. In fact, I pulled you over because you were witnessed by someone in Lauscha doing magic. Under the Thuringian state laws, I am arresting you because..."

"Excuse me. Isn't magic legal in Bamberg? We've just crossed the border."

His head jilted, but his expression looked serious. "What?" The officer seemed confused. The officer next to him started to look around, as if she was trying to work out where she was.

"This is the Bavarian border here." Sophie pointed to a sign about ten metres away. "That's Thuringia back there."

The officer stared at them; a flicker of anger started to come across his face before he managed to control himself. He took a deep breath, lowered his head, and assessed them all with a serious expression that sent a slight chill down Sophie's spine. The female officer crossed her arms, slightly annoyed for a minute or so. She then uttered, "Thank you and good night," and got back in the car.

The male officer spun on his heels and without saying anything, got in the car. The car turned around and drove off down the road, its blue lights turning off, disappearing into the darkness.

Harlan spun around, confused.

Sophie took a glance at him. "We're over the border in Bavaria. Here..." She pointed at her feet. "In Thuringia, magic is illegal, here...magic is fine. He can't do anything."

Raffaella crossed her arms and just shook her head. Sophie was now exhausted and slumped back on the scooter. Harlan came over and gave her a big hug.

"Dang...Sophie Wolf... girl, you are freaking amazing."

Sophie managed a small smile. "I have never done anything like that before. I just stood up to a police officer."

Tomoko put her hand up timidly. "Errhh ...can we make it the last time, please?"

"They really wanted to get us. We were lucky. Who were they?" Harlan asked.

"Stag people connected to Adeline? Not sure," Sophie said, shaking her head.

Tomoko went back and got her bow, it took Raffaella longer to find her sword, which had bounced off the car and ended up on the side of the road. They drove cautiously back to Bamberg. Tomoko dropped Sophie off at her house and she went straight to sleep.

***

Waking up in the morning, Sophie felt groggy from the night before still. She did the quick math in her head and realized she had only got five hours sleep. She was starting to get worried her dad was going to ask why she was coming in so late. So far, she had told him she was doing group assignments. Doing *group assignments* seemed to be everyone at school's excuse for hanging out at each other's houses.

She felt a tiny bit deceitful, but it was for a good cause. Essentially, they were assisting the Queen of England's Official Mage to do an investigation. Government business. Sort of. Sophie walked out of the room and Ernst was standing there, in the lounge room, holding a piece of paper.

He didn't look happy.

"Sophie Wolf."

That tone of voice... *I'm not happy at all.* Ernst only said her full name when he *really* wasn't happy.

"What is this?" He waved it in Sophie's face.

"Paper?" Sophie said, a last-ditch attempt at lightening the situation. It didn't work.

"The symbol. Here." He sounded like he was talking through gritted teeth. Sophie checked his hand; his fist was clenching and unclenching. She suddenly realized what it was. It was a piece of paper on which she had written a magic symbol for a spell. She did it after waking up, so she could remember it, and later put it in her spellbook but it must have fallen out.

I should have tossed it in the bin. Idiot

"This is... magic...like...spellwork." Ernst was so angry, when he was speaking his words, he was only just holding his anger in. Barely.

"You told me you had done one dreamcast session about magic. You are still doing it?"

"Well, er, yes, Papa." Sophie stared directly at him.

"SOPHIE!" Ernst raised his voice. "You can't be doing this! You must stop now!"

At that point, the door opened, and Hisako walked in. Sophie felt a sense of relief. When the two of them got together, they could always talk Ernst around. Hisako was always a calming presence. Hisako's face quickly morphed from her normal smooth, calm features, to the rugged features of concern.

"Er... morning," Hisako said, trying to judge the room.

Ernst glanced at her.

"I found this." He showed the symbol to Hisako.

Hisako peered at it, and then peered at Sophie.

"Ah...magic."

"Yes. Sophie has been doing some sort of magic, not telling me...us... hang on." He peered at Hisako.

"Did you know about this?"

"Well, yes. Ernst, she told me. I was going to talk to you." Hisako walked towards him.

"How could you let my daughter do magic and not tell me?" Ernst was raising his voice again.

"Papa. It's not her fault. If anyone's to blame, it's me. I didn't know you would react like this," Sophie said. She could see he was getting angry. She'd never seen him angry like this. There was something going on that she didn't understand.

"Please... please... calm down. Doing magic is important to her, she's good at it. She may be able to do great things, help people." Hisako was keeping her voice level, clearly trying to calm the situation.

"I can't believe you are saying this!" Ernst raised his voice. "This is dangerous! I don't want my daughter involved in magic. Magic was illegal here until twenty years ago."

"Ernst, it's not illegal here now. It's acceptable in Japan."

"We're not in Japan!!!I can't believe you endangered my daughter..."

"Endanger... I would never endanger Sophie. Ernst she's good at it, from what I hear. This is a rare art..."

Ernst glared at her angrily. "Hisako, you're finished."

"You don't want me here today? But I just got here..." Hisako momentarily glancing at her coat she had only just taken off, and then at her watch.

"No, you're finished permanently. I don't want you here anymore." Ernst was spitting his words through gritted teeth.

"WHAT! NO PAPA!" Sophie stared at Ernst, heat rising on her neck, her shoulders tense. Hisako had been with them for so long. Sophie felt tears welling up in her eyes, she realized how close she was to Hisako.

"No, Papa, it's my fault. Papa. It's my fault." Sophie started crying. "Don't take it out on her."

Hisako simply froze, her mouth half opened as to say something...then closed silently. She went into the kitchen, grabbed her cooking knives, her chopsticks, and a mug. She then walked to the door. Turning to them both, she went to say something again, but instead grabbed her jacket, and left, slamming the door.

Ernst stood there, breathing deeply.

"I hate you, Papa! How could you do this! Hisako has been so nice to us for years. So nice! How could you do this!" Sophie felt herself feeling a rage coming on. She started flicking through the list of spells she knew, trying to think of a magical way of solving this.

There wasn't one.

She went to her room and slammed the door.

In the morning, her father tried to talk to her, tried to calm things down. She refused to talk to him. She was so angry, if she had said anything at all, it wouldn't have been nice.

Chapter 26 - Mystery in the ground

Back at school, the four of them were once again in history class. Raffaella was now sitting up closer to them, in the seat next to Tomoko.

Mr. Freidrickson was talking about *The War of 1812*, something that was not particularly interesting to anyone in the class, but Sophie's mind was on Hisako being sacked by her papa. The magic was not her fault. Hisako was lovely and had been a part of her life for so long. How could he do this?

Sophie started thinking about magic. Was her father right in being worried? She knew magic was a good thing. She knew she could use it to do positive things, that it was a force for good. With the dreamcasting, it seemed they had access to advanced, arcane magic that not many others did. It was important, powerful knowledge that had been lost and now they could bring it back into the world. But the fact so many people feared it was a little disturbing.

Why was her papa so angry? Fear of something made people act weird, at times. His reactions were weird to start with, but his sacking Hisako was completely mental.

Suddenly, her life seemed to have a lot of responsibility she hadn't asked for, and while she liked the adventure of it all, it was unsettling. They had discovered a hidden community of beast people, and there was an errant mage on the loose, stealing things, and a rising was going to happen and possibly destroy her beloved Bamberg.

Her papa was really getting angry about the magic, just as she was now finally getting good at it. She had now learned six spells from Johannes, and thanks to her knowledge of Early New High German, they were all perfectly do-able in the real world. This was exciting, but the knowledge that she had the power to do them made her question herself. Was she the one that should have these powers? Wouldn't they be better with someone else that knew what to do with them?

Evidently, she and Tomoko and Adeline seemed to be some of only a few mages, in Bavaria at least and it made her a little nervous. The spells she knew flicked through her mind, the things she could do. Nothing incredible, but apparently, it was more than what most mages currently alive could do. So, on the one hand, she had the power of spells, and on the other hand there was the awful trouble she could get into for dabbling in magic. From the town. From the police. And now, this trouble from her father, and trouble for Hisako.

Sophie left quickly at the end of the class, heading to the school cafeteria. She decided not to bring it up, but put it to the back of her mind, and think of better things.

Once there, she adjusted the chair so she could see the entryway to the school kitchen area, where she expected her friends to come. It made her think of the new little group that had come together. She was growing to like the name, Circle 66.

It was the bond of people who had been through a shared experience. She smiled as she ate some of the school spaghetti Bolognese, eating slowly as recent events flitted through her mind.

She already knew Harlan before her first dreamscape, and he hadn't changed. Well not much. She was getting to know Raffaella, who was interesting but a little unusual, and thought a lot of Tomoko. Tomoko came off as smart, cautious, and she apparently knew a lot more spells than her, though Tomoko hadn't said how many. She was always friendly and upbeat, which Sophie liked.

As she ate her lunch, Harlan turned up. She felt like confiding recent events to Harlan, but then Raffaella appeared soon after, so she decided not to. Sophie wondered if it was only because Harlan appeared that Raffaella so quickly appeared as well. Did she sort of like him? It was hard to imagine Raffaella liking anyone.

"So, what's the plan, group leader?" Harlan asked, eating a pie rather   indelicately.

As Harlan said *group leader*, Tomoko. Harlan and Raffaella all stared at Sophie. Sophie stared back at each of them in turn.

"Group leader?" Sophie shook her head. "Why me?"

"Dang Sophie, you're loud. You always say what you think," Harlan said, now trying to digest a mouthful of pasta.

"Yes," Tomoko said, nodding slightly. "You always make quick decisions too," Tomoko said.

"Tomoko knows more magic than me... maybe she should be group leader?" Sophie stopped eating now and stared at the others.

Tomoko practically gagged on her food and took a second to clear her throat.

"Ie!..." Tomoko spluttered. "No thanks I don't want to do that, I would get us all killed. I feel I am too cautious, I think, to be a good leader."

"This marinara is good, Mama," Raffaella said, breaking her silence.

"What do you think about a leader?" Harlan got the conversation back before it was derailed.

"My vote, she is with Sophie," Raffaella said. "If you made me leader, I would have you all charging into combat and probably get you killed. If Tomoko was the leader, she says she is too cautious, so maybe that's no good. If you made Harlan the leader..." She frowned. "...Sophie... She is a good compromise."

"Hey." Harlan appeared mock offended, though clearly, he was getting used to Raffaella's jibes.

Raffaella took a mouthful of the marinara, and started talking with her mouth half full, and twirled her fork in the air for emphasis.

"...besides...she clearly is doing it anyway. My sword master has said, '*You don't debate who should be the best leader, a true leader will be obvious to all without discussion.*"

"Okay, I'll be the leader." Sophie shrugged, and realized Raffaella was right. She was sort of doing it anyway.

"Carbs.Mmm." Raffaella mumbled. She continued eating her spaghetti marinara from a plastic container, it smelled delicious.

"Raffaella, now you've let us know about the leadership issues, what do you think of our current situation?" Harlan took another bite of his pie. "I mean, we've had a little time to get used to it... but it's sort of new to you."

"I..." she said, between mouthfuls. "...I like it. Two mages. Spells." She nodded at Harlan. "A trained thief who helps out every so often."

"Not a thief," Harlan mumbled.

"...and a warrior," Sophie said, looking at Raffaella, who didn't react, but kept eating. No one had referred to her as a *warrior* but no doubt, with a proper sword in her hand... that's exactly what she was. Raffaella's warrior status was apparently well earned. She was being taught by one of the top Italian sword *maestros* of the fifteenth century. That aside, what Sophie had seen of her work, with her own eyes, was impressive.

The thing was, they were probably more likely to use the spells than combat. Plus... what use would a sword be against people with guns?

"So, what's next, *Green leader*?" Harlan checked Sophie.

"First up, we go back to the Obelisk, and I'm going to put some sort of ward on it. Johannes taught me. I don't like what Adeline was doing there. I'm scared she may be trying to summon something."

Tomoko had finished her sushi. "Oishi." She picked up a napkin and wiped her fingers.

"That horned creature. We saw glimpses of it. Adeline...It was starting to appear."

Harlan appeared worried. "Do you think she is a...summoner?" he said.

"Shh. Jesus Harlan don't say that so loud," Sophie said, grabbing Harlan's hand.

Tomoko glanced across at Harlan, who appeared apologetic.

"Okay, sorry," Harlan said.

"At the moment, the obelisk seems to be an important point for us. We can use it for travel, as can Adeline. Maybe she is using it to sum..." She lowered her voice. "Er... bring creatures in from another plane."

"Do you think she can do that?" Harlan said, looking at both Tomoko and Sophie.

"I don't know. I hope not," Tomoko said, looking concerned.

"I'll meet you at my house, I need to get something." Raffaella peered at them all.

"Oh, I have something new I want to show you. I will show you when we get to Raffaella's." Tomoko grinned, jiggling in her chair.

***

The day passed slowly; they were to meet up at Raffaella's house once again. It was a Thursday night, and a rare night when Sophie wasn't adventuring or doing magic. Harlan had suggested doing something different, so they decided to hang out.

Sophie was early, so was waiting with Raffaella for the others. Sophie noticed an old scooter coming towards them, but it wasn't one she recognized.

It pulled up outside Raffaella's house. The rider took off their helmet and goggles.

It was Tomoko.

"Harlan and Raffaella had one of these, so I thought I would get one as well," she said, taking off her gloves, and smiling.

Raffaella came out of the house, saw Tomoko standing there with a scooter, and took a double take.

"What is this?" Raffaella sounded vaguely serious. About as serious as her usual poker face would betray. Sophie decided not to say anything, Raffaella got somewhat unpredictable when it came to scooters.

"It's a scooter. My uncle over in Schweinfurt had this old one in his shed," Tomoko said.

Sophie now realized she was the only one that didn't have a scooter. Suddenly she felt reliant on the others. Maybe if she got some money together, she would get one. The group seemed to be evolving into a magical, armed, *scooter gang*.

"But... what sort? It is old. But it is not Italian. Is this an old German scooter?" Raffaella was stunned.

Tomoko tapped the headset affectionately, with the palm of her hand.

"It is called *Fuji Rabbit*. My uncle had it in his shed for many years. We went up to Dresden to get it on the weekend. It was the first scooter ever made."

"The first scooter ever made was the Vespa, in March 1946, in the Republic of Florence," Raffaella cited the fact by rote, like she had said it before, with her hands on her hips. Tomoko pulled out her smartphone, and quickly typed in something.

"Fuji Rabbit. The first production model rolled off the factory floor in *January* 1946, Nihon Ichiban!" she said, pumping her hand in the air, and a broad grin across her face.

She handed the smartphone to Raffaella, who read the text quietly. As always, Raffaella kept her poker face, simply staring at the phone silently. Raffaella then glanced down at the sledgehammer that was on the ground. Tomoko and Sophie saw her look at it, and both stood between Raffaella and Tomoko's scooter.

"Ah, how about I swap you one of my scooters for..." Raffaella began.

"Ah, no thank you," Tomoko replied, awkwardly draping herself over her scooter, trying to cover as much as possible with her body.

Raffaella's garage was convenient, because it was sort of central to where everyone lived (not that Bamberg was that big anyway) and from Sophie and Harlan's view, there was always the potential win that would be Mrs Cupertino bringing out lasagna or pasta for everyone.

Sophie heard the *putter putter* of another scooter, and Harlan turned up, putting his scooter on its stand, and hopping off.

"Hey, all." Harlan reached for the pizza box on the rack behind the seat.

The three responded with their usual greetings. Sophie was starving.

He noticed the new scooter. "New scooter Tomoko? Nice."

"I got my license," Tomoko said, with a slight grin, reminding Sophie getting a license was on her list of things to do. A long list.

Harlan put the pizza down and they all stood around. Sophie loved pizza but didn't get to have it too often. Harlan opened the pizza box, and on top of it, glaringly, were large, triangular pieces of pineapple. Here you are, foods up!"

"Wait a minute, it is cold." Raffaella stepped back and went over to a shelf. Harlan appeared confused.

"No...I just bought it, it's ho..."

As he spoke, Raffaella stepped forward with a handheld butane torch, a blue flame sparked up from it. Everyone backed away from her. She knelt and completely torched the pizza. She then stomped on it to put it out and dropped it in the bin.

At the door connecting the garage to the old house, Raffaella's father appeared.

"Raffaella, why are you burning something in the garage?!!!"

"Papa. Pizza with pineapple!" she called back.

"Ah..." He stared at everyone again for five seconds, and then went inside.

"Papa, Lasagne for four! Grazie."

"Si, Bella."

They all sat down, Harlan still confusingly staring at the bin where the pizza was. Tomoko seemed happier about the promise of lasagna than the Pizza.

On cue, Mrs Cuppertino appeared with four big helpings of Lasagne, and a fork in each plate.

Sophie took a plate, and grabbed a fork, holding it up as a dash of freshly grated parmesan cheese was added by Mrs Cuppertino. "Oh, thank you *soooo* much!"

"Okay, good lasagne. Let's clarify what we need to do next." Sophie stared at the group and tried to get them back on topic, as the vague swirls of pineapple and pizza crust lifted up into the air and disappeared into the ceiling of the garage.

"What's in the bag, Sophie?" Harlan asked, digging into his second helping of Lasagne.

"I have something I want to try," she spoke.

Sophie pulled out some tins of paints, and some brushes, and some notebooks. Tomoko walked over to have a look. "Sophie, what are you doing with all this?"

"Dang Soph...what's with the arts and crafts session?" Harlan said.

Sophie stood up and walked over to Raffaella.

"Raffaella I'm going to ask you something... don't freak out on me, okay?" Sophie said.

"Have you ever seen me freak out?" Raffaella glanced at her with her typical blank expression.

"Well, not externally," Sophie said. "I want to paint one of your scooters. One that you ride."

Harlan laughed, while Tomoko put her hand over her mouth to stem a yelp of surprise. Raffaella watched blankly, not reacting. "Paint my scooter? Why?"

"I want to put a magic glyph on it. A spell, I want to see if it works. These spells work on things, like buildings, and some objects like weapons. No idea if it works on a Vespa."

"Will it make her—" She patted the scooter on the headset, almost like it was a big dog. "—go faster?" Harlan obviously reacting to the word *faster.*

"No. It's a glyph of protection. It will protect it," Sophie said.

Sophie had been saving this bit up, to make an impression. "This one." She drew the Glyph for protection in the air and said, *"Hynded."* The symbol glowed orange in the air, long enough for people to see it before disappearing.

Raffaella nodded in approval and pointed to a shiny black scooter. "This one."

Sophie knelt in front of the scooter, with the brush next to her.

Sophie drew the glyph of protection in the air again. The ruddy orange glyph sat in the air, moving just slightly, like a red ember floating near a fire. It shimmered. Everyone stared at it. Then Sophie started painting, and after a few seconds, things were a blur.

***

Sophie glanced down at the scooter. Suddenly, it was covered in Glyphs. But impossibly, it seemed like only seconds had gone by. She shook her head, to get her focus. The scooter was covered in symbols, but she didn't remember painting them. She felt groggy, like she had been asleep.

"Ow... my legs." Sophie's legs were numb from kneeling for so long.

She scanned the room around her. Tomoko and Harlan were asleep, and Raffaella was sitting in a chair, looking at her, drinking a coffee.

"Raffaella...I...I—" She was rubbing her legs. "How did these glyphs get all over the scooter, I don't remember anything."

"What do you mean you don't remember anything? You were here. We were talking to you," Raffaella said, putting her coffee down and walking over to her.

"No. What? No... I er...all I remember is starting to paint and then... it was done."

Raffaella stared at her, her head askew.

"What? No, we were chatting to you for a while. Then you did go quiet." Raffaella studied her curiously, then the scooter.

"You don't remember doing the painting?" she asked.

"No." Sophie felt tired. "It's like I went into a trance. I remember starting the scooter, and it seemed like a second later, it was covered in these glyphs."

"Scooters," Raffaella said. She pointed behind Sophie. There were two others scooters also painted in the glyphs. Sophie studied them in shock.

"Raphaella... who... who did these?" Sophie asked, still staring at the two scooters.

"You. You did them all. You don't remember?" Raphaella glanced at Sophie, her face showing a hint of concern.

Sophie sat down on the floor. No wonder she was so tired. After a minute, she slowly stood up, patting her legs. Tomoko woke up with a jolt and dazedly came over, and then Harlan.

"Is it finished?" he asked.

Sophie nodded in response, a slight limp in her steps as she walked around the scooters, still looking at them in disbelief. They were covered in the most bizarre symbols, but she could see the protection glyph here and there, in the patterns. It was bizarre, and beautiful.

"It's amazing! Don't you guys think?" Sophie said.

The three glanced at each other and then back at Sophie.

"Sophie... *we've* been telling *you* that for the last twenty minutes," Harlan said, shaking his head. "Trance magic glyph painting. You could do a workshop at a new age resort."

Sophie checked her watch.

"Oh! look at the time, we need to go. Let's try this out." She grabbed her jacket. "Who's giving me a lift?"

Harlan pointed to his scooter. "Well... your ride awaits, my princess."

Sophie smacked him on the shoulder. "Oh, Harls." He started his scooter and she hopped on, as Raffaella and Tomoko scrambled around for gloves, jackets, and helmets.

#

The scooters took off from Raffaella's garage. Tomoko, Harlan and Raffaella on their own, with Sophie on the back of

Harlan's. They once again took the road to Dexheim. This time it dawned on Sophie that Adeline may be there using the portal.

They pulled up to the forest, and once again pushed their scooters off the road. This time they were careful. Harlan disappeared without a word into the bushes to scout ahead. He came back, with a simple wave, and a thumbs up signal, and they started to trek off into the forest.

Sophie cleared her voice to get their attention.

"Okay, I'm going to try casting the spell of warding on the portal side. It won't keep people away, but it will keep—" She lowered her voice. "—*summoning* from happening. I think."

Sophie reached into her bag and pulled out a sausage. Tomoko, Raffaella and Sophie all stared at her, and at the sausage.

Harlan bent over to get a closer look. "Sophie... er...why do you have a sausage?"

Sophie shook her head. "This is a ward. For warding off evil. You write the symbol for protection on the thing you want to protect. That is the ward. So, I have paint and a paintbrush for that. Then I put that down and cast the spell. I draw the symbol in the air. The spell binds to the symbol and protects the area with a ward."

Tomoko glanced at her, nodding. "So, it is like a permanent guard of protection. We have them in my magic path. We don't call it *ward*. We call it *Ashaki*."

Harlan seemed confused, and then peered at each of them.

"Okay... that's all good, ya know... but... why a sausage?"

"Johannes told me to use a German sausage... a sausage is essential for the spell to work. It's integral to German magic."

Tomoko stared at Sophie, blankly.

"When I have seen this done, we just do the symbol, we write it down, often to protect a house. Then cast it." She stared at the sausage and pointed. "Tabemono Jenai, we don't have any sausage or food."

Sophie shook her head.

"No, Johannes said it's essential. It's a ward sausage. A sausage of warding."

Harlan started laughing. Sophie glanced at the sausage as a look of realization came across her face.

"Johannes said... Oh damn... I should have realized...freaking Johannes and his stupid sense of humour."

She flushed with anger, but then started to grin as she saw Harlan, rolling around on the ground in fits of laughter, barely in control of his body.

"Sausage of Warding!" Harlan shrieked.

"Oh, shut up," she said, smiling and shaking her head.

As Harlan recovered, Sophie pulled out a brush and some gold paint from her bag. She walked around and found a nice big flat rock.

"Tomoko… this should work?" she asked.

"Yes, Sophie san."

Sophie brushed off one side of the rock, so it was clean. She then painted a symbol, for protection, onto the rock. After blowing on it so it was dry, she took out a can and spray painted the rock.

"Gloss spray protects it from the elements. It should be stable for quite a while."

Sophie then put the rock on the ground. She cast the spell, drawing the same symbol in the air. She put the rock in the dirt, just in front of the obelisk, and covered it over.

Harlan was smiling still. "I'm hungry. Anyone want some German sausages back in Bamberg?"

Sophie glared at him. "I'll shove a sausage…"

Harlan laughed. "It's a shame I'll never meet Johannes. 500 years later, and he is still pranking you."

"So typical. I just cast a spell to keep some sort of demon from coming into this world from another plane, doing God knows what, and you are still laughing at a sausage joke." Sophie said.

Tomoko rolled her eyes. "Boys! Anyway, I'm glad to see this spell done. I've seen it in the dreamcast, but I have never done it. Let us hope it works."

"Yeah." Sophie glanced down to where the rock was. "Let's hope she doesn't find that rock." Raffaella was sitting on the ground watching without comment.

Suddenly, Harlan stopped laughing, and stood up. He put his fingers to his lips, motioning for everyone to be quiet.

"Quick hide. Over here," he called, disappearing into the low bush of the forest and roughly pulled the three girls down with him.

The four waited. Sophie realized that Adeline, the blonde girl, could come back. They should have left Harlan near the road to warn them. However, Sophie also felt thought that Adeline may return, and she could see the spells she was casting once again. There was a sense of intellectual curiosity; Adeline could do things that she couldn't, despite being obviously young. However, to Sophie's surprise, after about a minute, three men came walking through the forest, straight to the obelisk. Men they hadn't seen before.

Tomoko appeared concerned. "Should we go?"

Harlan shook his head. "Nah. Let's wait and watch; we may learn something."

Sophie shook her head silently. The Obelisk was clearly some important relic that multiple people were using. *Were these people with Adeline or were they a different group?* Sophie squinted at them, trying to see. All three of them had long hair, about mid-twenties. One's hair was lighter, and he wore a black denim jacket, the other man wore a red shirt with some rock band logo on it, and the third, wore dirty, old worn blue dirty overalls and a dirty white T shirt. Their clothes appeared a little strange, Sophie thought. Like they were old fashioned, but not that old. They all appeared about the same height and the same age.

Sophie watched on. She had only just discovered this obelisk, and now the place was like the main railway station at Munich.

Two of the men left and then reappeared, trudging through the forest carrying timber, the other pushing a wheelbarrow. They dumped the materials next to the obelisk.

Sophie wondered, *what would they be doing with building materials?* It didn't seem likely they were transporting it to the cellar in London, the obelisk could take them to any number of places.

The four of them watched on as the three men wandered off and got more materials. They made multiple trips, until they finished piling the material in various stacks in front of the obelisk. Sophie realized they were carefully piling it in the area covered by the transportation spell, anything outside a rough four metre square area wouldn't transport. They were using the obelisk to transport building materials somewhere.

Harlan tapped Sophie on the shoulder and gave her a confused look. Sophie just shrugged. Raffaella and Tomoko also shook their heads, to indicate they didn't know what was going on.

Eventually, they stopped piling up the material. The one with the overalls left, and the other two stood next to the materials.

With the hand movements that were partially familiar to Sophie, the one with the lighter hair cast the two-part ritual. Sophie listened carefully, but it wasn't in a language that she understood.

Harlan muttered, "Oh damn, nearly forgot." He pulled out his glasses to look at them and the equipment. The expression on his face changed, his eyes widening. She once again felt the sense of frustration that his glasses did something and hers did nothing.

"What can you see?"

"Oh… damn. Through the glasses, they have pale faces and—" Harlan screwed up his face involuntarily. "—pointy ears."

Sophie grabbed the glasses to look, and Harlan tried to grab them back.

"No, Marcus trusted them to me, he said other people aren't allowed to use them."

Sophie ignored Harlan and took the glasses to look at the three men.

"Wow. They are using some spell that makes them look human. They're not. "Sophie was stunned by how their appearance changed when she observed them with the glasses. They were paler, with big blue eyes and their hair was lighter. They had the same clothes. They were both clean shaven when observed with the glasses.

"Pointy ears! Well, better looking than our half stag friends," Sophie said, keeping her voice down. She stared a little more carefully, one of them had tattoos on his neck. Strange, primitive looking shapes she hadn't seen before.

Tomoko whispered, requesting the glasses She watched on, smiling excitedly. Raffaella waited patiently, with a curious look on her face. She took her turn after Tomoko, putting on the glasses and staring intently.

All of them were, naturally, surprised. Being the most unused to magic, Raffaella took the glasses off and put them back on again several times to check what she was looking at was real. Sophie noted Raffaella seemed to have problems accepting that it was real. Her and Tomoko had by now seen enough weirdness that they could accept things like this, a month ago, Sophie would have probably thought she was hallucinating.

The men got all the building equipment in place and put it neatly in a pile. Whatever sort of creatures they were, they were neat. Sophie noted they didn't seem particularly dangerous, they didn't have any weapons, and they moved efficiently and quietly.

Soon enough, they cast the second part of the spell and they disappeared, as did the materials they had with them. Sophie kept looking at them, even though Harlan was trying to get the glasses back.

Sophie listened to the spell as the men were casting it and noticed something. She could tell it wasn't old German, but it sounded like a translation of the old German, into a different language; the rhythm of the spell, and the sentences were the same. The three men/things had cast the spell. But the last sentence, where Sophie normally said London, was changed.

They didn't say London, they said, "Daegsheim."

Sophie glanced at the others, a revelation dawning on her.

"Dexheim! They changed the destination in the spell. They were telling the spell, where to take them. We said London, and we went to London, but they said, "Dexheim.""

Rafaella raised an eyebrow. Sophie realized they may have to explain things to her a little more.

The blue blur of the spell started to dissipate and the men, and the building materials were both gone. Sophie had just got the glasses, after being passed around again. She wondered what to think about the men. They weren't doing anything threatening, in fact moving building materials was pretty boring. *Magic people going about their everyday magic lives* she thought.

At that point, Sophie went to turn and give the glasses to Harlan... She saw him, and screamed out, stepping back. Staring at Harlan through the glasses, *he* now appeared totally different.

It took a second or two for Sophie to register, Harlan was not as he appeared normally. Staring at Harlan through the glasses, Harlan's facial features had completely changed.

"Harlan." She stared at him, her mouth dropping. She pointed in the direction of the men who had just left. "You're... you're just like them!"

Harlan turned to Sophie. "What do you mean?"

"Through the glasses, you're different." She responded. She quickly turned her head to see how the others appeared. They still appeared the same. Back to Harlan, he still appeared different.

Like the men at the obelisk, Harlan's hair was now long. His skin was pale, and his eyes were pale light grey. He had long pointy ears. Sophie stared at him a little longer, transfixed by how he could appear different.

"Well, you actually appear better…"

Harlan grunted and grabbed the glasses off her, pulled out his phone, and using it as a mirror, tried to view himself.

"I look the same as I always do, I don't look like them. You're joking, right?" He touched his ears, checking if they were pointy. "Sophie, are you going mad? I just look the same to me."

Grabbing the glasses back off Harlan, she went to hand them to Tomoko, but handed them to Raffaella instead. Raffaella tentatively put them to her head to see through, and Sophie noticed both her eyebrows raised, an unusual level of interest, but Raffaella's standard monotone voice didn't show any emotion. "Yes… he…looks like them."

"WHAT!" Harlan tried to grab the glasses, but Raffaella handed them to Tomoko. "Oh…I want to see." Tomoko put them on, and her gaze tracked up and down his long frame. She started laughing.

"Sorry, Harlan. You appear to be… whatever those guys are. Do you have a tail?"

"No, I don't have a tail. Hey, stop staring at my butt!" His voice raising its pitch in frustration. Tomoko laughed in her weird, loud, maniacal laugh, and handed the glasses to Sophie. Sophie grabbed the glasses looking at him once more. He still appeared to be exactly like like one of the creatures the men appeared to be. Not the same, but close.

"How can he have long hair here, but not in reality," Rafaella queried.

"Dang it, give me those. I feel like a zoo exhibit." Harlan grabbed the glasses back.

"Harlan, do either of your parents have pointy ears?" Sophie asked, mostly joking.

Harlan went quiet, biting his bottom lip, apparently deep in thought. Sophie and Tomoko stopped laughing, sensing Harlan suddenly was serious. It started to click. Harlan had been searching for his mother in Bamberg. Was his appearance something to do with his genetic mom?

They pestered Harlan about why the glasses made him appear the same as the creatures, but he was clearly unimpressed and didn't want to discuss it. After a while, Sophie started to consider their situation again.

Sophie thought about the three men that had used the portal. It made her think that maybe she should try the transport spell, as the other men had, with the slight change in the wording of the incantation to what appeared to be their destination. Sophie glanced back at the group.

"Feel like another trip?"

Tomoko turned to her, with the typical face that she used to express concern over one of Sophie's suggestions.

"You mean... follow them?"

"Well...yes. Don't you want to see where they go?" Sophie peered back at the group.

"No, I don't," Tomoko said, stepping away from the Obelisk.

Sophie walked towards the Obelisk. "Well, I'm going. Come along   if   you   want." The others stood next to the Obelisk with her and Tomoko finally relented, actively frowning to show her reluctance.

Sophie started her hand swirls, her hands swiftly dancing through the air, drawing the symbol for *gate*, and she cast the spell once again. She felt the same warm energy come and flow over her body. Her body felt lightweight. This time she switched the word in the spell from London to *Dexheim*.

She felt the same feeling as she had the first time she used the portal, the world around them morphed from its many colours, into a blue blur. The four of them appeared once again next to an obelisk, not the same, but like the other two.

Instead, in this case, they were next to an obelisk, in a different lush green overgrown forest... and standing in front of them was one of the pale creatures, with no shirt, holding an axe in his hand.

Chapter 27 – Dexheim

Sophie froze. The words for the sleep spell as a gut reaction started going through her head. As she started to cast the spell, she checked around her, catching Harlan and Tomoko running off in the other direction, away from the creature. She took a deep breath, filling her lungs, and braced herself against the steady feeling of panic taking a grip on her.

She briefly glanced at the creature. It was still moving towards her. Panic took over. She ran after her friends.

"RUN," Sophie called out. "RUUUN!!!!" Tomoko was screaming.

Harlan had disappeared into the bushes quickly while Raffaella was running fastest, followed by Tomoko.

Sophie knew she was a good runner but looking over her shoulder quickly she could see the creature was gaining on her. It was all happening so fast, she hardly had time to think. He was calling out something, she couldn't quite hear it. He still had an axe   in   his   hand. She caught up to Tomoko.

Sophie could see Raffaella ahead of her; she was running away from the creature, as they were, but she veered off to the left, and dived onto the ground, rolling, then landed on her feet. When she rolled back up, she was standing facing towards them. She was holding a big stick.

Now she started screaming, running towards them... *towards* the creature... as they were running away from it. Tomoko was obviously frightened as she shouted, "Raffaella!!!"

Sophie ran faster, slightly taking over Tomoko, and glanced back. "Tomoko. He's catching us. SLEEP SPELL."

Amid the frantic confusion, Raffaella sprinted right through the middle of them, as the creature continued bounding towards them.

"Okay," Tomoko screamed.

They spun around, Sophie's hands swiftly making the symbol for *sleep*, a deft flurry of fingers drawing in the air. The command word, *slafen*, was on the tip of her tongue.

"Stop...Let's have a cup of tea and talk about this!"

Sophie glanced back. Rafaella initially aimed high at the creature as a feint, and then dropped to one knee, and was about to pummel the creature in the midriff. The creature was holding his hands up, naturally looking at Raffaella, with some concern.

On hearing this Sophie dropped her hands and stopped the incantation. She turned around. The creature was approaching them slowly, stepping around Raffaella, still with his hands up. Sophie noticed he no longer had the axe. Sophie considered, though it would be perhaps a nice trap for the unsuspecting tea lover, that anyone that was going to hurt you would never offer you a cup of tea.

"Ahhhh... you must have unlocked the portal. Thank you! We owe you a great deal of thanks." He was in his pale skinned, pointy eared form, but spoke perfect German.

Sophie looked at him. "Stay back. Both of us can do powerful magic." Sophie had no idea what she was saying, but her instincts told her to bluff. She put up her hands in what she thought would look like a threatening manner.

"You had an axe." Tomoko pointed at his empty hands.

He switched to English, once again perfect without an accent. "Well... I was cutting wood... OH... that's why you ran!"

At that point, several other creatures came over. There were men and women, all gathering around. At that point, Raffaella put the club down by her side. Sophie noticed it was roughly the length of one of her swords, so she could probably use it like one. Harlan, as was his stealthy nature, was nowhere to be seen.

An older man came up to them. He had a long silver beard, pale skin, shiny white teeth, and piercing blue eyes. Looking at him was confusing, he appeared old, but still seemed oddly young. It was almost unsettling.

He pointed to Sophie.

"You…just came through the gate?"

Sophie nodded slowly. It was obvious they had, in any case. She was not sure if it was a good thing or not, if they were in trouble, and if they were, how much. There was a murmuring coming from the group watching them. Some of them seemed to be upset, but others seemed curious.

Sophie sensed the mood of the gathering audience changed, and her gut told her something was happening. She put her hands in front of her, preparing a spell, as did Tomoko, who put her back to hers. Raffaella gripped her tree branch, clenching it tight, and resting it on her shoulder.

The older man gazed at them. "Please, forgive us. Some of the people here are confused. We've never seen anyone else, but Fae came through. It's unsettling, and your appearance through the gate has scared some of us."

Most of the crowd were speaking in a different unfamiliar language. But she picked up one of them, in German say, "…they are real. From the realm of men."

The older one pointed to himself. "I'm Aedan. I am a lord. If you came through the gate, we owe you thanks. Our mages have never been able to use it to get to Bamberg."

The original shirtless Fae stepped forward, buttoning up a white linen shirt with voluminous sleeves. "I'm Magwir. Sorry about all this." He waved his hand at the crowd ushering them back, who obeyed and shuffled back a couple of steps.

"Come with us. We'll take you to our town," Aedan said, very formally.

He noticed their hesitation. "I can promise on my honour, you will be able to return. Please come. We will have tea for you."

Sophie stared at Tomoko who looked at Raffaella in turn. Tomoko shook her head furiously, while Raffaella and Sophie nodded. "Okay, we'll come."

Raffaella leaned in closer to Sophie and whispered, "Harlan is still gone."

Sophie knew he would be hiding, but hoped he was in earshot. She called out rather obviously. "Yes, we'll come with you, but we need to return to this spot in an hour." She wasn't 100% sure about what to do, but Harlan obviously didn't trust the Fae. Odd, considering as far as he appeared through the glasses of true sight at least, he appeared just like them.

Aedan initially requested they put blindfolds on the three visitors. Sophie outright refused, she was keeping her hands and vision so she could use magic if she had to. Overall, the Fae didn't seem threatening, in fact a lot of them seemed to be frightened of *her*.

Running all the combinations, things she may have to do through her head, Sophie realized she was starting to get confidence in her abilities. The fact the Fae were concerned about her abilities sort of surprised her. It was starting to sink in, the magic she could do was powerful, and people regarded it as such.

A tall, pretty woman Fae appeared, with long flowing white hair, and introduced herself as *Anistula*. She joined them, walking along next to them as an escort. From the way she carried herself, and the way people behaved around here, she was clearly someone important, and she appeared to be calming the crowd by her presence. They were led away from the obelisk, and off to a rather dense part of the forest. There was a neat, well-worn path through the middle of it, but Sophie could see, just off the path it was dense enough that you couldn't walk through, easily at least.

A huge tree sat within the denseness of it. It was tall, but especially wide, a deep dark brown colour, almost black and it was covered in patches of bright green moss. Its roots were huge, like the thighs of a large man, and they were a dense mess, intertwined like spaghetti, with the roots from the neighbouring trees. Sophie had to bend her back slightly so she could tip back to look at the top of it. It was both huge, fearsome, and beautiful.

She peered back down, and in the middle of the tree's wide trunk, there was a faint shimmer. A large door opened within the tree trunk, allowing the three and their escorts to pass through it and into a dark tunnel. Evidently, this was the only way into where the Fae lived. Sophie touched her hands on the walls, which were made from interwoven tree roots. She couldn't tell if they were on the surface, or slowly going underground as no light came through the walls, except for a faint glimmer radiating from some glowing moss. She could see the aura in the light, which meant it was some sort of magical effect.

The Fae seemed to have some magic. Sophie suspected the power for it seemed to be tied to the forest and connected them with it.

Sophie glanced around as they were taken down into the tunnel. As they went in deeper, the side of the walls appeared damp, and she had a natural reaction to worry about the walls caving in.

After about ten minutes, when they exited, they appeared in a forest that was lush and green. It was different from the previous forest outside the big tree. The huge trees had thick wide trunks, which split into roots that reached down into the ground like a great wooden octopus. The grass was flat and bright green, and a little creek meandered through the middle, grass cascading over the side, hiding its edges with a green furry fringe. It was a lush little paradise. Sophie and Tomoko held up their hands to their eyes. At the exit was a small glade, and a little lake. Some of the Fae were sitting and talking, one of them weaving some garment in a wooden frame.

Tomoko stopped, and stared, her mouth ajar.

"It is beautiful." Tomoko said, slowly. "It is so green; the grass is glowing. Reminds me of Osaka in Spring. Or some of the forests in the mountains near Kyoto."

Raffaella gazed at the surroundings. "Tuscany…" staring almost rudely at the Fae, "But actually, more beautiful."

Until this point the Fae woman next to them, Anistula, had remained silent, except to introduce herself. Sophie studied her, wondering who she was. She carried herself with importance, her neck and head straight and proud.

"Uhm, excuse me Anistula… these Fae here." She pointed to the Fae lounging around, and going about their business, are they expecting us?"

Sophie could see her face properly, as she stared at her. She realized how stunning she was.

"They would be alarmed if they knew who you were. When word gets out about it, they may well be."

"What do you mean?" Sophie and Tomoko both said in unison, puzzled.

"Most of them probably suspect you are Fae returning in human form, who have not changed their appearance back to

Fae." She grinned wryly. "It is best that we get you somewhere before word gets around."

As they walked, they noticed small cottages built amongst the trees. The forest was still there, but it seemed to exist around, and over the houses, like the houses and the trees were happy and natural to fit in with each other. Tree roots came out of the ground and twisted around the structure of the houses.

They started walking past some small cottages, all made of wood, and painted various shades of Green. The houses were built on the ground, but they had elaborate roofs, with platforms that extended up, and connected to the trees. The woodwork was elaborate, Sophie noticing the inscriptions in the wood like Celtic knotwork.

The windows had no glass and were either opened or shuttered. Generally, the Fae seemed to be going about their business, talking, or carrying things. While most of them rode horses, or walked, she noticed oddly, one riding a motorbike.

Eventually the procession led them to a large building, surrounded by smaller buildings. It had the look of a cathedral but was completely made of wood. There were two huge doors, each with intricate carvings in them. Wooden steps led up to the doors, and two tall Fae stood guard, bare-chested, with their hands each holding a big axe in front of them.

Anistula and Aedan spoke to each other in some odd, but beautiful sounding language. It was soft and elegant, and wonderful just to listen to. They then spoke to the men at the door, before opening a smaller door within the larger ones, to step through.

Aedan motioned for them to follow. Raffaella stepped through, followed by Tomoko and then Sophie. Sophie worried what had happened to Harlan back at the obelisk... but really, it was his problem for running off.

They stepped through the large gates, and all three momentarily stopped. There were two large trees either side of the gates. Inside the doors was a long hallway, with the most elaborate pictures painted on the walls and ceilings.

Then Sophie noticed something odd. There were four men on the inside of the doorways. They were definitely Fae, and each had the pale white skin, the long hair. They wore traditional armour and held shields and big spears. But in this case, the hair was tied back in a ponytail. They wore green shirts, with ties around their arms, and little symbols, or perhaps writing on the armbands.

Oddly, they carried modern pistols, but they also had a sword over their back, held there by a big belt. The guards eyed the three suspiciously. While the rest of the Fae were wary of them, the guards stood statue-like, without moving, though their eyes followed them as they walked into the corridor. The Fae were clearly not trusting of outsiders.

They walked down the corridor, towards a chamber, and into an office. Inside this stood an older Fae man peering out through a great stained-glass window, which ran from floor to ceiling. He was tall, bald, the only person in the room devoid of the Fae long hair and held himself regally. He wore a simple shiny brass circlet in his hair, a subtle indication of rank.

In the centre of the stained-glass window was a huge tree, the light shining through the multi-colored glass, the ambers, reds, and greens of the stained glass shone down on the floor. The room was tall, and the visage through the window was a splendorous view of the middle of the forest trees, a clump of buildings here and there. Raffaella let out a breath at the impressive sight.

"Please—" The Fae motioned. "Come in." He had a deep, emotive voice. It was almost moving, and it conveyed the fact that he was important. He stepped towards them and awkwardly shook their hands, then seemed to step back to check their reaction.

"Oh. You're bald." Sophie said. Tomoko looked at her oddly, smiling.

He looked at her oddly for a second, before composing himself. "Yes, I am...I am Count Wystan," he declared. Sophie realized at that point; the Fae probably had little contact with humans. Hearing this, Tomoko fidgeted nervously while Raffaella froze, her hands open, prepared.

"You've opened the portal." He strode away from them, as four guards came in from the door. "Which has allowed people to come through the obelisks."

Sophie shook her head.

"No. We did not. Another Mage, Adeline, opened the portal."

"You led her to it. We saw her in the forest. She followed you," Wystan said, closely examining the three of them.

Sophie glanced at Tomoko. They both seemed surprised, Adeline must have somehow seen them the first time they found the Obelisk. It seemed they had led her to it.

Tomoko raised her hand to signal that she wanted to speak. "Sumimasen…er excuse me. We aren't with Adeline. We mean no harm."

"We think that Adeline is causing all sorts of trouble and plans for a *rising* that will affect Bamberg and the people that live there. We're trying to work out what is going on and stop this," Sophie said, trying to emphasize their innocence.

Tomoko spoke up, "Yes, Sophie and I just want to learn magic as the pure art it is, we don't want to hurt anyone."

Count Wystan ignored Tomoko. He put his hands together, regally, standing in front of the ornate glass, like he was the subject of a portrait, and the window was a huge frame.

"When you started using the obelisk for transport… The spell you used removed the portal lock that had been placed there a long time ago to protect us. You have now endangered us, as people can come here… *but…* it has also been good. We had to use a longer path before, this gate is shorter and more convenient. This has helped us, yes. We have used it to travel to Dexheim where we can get some things from *the men.*" Sophie had to think what he meant by saying "the men", then realized he was talking about humans, human society. Different from the Fae.

"It has helped those of us who choose to live among the men." Wystan said.

Sophie scanned the room. The four Fae guards in the room also had guns. However, she noticed Aedan subtly place himself between Sophie and the guards; presumably trying to protect them. His movements concerned her. Sophie eyes darted from the guards with the guns, to Lord Wystan and Magwir, trying to read what was going on. Her body was tense, she tried to remain calm, but could see Tomoko's pursed lips and nervous hands.

"May I ask how you came to learn your magic?" He titled his head down at them, and then vaguely around the room. Sophie thought he was trying to conceal how interested he was. "No one has come through that portal…in a long time. We thought there were no mages here, in this part of the world. All gone."

Sophie glanced over at Tomoko. Neither were exactly sure what to say. Tomoko had a look of concentration on her face, clearly trying to work out what to do.

Just as Sophie went to open her mouth, Tomoko spoke.

"I have trained as an apprentice to the Sorcerer Kentaro Ojima. Great Maho for the court of the Daimyo Obakanage, twenty-first inheritor of the title."

Count Wystan gestured to her. "You are from Japan?"

Tomoko said, "Yes… from Japan…" She added, awkwardly. "…my lord."

He then nodded towards Raffaella.

"…and you?"

"I am Raffaella Cuppertino. I train in the sword arts. My trainer is Achille Marozzo, a master of the Bolognese tradition. Also—" She paused. "—I am a trained Vespa mechanic."

Lord Wystan studied her momentarily, his face expressionless and dignified. If he understood what a Vespa mechanic was, he didn't show any reaction.

"And you?" he motioned to Sophie.

"I have learnt some spells from a mage called Johannes Von Abertwirder, he's a high-level Illusionist, I think." Wystan stopped for a second, and he squinted.

"High level Illusionist?"

Count Wystan glanced over to Anistula; his eyes momentarily widened.

Anistula went to speak, but Lord Wystan waved at her, shaking his head. Anistula ignored him and spoke anyway.

"You trained under a high-level illusionist? You *cannot* have. There haven't been any since before you were born." Anistula, who until now, had remained stoically regal, appeared to become a little bit emotional. Sophie was surprised.

"Well, whether you believe it or not, I don't really care. And in fact, he's from the fifteenth century," Sophie said.

Sophie noticed Wystan, Aedan, Magwir and Anistula were all now staring at her, with expressions that ranged from smiling to concern.

"May I ask how you take lessons from someone who died hundreds of years ago? Sophie?" He studied the three of them, looking them up and down "Are you using books they have written?"

Sophie shook her head. "No, technology." She decided to say no more of it, she really wasn't sure where the conversation was going, or what was the best strategy to play.

Count Wystan waved to his offsider, who left the room. He said a single word to Aedan in what she assumed was the Fae language. Sophie listened to it; it sounded somewhat like Russian. Aedan then replied with a few sentences, also in their language. She couldn't understand what he said, but there was concern in his voice.

"You three have come through the portal. You know the way here. You can let the men come here. Our rules do not allow us to let you leave. We must protect our people."

Sophie put her hands up in front of her, ready to do a spell if need be.

Aedan noticed her hands. "But…" He put up his hand to reassure them.

"Lord Aedan," Wystan continued, "has given you assurance you can return." He held out his hands. "And it would be dishonorable to bring you here under a false offer. The Fae will do our best to protect ourselves."

Tomoko, Sophie and Raffaella stared at each other, Sophie could see Tomoko let out a deep breath, clearly relieved. Sophie nodded to Lord Wystan.

"Thank you. We are sorry if using the portal has put you in any danger."

Lord Wystan pointed to the door. "Please feel free to go. We hope to meet you again, and perchance we can work together."

The three quickly backed out of the room, Aedan moving them back to the tunnel through the forest and then to the Obelisk.

***

At the obelisk, Aedan seemed relieved. "I am glad to get you back here. I was concerned for a moment… Lord Wystan can be overprotective. Take care, and good luck with your work against this errant mage, Adeline."

As they stood at the Obelisk, they thanked Lord Aedan. He walked off, looking back a couple of times smiling, before finally disappearing. Sophie spun around and noted they were finally by themselves, though she figured the Fae would be watching, making sure they went back. For her part, Sophie would have been glad to leave, but Harlan had disappeared, and they had to wait.

Tomoko stood closer to the other two, so she was completely out of earshot of any Fae, unless they were particularly well hidden.

"I liked Aedan, Anistula was very cool." She grinned broadly. "Wystan I'm not sure about' Tomoko glanced at the others, pulled out her phone, and started lining up Sophie to take a few photos of her. Sophie smiled briefly for the photos, then sat down as well, kicking a big log over to use as a seat. She eased down; her thighs were starting to hurt from all the walking.

Tomoko's eyes widened. "Oh, I just forgot. Harlan looks like the Fae! How exciting."

Sophie had not wanted to talk about it while Harlan was around. He was gone for the moment at least.

"He didn't want to talk about it. Is there some spell that makes him look like the Fae?" Sophie asked, thinking Tomoko may know.

"I don't know." Tomoko shook her head. "They were there, was it some kind of effect?"

"He doesn't like it much," Raffaella said, flatly. Sophie sensed that Raffaella thought it was amusing, not that she would ever smile.

"He does make a pretty Fae though." Sophie grinned. "I may try some magic and see if he can look like them all the time."

Sophie called out very loudly, "HARLAN!" and the others joined in, creating a chorus of his name being called out to the forest. They did this for five minutes before he finally appeared.

"I'm here. Is it safe?" Harlan's voice issued forth from the underbrush, almost like the plants were talking. He then appeared out of the bushes, cautiously. Sophie was relieved to see him, and gave him a quick hug, he patted her on the back.

Raffaella shook her head. "Ran away again." However, she leaned over and picked the odd leaf off him.

"Harlan, why did you hide from the Fae?" Sophie glared at him.

"Well...er... my TA told me Ogilvy's first law... ya know."

"Ogilvy's law?" Sophie said.

"Well, Ogilvy's law says *Don't put yourself in a situation where strangers control the outcome.*"

"Oh, okay." Sophie thought it was one of the better laws Harlan kept quoting.

Soon after Harlan appeared, a group of Fae returned to see them as well. They seemed like they wanted to approach them and ask questions, but Sophie very purposefully started her spell. The group of Fae stood there, watching them, with apprehensive faces as the blue mist appeared and took them back to Bamberg Forest and the Obelisk.

***

Leaving the Obelisk behind them and moving rather swiftly Sophie realised it was getting close to ten p.m. Sophie knew her dad would be worried, and quickly called him to let him know she was heading home. She spoke to him curtly. She still hadn't forgiven him for firing Hisako. She didn't think she ever would.

"Harlan... you missed out on... just some amazing things. We saw the Fae's village...or town...or I don't know what it's called."

Tomoko broke her silence. "Yes... and we almost didn't get out of it. That was frightening, I'm not particularly sure I want to go back there." She peered at Harlan. "Your people weren't exactly welcoming."

Harlan glanced back at her as he pushed a tree branch out of the way, stumbling over a large root on the ground. "My people? You're still saying I'm like them?"

"Yes, give us the glasses again so we can see the real you." Sophie put out her hand.

"No." He stepped away from her. Sophie smirked. It was good to harass him about something for a change. She'd discovered a new button she could push to get a reaction from him. Always handy.

"They appear to be able to change their appearance to human, that's how they live in human society," Sophie said.

"I don't care. I have both my parents back home, in Wyoming. They are my parents. I don't feel any different. I can't see that I'm the same. They are just farmers, in Wyoming, normal people, not Fae. No pointy ears, and he doesn't have long hair or use magic. I doubt there was a mix up in the hospital between the human and Fae babies."

Sophie realized he was becoming agitated, unusual for him. "Harlan." She touched him on the shoulder. "I've met your family, you are right. Your parents are wonderful. They are obviously yours." Sophie was thinking about Harlan's father, who appeared exactly like him. But he didn't resemble his mother, a beautiful woman, with a darker complexion and jet-black hair.

The three glanced at Harlan, and decided to drop the issue, Harlan seemed to have lost his sense of humour about it.

As they walked back to the scooters, Sophie felt a sense of relief lift from her shoulders. The crisp air of the forest was refreshing. It was a relief to get back through the Obelisk.

"So, what next?" Harlan said, staring at them all.

"We need to find Adeline. Track her down. She knows about the portal now, and she may be able to use it. Who knows how close we are to this rising happening?"

They headed their separate ways, Sophie considering the Fae and their place in all of this.

Chapter 28 - The "Electric Light Kafe'

Sophie stood reading an interesting sign that had appeared on the wall in their upstairs mages level of the Electric Light Kafe. It was starting to give her an idea of the sort of people that used to meet here. It was a list of rules.

1 No weapons to be used in the café
2 Once a job has been allocated to a crew, it can't be taken by another
3 Please clean up after any familiars or other creatures that may make a mess
4 Do not rest your elbows on the table if you are wearing metal armour—it damages the wood
5 Anyone casting offensive spells will be banned *permanently* from the premises. Fireball is an offensive spell and is not "a spell to keep us warm". This includes spells that destroy property and cause withering of limbs.
6 Please check the symbols on the archway regularly to see what activity there is in the town
7 Wizards and warlocks may exchange spell casting techniques, and vials, but no chemical or plant materials are to be prepared in the café. Arsenic is not allowed near the kitchen.
8 Non-humans should remain in human form at all times.
9 These artifacts are banned from the café: (1) Artemis's shoes of crotch kicking (2) Ruprecht's mallet of furniture destruction (3) Any vorpal swords (4) Magic pudding bowls (the walking variety)
10 Creatures of burden and horses must be kept in the barn next to the Kafe, even if they are partially sentient.

Jeff appeared up the stairs, saw her reading the unusual text on the wall, and came over. "Ah, Sophie of the infamous Circle 66!" He pointed at the wall "I had this old sign in the attic, it's probably, maybe 100 years old. I've never put it up, but you lot are 'ere so it seems the time. Anyway, coffee love? The usual?" Jess asked.

"Yes, thanks Jeff." Sophie smiled. His enthusiastic cheeriness was contagious.

After a few days of a break, the three had met up at the Electric Light Kafe once again.

"You know... all this is moving along so fast, I'm having trouble processing it," Harlan said, sipping a coffee and eating a donut. "So where are we? We were trying to track down that mini wizard girl."

"Adeline," Tomoko corrected.

"Yes. Track her down. Except we don't know how to do it. She's not at our school... The next likely school is the school at Dexheim, we could try there first, then the others."

Tomoko thanked the waitress for the green tea.

"Well, er, yeah, we could sit in the café opposite and just watch who comes out." Harlan said. Sophie noticed Raffaella pull up on her scooter outside. She walked into the café, took off her helmet, and started reading the list of rules, before coming over.

"Hi, everyone. We need to go." She kept her helmet in her hand but didn't take off her gloves.

"What's up? Go where?" Harlan glanced at her.

"Another break in, my papa told me about it this morning." Rafaella pulled her phone out of her pocket and showed them the web page for the local newspaper.

"Oh, I missed it," Tomoko said, frowning. I've been scanning the news sites for anything unusual. I've got SMS alerts set up as well."

"It's only just happened. Papa drove past it," Raffaella said. "It seems a bookshop was broken into overnight. It was definitely our wizard."

"Adeline," Tomoko added, again. "How can you tell?"

"She shifted the bricks," Tomoko said, and waved at the waitress to come over. "I just worked it out. She never breaks windows or opens the door. She melts the bricks or removes them."

Tomoko glanced at the three of them.

"Oh!" She put her coffee down. "I know why. She is an elementalist. My Sensei told me about them."

"Ah... I've heard of them." Sophie seemed curious.

Tomoko continued, "It's one of the types of Mages. Sophie said Rupert mentioned them, and like I said, my sensei mentioned them as well. Their magic works using the elements. Earth, wind, fire, and water." Tomoko pointed to the sugar bowl and pushed it with her spoon.

"She is moving bricks and earth and soil around... she is an earth   elementalist."
Suddenly things started to make sense to Sophie. The bank. Her Bedroom. She could shape stone, make holes in it, like it was clay. It was a handy ability.

"Let's go check out the shop before we go, it's a ten-minute detour to school."

Tomoko cancelled her food order, and the three of them quickly tossed down their coffees and left the café. Sophie noted to herself it was a mild victory that they could sit in a café, talk about magic, and not be kicked out.

***

The three scooters pulled up at the front of the bookshop. It was in the old part of the town once again, surrounded by picturesque little medieval shops, all colorfully decorated for the upcoming Winter festival. Once again, the area of damage was taped off by police, and media people were walking about.

Sophie examined the side wall of the bookshop. It was the same effect, it seemed exactly like the bricks were melted, but there was no heat or burning. Tomoko leant over and touched it with her hand, her eyes wide, taking in the strange effect.

"Be careful." A young man was standing there. "I don't know how stable the wall is. I've propped it up from the inside. It might fall down."

Tomoko shyly backed away from the wall.

Sophie glanced at the young man. He had brown hair and was wearing a T-shirt, with black glasses. His clothing and appearance seemed studious, the sort of person that may spend a lot of time in a bookshop.

"Do you know what happened?" Sophie asked.

He stood back, not quite sure what to make of the four kids on scooters.

"Ja. Mannfred Oltderfer. My father owns the shop. I'm just trying to make sure no one gets hurt while he talks to the police." He pointed to an older man, with long grey hair and beard, talking to a policeman, with a couple of reporters standing around listening intently.

Mannfred scanned the four intently. "Are you from the International School?"

They all nodded.

"Could we ask you about the break in...?" Sophie paused to think for a second. "We are doing a group assignment at the moment on crime reporting in the news, and we would get great marks if we could actually talk to someone about a real crime."

Mannfred examined them momentarily, still assessing them, as Harlan hopped off his scooter and set it on its stand on the road. Mannfred seemed serious.

"Why... do you all ride motor scooters?"

"Cheap. You can get a license easily if you are fifteen," Harlan said.

"Italian style," Raffaella added.

Mannfred glanced down at the scooters and then at Sophie. He seemed to be considering something.

"Well, I don't mind telling you. It's just sad someone broke into our shop...it's going to cost thousands to fix this. Papa... he doesn't know if the insurance is going to cover it. The security camera didn't show much—" He pointed at the hole in the wall. "—but yes, anyway, what did you want to know?"

"What was the book that was stolen?"

"Well, that's the odd thing. *Der Lunstaden Odes*. I mean it was old, but it wasn't worth that much," Mannfred said.

"How old was it?" Sophie asked.

"It was the seventeenth century. 1612. The odd thing... nothing else was stolen. Nothing." The man stroked his beard, apparently still processing the recent events. "All this for the one book."

"What sort of book was it?" Tomoko asked.

"It was a book of Poetry," Mannfred said. He put his hands in his pockets.

"Hang on, you said the security camera didn't show *much*. Did it show anything?" Sophie asked.

Mannfred studied her curiously, Sophie realized he may think they were asking strange questions. The expression disappeared from his face quickly, and he shrugged.

"Not much. The police told me not to talk about it. It was odd.

"Odd?" Sophie's interest picked up.

"Yes. Well, it wasn't clear, but it seemed like a short woman, with a taller man," Mannfred said, a curious expression on his face.

"Was the short woman really blonde?"

Mannfred screwed up his face. "Yes, she was, how did you know?"

"Oh, the police mentioned it," Sophie lied. Sophie watched her friends, and they all nodded. Everyone was clear who it was.

As they left, Tomoko glanced over at Sophie.

"Well, there's a pattern here. Someone is stealing books. Security Camera, short blonde woman, this is almost definitely Adeline." Tomoko glanced at them all.

Sophie made eye contact with Tomoko and appeared doubtful.

"Why would she be going to all this trouble to steal poetry books?" Sophie said. She waved and gave Mannfred a respectful nod of thanks, and they walked over to the scooters.

"So, what do we do next?" Harlan said, leaning on his scooter, helmet in hand.

Sophie crossed her arms. "We know she's stealing these books. She's preparing for the rising."

"Yes, we don't know very much," Tomoko said.

They were all quiet.

"Okay, first thing we track her down. We go to all the schools, see if we can see her, and then follow her," Sophie said. "It's all I can think of doing."

Chapter 29 - The Art of Following Mages

They rode back to school, the four of them making various excuses about why they had to leave. Fortunately, they were in different classes. They hopped on the three scooters, taking the quickest route on the town's cobbled streets. Harlan, who knew the town the best, led.

They pulled up outside the school in Dexheim, just as the students were coming out. Conveniently, there was a café opposite, so the four of them quickly ordered coffees and sat down. Harlan stared out at the gate.

"Yeah, well, there's a lot of them, all wearing the same uniform. Bit like looking for a needle in a stack of...needles," Harlan said.

Tomoko stared at them all. "Yes, but she is short. With very blonde hair. She will stand out. If she is at this school, we will see her."

"Short. Seems to be a requirement to be a mage." He grinned.

Sophie gawked at him. "Hey, I'm not short."

"Heh, well from my perspective, you're all short," he said, wryly.

"I just want to find and deal with this," Raffaella muttered. She was playing with her phone, trying to see if she could use the magnification to see across the street.

The four of them waited for about half an hour watching a lot of kids pile out of the school.

Finally, Sophie's eyes widened, and Raffaella let out a gasp.

"That's her," Sophie said.

Harlan spoke, "Dang. Yeah, it is. She is little. Such a little girl causing so much trouble. You would never guess."

"With magic, never judge *anything* based on looks alone," Tomoko said. "My sensei told me that many times."

The four of them quickly paid for their coffees and hopped on the scooters, careful to stay out of sight of Adeline.

Adeline went up to a bus stop and waited. After some time, a bus came along, and she got on. Not really knowing what to do, they followed on their scooters, at a distance, driving slowly. Tomoko took the lead, making sure not to turn a corner and bump into the errant mage.

***

Tomoko kept going ahead, with the others lagging her, just keeping her in sight, so if anyone on the bus looked behind, they would only see Tomoko by herself.

Peering up ahead, Sophie saw Tomoko waving her open hand back at them. They stopped. Tomoko then turned around and came back to them.

"She got off the bus. I think we should put the scooters somewhere and follow her on foot," Sophie said.

"Let us not approach her, please," Tomoko said, a slight waiver in her voice.

Sophie quickly shook her head. "Let's just see where she goes."

By this stage, they were out of the town and up in the mountains. Sophie wasn't sure if they had gone over the Bavarian border. It was the wonderful green forest, the sharp outlines of the pine trees, intersected by the curvy black roads, the odd house here and there.

They quickly hid their scooters in the underbrush, Raffaella grabbing her longsword and putting it over her shoulder with a leather bandolier, and followed along on foot, careful to stay back far enough that she couldn't see them.

Adeline turned off the footpath and started walking to her house. As they got closer, they could see some old castle ruins on top of the hill nearby, looking down on the three houses in the little, bright green valley. It was postcard level beautiful Bavarian countryside.

They were just about to turn the corner when they heard a car.

"Hey, look normal," Harlan quickly called out.

They all put their hands in their pockets and walked along like they were just going for a walk. Sophie realized this must have appeared strange to whoever was in the car, as they were in the middle of nowhere.

Sophie caught a quick glance of the car. It was Adeline's parents, with her in the back. The car took the corner and disappeared.

"Did they see us?" Sophie's head turned to check the others, alarmed.

"I didn't want to look directly at them, but I think they were just looking straight ahead," Tomoko said. The lack of alarm in her voice was reassuring.

Raffaella put her hands in her pockets. "What do we do now?"

Harlan reached into his pocket and pulled out a little leather wallet. "I always carry this with me."

"What is it?" Tomoko gazed oddly at it.

"It's my lockpick set." He gazed around, then hopped a fence and disappeared into the bushes.

"Harlan... No!" Tomoko called out, but he was gone, apparently trying to sneak around the back. The three scampered after him.

The house was by itself, part way up the lower section of the climbing road that went up to the mountain.

By the time the three girls had made their way to the house, through the forest, and then into the backyard, the backdoor was already opened. They crept inside.

"We are going inside?" Tomoko said, worried. "I thought we were just following her?"

"Yes, we're going inside. We need to work out what's going on. So far, we know very little about her," Sophie said.

"Should we take our shoes off?" Tomoko scanned around, then proceeded to take hers off.

"Why?" Raffaella asked.

"You know, just in case," Tomoko thought. "...footprints?"

They all took their shoes off, except for Harlan.

"I'll keep a lookout in case they come back," Harlan said. "You guys check for... er, what is it we are trying to find?"

Sophie was investigating the room, picking through things carefully. "Harlan!" she said, slightly frustrated at his forgetfulness. "The books. The poetry books. Everyone looked for anything interesting. But the books are probably what we need."

They opened doors into various places. There were bedrooms, with nothing in them. "They have taste. There's even an Italian horror movie here," Rafaella picked through a collection of videos and DVDs on a shelf. "They have Suspiria."

They couldn't find anything else. The last place to check was a closet.

"Don't bother." Sophie appeared frustrated. "There's nothing here."

Tomoko shrugged and opened the door. "You guys... er... come here."

They all gathered around the closet door. Tomoko had opened it to reveal that it was actually a door to a staircase heading down, directly into the ground.

Raffaella peered down. "Oh...a dungeon, cool."

Tomoko bent down and touched the rock.

"She has used her magic to cut this staircase into the rock. If it was cut by machine, it would be rough, but it's smooth... like it's been melted." Sophie pushed past and went down the steps, motioning for them to follow.

The steps went down for about twenty metres, and they then felt them go straight and level, Sophie guessed they were going parallel with the surface.

Tomoko appeared concerned, stopping momentarily. "What do we do if they come back?"

"They've only just left. Don't worry."

They kept going. Tomoko scanned around. "As an elemental, she can carve rock with spells. So, she can basically carve out tunnels and rooms beneath her house." She ran her hand along the smooth surface of the wall. "It is an amazing ability. I am jealous of her."

"It is cool." Raffaella peered around. "There's probably going to be some sort of demon though."

"Demon?" Tomoko said. Harlan glanced at Raffaella.

"A place like this...There must be some sort of creature here," Raffaella said.

Sophie was surprised how far they were going. The tunnels were incredible. As they walked along, they heard a murmuring up ahead.

"What's that noise?" Sophie said.

Tomoko immediately started going back to get out before Sophie grabbed her by the arm. The tunnel opened out into an open space, and to the side, there was a room.

It had a wooden door attached to the outside of it. The workmanship wasn't very good—evidently Adeline's work with stone was good, but the wooden doors and other fittings needed a good carpenter.

"This is probably her storage. Underground, no one is going to find it. From the surface it seems like a house, but well, she obviously has a lot more space down here. She'll probably have all the books down here... somewhere. If we can find them." Sophie said.

It was only bolted from the outside, which Sophie realized was lucky, as Harlan was back in the house. Sophie opened the bolt, and opened the door, to peek inside.

Sitting in the room, on a table, with a computer to one side, and a small desk... was Marcus.

Chapter 30—Marcus

"Professor!" Tomoko rushed over to him, obviously overjoyed to see him. He had his hands tied behind his back. Tomoko knelt next to him and untied him.

"We thought you had left Bavaria?" Raffaella said.

"Are you okay?" Sophie held his shoulder sympathetically, overjoyed to see him. Touching his arm, her joy switched to concern as she realized he seemed somewhat frail and unsteady, certainly more so than he was last time. She guessed he was in his 60s, but he had seemed an energetic healthy man when she saw him last.

"Thank you all so much. I haven't seen daylight for quite some time. Is my wife with you?"

"Your wife? No," Tomoko said.

"Oh, good… she is probably safe." Marcus appeared relieved.

Tomoko went over to a table and picked up a book.

"Oh! This…this is the poetry book that was taken from the bookshop."

Marcus shook his head.

"Yes. The spells are written in verse, in the middle of poems. Medieval mages would do this to hide their spells. Also, in hymnals and songbooks. Adeline has had me trying to decipher it. She was trying to use it to activate the obelisk gate. But I've been delaying. I gave her a partial translation. We can't let her get through the portal."

"Ah, well she has got through now," Sophie said, trying to disguise the guilt in her voice. Hearing this, Marcus' expression changed, and he appeared dour. His head snapped quickly, staring at Sophie.

"Sophie, how did she...?"

Sophie scratched her head, her hand nervously touching the back of her neck

"She watched me do it, and then copied the spell."

He just shook his head and muttered something Sophie couldn't hear. Tomoko tried to support the professor's arms, but he batted her away.

"I'm okay, it hasn't been that long. Let's just get out of here."

"What are you doing here, Professor?" Raffaella asked, just before Sophie could.

"Adeline... She kidnapped me with her parents. She's very capable, she knows a range of spells... more than she should know. This whole thing... just turned out so wrong. She has all these Goatkin, half goat half human, and the stag creatures. Lots of them." He shook his head. "I've made a huge mistake with her." He put his hand to his head, clearly upset.

Tomoko turned to the professor. "What do you mean more than she should know?"

"Well," he started putting a few things in his pockets and went to the doorway. "She knows elementalist spells and spells from the Illusionist path. She knows the different spells from the two separate paths. Which is concerning and probably dangerous. I don't know what is going on with her, but she is acting in concert with her parents. And she's teaching them how to do magic."

"Hai, yes," Tomoko continued; her voice strained. "They control the poor girl. They are using her, controlling her, making her steal books. Planning for the rising."

"No. No." His brow furrowed in an anxious expression; he shook his head. "I've seen her here, up close. SHE is controlling them. She was just a little girl, a nice little girl when I met her. She was twelve, and I normally only accepted fifteen- or sixteen-year-olds into the program. I don't know what has gone wrong. But there is something here I don't understand. Why a 12-year-old girl would behave like this, I don't know."

Marcus stopped getting his things, his hand went to his temple, holding his head for a few seconds. His eyes moistened, and it seemed like he was getting emotional, but then shook his head.

"Oh, are any of you using a headset with a ginger cat in it?"

"I used one once or twice from Rupert, but switched to the one you sent me," Sophie said.

"Good the ginger cat is a program hack and reports to them what he sees. Destroy that headset," Marcus said. He scanned the room grabbing books and a jacket. "We need to..." He grabbed a final book and made for the door. "Take this book and get out of here." He was walking, but unsteady.

Sophie saw the professor study her momentarily.

"Sophie... you're wondering how I know all this? There is a good explanation. I'm a mage like you and Tomoko."

"Yes, Rupert pretty much gave us that impression," Sophie said.

"Hai. That's what things seem to be indicating," Tomoko said.

"Well, actually, I'm a magicist. I work with science, interfaced with magic. So, where I do science, and it can't progress, I finish off the process with magic. So, it's a combination."

"Yes, it's okay, Marcus. We met a man from England. The Queen's mage, Rupert."

Marcus smiled, nodding his head.

"You met Rupert? Oh good, he is a good friend. He is probably keeping an eye on you."

"Well one of them is probably a good friend. We've met two Ruperts."

"Two? Be careful, one of them must be fake," he said, in an earnest expression.

"Thanks, Captain Obvious," Sophie said.

Harlan's face was an instant expression of annoyance, but Marcus didn't seem to pick up on Sophie's sarcasm, or he was too dazed to realise. Tomoko stared at Marcus in a way that made it obvious she cared for him. Sophie realized Harlan, Tomoko and Raffaella all had a lot more sessions with him and were closer to him than she was. They seemed shaken seeing him being kept in prison and looking a bit worse for the experience.

Sophie started to feel awful about Marcus...and felt anger towards Adeline swell up inside her.

"Let's just get him out of here as fast as possible. We don't really know what is going on here," Sophie said.

They left the room and headed back along the tunnel to the house. Marcus stopped at a door and examined it.

"Wait, we need to let him out. There's a man in here."

Marcus unbolted the door, and cautiously opened the door. Inside was a blond man, wearing a slightly dirty grey suit and a white shirt, sitting on the edge of his bed. His hair was greasy, and he had a short unkempt beard. He was rocking back and forth, muttering to himself.

Tomoko ran over to him, concern on her face. "Are you okay?"

"Kannst de Laufan? Can you walk?" Sophie said.

The man stared at them all. His wide eyes darted from person to person, his mouth was open, but said nothing. He shook, nervously, clearly bewildered.

"Herr doktor." He shook his head. "Herr doktor." He gazed at them all, and then closed his eyes tight and turned his head away from them. He started to disappear back under his blanket.

Marcus shook his head. "No come along my friend. We're not leaving you here."

"Let's help him out, I don't want to leave him here." They lifted him off the bed, but he was slow moving.

As they were heading back to the steps into the house, they heard footsteps up ahead. It was Harlan.

"It's too late, they are back!!" He was running down the tunnel. I've shut everything up upstairs, oh Professor!! Oh, who's this guy?"

"Hello, Harlan." Despite all the chaos, the professor was happy to see him. "We don't know who he is, but we can't leave him here."

"We can't go back to the house, let's go further into the tunnel, maybe there is a way out this way, or maybe we can hide," Sophie said, glancing back over Harlan's shoulder towards the house.

"We can fight her?" Tomoko said to Sophie.

The professor shook his head.

"No, she's too powerful, you won't beat her... you don't know enough. I also don't know what her parents are capable of. I'm not sure if they are mages."

The five continued down the tunnel. They went past the room where the professor originally was and continued down past the smooth, almost glass-like walls.

The impressive tunnel continued for some time.

They crept along the passageway. Without explanation, Harlan scurried ahead of the party to scout ahead, moving quieter than everyone else. Harland had explained to Sophie before, people wouldn't hear him coming, but his senses were better because of his thief training; he could see and hear anyone before they heard him. Sophie could see him hugging the shadows, he knew exactly how to move in the dark, so he was hard to be seen.

Drums.

Up ahead they could hear a loud rhythmic beating noise. The noise was powerful, Sophie could feel the steady bass sound rhythmically thumping her chest.

"War drums," Raffaella said.

"Well, you're being a little overdramatic, aren't you?" Harlan glanced at her.

"I've heard war drums in my dreamscape. I've seen war. I've been in two," Raffaella said flatly.

"Let's keep moving, there must be a way out up ahead," Sophie said.

"We are moving *towards* the war drums? Shouldn't we be moving away from them?" The questioning was evident in Tomoko's voice.

"We don't have any choice…we can't go back," Harlan shook his head at her.

Sophie noticed Raffaella had a grim expression of pure focus on her face, she realised she'd seen that expression every time Raffaella faced combat. Marcus wore a thin, weary smile on his face, maybe he was just happy to be free and out of his cell. He held the blond man by the arm, guiding him down the tunnel. The blond man appeared confused.

They continued along the passageway. Light appeared intermittently from electric lights mounted on the walls, power cables draped from each. However, up ahead, it was clearly dark. There was a quiver of nervousness in Sophie's hand, she shook it a couple of times to try to get it steady.

Tomoko quickly drew the glyph for light and the symbol glowed in front of her, providing a faint light that was enough to see where her feet were landing. Sophie realized she knew the same spell, and cast it, illuminating the passageway. It was the first time she had used it.

The little glyph for light, a circle with a line above it and through the middle, glowed orange red sitting just in front of

Sophie's hand. She waved her hand about, and the little glyph glowed and followed her hand, fluttering just a tiny amount, with the flourish. Despite what was going on, Sophie noted how beautiful it appeared.

It gave her just enough light for her to see where she was going.

Raffaella glanced at them both. She pulled out her smartphone and used the torch. It was a lot brighter than the spells. *Smartass,* Sophie thought, momentarily thinking about getting her own phone out, but deciding to stick with magic. *Tradition!*

As per usual, Harlan had scampered up ahead, moving silently, and using his hearing to listen for anyone else around.

He came back to them and let them know there were two doors up ahead. About a minute later, they continued along the passageway. It was the typical slightly smooth finish, made with magic.

There were two openings. The one on the left was a roughly hewn archway, with no door. The one on the right was different. It was an ornate opening, carved from stone. It was fitted with an ancient wooden door.

Harlan pointed to them and whispered, "The doors are different. This is the normal type one. This is… something else."

Tomoko examined it. "One is older, one is new?"

"What is this old door doing here?" Sophie asked.

They all glanced at each other blankly, until Marcus chimed in, "Maybe it was already here? It was built underground, and somehow Adeline has tunneled underground and connected to it."

Harlan examined the door frame, then slowly opened the door. He told them to wait, went through, came back a minute later, and motioned for them to follow. As she walked, Sophie noticed the walls here were traditional stonework, clearly hundreds of years old. They were in a passageway that appeared to be normal old medieval stonework building. It was wet on the walls, and occasionally there was a roughhewn rock on the ground. Some roots poked out on the left-hand wall, but apart from that, it was safe to walk down.

The passageway continued, until they got to another door. Harlan was checking it, to see if it was somehow trapped. Sophie had no idea if he could do it.

Harlan carefully opened the door, and he stood staring out. They all shuffled up quietly to see what it was.

Everyone went quiet. The room was amazing. It was a huge, cathedral-like space, but built underground. They were on a balcony, with stairs on their left to take them down to the main gathering space. But peering down, they could see an altar, with some statues on it. The room was empty apart from two half stag men setting up a table, some big speakers, and a microphone. A particularly muscular stag man was wearing a flannel shirt and putting a speaker on top of another one. The Cervitaur "DJ" had started playing the war drum music.

"Ah." Marcus nodded. "It's an *Unter Kathedrale*. Built during the religious wars. It's an underground cathedral, people used to worship here to get away from their enemies." He paused gazing around in wonder. "In a time in Bavarian history when we weren't perhaps as civilized."

Sophie tilted her head back, so she could take it all in, her mouth slightly open in awe. The building was amazing. The roof must have been four metres high. Sophie tried to guess how many people it could hold. Maybe 300? The stonework was ornate, with stone relief creatures, scrollwork and filigree carved into twenty or so decorated columns, lining the walls and supporting the ornate roof. There were a few torches lit here and there, but overall, it was sparsely lit.

Tomoko stammered, pointing. "The statues."

Sophie peered down. She realised why Tomoko had gasped.

The huge room was dedicated to an altar, which it seemed to focus on an altar, and on it were three statues.

Her eyes widened, as she stared. The three stone statues were stone carvings of Adeline, and her parents standing beside her.

Sophie shook her head, trying to get some focus.

"She created these half stag creatures. Apparently, she is now getting them to worship her as a *god*. Akshay needs to talk to them to set them straight. She is a mage …using magic… to make herself a god."

"This has gone so wrong. So very wrong." The despair in Marcus's voice was all too obvious. It was wrong. Sophie was aware she had powerful abilities, which could grow as she learned more spells. And Adeline, very clearly, seemed to be abusing them for who knows what personal schemes.

"She was so nice when I met her. How could a young girl turn so bad?" Marcus's voice was full of lament.

Tomoko scanned the room. "Let us get out of here. There is no one around. We cannot wait for them to come."

***

Tomoko strode towards the stairs, Harlan quickly jumped in front of her to stop her from leading, and instead went forward, beckoning people to follow. Once down the stairs they came out into the actual cathedral, Sophie presumed where people would have gathered to worship. It was like a normal cathedral, but ancient stone, and dark. No beautiful stained-glass windows. Partially illuminated, you could only see the parts of it where the torches were, the rest was in blackness.

Tomoko peered over at the statues, and at the stag men fixing up the speakers.

"Creepy," she said, staring at them intently.

Harlan had disappeared and scouted ahead. He came back to them and whispered.

"Errrh, there's a door up ahead. I think we can get out that way." He twisted his head.

"WAIT!" He pointed towards a door at the other end of the Cathedral. "Noise... a door..." He looked at the direction of, the door, and the direction of the noise.

"No time. Quick hide," Harlan said.

There were some boxes and pallets of various supplies. Not particularly fitting for a Cathedral, but the room was big enough they could sit in the corner and be out of the way. Raffaella had her sword out, and was in a combat stance, ready to react.

They all got down behind the boxes and supplies.

"Sh...quietly." Harlan was cursed by their clumsiness. To him, normal footsteps sounded incredibly loud and clumsy.

Sophie tried to practically bury herself right down. She noticed Harlan had covered his hands and face with his clothing, so you could not see any of his white skin at all. He pushed Tomoko's head down.

Marcus watched on intently, occasionally glancing at the blonde man, who was simply staring straight ahead, apparently dazed. She would have thought that Marcus would just be happy to get out of there, considering he had been kept against his will in such an awful place, underground with no sunlight for God knows how many weeks.

As they watched, the door in the far wall opened. A trail of black hooded people came through. They were holding fiery brands; each one held a torch.

"Death cult!" Raffaella said. She almost sounded happy to see it. Sophie realized that with the usual fantastic outcomes Raffaella generally proposed, she had been correct about this one.

On the other side of the Cathedral space, not far from the altar, Sophie noticed two doors were opening. The first door opened, to the right of the altar, and the bulky tall silhouette of a Stag man filled the doorway. It walked in slowly, followed by a line of them, walking proudly, in pairs. Sophie was struck in awe, the ghostly dark, ethereal procession of the horned figures hardly seemed like it could be real.

She hadn't seen so many of the stag men and while she was all too aware of the fear creeping into her chest, the figures struck her as proud and sort of majestic almost, in the way they carried themselves.

The stag men, in a column of pairs, continued to file into the great space, walking slowly. Their antlers sprouted from their heads, making them slightly demonic, and imposing.

Sophie's gaze quickly diverted to the other door, on the left of the altar. It had opened at the same time, but only now, a row of Goatkin appeared, shuffling through the doorway. They were shorter in comparison, but their horns were pointier and straight, jutting back from their heads. The front of their heads was bony. A dimly lit carnival of grotesques, the vaguely illuminated silhouettes painting images of horned demons on the walls, using shadows as paint

The Goatkin grunted and shambled, whereas the Stag men were more upright and were quieter or speaking to each other in German. The Goatkin's drooling muzzles swiveled, scanning this way and that. Long snouts and mangy beards. Bleating, roaring, grunting, a cacophony of noises. Sophie noticed they tended to glance over at the stag men, and around the room, whereas the stag creatures walked staring straight ahead, almost noble.

Every second or third stag creature/Goatkin that walked bore a fiery brand, the dancing orange flames providing just some local light, flickering, and playing off the carvings on the wall, catching the glints of their eyes, the odd reflection of a metal object here and there. The silhouettes of the horns cast on the wall made from the fiery source of light cast a shadow of a mass of devils. Slowly as more of them walked in, the room became brighter. Towards the end of the entrance, the room was practically fully lit up, though the light didn't reach up to the roof.

They filed into the area like demonic half beast altar boys attending a grotesque mass. The Goatkin continued to mutter to themselves, and the Stag men had the odd quick conversation to each other but were mostly silent. They all started gathering around the statues.

Sophie glanced at the others. They were all watching with intent. Most of them appeared nervous, particularly Tomoko. She stopped her light spell, the flickering symbol disappeared from the front of her hand. Raffaella glanced on, focusing, and Marcus, a curious interested expression on his face.

They all continued to gather around the statues, until there were none coming through the doors, and the room was full. They stood in front of the statues, chanting, which went on for a couple of minutes.

Then quite obviously not a stag man or Goatkin, a man appeared and stood behind the statues. He stood among them as a lone human in a sea of half beasts. His hair was slicked back, shoulder length and grey, he wore dark glasses, and wore a suit. He looked around for a while, observing things, and then left.

"Who's the random human?" Harlan said.

Sophie looked and shrugged. Harlan shrugged back.

Sophie leant over to Harlan.

"Maybe this is it? They gather around the statues, chant, and then leave. Seems a bit pointless."

Raffaella gazed at the ritual. "I thought it would be eviler. I expected more drumming and wild dancing. I wanted a demon."

Sophie turned back to see. She noticed there was a murmur moving through the crowd, heads turning and peering, like ripples through water. The horned crowd suddenly was all turning and reacting to the statues, some pointing and the occasional loud shriek of nonhuman delight.

Something was happening with the statues.

Sophie scanned around the room, to gauge the mood, then she noticed the reason for the attention.

They were starting to move.

She saw their hands come to life, slowly at first. Then their arms. Their upper torsos. Almost like they were waking from a stony slumber. Only the parents became animate, not the statue of Adeline herself, which remained stone. Sophie momentarily wondered why that was, then fixed her focus back on the statues.

Both parents' statues were now moving.

As the male statue, transformed into a human shape, something struck Sophie about his face. His eyes, his cheekbones, something about his face appeared familiar, though other parts didn't. It was a frustrating feeling of partially recognizing someone, but not being able to place them. Then the penny dropped.

"That man, they called him Lars, he was the first Rupert I met! He was pretending to be Rupert. He must have had a disguise, but that's definitely him."

The others peered at her, but before they could say anything, the mother statue started to speak, and they went quiet.

"Welcome... children." The mother had now partially transformed from stone to human. Sophie watched on; the whole effect was quite disturbing and made Sophie ill at ease. The stag men and Sophie saw the mother statue slowly swivel, and stopped, facing towards where Sophie and her friends were hiding.

At that moment, the drumming music stopped and there was a peculiar quiet. Sophie peered over at the man at the speakers, who had been playing the drumming music. He was holding his smartphone and seemed to be plugging it into the sound system. Then some new music started.

"AC/DC?" Raffaella said. The first to recognise the opening guitar riffs.

Sophie listened. It *was* AC/DC. Sophie stared directly at Harlan. "I hate this band, they follow me everywhere, it's like I'm cursed."

Harlan appeared confused. "I love this band, but why do we hear them all the time?"

Tomoko whispered, speaking excitedly and fast. "Oh!!... I know, I think Sophie, you *are* cursed. The boxes you opened were cursed. This is a musician's curse, the musician will follow you everywhere you go, playing a song you hate."

Finally, the penny dropped. Sophie realised she had been hexed with *the curse of the annoying bard*. Johannes had cursed his buried box, a magical buried time bomb, triggered when she opened it! She peeked at the central figures on the altar, all three of them had now turned from stone to actual humans. There was a commotion with stag men yelling at the DJ. Clearly Adeline's devotees were wondering why they were listening to classic 80's rock music, instead of their moody rhythmic drums.

With all the commotion, Adeline's mother was scanning the giant room, from left to right. She then raised her arm and pointed directly at them.

"Our enemy. THERE!"

The stag men and the Goatkin, some of them confused, turned to investigate the pile of things they were hiding behind.

Sophie could have heard a pin drop from her group. Everyone froze, not even daring to take a breath.

"Er...Crap," Harlan said. "LET'S GO!"

As soon as Harlan called out, the Goatkin and stag creatures turned and started to stride towards them. The group grabbed themselves and ran towards the door that Harlan had found, in front of them, leading out of the Unter-Kathedrale.

Raffaella stood at the door, with her sword out, waiting till the last person had gone through. Sophie glanced back as she went through the door. She could see that the two parent statues now appeared to have turned completely into Adeline's parents, Birgit, and Lars, and were continuously pointing at the party and screaming for people to follow them. Adeline's statue was now gone, but she couldn't see Adeline herself.

They went through and closed the door.

"Tomoko, do you know a spell to keep it locked?" Harlan called out.

Tomoko shook her head. "I know twenty spells, none of them will help here."

"Ok let's keep going," Sophie said.

They continued going down a passageway, running. Sophie could see that Marcus was moving slower than the rest of them.

As they ran, Sophie started thinking of a lightning bolt spell. If she used Fireball, in these narrow tunnels, she would kill everyone as the blast would come back along the tunnel and kill them. She realised she should have used it back in the bigger space of the Unter-Kathedrale.

"You guys run up ahead, we'll stop here and be ready to get them."

Sophie knew they had to prepare and make a stand here, otherwise, they were likely to get attacked while they were all running. She prepared a lightning bolt spell, remembering the complex glyph, she drew it in the air in front of her hand. Tomoko stood to her left and prepared another spell. Raffaella stood in front of them, sword over her shoulder, ready. They could cast over Raffaella's, shoulder, while she kept the creatures from getting to her and Tomoko. There was a faint blue shimmer... Sophie realised that Tomoko had cast a shield spell, that would protect them from non-magic projectiles.

"Can I take a photo of you now?" Tomoko asked, still staring straight ahead.

"Tomoko no, now is not a good time," Sophie muttered, through gritted teeth.

Glancing around, she judged that in the narrow confines of the tunnel, they may be able to hold them off for a while. But there were so many. Back in the main area of the Unter-Kathedrale, Sophie had counted perhaps 150, or more, of them.

Too many.

Sophie knew they couldn't outrun them. Professor Marcus was okay, but the blond man was tiring quickly. She wouldn't leave them behind. If they could delay Adeline's devotees, this would give him time to perhaps get out with Harlan.

There was a loud group sound of shrieking and howling, the steady stamp of feet, the sound of a mob, first. The thumping of feet, shouting, cursing, braying. Then Raffaella saw them first. She lowered her head, fixing her gaze on them, setting her feet, and raised her longsword above her shoulder.

Tomoko started preparing her spell. A dark figure appeared in front   of   a   screaming   mass. Sophie could make out the creature's face, and momentarily something twigged as being not right. He was *familiar*. The first creature, running towards them, with an outdrawn sword in one hand, was the one they had called Redbeard, the red-haired stag man from the convenience store. Redbeard was running hard, just in front of the others. Sophie studied his face; it was an expression of anguish, and fear, but curiously, not anger.

He saw her and mouthed the word, "RUN." His face lit up with desperation.

Sophie screamed at the others, "RUN!!"

They turned and fled. As they ran, Tomoko screamed out, "The first one is Redbeard."

"From the Convenience store?" Raffaella called out.

No one answered. They kept running as fast as they could, losing sight of the mob again.

As they ran through the ancient stone corridors, they caught up to Harlan moving slowly with Marcus. Harlan took a fork to the right.

"Keep going," Sophie called out.

They kept down the fork. Sophie checked Marcus; he wasn't going any further.

"Okay, we aren't going anywhere for a while. Here we fight them," Sophie declared.

"Here we stand!" Raffaella called out, raising her sword high once again.

"They're coming," Tomoko called out, her voice breaking in fear. "Sophie, get your spell ready."

They heard the creatures coming towards them getting louder. They waited.

"Get ready." She scanned either side, to see the others bracing themselves for a fight.

Sophie listened, the creatures momentarily got louder as they approached, but then… started to fade.

The mob of Goatkin and stag men didn't come. They heard the creatures moving away.

Tomoko smiled. "They are sounding more distant, are they going back?"

It dawned on Sophie. "The fork…where the tunnel forked… Redbeard was leading, could he have taken them down the wrong fork?"

Marcus piped up. "Okay, I've got my breath back, and our friend here has had a rest, let's keep moving."

They continued to stride down the tunnel, at a brisk walking pace. There were doors to small rooms to each side, but no one was in them. Apparently, everyone had attended the altar service.

They got to the end of the corridor.

"This is an incline. I can feel us going up," Harlan said, he was squinting, sensing.

Sophie glanced at Harlan. "How can you tell which way we are going?"

"I have good direction finding, I never get lost... It's part of my training. In darkness I can feel whether we are going up or down."

Sophie realized she had no idea where they were or which direction to take, and instantly felt thankful Harlan was with them. They'd be lost without him.

The tunnel continued for a while, Harlan came back to them, out of the dark.

"We have a problem, the tunnel ends," he whispered; his voice sounded tired. She read his face, a stoic brave expression, but his eyes flickered at the wall, uncertain.

"Why would a tunnel come all this way, and just finish in a brick wall?" Harlan said, almost muttering to himself. He started pressing on it, feeling it in the dark.

"Checking for secret doors?" Raffaella said, watching on.

"Yes, something, anything." Harlan was peering at it from different angles, and pushing his fingers into crevices, hoping to find an activating device.

Tomoko's eyes widened, her voice getting momentarily excited.

"Harlan, ooh, the glasses," Tomoko said.

Harlan watched her, thought for a second, and quickly put them on.

"Ahhhh!" he exhaled in shock, and a big smile came across his face, as he glanced back at Tomoko.

He reached down and put his hand on one of the bricks, giving it a hard push. It nudged back into a recess in the wall. A door appeared, from nowhere, morphing out of the brickwork magically, and they walked through to find themselves in the bottom of a medieval ruin. They could see the night sky above them.

There was light, natural light. The professor immediately stopped   and   adjusted   his   eyes.

Sophie realized he probably hadn't seen the actual light for a while. Sophie put her hand on the wall, it was cold and wet. She glanced up and saw an old stone staircase, leading the group up to it. They found themselves in the castle on top of the hill, and they could all peer down at Adeline's house below, with the family's black Volvo sedan in the driveway.

"Let's get away from here." Sophie's head swiveled to check the professor was okay, and that Raffaella still had the book, while Harlan led them down the hill on a circuitous path that kept them out of sight. Despite being locked up for two weeks, now they were out of the underground, the Professor perked up and was in good spirits, wanting to know all that had happened. Tomoko and Raffaella told him briefly about the break-ins, and what they knew of Adeline. He was most interested in the Obelisk, and how it was used for travel.

They got down to the road, but still stayed off it, cutting cross country to get to the scooters.

"Professor, I don't know if it's polite to ask this, but what path of magic are you? Is magicist a path of magic?" Sophie asked him, still checking around. It was getting cold and dark, and she noted she could see her breath in the damp air.

"I'm a magicist, but yes the magic component still has a path. My mage abilities are from the Illusionist school," he answered. He glanced at Tomoko and Sophie. "Tomoko you are from the Bright school, yes?"

"Yes. Kentaro is the fifteenth inheritor. Well, that's what he tells me," Tomoko answered.

"Sophie?"

"I'm from the illusionist school as well." Sophie deliberated, thinking. She trusted the Professor but was still unsure about the whole situation. "We visited the Illusionists in London...it...er... didn't go very well."

"They're magic is weak, isn't it?" He glanced up at Sophie as he walked.

"Yes, they... tried some magic. It was pathetic."

"Most of the magic in the west that has continued from the past has weakened and in fact, many of the spells have been lost. The six mage dreamscapers are the only ones with the more powerful magic, because you are learning directly from the original teachers. The rest have been taught in a hand me down fashion. Time, distractions of worldly pleasures, and the simple mundanity of life destroys magic, there has been plenty of that over the eons."

Tomoko butted in, uncharacteristically.

"Professor." She paused. "You said six mage dreamscapers. *Roku, six?*"

"Thirty dreamscapers in the program, but only six were studying magic." He peered at them all, thinking. "Maybe I shouldn't have told you that." He put his hand over his mouth. "The three are you two, Adeline, and another three who I shall not tell you. It is best for them and best for you."

***

Eventually the group came to their scooters and hopped on. Sophie doubled on Harlan's scooter, with Marcus awkwardly hopping on the back of Raffaella's and the blond man on the back of Tomoko's. They rolled the scooters down the hill for a little while to keep quiet, and then started the engines once they were clearly out of earshot of the house.

Harlan's scooter moved into the front of the small group, and they sprinted at speed along the regional road, which quickly turned into the cobbled streets of Dexheim. The professor, calling out over the engine noise, directed Raffaella, who sped up to get in front. Eventually they all pulled up outside a small terrace in a pretty, old part of the town near the river. The professor pointed at a house.

"This is mine. Thank you, Raffaella." The professor awkwardly started getting off the scooter. "Well, this is goodbye I'm afraid." The professor held Raffaella's shoulder, steadying himself, as he hopped off. He took the blonde man in through his front door, and then quickly popped his head back out.

"Considering the circumstances, I think it best that I disappear. I need to find my wife." He turned to Sophie and Tomoko.

"Can I have both of your numbers?" I may need to contact you." They both pulled out their phones and gave the numbers to him.

He peered at them before he turned to go inside, clasping his hands together, his expressive face showing both gratitude, and a touch of concern.

"Thank you so much for coming to get me, and for saving our bewildered mysterious friend. Not sure what I will do with him, maybe try to work out who he is. I don't know what Adeline had planned. Please, you need to keep that book from her, and keep an eye on her."

He paused, then glanced at them all. He went to speak, shut his mouth, then opened it again. Then silently stood there gazing at them, before finally speaking.

"I am torn here. The more I tell you, the more you are likely to be in danger. You four are all very young, but you are part of a small group of people that have the skills to deal with it."

His hand went up to his brow, an expression of consternation on his face.

"I really am not sure if I have done a great thing here, or created a great mess... I wonder if all magicists and scientists feel like this when they discover some great thing." He ran his hand through his hair. "Please wait here." He then trotted off to his house, reappearing a minute later.

"Here." He gave Tomoko a small box. "Don't lose it...it's extremely important. You need to give this to someone who is lost, a countryman of yours. Don't just give it to anyone. I'm trusting this with you, okay?"

Tomoko was taken aback but nodded. She studied the box.

"Marcus, what if I give it to the wrong person."

He observed her, thinking for a second, then touched her on the shoulder.

"Trust me, you will know."

He turned to Raffaella, frowning at her Metallica Metal T shirt.

"I stopped liking them after their third album." With that he turned away and walked back to his house. Sophie called out to him, her hand reaching out.

"Wait... Marcus... Do you have to go? We... we could use your help."

He turned back, his face full of worry and concern.

"Yes, sorry. I won't be here tomorrow. I need to get away from you all, and... all this." Fear was evident in his voice. With that, he walked back into his house and closed the door.

It was about nine p.m., and Sophie momentarily considered the homework she needed to get done. Her exhaustion was buoyed by this wonderful feeling she had done something right. Saved Marcus, and the blond man.

"Let's go," she said.

She felt bleak that Marcus couldn't stay and help them, he knew so much. She turned back to her friends. The three of them were putting on their helmets. Harlan grinned, came over to Sophie, gave her a hug, then patted Raffaella and Tomoko on their helmets, nodding at them both. Tomoko smiled, and Raffaella nodded in return.

"Well done team," Sophie beamed at them all.

It struck Sophie how circle 66 were coming together as this group, but how they had now come together as a group of friends. And now, they had actually accomplished a great thing. They all put on their helmets, started their scooters, and headed home.

Chapter 31—Akshay

Mr Freidrickson was reading his phone, glancing up occasionally to watch the students as they filtered down the rows of seats and sat down, filling the chairs as they occupied them from back to front, like Tetris blocks.

Raffaella walked into class, wearing a sword strapped over her back, with a brown leather belt down the front.

"Hey, little matey, you can't wear that," he said. Sophie was taken aback by the tone in his voice. Raffaella stared at him blankly for a second and then spoke.

"Yes sir, I adjusted the belt, so it fits over my clothes. I can still carry my bag." She swung her arm to demonstrate. She was pleased with herself, as much as you could ever tell whether she was pleased or not.

"No, I mean you...well. Bugger me, you're not *allowed* to wear that in here," Freidrickson said.

"I'm in the fencing club," Raffaella responded.

"I don't care if you invented swords and are showing off your new invention to your fans. Nooo... No swords in here mate. Swords, no." Freidrickson raised his voice slightly. The class muttering lowered in volume in response to his voice, bubbling down to a quiet murmur.

"I'm the instructor," Raffaella responded.

"Oh, you're the instructor? Well in that case, let me see... it's still no," Freidrickson said, lowering his voice and maintaining his composure.

"This is history class. Swords." Raffaella said.

Sophie grinned, she knew Raffaella may sound like a smart Alec, but she was saying it straight, as she had no sense of humour at all. Anything that *sounded* funny with Raffaella was never meant to be.

"No." Freidrickson stood up from his chair. "It's a sword. It could smack one of your little mates in the noggin or something."

"It's a longsword. Longswords don't hurt someone. Someone with a longsword hurts someone."

"Raffaella, maaaate." Sophie noticed he always elongated the a's in mate when he wanted to make a point. "I'm not having a nonsensical NRA type circular debate with a sixteen-year-old sword bearing goth. Away with the sword mate. Now." The anger was gone from Freidrickson' s voice, and now he just sounded tired.

"Yes, sir," she acquiesced, though not a hint of defeat in her voice.

"Go and put it in your closet or the... or the sword storage area... or in a big stone where the bloody future king of bloody England can pull it out or something." He sat back down and started flicking through the class textbook. Sophie decided this was not the time to ask about how far you could see with a medieval lantern.

Sophie glanced down; her phone ring was turned off, but it was vibrating for an incoming call. Freidrickson hated phones going off in class, she didn't answer. She pulled it out and a text message came through. She had to check the name twice to make sure it really was who it was.

Akshay, the librarian from Bamberg University had sent her a message.

Please come and meet me this afternoon. Bring the others.

"Oh. What. Akshay?" Sophie glanced down at the phone. Akshay had always been nice when they visited, but they didn't know him that well. Sophie didn't even know how he got her number.

Harlan seemed surprised. "Akshay? Er, he wants to see us? Important Librarian business?"

"Maybe something else has been stolen. Maybe he has some relic he wants to give us," Raffaella said. Raffaella was prone to fantasy, but it was hard to tell if she was being sarcastic at times. Raffaella didn't do humour, and didn't laugh, but Sophie guessed if she was going to be funny, it was most likely going to be sarcastic.

Sophie glanced up. Freidrickson was staring straight at them. They went quiet till after the class.

The reasons why Akshay might want to see them kept Sophie distracted enough that once again, another trigonometry class suffered from her *partial* attention. It came to the end of school, and they all climbed onto their scooters and drove to the University. The scooters were convenient in many ways. Cars were restricted by the boom gates, but the scooters could go straight around them, and it was easy to park.

They parked at the front of the library, and Sophie walked past the large front reference desk, the research librarians at their big desk staring at them like they were going to say something but didn't. She went down the stairs, walking briskly to the rare books section.

There were the three, as per usual. Thomas, with startling blond hair, was on the computer as usual. Akshay and Marxo were perusing what appeared to be a big fashion book. Akshay seemed to be scanning the book, unimpressed, while Marxo was pointing out some elaborate alternative wedding dresses.

Akshay piped up when they arrived.

"Oh ladies. Harlan." He nodded politely. "Thank you for coming."

Thomas stood up with a shock. "Oh Raffaella... I have something for you." He glanced around on the desk, picked up a CD and gave it to her.

"Thanks." Raffaella seemed vaguely confused, glancing at the CD.

"I've got something to show you all, come through here." Akshay directed them into another room. Sophie glanced back to see Marxo had quickly gone back to his fashion book. Thomas was trying to appear cool, while still watching Raffaella, and turned away when he saw Sophie notice him. She obviously had a fan.

Akshay took them into a little room, for which the door was labelled *Audio-Visual Room Number 3*. It seemed like a little room for showing presentations.

Akshay observed them all.

"I picked this room for privacy. Please take a seat." When Akshay said privacy, Sophie checked the windows and noted no one could see in.

There was a click as Akshay shut the door. He had locked it.

"This is something you may be interested in." He pulled two old books out of his bag. Sophie thought, maybe from the 1950s. The other one appeared to be an original medieval text, at least 500 years old. He opened them both to where they had bookmarks stuck in them.

"Oh." Tomoko put her hand to her mouth.

Both the books were, from their titles, about *Cervitaurs*. Which evidently was the proper name for the stag men.

Harlan picked up a book and started scanning through it. Sophie decided not to say anything and see what Akshay did next.

Akshay regarded them both.

"Yes. That's not the only thing I wanted to show you. I don't want you to be alarmed."

Akshay pulled his shirt aside, enough to reveal a strange tattoo on the top of his chest, above his head. He touched it, and there was a strange blue hazy effect, and Akshay's form shimmered and blurred before their eyes.

Standing before them now...instead of a human Akshay, was a Cervitaur. He crossed his arms and grinned.

Chapter 32 - Allies

"Wait… I'M A FRIEND."

"You guys were trying to kill us two days ago." Harlan stood up, his fists clenched, shaping up to fight Akshay. Sophie was already prepared. She had been wary of the invitation; in front of her hand floated the glowing orange sleep glyph, the reflection of the light flickering off the shiny gloss painted yellow walls of the room.

It was ready to cast in an instant.

Akshay peered at the flickering orange symbol and took in a breath.

"Okay, wait. I came here to tell you about them. I want to help you. I am a Cervitaur, but I'm not with *her*. We are a different group. I think we can be allies against Adeline," Akshay said.

He was in his Cervitaur form, and was tall enough now, with his full antlers, that he had to duck below the light fittings. It was an impressive sight.

He glanced up, slightly annoyed at the ceiling lights, held his hand over his heart, and changed back to human form.

"How do you do that spell?" Tomoko asked.

"It's a permanent morph spell." He undid a button and lifted his shirt slightly so you could see the symbol on his chest better. "The glyph symbol is tattooed on our skin, and we can cast it at any time. All creatures that want to live amongst humans, and appear as they do, have them."

Johannes had told Sophie that you could cast them on property, but she hadn't realised you could put a magic glyph on a *person*.

"Your people tried to run us over with a car the other day." Sophie said, through gritted teeth.

"I told you... they aren't *my people*," He shook his head, pausing for a second. "Well, they are Cervitaurs, but not *my* Cervitaurs. My people are nice and won't run you over with a car."

He thought for a second. "Well... they might if you really annoyed them, but that's not the point. We've been watching Adeline for some time, since we noticed some new Cervitaurs in Bamberg, and we tracked them to her. She has been using a spell or some magic item for some years... to *create* them. That's who *they* are. They are loyal to her... they see her as a creator, God-like figure."

Tomoko winced. For some years? Adeline was only twelve or so. How could she be doing all this since she was seven? Presumably, it was her parents controlling her. They'd already seen her in action at the Under-Kathedrale.

"Adeline being a god to them is just crazy. She is only twelve years old," Sophie said.

"She created them, using magic. That's how they see her," Akshay said, sounding a little tense. "The Goatkin are even worse. They are blindly loyal to her. Idiots."

"Well—" Sophie stared at him. "Well... what about you?"

"My community has been living amongst humans since the medieval period. You even occasionally see us in medieval paintings. They aren't allegorical pictures...that's actually a painting of my people at that time."

"Like the famous Cervitaurs in armour, you see in some Renaissance paintings?" Sophie was surprised. She remembered images of various paintings she had seen showing Cervitaurs in medieval and renaissance art. They were occasionally mentioned by people writing at the time. But everyone always assumed the artist was mixing mythical beings or devils with real people. Cervitaurs were assumed to be ancient myth, the same as Santa Claus or the tooth fairy.

"Yes. Exactly. But we learnt the magic for morphing to appear as humans, and now we hide our identities. Because... well—" He waved at them all. "...humans freak out." Akshay sat down. Everyone else was still standing up, though Harlan had put his hands down, from a boxing guard type position.

"Please relax, everyone. Sit down. You're putting me on edge. There's two mages here, a warrior, and..." He waved flippantly at Harlan, without referring to him. "...so, I'm outmatched. In any case, ... I'm on your side."

Sophie slowly sat down, keeping a direct gaze with Akshay.

"How many Cervitaurs like you are in Bamberg?"

"Twenty of us in Bamberg. 564 in all the German states. Oh, there was a new little boy born on Sunday, so 565."

"Oh, a boy. That's nice," Harlan said.

Sophie frowned. "I don't understand. Do t*hey* know?" Sophie pointed outside to Akshay's two librarian workmates.

"No. No, we don't tell anyone who we are. We blend in. That's how we have survived for 2200 years. We *become* the people we live with. We adopt their language. Religion. Dress. Music. But we are still Cervitaurs. It is our way. But it has kept us alive for thousands of years."

"How do you make new Cervitaurs? With Magic?" Harlan asked.

Akshay smiled. "Our babies are delivered by a stork... what do you think? The same way humans do." Akshay glanced at Harlan with, one eyebrow raised.

"Oh...yeah, of course." Harlan seemed embarrassed and rubbed the back of his neck.

"Sooo... what about the new Cervitaurs?"

"They are created by Adeline. They see her as a god. She is a false god; she doesn't own them. They should be free, as we are."

"We are trying to stop Adeline. We don't exactly know how," Sophie said.

"We share a common purpose. You can help us. We can help you." Akshay regarded them all, his expression sincere.

"Well... ya know, there's only four of us," Harlan said.

Akshay glanced at them all, shaking his head to show he was not concerned by the statement.

"It's not *how many* there are of you. It's *what* you can do. Besides, there are more than four of you." Akshay grinned and checked his watch. "I've only got limited time; I have to let you know a few things that can help you. I hope you don't underestimate Adeline."

"Well, she is…well scary," Sophie admitted.

"Hai, yes." Tomoko nodded.

Sophie caught Raffaella doing a slight eye roll. Evidently Adeline didn't scare her.

"Good, you should fear her. That may keep you alive," Akshay said. "She has a formidable knowledge of spells, and I've seen her work up close. She is powerful." He squinted at Tomoko and Sophie. "Though… you two. Together…"

Akshay changed the topic and flicked to some pages in the first book, which he had bookmarked. It was entitled *Creatures of Calligraphy*. It was a book of bizarre creatures, taken from calligraphy, where monks would draw strange creatures in medieval illuminated books.

Tomoko scanned the book intently, her head turning from page to page.

"This book is… amazing," Tomoko said, flicking past the bookmark, and reading the rest. A variety of medieval paintings of strange creatures.

"Here I need to show you something else, it's important." Akshay raised his voice momentarily. He flicked to where a second bookmark was. On the page, there was a fanciful medieval illustration, but even with artistic license, you could see the pictures were clearly similar to their creatures. There were huge medieval gothic fonts next to it. There was English text next to the pictures.

"These are Goatkin. They are stupid, but strong. They can't cast spells. They also can't shapeshift like us into humans. Thank the gods, I don't know what sort of chaos that would cause." He thought for a second. "Adeline uses them as her grunts, her front-line muscle. She configures them from normal goats." He frowned. "It's not pretty to watch."

"Yes, we've seen them," Sophie said simply, not going into detail.

Tomoko squinted at Akshay, a curious expression on her face.

"Akshay… how does Adeline create Cervitaurs?"

Akshay glanced back at her, and hesitated.

"I don't normally talk about it. I shouldn't tell you, as you are mages, and you may decide to go and do it. The process is a bit horrific to us, we'd just like it to be stopped forever. But we think she has some magical relic item. Each Cervitaur is created from a human mirror… a human counterpart."

There were a few seconds of silence, while the group took it in.

Akshay continued.

"Yes, it's a tad disturbing. Each Cervitaur comes from a human. They are created by humans as part of the spell. She needs a piece of human bone."

"Human bone!" There was a clear shock in Tomoko's voice.

"Er... that's well, disgusting. Where is she going to get human bones from?" Harlan said.

Akshay just shook his head. "We haven't worked that out yet. I shudder to think."

Akshay glanced down back at the book and flicked to another page.

"This is us. Historically, we are called *Gartner Hytoof* in old Low German. So, this creature appears as one of us. You'll see us commonly shown in German manuscripts and illuminations, but nowhere else."

Akshay smiled, glancing at Harlan.

"Harlan, with your glasses, you'll see Cervitaurs in one or two bars in Dresden."

Akshay read out the text from the book.

"Gartner Hytoofs were mythical beasts. They had the body of a man, cloven hooves, muscular." He glanced down at himself briefly and grinned. "Ahem... and the head of a stag. When they speak, they have loud, booming voices. They would attack people with a sword, but mostly kept living in the forests, away from people. We see few of them in this good year of our lord, 1476."

Akshay scratched his beard.

"Even back in 1476 we were making ourselves scarce. Interesting. True about the booming loud voice, my mother and father both had one. I was temporarily deaf up until I left home when I was eighteen."

"What this picture?" Harlan held up the book showing, a rather graphic painting of Cervitaurs destroying a town and killing it's in habitants."

"Oh, that's the rising that happened in the city of Ventenberg," he said, a slight waiver in his voice.

"Er, the rising." Harlan looked at it silently. There was a pause as the four looked at the picture silently.

"I've never heard of Ventenberg?" Sophie said.

"That's because after the rising, there wasn't any Ventenberg," Akshay said, in a low voice.

"We need to stop the stag men from doing this here," Tomoko said.

Akshay shook his head.

"We do, but please don't call us *Stag men*. It's speciesism. It's like if I called you *Ape men*. Call us Cervitaurs." They all nodded.

Harlan pointed to the books. "Can we borrow these books?"

Akshay smiled in a way professionals smile when they have bad news to tell. "No, sorry, I could normally lend them to you on your father's account, but his account is blocked. Unpaid library fines. You can take some photos."

Sophie rolled her eyes. "Librarians and their rules!"

"One last thing, before you go. You'll need to see these people; they can help you. Hopefully, they will. Here."

He handed her the paper. On it was an address, with instructions about meeting the people. Sophie glanced at what was a barely understandable scrawl. It was an address, in Japan.

Chapter 33 - Stone Circles at Ozu

They managed to get back to school before the end of lunch. Sophie smirked to herself. While the rest of the students were doing typical high school students' stuff, eating their lunch, gossiping, or playing ball games... they'd gone off and met a half man, half stag, and heard the history of his people.

Tomoko walked past Sophie, who was sitting on the stairs, waiting for class to begin.

"Tomoko, you know what Akshay said about the people in Japan? The information he gave us." Sophie glanced at Tomoko, who typically was hesitant.

"Yes... He mentioned people in some town in Japan...nande? Do you want to go there... now?" Tomoko seemed surprised. *Always the cautious one,* thought Sophie.

"Let's go after school," Sophie said.

"So, we are going to Japan, using the obelisk after school...?" Tomoko said.

Sophie nodded, and felt a rush of excitement, the instant rush of pleasure she would get from travelling overseas.

"Hai, er, okay." Tomoko nodded and smiled. "I'll plan it in my geography class. Leave Japan itself to me. You just need to get us there. Can you ask Harlan and Raffaella?"

"Okay." Sophie could hear the hesitation in Tomoko's voice." See you later. Let's meet at my place."

#

Sophie sat at the front of the house, waiting for Tomoko, who arrived exactly on time. Tomoko was always punctual, and on the rare occasion she was late, she would profusely apologize.

"Where's Raff and Harlan?" Tomoko glanced around.

"They can't come...Raffaella is working on Harlan's scooter, something about adding a thingy to make it go faster but stopping it from exploding. We don't need them, do we? This doesn't sound particularly dangerous or anything. We appear to be dealing with friendly sorts of people." Sophie said.

"Sophie san, what do we expect to get from these people?"

Sophie wasn't entirely sure herself but following up the few leads they had was some sort of progress." I was hoping they may be able to help us. Give us some clues, give us advice."

Tomoko squinted, clearly a little concerned, but then seemed to reconsider and grinned, if a little hesitantly.

"Okay, well, I am very happy to go back to Japan, I haven't been in a year or so." Tomoko fidgeted nervously with her gloves as she spoke. They both put on helmets and hopped on the back of Tomoko's *Fuji Rabbit* Japanese scooter and took off towards the Obelisk. It was just getting dark, and Sophie noticed how careful a rider Tomoko was; it took a little bit longer than usual because she slowed down around corners, very careful of oncoming traffic.

There was no one around, so they hid Tomoko's scooter, covering it with branches, and started their way along the path to the obelisk.

"Sophie san. I've been meaning to ask you. Do you think Raffaella likes Harlan?" Tomoko said.

"I don't know. She seems to mainly like fighting and mechanical repairs. It's hard to work out much beyond that." Sophie considered, then realised the motivation of the question.

"Tomoko, do you like Harlan?"

Tomoko seemed blank, then embarrassed "Oh, no. I like someone else at school, but not him."

"He's been a great friend to me while I've been here. I'll be incredibly sad when he leaves," Sophie said.

"I'll miss him. I get attached to people, I need to have people around me, that is when I am most happy," Tomoko said. Sophie noted a genuine, sad lilt in her voice.

They soon came up to the Obelisk, sitting on its side. They were wary approaching it, but Sophie noted that at least if they encountered the Fae here, they would be able to talk to them. The Fae were basically allies now. Sort of. As far as Sophie could work out. Sophie stood in the usual spot, and cast the spell, this time replacing the destination point with the name of the place they were going to Ozu.

As Sophie cast the spell, she noticed Tomoko studying her and mimicking the hand signs. The usual blue blur... the shimmer... the slightly unsettling feeling... then the *glorious* rush of energy/power through the body.

***

Their surroundings changed, and now they were standing in the middle of some stone circles. As they landed, they noticed a man walking away from them, with his back to them. He hadn't noticed them, and he walked over to what appeared to be a tourist information board and started taking some signs off it, replacing them with new ones. There were several huts all around them. He turned around to study them.

"Nande? Er... excuse me, what are you doing there?"

"We just arrived," Sophie blurted out, then realised that would be hard to explain.

He crossed his arms in front of his chest, making a cross sign, the Japanese hand signal for *forbidden*.

"*Gaijin.* Dame... You cannot stand on these. They are very old." He then glanced at Tomoko and said something in Japanese. She appeared embarrassed, bowed, and Sophie assumed, apologised profusely. They scurried off.

"This way, we need to get into town. I printed out the details. It's a little bar in the old part of the town." They went up to a bus stop, and Sophie realised they were actually a fair way away from houses or much of anything. Tomoko checked the bus stop sign.

"Oh... the bus only comes twice a day."

"Twice a day?"

"Next time is tomorrow." Tomoko glanced at her.

"Shall we start walking?" Sophie spun around; the place was deserted.

"Hai... ahh yep." Tomoko pointed in the right direction.

They had only been walking for about five minutes, when they saw a little white truck coming along the road. It pulled over, and there was a tall, young man driving. He said something in Japanese to Tomoko. Tomoko nodded.

"He said he can give us a lift! Hop in the back." The little truck took off, driving fast. They both sat in the back, Sophie saw a chainsaw and a helmet, some ropes.

"Forestry worker. Very tough life. But very respectful to the trees,"   Tomoko   told   Sophie. Sophie looked around. It was beautiful countryside. A beautiful, lush valley, tree covered mountains. As they drove along, Sophie noticed a whole lot of little statues on the side of the mountain.

"Tomoko, what are those… the little stone statues there, on the side?"

"Ah…they are graves. We often bury family together, on the mountains out here. They will have a beautiful view forever."

Sophie smiled. The concept of being buried, and having your soul see out across a beautiful scene for the rest of eternity was an amazing idea. Sophie had always thought of Japan being built up skyscrapers, castles, and little squashed apartments, but here in the countryside, it was as beautiful as the lush deep forests back in Bavaria.

There were a bunch of workers in the back of the truck, all men, ranging in ages from twenty to sixty, coloured overalls, boots, and most of them wore bandanas made of some traditional material, except for an older guy with a faded baseball cap.

They all laughed and cheered when they saw the two girls, and helped them up into the truck, clearing some gear and lunchboxes to make room for them.

Clearly, they weren't expecting two girls to appear, Sophie thought.

One of the men spoke in Japanese to Sophie, who just shrugged. They spoke slower, and louder, emphasizing something with their hands… it was still Japanese, and it didn't make it any more understandable.

The men then turned their attention to Tomoko, who responded to their questions, laughing.

"They asked why two young tourists were out on the roads by themselves."

Sophie stared at Tomoko. "But you're not a tourist. You're Japanese."

Tomoko shook her head. "I'm not from the mountains, not from Akita, so I'm a tourist."

She leaned in slightly. "The old guy with the baseball cap, his accent is so strong, I can barely understand him."

"Hei o Hei, Hei o Hei." Suddenly, the men started singing.

Sophie gathered it was like a traditional work song. The men were happy, their workday was over, they sang, and the old man motioned to Sophie. Sophie joined in, as did Tomoko. They both laughed as they sang. For that ten-minute truck trip, Sophie sat in the back, watched the huge forest trees and the traditional Japanese houses rush by, and forgot all the worries and complications in her world.

The truck driver called out to Tomoko in Japanese. Tomoko spoke to him, with a quick bow of her head. Sophie recognised one of ten words in Japanese she knew *arigato*: thank you.

"He's going to drop us close to where we want to go," Tomoko translated.

The truck headed towards the town. It was a small town, but it all was new and interesting to Sophie. The whole thing was such a huge buzz. Normally if you were going to an overseas holiday destination, you have weeks of preparation, and then a long flight. However, Sophie had had literally two hours advance notice that she would be in Japan from Tomoko, and the travel through the Obelisk Portal was about fifty seconds.

The truck turned off the main highway, and down to a small village.

There were about twenty houses, and the village encroached on a forest. There was one small building that appeared to be a café, or a bar... it was old and hard to tell. It was a traditional Japanese style; it was beautiful to Sophie. Wooden, it must have been 100 years old or so, with a few paper lanterns out front, some windchimes, a motorbike and an old Japanese scooter out front.

A few little cars were parked out the front.

Sophie checked her watch, realised Harlan had stolen it again, so checked her phone for the time. It was seven p.m., and it was Friday.

There were people inside, and she could hear laughter and loud conversation, and some music. Tomoko watched Sophie.

"Okay, so this is it. Friends of Akshay... should be friends of ours, too."

There were no open windows, so Tomoko couldn't see in. She pushed the traditional wooden door to the side and stepped inside, with Sophie following.

They walked into a full room; the place was packed with at least thirty people.

Everything stopped.

Everyone stopped talking and eating.

The bartender stopped pouring beer.

They all stared intently at Sophie and Tomoko. *Uncomfortable,* Sophie thought.

Sophie's heart stopped. She wondered if they were checking her because she was a foreigner. But they were staring at both of them.

Tomoko panicked and started moving backwards to get away from the collective intense gaze. She backed into Sophie standing in the doorway, who then pushed her forward, back into the bar. The bar appeared sort of old, the wall was covered with pictures and album covers from the 1970s.

Some old American rock song was just finishing as they entered, almost exactly as they walked through the door. There was silence for two or three seconds, then an AC/DC song started. Momentarily annoyed by it, Sophie's attention quickly came back to the room.

"Look!" Tomoko peered at Sophie, then nodded towards the wall. It was a human head, stuck on a wooden board on the wall, like a hunting trophy.

Sophie was alarmed for a second, then realized it was made of plastic. "It's not real," she whispered to Tomoko.

"You need to talk," Sophie whispered.

Tomoko shook her head. "*Ie,* I don't want to. I'm nervous. You do it."

"I don't speak Japanese," Sophie replied, curtly.

"Oh…yes…" Tomoko nodded. She moved ahead slowly, reluctantly, up to the bar.

By now, some people had started talking again. Others were still staring at them, their heads and collective gaze slowly tracking the pair as they walked from the door up to the bar. Sophie felt every gaze. The walk was two metres but felt like two miles. Despite the cold, she started to feel the sweat on the back of her head and took off her jacket.

They got to the bar. The bartender stared at them.

"Watashi tashi tomodachi no Akshay desu," Tomoko said.

"What did you say?" Sophie said.

"We are friends of Akshay," Tomoko translated.

The bartender stared down at them from across the bar. "Anata wa miseinendesu. Deteike."

"What did he say?" Sophie said.

"You are underage. Get out," Tomoko translated.

"MINASAN!" Sophie called out.

Tomoko head jerked back, to face Sophie, her mouth agape. The whole room stopped.

"We are friends of Akshay!" Sophie said to the room, scanning the room.

Everyone in the room stopped talking, their heads turning to the two girls. They all stared. Sophie eyes met the bartenders. The bartender's face slowly lowered, but he kept his gaze on them, under his brow, scowling. He pointed to the door. Two burly men stood up, the noise of their chairs screeching on the floor as they pushed them out from the table. They headed towards the two girls.

Sophie and Tomoko saw the two men moving towards them. Sophie glanced behind herself, and then slowly backed up towards the entrance. Tomoko was backing out even faster than her, pulling on her jacket sleeve. They both got to the door before the two men got to them. They slipped out of the door and began to trot fast, Sophie fighting the desperate urge to break into a sprint.

Sophie heard the door behind them swing shut. She kept walking fast, taking big steps. She then heard the door open again. Someone else was leaving through the door as well, coming after them. Sophie didn't gaze back, but just kept walking faster. She could see Tomoko was walking fast as well.

The street outside the front of the little bar was deserted. Sophie peeked past Tomoko at the window of a house, using the reflection to try and get a view of the street behind her. She could make out about five men were following them, and they didn't appear happy.

Chapter 34—*Sono Ojika*

Glancing up ahead, Sophie could see the main road. It was dead quiet in this village, and it appeared that some of the houses were deserted. She knew there were cars up there, more traffic, more witnesses. She started thinking of the sleep spell in her mind, nervous fingers twitching, ready to create the symbol if needed.

She picked up pace, and Tomoko took her lead and started walking faster as well. They turned the corner of the deserted street, and they could see the highway.

Sophie was surprised to see the forestry truck still there, sitting pretty much where it had stopped, with the men sitting on the ground next to it. It hadn't left after it dropped them off. One of them had out a chainsaw, and was oiling it, rather obviously.

Sophie breathed a sigh of relief, she double checked that these were the forestry men they had been singing the song with.

The five men following them now turned the corner. They saw the forestry men sitting around the truck and Sophie could see they slowed their pace.

One of the big burly men walked right up to the man with the chainsaw. The man with the chainsaw stood up and held it in front of himself. He walked right up to him and stared at him in his face.

Then they both laughed, and the burly man gave him a pat on the shoulder. The seriousness on all the people's faces dropped away. Evidently, the men all knew each other, and they started to greet each other with pats on the shoulder and nodding.

"Akira san, I think they need a lift somewhere," the big burly man said, speaking in English. They then spoke in Japanese to each other briefly. The burly man said, waving over his shoulder as he walked back with his four other friends, in the direction of the bar.

Sophie's gaze met that of the forestry man who she knew spoke English.

"What is going on?" she asked.

"When we dropped you off, we wanted to know why two gaijin would want to go to *Sono Ojika.*"

"*Sono Ojika?*"

"*That is the name of the bar.* We decided to wait and see what happened. It went pretty much how we expected it to." He grinned. "Hop in, we'll give you a lift back to where we picked you up."

The two both hopped in the truck, and the forestry men started singing again. Before long, despite the bar incident, Tomoko started singing with the men, clearly happy to be back in Japan. Sophie started singing with them as well, mangling the words, and the men chuckled at her efforts. Sophie's adrenaline had been pumping hard, in the little village when the men had followed them, but she was surprised how a good sing along, in the back of truck, with happy people made her forget.

She had an odd feeling, they hadn't found out anything, but she couldn't say that her first trip to Japan had been boring at least. She chatted to Tomoko on the way home. She wasn't sure they had achieved much, but she gathered Tomoko had a good time.

Chapter 35 - Coffee with Hisako

It had been a while since Sophie had caught up with Hisako. In the past, apart from the odd holiday when Hisako went to Japan, Sophie had seen Hisako regularly since she had known her. Now that she wasn't around, she really noticed her absence. She thought of the saying, *Absence makes the heart grow fonder;* something her papa would say.

Hisako had made the time for them to catch up before school, but Sophie suspected Hisako had just made it early to make sure Sophie was up out of bed on time. Sophie waited at the front of the café and saw Hisako coming down the street. Hisako gave her a hug and they went into the café.

It was the Electric Light Kafe, they were downstairs in the general area, but there were not really any other customers.

"I'm so glad we are catching up, let us keep regular contact, shall we?" Hisako said.

"Yes. You know, I'm so sorry about Papa. I do not forgive him. I won't. Ever." Sophie shook her head as she spoke, she felt her mouth pouting like she was going to cry and had to stifle the emotion.

"Sophie... there is something important I wanted to tell you. You need to keep up with your magic. This is something that not many people can do." She shook her head for emphasis.

"This is a gift, a rare gift."

Sophie nodded. "I guess when you put it like that. I really enjoy it."

"Well, yes. I've known you for... eight years now. I've seen you change a lot over that time. You are happier. You've grown up, you have some good friends now."

Sophie thought of Tomoko and Raphaella. They had really become a big part of her life recently.

"I know here in Bavaria, the German states, everyone fears magic, but in Japan, people would see this as something special. You can do good with it," Hisako said. "I had been working for you and Ernst for a long time. Ernst needed someone to help care for you when you were eight, and Ernst's cooking is not great.

"He does a good sandwich!" Sophie said, obliquely defending her father.

"Yes, and so many types."

She smiled.

"That is really his area of specialty," Hisako said, a wry smile on her face.

"Because that's all he can make..." Sophie said, with a smirk.

"Anyway..." Hisako smiled, but then Sophie noticed her expression change, and she was instantly serious. "...to be honest, I don't know what I was there, at your house. I was a nanny when you were younger. Then I was a cook, a cleaner."

"Well, I don't care what your official job was, you're *really* important to us. I don't know why Papa reacted like that."

Hisako paused for a minute, seeming like she was thinking about something serious, then spoke.

"Thanks Sophie." She paused before continuing. "I don't know what I am to you Sophie. I hope this doesn't sound strange, but I've watched you grow up. At times, I *almost* feel like your parent. Other times I feel like your friend."

"Oh Hisako. Does it matter? I'm glad to have you as both, or either."

Hisako gazed at Sophie, reached out and touched her shoulder.

"Thanks, that's nice of you to say that. In some ways, it doesn't matter I think, maybe in other ways it does...but your dad and magic... I just don't know."

Hisako glanced down at her coffee, then back at Sophie.

"Don't worry about the work, money, if you're thinking of that. I have other work. I just started doing some great chef work and..." She raised her head proudly, to emphasize the importance of the announcement. "I am going to start teaching naginata, which I did a lot when I was younger."

"I won't let Papa continue on with this. He's just a big idiot. I honestly don't know what he is on about, why he is unhappy about magic… but it's not your fault, he didn't need to take it out on you."

Sophie gave Hisako a little bow, Hisako grinned and returned it, then Sophie gave her a big hug. She felt a pitiful feeling in her stomach, she missed her so much. Hisako left and Sophie went over to pay the bill.

As Sophie paid Jeff the bill for the coffees, she momentarily considered all that was going on. They needed to stop the rising. Adeline seemed to have more power than they did, except for maybe Tomoko. And Adeline's father seemed intent on learning about them, she thought. At least she had stopped using the headset with the ginger cat. Sophie felt momentarily annoyed at him.

Then it struck her, maybe Jeff knew something, or someone that could help. He was one of the few people who wasn't too bothered by magic.

"Jeff, do you know much about magic, what happened in town, the people that were here?" She wondered if there was some sort of clue.

"Oh, sorry love. I'm a Barista, not a Bamberg mage historian. When I got the Kafe, all that was long in the past. Just a few little stories and the rules sign left."

"Oh," Sophie said.

"But I do 'ave the address of the previous owner. Von Strizel. He's still alive, last I heard. He could probably 'ave a word or two," Jeff said, a cheeky grin on his face.

***

After calling the others, Sophie quickly hopped on a bus to find the man. Gazing at her smartphone to get directions to the place, she navigated between ancient houses searching for street numbers that weren't always there. Awkwardly, she didn't have his phone number, so she had no idea if he was going to be there or not.

She eventually found Herr Von Strizel's house, older style, brightly coloured, with a well-cared for small rose garden in the front. Tomoko and Harlan arrived soon after, both on their scooters. Raffaella was off doing her longsword class.

Knocking on the door, a woman appeared, she seemed to be a cleaner or nurse, Sophie gathered, from what she was wearing. A largish woman, with big brown eyes and rosy cheeks and attitude.

"Hello, Is Herr Von Strizel at home?" Sophie asked.

The woman stared at them all curiously, pausing a long moment.

"I'll get him for you." She disappeared into the house.

Von Strizel appeared at the door. He was a big man, moving slowly, probably in his 80's.

He had thin brown hair on the side of his head, and a brown beard. He wore brown suspenders over a voluminous white shirt.

"Yes? I am Eric Von Strizel." He seemed mildly perplexed as to why there would be a group of three young people at his door.

"I've come to talk about your old Tavern. Jeff bought it from you. It's called the Electric Light Kafe now."

"Oh?" His face changed. "I don't like magic. I don't support it. I wish it was banned. No good will come of it." He said it by rote, mechanically, like it was a prepared line, and very defensive. "How did you find me?"

Sophie had an idea what was going on. She realised he probably had people asking him about the old tavern and mages, and some people didn't like magic.

"Jeff told me. Herr Von Strizel, I'm not anti-magic. I'm not here to harass you. Let me show you something," Sophie said, thinking fast and trying to put him at ease. She realised she had one chance at this; he could just slam the door in their face, or he could really help them.

Sophie decided to play her trump card. She opened her jacket, facing it towards him from the street, and quickly drew a symbol for the light spell on the inside of it, so only he could see.

She stepped back and she could see he was shocked. He stepped back and fell into a chair.

The lady ran out, screaming "He's got a weak heart! What did you do?"

Sophie suddenly considered in horror; she may have given an old man a heart attack by showing him magic. They all stepped into the house to help.

"Helga, I'm okay. Please leave us." He got up from the chair by himself, and was evidently not dying, to Sophie's relief. He motioned for the three to come in, and they sat in his lounge room. It was decorated with glass cabinets, and old photos of Herr Von Strizel in various locations around the world. Though no photos of the old tavern or anything magical

"You're a mage," he said. "How...?"

"Ah, it's a long story, and I shouldn't talk about it."

"Are you a mage?" he asked Harlan.

"No..I'm actually a stealth..."

"He's a thief," Sophie replied.

"I'm a mage," Tomoko said. "Do not worry Herr Von Strizel, he doesn't steal things... most of the time."

"Well, I'm glad to see them back in Bamberg. *Mages* that is. The Von Strizel's have been loyal retainers to mages for many generations. Nowadays, it's best not to talk about magic, and I don't talk about the old days, even when people ask. But you are mages yourselves." He pointed at Harlan. "And er, whatever..."

"I have so many questions to ask," Sophie said. Tomoko was leaning in, keen to hear.

"Certainly, what would you like to know?" Von Strizel smiled.

"We are dealing with a young mage who is causing problems. Her name is Adeline. She is starting a rise of Cervitaurs. We initially were met by a fake Rupert," Sophie said. She realised she was blurting it all out, hoping to get an answer, anything that would help.

He seemed blank. "I don't know anything much about that. There's always been Cervitaurs in Bamberg of course, in secret. That is their way. I don't know any *Ruperts*. What did you mean by fake Rupert?"

"Oh, someone was pretending to be him. Someone wore a disguise," Tomoko said.

As soon as Tomoko said the word *disguise*, Von Strizel's whole manner changed.

"Ah, well. Hmm." He appeared serious, gazing at the three, contemplating something. He seemed to be deliberating, but finally spoke. "There was a troublesome fellow, a criminal. Very intelligent, back in my time. He used disguises, and he was very good at it. Hypnotism. He wrote a manifesto, techniques for changing the world."

"Back in your time, so he would be old?" Sophie realised it couldn't be Adeline's father. He was too young.

"Not old. Dead. He died a long time ago," Von Strizel said, clearly still thinking.

"What sort of mage was he?" Sophie asked.

"No. Not a mage, just a man, a very intelligent man, charismatic. A very driven man. He wanted things and would do anything to get it." Von Strizel appeared slightly serious, his words slowed as he seemed to be in thought.

"What was his name?" Sophie asked.

"Mabuse," Von Strizel said. "They called him *Mabuse Der Spieler.*"

Sophie had another ten questions lined up in her thoughts, ready to ask, but she fought against the urge to ask them. They needed to get to school, and they were already late.

Sophie thought about the developments on the back of Harlan's scooter, as it zipped along to get to school. Adeline's papa had used hypnotism on the two men, when he first pretended to be Rupert. He was excellent at disguises. Clearly there was some connection with this Mabuse person.

Chapter 36 – The Electric Light Kafe: Part 4

Another cold tram. As the tram rattled along the cobblestoned streets, the odd high-pitched squeak as the brakes were applied, Sophie stared out the window, and shivered. Moving her shoulders, she tried to pull her black beanie down, and her scarf up, so they met ninja fashion and left no skin exposed to the cold. There were people milling about on the footpath. It was still cold, but it was better weather than previously, and the tourists were out, doing things.

Sophie bunched her jacket and clothes together and put her bag on her knee.It was back to the Electric light Kafe.

Alighting from the tram, Sophie went to make the wrong turn in the old streets. As she walked, she slipped slightly on the wet stones. Glancing up, she noticed an old sign stuck on the wall. It was a picture of a Wizard. An old 80s graphic of a wizard, with a big hat and beard. He was holding up his hand; a lightning bolt was coming out.

> Achtung:Magick
> Gebrauch Verboten!
> 400 Silvermack
> Bussgelt: 9889 356 32

It was faded and hard to read, but it was an old warning, telling people to report magic use to the police. Sophie realized she had not noticed these signs before, they were left over from that dark time in the past when magic was illegal... just something that older people spoke about, generally not in much detail and it never meant anything to her. But now she was a mage...she noticed things like this, and people's attitudes a lot. Like when you buy a new dress, and then suddenly, everyone seems to be wearing it.

She observed the rather stereotyped graphic of the wizard. A month ago, she would have thought it was probably an apt representation of a mage. The long grey hair, the hat, the cloak. Now she realized how stupid the picture was. I guess it was the obvious image that came into people's minds when they thought of a mage.

A month ago, she knew practically nothing about mages and magic.

Now, she was in the thick of it.

***

The Kafe building was old, but not particularly impressive, and not in the main thoroughfare, so not packed with tourists. There were more locals in it. Sophie stared in the window; the turntable was spinning around and some weird 70's rock was playing; She didn't recognize it. The window was full of 70's rock memorabilia. Mostly English (as Jeff was) and some German. There was a cool shoulder bag with a picture of a plane and the words *Pan Am* on it, she guessed it was an old airline.

Harlan and Raffaella's scooters were out front, Sophie noticed Raffaella was now using the scooters with the glyphs painted on them and was chuffed that she could use her magic to help someone. Though, the glyphs were still unproven; Sophie didn't know if they worked or not. She wondered if Tomoko and Harlan wanted the glyphs on theirs as well?

Jeff appeared, putting a vinyl record aside, and wandering over from the old turntable in the corner. He was his usual happy self.

"Hello, love. The rest of Circle 66 is upstairs. Would you like a coffee, it's cold out, isn't it?"

"Hey, Jeff, yes, cappuccino, danke. Yes, Bamberg is chilly today."

Sophie sat down, feeling sort of comfortable that they once again were sitting around in what they saw now as *their* cafe, planning the next step.

Sophie quickly briefed Harlan and Raffaella on their short and fruitless trip to Japan, and then briefed Raffaella on what they had learned from Von Strizel.

"That sounds like the lamest overseas holiday ever," Harlan said, sounding depressed.

"Well... we met some nice forestry workers and sang a working song with them in the back of their truck," Sophie said.

Tomoko appeared from the amenities.

"You talking about the men in the bar? In Japan, I was worried. I'm still worried about Adeline." she said, opening up some pasta, which she proceeded to eat with chopsticks.

"You're always worried. You know, you shouldn't be, you two can cast magic spells." Harlan pointed at Raffaella with a food laden fork. "Raffie is an expert warrior, and master scooter mechanic. A big fight breaks out and I'm likely to get wiped."

"You can *run and hide* really well. Don't call me Raffie." Raffaella tapped her finger on her chest, again wearing a different tight heavy metal T-shirt.

"Raffaella, are you saying Harls is cowardly running away all the time?" Sophie asked.

"Yes," Raffaella said. Straight to the point.

"Well, I agree." Sophie glanced over at him, eyebrow raised, waiting for the reaction.

"Arsene Lupin, my talented ancestor..he has a saying, Piotrs rule. *Those who avoid fighting and do some crime, live to steal another time.* Hey. I'm a thief. I do thief things, then I run and hide. It's my job. I'm not a tank like Raffaella." Harlan stared at them all, his voice raised in a desperate bid to defend himself.

"Tank," Raffaella muttered, nodding in approval.

"Listen," Sophie stepped in, "we don't have any real reason to worry. Adeline is active, and apparently powerful, but she has left us alone for a while. I've put wards on our houses so she can't break in. She seems to be focusing on her plans, not on us."

Taking a sip of her drink, Sophie leaned in.

Raffaella piped up, "What about Von Strizel, and this *Mabuse* person?"

Sophie shook her head. "It can't be Mabuse. He died a long time ago. But it could be someone using similar techniques."

"Disguises." Tomoko nodded.

"A coward's way of hiding. Face your enemy with your true face," Raffaella said

"It's not cowardly." Harlan appeared unimpressed. "It's about getting knowledge. Arsene would often quote Markovic's rule to me."

"What is that?" Raffaella said, raising an eyebrow.

"A thief who works with no information, is blind," Harlan said, proudly.

"So, Adeline, we know *who* she is, we know *where* she lives." Tomoko was talking, while stirring her tea with a spoon.

"She is a talented Sorceress. Tomoko and I are just beginners. I don't know what to do. We know a little about the Cervitaurs, we have some information about this Mabuse character, how do we put it all together to stop the rising?" Sophie said it out aloud, almost trying to process the current situation in her mind.

Everyone was quiet, which made Sophie realize there wasn't an obvious answer.

Raffaella decided to contribute.

"She probably does more powerful magic than us. We need to attack her and remove her as a threat."

They all gave Raffaella a collective strange expression.

"…She is planning the rising. We don't know what it is, but if we eliminate her, the problem is solved," Raffaella added.

Harlan pulled out his glasses and scanned the room randomly. Then put them back in his jacket.

Sophie took out *her* glasses and scanned the room with them. Nothing.

"These glasses are useless. I don't even know why I carry them." Sophie put them back in her pocket. "Getting back to Adeline…I know what we can do! We can put a lock spell on the Obelisk gate, using a lock spell."

Tomoko stared at her.

"Nande *lock spell*? Sophie... do you mean a *glyph*?"

"Yes, a glyph of warding. I don't think she will be able to break it. At the least it means she can't connect with the half men beast creature friends of hers… At best it will keep whatever trouble she is up to just to Bavaria. She can't go off causing trouble in other parts of the world." Sophie thought about the lock spell. *It makes sense we can't stop her, but at least we can limit her ability to travel, and the amount of damage she can do.* She finally felt good that they could do something, get back some possible control over a situation she had felt hopeless about.

Harlan glanced back at them all.

"Okay... can we just destroy the obelisk? Shift it somewhere, like, er, dump it in the ocean?"

"No..." Sophie shook her head. "The ley lines, the natural flow of magic in the earth, they are in the earth. They are a natural force; they can't be relocated. The obelisk is just a marker where they are, you can relocate *it*, but they will still be there. It won't matter."

Tomoko glanced at them both.

"Okay, we go back there tonight." She paused, picked up her tea, then put it down. "Let's lock up the gate with a spell... so no one can use it."

Raffaella piped in.

"The Fae won't be able to use it as well."

"Well, I don't know. They said they have another one they use?"

Sophie furrowed her brow, thinking. It was hard to work out what to do. But getting together and working it out seemed to be a good idea.

"Oh AC/DC. I love them," Tomoko said, vaguely swaying in her chair.

Sophie screwed up her face. Jeff was apparently playing AC/DC again.

"Who?" Raffaella said.

At that point, she noticed Harlan gazing past her, with a weird expression on his face. He was staring at someone who had just appeared at the top of the stairs, gazing into their room.

Raffaella glanced up from her coffee as well and started to rise out of her chair.

Sophie spun around and saw a man standing there, he took off a broad black hat and glasses, but from his beard it was obvious who it was. It was Redbeard, the Cervitaur with the red hair, they had seen first behind the counter at the convenience store, and then at the Unter-Kathedrale. *The Cervitaur that was in the mob of Cervitaurs that had chased them.*

He stood there staring at them, as he did, he shifted towards them, with his hands out of his pockets, palms out, showing that his hands were empty. Sophie stood up and her hand instantly drew the sleep symbol. It flickered to life, floating in front of her hand.

"No." A figure appeared next to him at the top of the stairs.

It was Akshay.

"It's okay, he's with me. Darlings, calm down." Akshay came over and gently put his hand on Sophie's shoulder to reassure her. She took a step back.

"What are you doing?" Jeff had appeared at the top of the stairs and was pointing at Sophie. Sophie stared at Jeff, who seemed alarmed at her for making the symbol.

He stepped in between Redbeard and peered at Sophie.

"You can't be hurting people with magic here," Jeff said.

Sophie gazed at Harlan, who then in turn gazed at Tomoko.

"Sophie, using spells, no. We need to follow Jeff's rules," Harlan said.

Sophie saw his eyes flick from her, and then back to Redbeard. Sophie knew Harlan would be worried about them being booted out of yet another café. She hadn't meant to get offside with Jeff, and her heart sank from instant regret.

Tomoko appeared taken aback by all this, while Rafaella had stood straight up to Redbeard, standing protectively between him and Sophie, her jaw set firm and determined.

"Please, no huge magical battles in the electric light café, Rule number 5!"

Jeff pointed to the rules on the wall. Sophie quickly glanced down to the rule marked with a big red number 5 in front of it:

5 Anyone casting offensive spells will be banned permanently from the premises. Fireball is an offensive spell and is not "a spell to keep us warm". This includes spells that destroy property and result in the withering of limbs.

"I'll give you one last chance." He raised his voice. "I will not have any magic happening in this cafe, it's just not on, all right?" Jeff pointed to Sophie. She sheepishly put out her sleep spell, the bright orange glyph disappearing in an instant.

All appeared confused. The four made space at the table for Redbeard and Akshay, who sat down. Redbeard's eyes darted around the group, and he swallowed as he and Akshay sat down. Sophie noticed him move his chair away from them, and his eyes flicked from scanning their faces, to peering at Tomoko and Sophie's hands.

"Okay, what is going on here?" Sophie said.

Jeff gazed at them all, apparently satisfied they were peaceful, and went back down the stairs.

Akshay's expression changed to annoyance, as he spoke.

"First of all, I have to ask, what the hell were you doing in the Unter-Kathedrale?"

They all peered at each other.

"We were investigating Adeline," Sophie offered.

Sophie turned to Akshay.

"Hang on, why is he here?" She pointed at Redbeard. "We saw him at the Unter Kathedrale."

"Yes, you did. That's the issue. He's our *plant* there. He's living there with them." Akshay and Redbeard gazed at each other, annoyed, then back at the group.

Redbeard turned to them.

"And you almost blew my cover. I had to get in front of the group and then lead them away from you. That's how you managed to get away."

"Yeah? Dang, Redbeard," Harlan said, leaning into the table.

"There were about forty angry Cervitaurs, and a bunch of smelly Goatkin following you. I deliberately took them off to the right fork in the passageway. Fortunately, they had stopped and weren't sure which one you had taken," Redbeard spoke, scratching his beard. "It was tricky. They could have killed you."

"I would have taken plenty with me." Sophie smiled.

Harlan glanced at Sophie; his eyebrow raised.

"Hang on, you didn't tell me you were going to fireball us all! I'd prefer to be taken prisoner!"

"I do not want to be fireballed." Tomoko shook her head.

"There is honour in mutual slaying," Raffaella said, crossing her arms.

"I think you have drifted off topic..." Akshay gazed at them.

"Let me explain..." Redbeard started again.

Akshay cut him off, putting his hand on his shoulder.

"...actually, it's probably better that I do. As I said, Redbeard here is our plant with Adeline's Cervitaurs." He paused, thinking, before he spoke. "There is a lot at stake. As you know, my main job is to save them from Adeline. Make them realise they don't need to follow her around like her personal slave army," Akshay said. "He is one of the main SCK operatives."

"What is the *SCK*?" Harlan asked.

"SCK, it is our *Spezial Cervitaur Kommando.*"

"Oh," Harlan said, appearing impressed.

"I actually was really against telling you all about our work. Not that I don't trust you, I do. But... you just don't reveal operatives. The only reason I am is, you have encountered him twice in your operations. I'm worried you may get in a fight with *them* and kill *him!*"

"Okay, we'll try not to kill him," Raffaella said, sounding slightly menacing, but probably not meaning to.

Akshay's tone of voice was getting angrier, even more heightened than Redbeard's.

"Adeline is serious business, for *my* people. These are my people, and someone is controlling them, basically using them as her slaves. She is telling them all sorts of untruths, about humans being bad to them, and how they need to rise up and attack humans." Sophie noticed Akshay was starting to raise his voice.

Harlan, Sophie, Tomoko and Raffaella all went quiet, but Sophie inside was questioning the way these two behaved. They had their own mission, but they didn't seem to care that Sophie and her crew also had theirs. Akshay, however, was not budging. His face appeared grim; his jaw clenched.

"Stay away from her," he said calmly, but his tone was very serious.

Sophie glanced at Akshay.

"Hang on, Professor Marcus was kept imprisoned there. We got him out. Poor Marcus had been there for weeks."

Akshay shifted back in his chair, clearly was taken aback by this news.

Redbeard, who had been sitting there silently, clearly letting Akshay do the talking, suddenly spoke, surprising Sophie.

"Yes. Well, we had heard there was someone there." Sophie thought she detected a slight note of guilt in his voice.

Tomoko piped up

"Poor Marcus! You knew he was there, and you were just going to leave him?" She sounded like she was about to get angry.

"He was not part of the mission," Akshay said, shaking his head, and sounding serious still.

Harlan suddenly piped up. "Hey, just wait a minute here. You left him in that cell because he was not part of your mission. Then you're angry with us because we successfully rescued him!"

"There's more at stake here than this one man. We have all those Cervitaurs to save from Adeline," Akshay said, pointing a finger at Harlan. Harlan glanced at the finger, and then squinted at Akshay.

Sophie sat back and held her head, things were moving fast. Akshay had seemed friendly before, but clearly the situation, or something, was putting him on edge. He was clearly trying to help his Cervitaurs, but she wasn't sure how much he wanted their involvement. She was trying to think fast.

"I had wanted to work with you, but I'm sorry, I can't risk it." He sounded disappointed. He got up, pushed the chair in…and started to walk out of the room.

"We care about people and wouldn't leave someone locked up and being tortured because it got in the way of our mission!" Sophie shouted at him. He stared at her, seemed like he was going to say something, but just shook his head sadly and stormed off.

Redbeard appeared surprised that Akshay had left, he uttered a simple, "Thanks, bye," and followed him quickly down the stairs. They all leaned back in their chairs, quiet for a few seconds, looking at each other.

"Did we do the right thing?" Harlan was the first to speak.

"We did the honorable thing. The brave choice. We rescued Marcus." Raffaella nodded.

"Is he right? Are we reckless?" Harlan gazed at them all.

"Ahh… maybe?" Tomoko said.

"Brown's law… playing safe with money always keeps it. But risking it to get more is always more fun," Harlan said, repeating it by rote, indicating he knew a lot of rules by heart.

At that point Jeff appeared. It was another coffee, and three donuts for Harlan, before they all agreed they had spent too much time on magic, and they were getting behind in their studies. There was a quick vote, and they all agreed to give everything a three-day rest to catch up on their studies…and meet Friday.

Sophie sat on the back of Harlan's scooter, as he drove her home. Her thoughts had already, strangely drifted to schoolwork, and she absentmindedly put a history assignment together in her head. The dark medieval buildings, lit prettily by traditional lighting, passed by. Harlan leaned into a corner, taking it at some speed, and Sophie leaned in too. He got to her house.

"I'll see you, Sophie."

"See you, Harls." She gave him a quick hug and he drove off on his scooter.

She fumbled for her keys in the dark, and went to go inside, but was startled by the movement behind her. A figure came forward to her, out from behind the shadow of a tree on the footpath, crossing the street, towards her at the front of her house. It was a man, wearing all black, and was wearing a black hoodie over his head. Her hand flickered quickly, the sleep glyph appearing before her fingers, the incandescent scarlet reflecting off her shiny black jacket.

"It's okay, calm down old girl. I'm just here to check up on you."

It was Rupert.

"We really need to talk," he said.

Chapter 37 - Two Ruperts

"Do you mind if we go for a wee walk? And chat?"

Sophie regarded this Rupert, who she finally had decided was the real Rupert, as non-threatening. However, his appearance out of the blue was a little suspicious and made her wary.

"Rupert... let's go to The Electric Kafe... okay, yes." Sophie said.

Rupert had an older white Mercedes sports car, as he drove back to the Kafe, he continued talking.

"I have felt bad. I have tried to help you out from behind the scenes. I know you have been dumped into all this, and as the only person around, I thought maybe I could assist. But...the fact that someone was impersonating me, made it a smidgeon odd. And there are other things," Rupert said. He had an odd expression on his face.

"Oh, Adeline's father...he was the one impersonating you. Probably trying to get information out of us."

"Really?" He appeared surprised. "Listen, let's not worry about that for the moment.

"Hang on, new Rupert."

"Don't call me that. Just Rupert is fine."

Sophie ignored him.

"New Rupert. How did you get here? Weren't you in England?"

"I came via the Obelisk in Munich."

"Oh," Sophie said. She still didn't understand how the obelisks were used, but some of them seemed to be common for everyday travel.

They got to the Kafe, and both hopped out. Jeff was there reading, he seemed mildly surprised to see Sophie back again so soon, but then stared with interest at Rupert. As they both went upstairs, Sophie heard the music change to AC/DC again. *Stupid Johannes and his stupid frigging curse.*

They sat at a table, opposite each other. Rupert pulled his floppy hair out of his eyes, remarkably like the first Rupert. Sophie noticed Rupert appeared a little nervous, which made Sophie nervous. He was fiddling with a ring on his finger. Sophie gazed down at it, and noticed it had glyphs around the band. She recognised some of them, clearly it was magic.

"Well old girl, I guess there's no easy way to do this."

Sophie senses heightened; Rupert seemed uncomfortable.

Under the table, she drew the symbol for sleep, and suspended it there, ready to use in an instant, so he could not see. She could feel the slight warmth of the symbol, floating in front of her hand.

Rupert stared at her, with a raised eyebrow.

"I know you have a spell under the table. I can sense the magic. Look, just watch."

Rupert grabbed the ring on his finger, he had been fiddling with. He pulled it off.

There was a blue blur.

Suddenly, his face morphed, and became fluid! In an odd morph of facial characteristics, and hair, Rupert's face started to change. It was rather like how the Cervitaurs changed, and clearly the same type of spell. *Transmorgraphation* Tomoko had called it.

It took about five seconds for the change to happen.

Rupert was now a woman.

About the same age, and build, but with long brown hair. And no moustache.

Sophie's eyes widened, and she stopped the sleep spell under the table.

"Er… Mama!!!?"

Sophie gazed upon her mother's facial features, staring back at her across the table. Sophie's mum just nodded.

"MAMA!" Sophie pushed the chair out from the table. It screeched loudly on the floor. She stood up.

"What is going on? I barely see you for the last eight years, I haven't seen you at all for the last three. A few phone calls… and you are talking to me, pretending to be some weird English guy." Sophie, her mouth agape, stared at her mother still sitting there just gazing at her. Sophie could hear her own voice waiver as she started to get angry.

At that point Jeff came up the stairs and went to give a coffee to Rupert. Instead of a man, turning to thank him, a strange woman turned to him instead. Jeff let out a high pitched, particularly girlish scream and jumped back. He glanced around at Sophie confused, for her to explain.

"Hello, I'm Anastasia. Anastasia...Wölf." Sophie's mum held out her hand smiling.

Jeff shook her hand slowly, robotically, and tentatively, clearly still stunned.

"Magic... I'm going to have to get used to this," he said, shaking his head. He walked off.

Sophie ignored him. She was still fuming, too angry to say anything. She glared at her mother.

"Mum. I...I... Why? Why did you do this?"

Sophie's mother shook her head.

"I'm a mage Sophie. I'm an important mage. I have to keep my head down. Plus, I like it."

"So, this is how I can do magic? It's in your family history?"

"Yes. Well probably. Your grandfather Rupert was," Anastasia said.

"Hang on. Is that who you are pretending to be?"

"Well yes." She adopted her Rupert voice. "I am acting as him while he is away, off doing something secretive for HM. And I may say I am doing a spiffy job of it. Your grandfather looked around my age, because he has a relic that keeps him young. Very valuable. This ring, a gender reversal artifact does the job. And I happen to look a lot like him when I change gender with this." She waved the ring in the air.

"Mama. Does doing magic for a long time make you crazy?" Sophie asked.

"I am not crazy. I have a mild dissociative disorder, which I am under professional care for. You should be a tad more respectful than that. You haven't seen me in three years."

"Yes, Mama, because you didn't visit us!" Sophie felt her blood boil and tried consciously to calm down.

"You could have tried to see *me*," Anastasia said.

"How? I'm a fifteen-year-old at school, with no money...and you are in a man's body living in London. How would I have worked where you were?" Sophie stared at her mother, incredulously.

"Well... that is a point... but... Sophie, there is a reason I didn't come and see you."

"Why? Because you were having such a good time doing magic. Hanging out with your mage friends. You just left us!" Sophie bellowed.

"No. Sophie." She appeared both angry and sad, and shook her head, reaching out to touch Sophie's hand on the table. Sophie pulled her hand back.

"I was trying to protect you from all this. Everyone knows people don't like mages. Particularly in England. I had to keep you separate from the work I do... to protect you."

Sophie could see she was sincere. It didn't matter. The anger was building up inside her, the muscles on her neck tense. It was almost like she was a boiling kettle, steaming and about to boil over. Things, feelings, images, all the time her mum had been missing from her life. All the time her friends did things, their mothers were there, and hers wasn't. She had grown numb to it over the years, suppressed her feelings, but now her mother was here, it was like it was starting to become apparent, starting to boil over.

"Why, Mama? Why did you leave us like this?"

"I had to, Sophie. I couldn't..."

Sophie peered at her, she was clearly finding it hard to say.

"I couldn't be a mage and a mother. Being a mage... it's... what I do, Sophie. All those years, I kept away from you to keep you safe. But it wasn't just that. Being a mage, it's important to me. It's what I do. I'm good at it."

Sophie stopped for a second. She realised she herself had said something like that to Hisako. Now her mum was saying the same thing to her. She went to open her mouth, then closed it again. Sophie had a sinking feeling in her stomach. Her mother had basically got the same calling as she did, to be a mage. That ridiculous, powerful calling, that consumes you and makes you feel so... important. The feeling of power, knowing you can do things that other people can't do. At the same time, the prejudice, the fear that people had.

While she felt pure rage towards her mother for leaving her, a part of her empathised that her mother was reacting to a calling, the same way she was.

"Sophie, I know you're angry. Please, just take some time. But I do have a smidgeon of information for you. There is a factory, a metal working factory, they are making sword blanks there. An informant spotted it as weird; they are making hundreds of sword blanks. I followed up and found that Adeline has had them being made for months. I know what she's got planned."

"Sword blanks?" Sophie was still incredibly angry with her mother.

"Yes. She's going to enchant them. It means they cut through magic protection. Normal bullets or swords won't go through magic shield spells. But a sword, well, a spiffy sword, designed the right way, with the right rituals and enchantment becomes a magic sword of its own."

"Magic sword, cuts through magic protection."

"Precisely, old girl."

"If you can't get them from the factory, I don't know, destroy the swords somehow, she's not going to be able to do anything, for the time being. The Cervitaur Kommando may be able to help you more after that. You need to work with them. I can talk to them for you."

Sophie was still fuming at her mother, but she had to put that out of the way for the moment. The information was vital, and it may give them a chance to set back the plans for Adeline's rising.

She peered at her mother across the table, as she continued talking. She could see her mother, in a clumsy way, at least partially, was trying to protect her from it all by removing herself from her life, but Sophie was still furious. Walking out on her and her papa for her own sake was unforgivable.

Sophie leant back in her chair, and took a breath, her tense shoulders slumped a little. It was a lot to take in. Her life, without a mother, for the last eight years. All of it explained now. In a minute. She could feel her fists clenched so her nails were almost hurting the palms of her hand, and her jaw set tight. She realised she'd spent years putting her mother out of her head, and now she was back here, unexpectedly.

Chapter 38 - Friday

It was Friday and they decided that it was time to get back to things. Sophie had spent the last couple of days mainly trying to think about her mother, all the bad she had done, and now reconcile her as being Rupert. It was hard to get her head around it. Good or bad, it probably meant they would have closer contact with her mother, Rupert. She shook her head. She wasn't even sure what to call him/her.

Tomoko came past Sophie's house, with Sophie waiting out the front so there wasn't any fuss meeting the family. They were meeting at Raffaella's. Her house was turning into a popular meeting place, largely because of Harlan. Harlan seemed to be spending more time there, working on his scooter. Coming from a farm, he had worked on motorbikes and equipment, so he already knew stuff about engines and repairing them.

There was also what Sophie and Tomoko jokingly called, *The Lasagne factor*. Whenever he was there, Mrs Cuppertino would bring out lasagna, and insist he ate it. Everyone else could only eat so much or didn't want to. But Harlan loved it.

They drove through the little cobbled streets. As Tomoko was moving into high gear to get some speed now they were on a longer road, Sophie wondered *but what did Raffaella think of Harlan being there?* Raffaella was generally standoffish with everyone, and she apparently was annoyed by him at times. While more than once she had expressed that thieves as party members were useless, at other times she liked and appreciated him.

Tomoko's scooter pulled up at Raffaella's, and they both hopped off and took off their helmets. Raffaella and Harlan were both in the workshop sitting at a table, Harlan wearing slightly dirty navy-blue overalls, Raffaella wearing even dirtier black ones, with the arms tied around her waist, and just a black T-shirt. Harlan was concentrating and examining three pieces of machinery, Sophie guessed they were from a scooter.

"Can I interrupt? I have some big news. I met Rupert last night," Sophie announced to the group, trying to think how she could explain everything, so it made sense.

"You met Rupert?" Harlan said. Everyone immediately gazed at Sophie.

"I met him, and he told me something important. Rupert is my mama."

Everyone stared at her blankly. There was absolute quiet.

"Soph. What do you mean?" Harlan asked. The waiver in his voice sounded like he was scared she had gone crazy.

"Mama is using a magic relic. A gender ring. It makes her physically change gender; she appears very much like the real Rupert. Because Rupert is her father... my grandfather, though I've never met him."

"Ah, so was he a fighter pilot in the war? Cool." Raffaella crossed her arms, nodding.

"So, there are two Ruperts. Someone pretending to be Rupert, who you first met ...and your mom, who is the new Rupert?" Harlan asked, sounding confused.

"Actually three. Original fake Rupert, my mama pretending to be Rupert, and, actual Rupert, my grandfather."

"Wait. Wakarimasen. Your grandfather was in the war, and he is still alive?"

Sophie shrugged, "Apparently. He's still doing things. Mama is pretending to be him while he is off doing...something she can't talk about."

The four were silent for a little while, while it all sank in. Sophie felt weird, explaining it all.

Finally, Tomoko broke the silence. "This is exciting. So many interesting people. We have two Ruperts to help us," she said, smiling.

"Well, I guess that's one way of looking at it," Sophie said, slightly frustrated but glad she had spoken to someone about it at least. She felt like she had got it off her chest.

"Anyway—he told me some good info. Apparently, we need to find a factory which would make sword blanks. They are making them for Adeline. She's going to enchant them. We need to find the factory where they are and destroy them – that should stop or delay the rising."

Sophie sat thinking about her mother, and the factory, then realized the conversation had gone quiet.

"Anyway, I didn't mean to interrupt, Sorry Raffaella, you were doing something with these… things." She pointed at what she assumed were car parts on the table.

Sophie didn't know what they were, but they were all grey steel, roughly the same size.

"Harlan, back to the test," Raffaella said pointing at the objects.

Harlan shook his head, possibly, trying to get the Rupert conversation out of it, and sat down at the table.

He started investigating the objects again. Concentrating, moving them around in his hand.

Raffaella glanced over her shoulder at them.

"It's a test," she said.

"A test?" Sophie said.

"Yes, to see if he can be my apprentice."

"Apprentice…are you training him with a sword?" Tomoko asked.

"Apprentice mechanic," Raffaella responded.

Sophie and Tomoko both nodded, slowly.

Harlan stood up. "Lambretta carburetor. Early model."

"Yes. Where does it go?" Raffaella nodded.

Harland glanced over his shoulder, stood up and put it in a box on the shelf.

"So, this one... Late model Vespa carburetor." He glanced at Raffaella,   and   she   nodded. He walked over to another box, after scanning around the workshop, and the part in it. Raffaella nodded again.

Then he came back to the last one. He stared at it intently. He sat down on the chair, both elbows on the table. He was staring at it, as if this would somehow make it speak to him, to tell him its origins.

Realization suddenly crept across his face.

"Honda! Japanese Carburetor!"

"Yes. Good. But where in the workshop does it go?"

"Oh... dang...wha...? You don't have any Honda parts in your workshops."

"Where does it go? Fail this... no apprenticeship."

"Fail...what? Are you serious?" Harlan appeared horrified.

She nodded, in her blank expression.

He gazed at them all, concentrating, his head askew. He examined the Japanese carburetor, then stared at Raffaella. He picked it up, walked over to the wall, and dropped it in the bin.

"Congratulations Harlan. You are my apprentice motorbike mechanic." Raffaella nodded again. Harlan collapsed into the chair, while Tomoko walked over to him and politely shook his hand.

"So, you are a multi class Thief/Vespa Mechanic? Interesting combo Harls," Sophie said, adjusting her stance and giving him a congratulatory smack on the shoulder. He nodded and grinned.

"Ok let's go guys. Let's see if we can find this factory." Sophie put her helmet back on. Raffaella and Harlan took their overalls off to reveal their normal clothes underneath, ready to go, and grabbed their helmets.

Tomoko put her helmet on, before sliding on to her scooter.

"Ikimashou! We go?"

Sophie nodded. "We go!"

Tomoko nodded. "Ikimasu!"

***

The three scooters took off. Tomoko had used her phone to search for the sort of factories that could do this work, and in this part of Bamberg, there was only one.

As they pulled up into the carpark, walked up the stairs to the office, a man in a dark suit with long dark hair and a beard was leaving. Sophie noticed that he stopped and stared at her momentarily, put his hand in his pocket and then kept walking. Harlan glanced at him, but Raffaella and Tomoko ignored him.

They went through the door. Inside, it was a normal factory, calendars on the wall, books, and catalogues about. There was an older woman with brown hair at the reception area, technical charts and photos of their various metal products decorated the wall behind her.

They all went in. The lady peered at them, and then out the
door at their three scooters. She raised an eyebrow. Sophie
realized she wasn't their usual sort of customer.

Sophie walked up confidently to the desk. "Excuse me, this
may be a strange question, but can you cut out sword blanks? To
make swords?"

The lady studied Sophie momentarily. "That is strange you
ask that. We just did that here."

Sophie smiled. They had the right place.

"We'd like to get some done ourselves. Er, could you show us
what they look like?"

The lady nodded. "Of course, come through."

She led them through the office, to the factory itself, and over
to a workshop area, and then stopped at an empty table.

"Oh, they were here yesterday." A man was standing there
having a coffee. He dropped the cup from his mouth to speak to
the lady. "Schwerter? Sie Wurden gestern abgeholt."

Sophie saw Harlan's blank expression and translated. "The
swords were picked up yesterday."

**

Harlan shook his head. "We were so close. If we'd got those
swords, destroyed them,

We could have stopped the rising. How much death and
destruction can hundreds of swords do?" Harlan said.

Tomoko nodded "We've missed them now. She's got them.
Hundreds of angry, armed cervitaurs."

As they left, Sophie glanced over at Harlan.

"Harlan, you were eyeing off that man, as we walked up."

"Oh yeah. I was. I just…saw something I hadn't seen in a
while." He grinned.

"What do you mean?"

"The man who was coming out as we came in. He had a pipe.
He put it in his pocket. He was probably embarrassed." Harlan
looked thoughtful.

"You know all about pipes, being into Jazz." Sophie froze.
"Oh my God… that guy. He was the one pretending to be
Rupert. Adeline's father."

"Adeline's father? What? How do you know?" Tomoko said.

"He was looking at me, and then turned away. He wouldn't have expected us to be here.

He had long hair, and a beard, but it's the eyes, they were the same as Adeline's father and from when he was pretending to be Rupert." She nodded, as she got more confident in the story "He had a pipe when he was pretending to be Rupert. It must be him. People just don't have pipes these days!"

They ran off in the direction he had gone, but the street was empty. Raffaella ran off further down the street, but soon came back shaking her head.

"But he looks nothing like Rupert?" Tomoko said.

Harlan nodded "Yeah, disguises can work really well, make you appear very different. Arsene does disguises. But Sophie's right, the eyes, they are hard to change. Was he the same height, Soph?"

"Well, yeah roughly the same."

"So, it was the guy, Von Strizel was speaking about? Mabuse?" Harlan asked.

"Well no. It was Adeline's father, Lars." Sophie said.

Sophie was quiet for a few seconds; she felt shocked that someone like that had just walked past them, been close to them.

"This is really weird. And scary. He walked right past us," Tomoko said.

Shaking her head so she could focus, Sophie realised she needed to get back on track.

"Okay, he's gone. We *need* to focus on the swords, I'm starting to get a bad feeling about this. What does it mean that they had them? That they got them yesterday?"

Tomoko shook her head. "They could enchant two hundred swords in a day."

"A day? That means they are ready now." Sophie said. Her hand went involuntarily to the back of her neck, rubbing it in frustration.

Harlan asked. "Oh damn. This is bad. I'm thinking of that picture that Akshay showed us, with the Cervitaurs killing everyone in that town. Can we attack them at their house? May be destroy the swords, or get to them before they get to Bamber... head them off?"

"Yes," Raffaella said, nodding.

"No." Tomoko shook her head. "Can we call someone for help?"

"There's no time, and who is there to call? The Fae don't owe us anything, why would they help us?" Harlan said, shaking his head. "Rupert?"

"I'm not calling him, he's In London, anyway." Sophie shook her head.

"They are likely to be prepared at their house for us. We've already surprised them there once; it won't work again," Sophie said.

Tomoko shook her head. "Yes, they could expect us to go Adeline's house. Why don't we get Harlan to sneak in and see if anything is happening at the Obelisk?"

Sophie nodded. "They could be using it to transport people or weapons. Or bring in help."

They decided to check that the Obelisk was not being used first, before going to the house. They took the usual route out of town, up the hill. It was still daylight, and the scenery going up the winding hills was beautiful.

Sophie noted that Raffaella had a sword shaped thing strapped to the seat-rest of her scooter. It was just a vague, longish shape wrapped up in cloth to the average person, but knowing Raffaella, it was clear what it was.

The scooters took the winding road and then pulled over to their usual spot, far enough from the road and the obelisk that if someone was there, the scooter engines wouldn't herald their arrival. They fitted neatly into some dense bushes and branches pulled over them made them invisible to the road. Sophie noticed Harlan gingerly putting his Vespa behind a bush. For a guy that used to ride motorbikes on a farm, he had grown quite attached to the smallish scooter.

Considering that the Obelisk had three separate groups of users now, they were more careful than usual.

"Okay wait here. I'll go ahead," Harlan said in a low voice. He crouched down and moved off stealthily into the bushes. Before they had a chance to start following him, he quickly returned.

"We need to leave!" He appeared very concerned.

"What's wrong?" Sophie said.

"There's about 200 of the creatures there, with Adeline, they must be guarding it."

"200? I need to see," Sophie said.

Tomoko grabbed her, almost pleading. "No, Sophie. It's not safe, let's go."

Sophie gazed at Harlan and Tomoko.

"Someone else can do it…" Tomoko said, her eyes wide. Sophie stared at her. She seemed like she was going to cry.

"Tomoko, we can't just walk away from this. We can't just leave this here, who knows what she plans to do with a small army of creatures and a huge pile of weapons. It's *us*. We are the ones here." There was a sound of exasperation in her voice, mixed with determination.

The rest were quiet, staring at Sophie.

"We're the ones… we're here. There is no one else." Sophie said, gazing back at them.

"Sophie is correct. Let's at least stay and see what is going on." Raffaella, as usual, wasn't fazed. With that, Sophie pushed off gingerly into the forest.

Harlan disappeared up ahead, Sophie could see he was eager to scout before she stumbled into something. This meant he was making sure their path ahead was safe, and they wouldn't get spotted.

They snuck to their usual observation spot, with Harlan appearing and then disappearing once again.

As Harlan had said, they were there. Cervitaurs. Lots of them. Sophie spotted they had done digging around the site and must have found her ward. *Damn should have buried it deeper.*

It was really the first chance they had had to examine them and see what they wore, this close, and in the light. They were all in their Cervitaur form, none of them were in their human appearance. They were all tall, which as a group, made them foreboding. One appeared to be the leader, as he barked out orders. He was taller than the rest. The Cervitaurs were armed with big, curved swords that seemed almost like oversized machetes, however some of them had guns, some had shields. They had big leather belts, and knives stuck in them.

"As Arsene would say, Rachov's law; *War is bad for business*, though it always seemed to contradict Simonov's law," Harlan said.

"Simonov's law?" Sophie asked.

"Simonov's law; *War is good for business*," Harlan said.

Tomoko lowered her voice, to a bare whisper, speaking to the group, while keeping her eyes on them.

"They are armed. I haven't seen them like this. Are they getting people to come in via the portal to help with the attack on Bamberg?"

Sophie nodded.

"I guess they must be, we've always thought the rising is about attacking the humans in Bamberg. Unless—" Sophie watched on, thinking. "Are they using the portal to launch an attack?" Sophie asked, more to herself than expecting an answer. The portal could go to so many places, including places they hadn't been.

Tomoko grabbed them all on the shoulder and pointed silently. To the right appeared a group of the half men, half goat creatures.

"The Goat people. We saw them in the Unter Kathedrale," Tomoko said.

"They are called Satyrs," Raffaella added. "Also, the name of a German Thrash band. They have them in their music videos."

"No. Satyrs have the body of a man and the legs of a goat," Harlan said.

"So do they." Tomoko said, pointing.

Harlan examined them again.

"No. Yes. But Satyrs have the head of a man. They have a goat's head," Harlan corrected.

"They look like Satyrs to me." Tomoko shook her head.

Harlan shook his head. "They are goat people."

"Goat people…that is a stupid name for them. I'm calling them satyrs," Raffaella said, shaking her head.

Sophie turned to face them all. "Geez… shut up guys." Sophie shook her head and glanced at Harlan, giving him a particularly nasty stare, just to see him once again disappearing into the bushes.

Suddenly Adeline appeared out of the forest, with her mother, and the man with the slicked back grey hair and dark glasses they had seen at the Unter-Kathedrale. She noticed he was wearing black gloves. The large leader of the Cervitaurs was there to talk to her. He was arguing about something. His huge size loomed over the little girl, and she stepped back, keeping her distance from him, but glared back at him defiantly. Sophie glanced at her; it seemed like she was keeping enough distance to cast a spell if he moved towards her… certainly what Sophie would have done in that situation. Adeline stood her ground and stared back at him without a hint of emotion on her face. Similarly, her mother stood, just staring at him, but Sophie couldn't see Lars, the father. The man with the grey hair and dark glasses stayed back behind them all.

"Where's Lars, the father?" Sophie whispered.

"I was wondering that too. The grey-haired guy that wears the sunglasses is there though." Tomoko muttered, in a low voice.

Adeline moved into the usual position for opening the Obelisk portal.

"She's opening the portal!" Tomoko whispered; the emotion was clear in her voice. Tomoko took out her phone and started recording it.

"I got a bad feeling about this. They hate humans, and they are all armed," Sophie whispered.

"Wherever they are going, there will be much death," Raffaella said.

Adeline started the spell once again. The portal opened.

She raised her hands. *"Ich öffne dieses Portal, mit der Kraft der Stimme, Magie und Natur Fae Dexheim obelisk!"*

It clicked…*Dexheim.* Sophie suddenly realized what was going on. Adeline was taking all these armed creatures through the portal…   *to*   *attack*   *the*   *Fae.*

Chapter 39 - Peace is Broken

The spell was cast, and they were gone. As they were gone, Harlan, having made himself scarce reappeared through the bushes behind them. Sophie spun around not expecting him to come from that direction, her hand ready to spell cast in front of her as an automatic reaction.

"There's a lot of them, all armed. This is not good. We should have locked the gate better. The Fae." Harlan's voice wavered, full of concern.

"We can't get involved; it is too dangerous. We aren't trained enough for this, we could all be killed." Tomoko seemed panicked. Sophie was equally ill at ease.

"I don't know if the Fae can defeat them. Maybe they could fight off those creatures, I think there are more Fae. But we don't know what powers Adeline has. The Fae don't have mages, just superficial personal magic." Sophie seemed worried, then double checked the area to make sure they were all gone, before standing up out of the bushes and making her way to the obelisk.

"I think we need to help them. The Fae need our help," Sophie said. She'd made up her mind. It was the right thing to do.

"Dame!!! Did you see how many there were? This is not our battle; it doesn't involve us." Tomoko faced them all, concerned written all over her face.

Raffaella stood there regarding them all, seemingly waiting for a consensus.

"Errhh guys I need to show you something," Harlan said, standing up.

"Now?" Sophie said, surprise in her voice.

"Something has been on my mind for a long time. I rang Akshay, then went and saw him, he showed me how to do something," Harlan said.

He stood up, his hand flicked through an intricate motion, just above his heart.

The blue blur of a spell morphed around his face. His skin went white, his eyes pale, his ears went pointy, and his hair went straight, and light coloured. Harlan changed into a Fae.

Everyone went quiet.

"Harlan, you look like a freak," Tomoko said.

"Er, wha...?" Harlan seemed shocked.

"No, I like the word freak. You look individual and cool. I think I used the wrong word?" Tomoko appeared apologetic. Harlan gave her a dark look.

"Yeah, er, the tattoo to change is invisible, but it's here, I can feel it under my skin." Harlan touched his chest. "Guys, I need to go, to help." He paused. "I've spent a lot of time thinking about it. You know, I am Fae. My mother must have been one, so..." He paused, his face clouded in concern and emotion. "I am too."

Sophie nodded. "Okay Harls. We all go. We're all in this together."

They went to the clearing, and Sophie started to cast the spell. Just as the spell was being cast, and the blue shimmer started, Sophie saw Tomoko back away from the shimmer.

"Sorry... I can't," Sophie heard her say indistinctly.

The blue shimmer stopped, and they had gone through the portal.

***

They appeared at the Obelisk in the Fae Forest. They were all in a defensive posture, with Sophie preparing, ready to cast if needed. Sophie scanned around the area, and her heart sank when she realized Tomoko wasn't with them. She felt betrayed that Tomoko had backed out, she was counting on her and her spells helping them. A pang of doubt struck her, she didn't know what she was heading into, she wasn't even sure if two mages could go up against Adeline if they had to, and now, by herself...

"Where's Tomoko?" Raffaella said.

Her question went unanswered.

"Oh wha… hell!" Harlan gazed all around them.

The scene was chaotic. All around them were broken bodies, weapons, and people fighting. Screaming furious Goatkin were fighting Fae warriors, who appeared desperate and determined, screaming battle cries in their Fae language.

"Get our backs together. Keep an eye out." Raffaella reached into the bag over her shoulder.

"This is insane!" Harlan turned, spinning, taking in all the surrounding chaos.

Raffaella drew her sword. "It's WAR!" She gazed intently around, trying to gauge where the enemy was coming from. She stepped over to put herself between any danger and the group.

Sophie felt adrenaline start to kick in. She took in a deep breath; she could feel a vague quiver in her body. There was so much going on, but her mind focused and took it all in. Her hand was a blur, and instantly she had the glyph for the sleep spell, floating in front of her hand, the dull blue circle with a wavy pattern through it. She scanned her surroundings quickly, to see where the obvious danger would come from.

There was a lot of individual fighting going on, between Fae warriors, Goatkin and Cervitaurs… oddly both the Fae and the Cervitaurs ignored them, clearly their priorities for staying alive made them focus on the obvious enemies.

Raffaella saw a Fae about to get killed, checked that Harlan and Sophie were safe, and ran off to help. With a furious but efficient flurry of blows, she attacked the Goatkin from various sides, but then stabbed it in the chest. The Goatkin tossed its hairy head back, and screamed, held its side, and collapsed.

Sophie was shocked, at seeing the Goatkin fall. It was all too real. This was the real danger, and it was happening so fast. Raffaella seemed to be in a state of pure focus and precision, her blows and movements were quick. She didn't hesitate or show any emotion.

"Sophie!" Harlan screamed at her.

Sophie shook her head, snapped out of her momentary daze, and started casting a spell, the glyph for *fireball,* a circle with a little flame appearing before her hands. She then realized…she just couldn't cast it, the huge ball of flame would cover a big area, and kill everyone, friend, and foe. She instead cast a succession of sleep spells, putting a few Goatkin to sleep. It would save some Fae lives.

The combat continued around them, with the combatants focusing on their obvious opponents, and mostly not engaging the three. The Goatkin still largely didn't seem to recognize them as enemies. The Fae were too busy defending themselves.

"Look." Harlan pointed over to the edge of the forest, away from   the   giant   tree   entrance. It was a group of Fae, with shields and swords, standing in a formation. Anistula stood with them, with a banner. Her height made her stand out in the battle, with a grand blue and silver helmet, and a horsehair plume sticking out of it. They were gazing off to their right. Sophie glanced over to what they were looking at.

Facing off against Anistula, was a larger group of Goatkin who were collecting themselves into a group and forming up.

"Oh my God. Look at that!" Sophie pointed over to the Goatkin.

"Dang... What is that?"

"Minotaur. Hell, it's huge," Sophie said.

They were gathering around a big minotaur, who seemed to be getting them to rally towards him. He towered above them.

They formed into a rough formation, and the minotaur pointed at Anistula. The group of Goatkin then started moving towards Anistula's Fae, keeping together in a rough formation. The Minotaur had a huge Axe. The odd arrow from the Fae arced towards him through the air, and the minotaur batted it out of the way. One stuck in his shoulder, and he simply ignored it.

"Quick, let's help Anistula," he yelled out.

Sophie assessed the chaos around her, she wasn't sure who would win, but helping them seemed to be the best option. She started running spells through her head, trying to work out what was best. They ran and joined the group. Anistula saw them come. As they joined them, Anistula called out

"Form ranks! SHIELD WALL!"

The Fae at the front formed a shield wall, the archers stood behind. Sophie, Harlan and Raffaella formed up behind the shield wall.

Anistula faced towards Harlan, nodding. "Finally, you've realized you're one of us, eh?" She smiled. "Take this. You are our bannerman." She handed him a banner. It was brightly coloured, a dragon's skull, with a long tail, made of cloth. It was beautiful but had a certain fierceness to it. It caught the wind and floated like it was a real little silk dragon, flying above them, observing the chaos below. Harlan instantly grabbed it and held it proudly in the air.

She nodded at Harlan, and then picked up her huge naginata. Anistula was tall, and the naginata was extra-long to match. She was certainly a heroic leader, the sort of person that inspired her troops to fight for her.

Sophie started contemplating the oncoming small horde. Tomoko not being here clouded her thoughts, she tried to put it out of her mind and concentrate.

"Fireball!" Harlan screamed above the din.

"No, I'm not good at it. I'll end up killing us as well," Sophie yelled.

She had an odd feeling in her stomach. She really didn't expect to be in the middle of a pitched battle when she woke up this morning. But it seemed right. Like she was supposed to be here. Like Johannes would have wanted her to use what he had taught her to help. They could have run away. They could have left the Fae. But that would have been wrong.

"Hold your arrows," Anistula called out.

The odd Fae had been loosing arrows. Now they held them nocked, half drawn. They stood still. In front of them, the group of Goatkin started moving towards them. Sophie peaked over the top of the shields. There were about twenty Fae with shields, between them and the oncoming group.

Sophie tried to roughly count them, they were facing a larger group of about forty Goatkin and Cervitaurs who were chanting and smashing weapons on their shields, making a terrifying noise. Sophie realized there were twice as many of the Goatkin facing the Fae: it was up to her and Raffaella to make the difference. The huge Minotaur stood amongst them, walking as they did, his shoulders swinging side to side, slowly. His broad, huge, two-handed axe hung resting casually on his shoulder.

Both sides had their shields all together, locked into the person on either side. The Goatkin's shield wall shuffled closer and closer to them.

"Loose!" Anistula yelled. The Fae archers loosed their arrows, the sounds of the bow strings being released in unison, making an inspiring *twang*. A flurry of arrows filled the air, some getting stuck in shields, some slipping through gaps in the goatskin shield wall. Some of the Goatkin fell down. Sophie watched as arrows arced over the Fae, spiraling down into the shields, and sticking there, some broke against them, or deflected off. However, the shield wall didn't stop, continuing moving towards them, walking over the top of the fallen.

Sophie knew the minotaur was just coming in range of her sleep spell.

She had to time it right, if she cast it and he was too far away, it would be wasted. Just as she judged he was in range to be affected, she cast it. He shook, felt the spell, and stopped for a second. Then shrugging it off, he kept coming. Sophie's heart sank, but she knew she needed to keep hitting him.

Suddenly, the Goatkin ranks picked up speed. There was a roar as they all called out a war cry in unison. They surged forward, shields still together, but moving faster. Sophie could see between the shields now, they weren't as tightly together, they opened up to get around tree stumps and bushes they couldn't walk over. Some of the Fae fired a few more arrows in the gaps.

"HOLD YOUR GROUND!" Anistula screamed.

The wave of shields smashed into the Fae. There was an almighty crash, a wave of force hit her, and Sophie was thrown to the ground. She could see Raffaella defiantly swinging a sword, concentration on her face, trying to hit something, but not able to   reach.
There was Fae all around her, getting pushed back; she realized she was close to being trampled.

"SOPHIE" She tried to see around her in the chaos of armoured legs and bodies, and Harlan had grabbed her by the arm, and helped her back up off the ground before she was trampled.

The minotaur towered above them. His giant axe crashed down on the shields, splitting them, bits of shield flying. Some of the Fae were shooting and hitting him, but the arrows just stuck in him, and he ignored them.

Sophie quickly got back on her feet. Her hand flurried through the air, and she cast yet another sleep spell on him. She could see it stunned him, he appeared vague, and gazed around confused for about five seconds, before grimacing once more.

She cast it again, and once again he seemed confused, and then closed his eyes.

"AGAIN," Harlan called out.

Sophie cast it again, and he closed his eyes. This time he stood still. His eyes closed. After ten seconds, his eyes slowly opened again, and he started to refocus. Some of the Goatkin now stopped and were glancing up at him in confusion.

"AGAIN," Harlan called out. Sophie felt weak. She felt drained. She started to feel sick.

She drew the glyph in the air in front of her. She could see her hand was slowing. Shaking. Things around her were moving slowly.

She finished the glyph, and then cast the spell. It hit the minotaur. She watched as his eyes opened, his arms holding the axe went slowly over his back, preparing to swing it down. But he was now moving slowly. Sophie watched as his hand opened and the axe fell out of his hand and over behind his back. The fighting continued around them.

Fae were continuing to fire arrows at him.

The minotaur's eyes slowly closed, and he toppled backwards, falling back into the crowd of Goatkin.

"SOPHIE! you did it!" Harlan called out.

Sophie collapsed on the ground. She was tired and weak, and felt nauseous. The Fae were still fighting around her, but she was too weak to stand. She realized the Fae ranks of soldiers were still getting pushed back. She was going to get trampled. She was too weak to care.

Harlan grabbed her off the ground, picking her up, supporting her weight.

"Sophie what's wrong?" Harlan tossed the banner to a Fae warrior, and started pulling her back, away from the front line of the combat. The combat continued, but Sophie could see that the Fae were no longer being pushed back. They were standing their ground. Anistula was amongst the battle, swinging her great two handed Naginata at the Goatkins, who were rushing in with jagged edged, rough swords.

"I don't know. I feel sick, and weak. I've never cast so many spells before. It's made me tired."

Anistula stepped back from the battle, she called out to them, across the din.

"Sophie, go. Go through the gate. Help Lord Wystan. Adeline is through there." She beckoned to Harlan. "You are Harlan, aren't you?" It was more of a statement, than a question. He nodded.

"You have helped us greatly here. Take the banner Harlan, it's important, you must keep it with you." She stepped towards them and handed the great white and green triangular banner to Harlan once again.

They ran to the huge tree-gate, Harlan helping Sophie to walk. Suddenly Raffaella, who had been in some combat, appeared and held Sophie by the other side.

"Sophie, you took out... that huge minotaur. You saved many lives. That was a great thing." Raffaella was slightly out of breath, spitting out words as she tried to breathe. She held Sophie by the shoulder.

Sophie nodded. She barely had the energy to talk.

"What is wrong with her?" Raffaella gazed at Harlan, her face a question.

"When she casts a lot of spells, she gets weak. We think. That's the greatest number of spells she has ever cast at once," Harlan said, the concern evident in his voice.

Raffaella was scanning the area, making sure they were safe while talking.

"Well, what do we do? We have a chance here; do we take her back home? She needs rest." Raffaella was peering back towards the obelisk.

Harlan peered into the tunnel that led to the Fae.

"I want to go... help the Fae," he said.

Sophie was weak and concentrating on walking. She pointed into the tunnel.

"We must go..."

"Okay. "We all go together," Raffaella said and nodded.

They stumble-walked together. Raffaella and Harlan on either side of Sophie, they pushed through the broken gates of the tree and stumbled through the tunnel.

Dead Fae and Goatkin lay around the door, evidently a small battle had taken place to defend it. They pushed on through the tunnel, stepping over the occasional unfortunate. Sophie could feel her energy slowly returning to her. She didn't feel nauseous anymore.

They moved through the tunnel, slowly, though they were gradually starting to pick up pace. They could hear some fighting, and up ahead they could see some figures holding weapons. Two Cervitaurs up ahead stood guard, with crossbows, and another with a shield. They appeared to be watching the end of the tunnel.

"Watchout!" Harlan screamed.

The crossbow bolt whizzed through the air, but then abruptly stopped in front of them and dropped to the ground.

"Thank God, Sophie. Blocking spell," Harlan said.

"No." Sophie weakly shook her head. She noticed the bolt on the ground, wondering what had shielded them.

"Look." Harlan pointed at the Banner. The banner was glowing. It had some sort of ability to shield them from arrows. The Cervitaurs with the crossbows appeared confused and were reloading their crossbows.

Raffaella started counting. "One thousand, two thousand..."

They fired again. Sophie winced and crouched down, as the bolts flew. Raffaella was counting to herself. And once again stopped. The banner glowed once again.

"Fifteen seconds!" Raffaella screamed and charged them. She attacked the two while they were trying to reload. They yelled out, confused. She quickly incapacitated them, cutting through both their crossbows, and wounding their arms, at which point they simply ran off. She maneuvered around the two, so the third one with the shield and the sword couldn't get at her, then she engaged him. She thrusted high at his head, then ducked down on one knee below his shield, so he couldn't see. As soon as he lowered his shield to see over the top of it, she jumped back up and struck him in the head, he fell, holding his head and she kicked him out of the way.

Their path was clear, and they now came out of the tunnels.

It was a sight...like nothing Sophie had ever seen before.

Chapter 40 - Confrontation.

The view before them was frightening. Arrayed to their right, was a group of about 150 Cervitaurs, Goatkin and two large mud creatures, the golems. A mass of chaos, weapons pointed this way and that, the odd battle flag. Random battle cry-like screams coming from different individuals permeating the scene, in contrast to barking orders coming from the Fae side facing them.

Two huge mud golems stood amongst the crowd of Cervitaurs and Goatkin, two or three metres taller than the soldiers below them. They stood still as rock, straight ahead, patiently awaiting command, their emotionless faces, slits for eyes and mouths roughly carved into a square block of clay for a head.

From the way that both small armies were positioned, it seemed like Adeline's half beast half man army had fought its way out of the tunnel, coming from the gate-tree. Strewn weapons, and figures lying prone on the ground.

On the left, the Fae were lined up, with shields, bows, crossbows—long naginata type pole weapons, pointy sticks jutting out, towards the sky.

They were organized in tight lines, both facing off against each other. Both sides showed signs they had clashed, there were dead and wounded lying around. Shields were dented.

Sophie surveyed the field. She knew she was in trouble. In her present state, she was too weak to take on Adeline. In a straight up spell battle, the small blonde mage would defeat her easily.

"Adeline." Raffaella pointed towards the middle of the Cervitaur/Goatkin group.

In the middle of the army, Sophie could see Adeline, with her parents standing behind her. All three watched the opposing army intently, intermittently checking their own army. None of them wore any armour or bore weapons. Clearly, they didn't intend to do any fighting themselves.

Then Sophie noticed. Her parents…were holding Adeline up. Of course… Adeline was weak from doing spells as well! *She* had obviously expended energy in the combat, she'd probably been casting more spells than Sophie. So, they had a chance. Both sides had a mage, but they were both weak.

"Soph…let's get over to the Fae, to their lines," Harlan said, lifting Sophie up.

"Yes, watchout… arrows," Raffaella said. The odd arrows were now coming down from Adeline's small army. Adeline had spotted them. Sophie could see the determined expression on her face. It was the same look as her parents. Adeline was staring, watching them intently as they moved. She clearly was focusing on what they would do.

Sophie tried her hardest to make a show of being fit and normal, but it was no use. She still needed Raffaella and Harlan's help to walk. They tried to scurry as quickly as possible, arrows just falling short. They then got to the shield wall, and Lord Wystan came over.

"Did you see Anistula? How is she?" Wystan came over and helped Sophie walk, his brow furrowed in concern.

Harlan spoke first.

"She was fighting a group at the entrance to the tree tunnel. They were holding their own. There was a huge minotaur, but we got it. Soph got it." Harlan gave Wystan a triumphant grin.

Wystan nodded.

"Well, that is something. Thank you all for helping…I…we will forever be in your debt. *We* now have a mage…things will be more even."

Sophie shook her head.

"I'm weak. I'm waiting for my energy to come back before I can cast another… spell."

Harlan glanced up at Wystan. "She casted too many outside, and nearly collapsed."

Raffaella shook her head. "She did collapse."

Wystan appeared concerned, he waved and one of his men came over, evidently a healer.

"Don't be so dramatic." Sophie glanced at them and smiled. She nodded at the healer. "I'll be okay, I just need time to get my energy back. I need to deal with Adeline."

"Same thing happened to her." Wystan pointed at Adeline. "She was casting firebolts. She made the earth rear up and it swallowed up some of my men. She created the golems, but then collapsed."

A voice called out from Adeline's massed ranks.

"We wish to speak," It was Lars, Adeline's father.

"We will make an arrangement with you." He paused, then waved his hand at all the long line of shields and weapons either side of him.

"We take this land, and you leave via the gate. You can go anywhere you want to. We will assist you to leave."

Wystan appeared furious at the proposal, and there was shouting coming from the ranks of the Fae, accompanied by a general waving of weapons in the air. It was a touchstone to set off fiery tempers.

Lord Wystan called out "What other things do we need to know of? What other conditions?"

"You have six hours to leave!" Adeline's father responded.

Wystan shook his head. "This is our home. We will not leave."

Sophie stared at the arrayed forces. It seemed to her that Adeline had more, and the mud golems were huge. Quickly counting the ranks, there were at least a hundred Goatkin, and around that many Cervitaurs. She noticed the Cervitaurs were generally bigger, and they were all grouped together.

"Even with Anistula coming to help...the Fae will lose."

Raffaella nodded. "There will be a lot of blood shed here today, and even after it all, the Fae may lose their home. We will fight valiantly. The numbers are against us, but the Fae fight for their families and their culture, and there can be no better motivation."

Wystan stood up, holding his hands up, and the Fae turned to face him.

"Fae of the forest, we fight for our homes. The forest has belonged to us for thousands of years. It is our home. *No one* should take it from us!"

The Fae all roared a battle cry, and started waving their weapons, huge lines of uniformed men, now filled with spirit.

Harlan grinned. Sophie was weak, and things seemed bad, but all the men shouting, and Wystan standing proud, was inspiring.

Adeline's father spoke. He made a rallying speech to the Cervitaurs and the Goatkin. Sophie couldn't hear it all, but it was about having a home, and not having to run from place to place. He spoke about the oppression of the Cervitaurs at the hands of man, and how they would be free. Sophie didn't know about the grievances of Adeline's Goatkin and Cervitaurs. She didn't understand the issues, maybe humans had done something to the Cervitaurs in the past? But she knew one thing. Taking the Fae's homes for their own wasn't the solution.

"What the... what is he talking about? The humans taking the Cervitaur's homes? It's utter BS!" Harlan said, shaking his head. Sophie dipped her head in agreeance, still focusing on what Adeline was doing.

It appeared that the talking was over. Soldiers on both sides were shouting at each other, but the leaders had stopped their speeches.

Sophie felt some energy come back to her and felt strong enough to stand. She still felt exhausted, and nauseous. She probably could do one more spell, but she had felt so bad casting before, she felt it might hurt her. She decided to ready herself and wait to see what Adeline did.

Adeline was now standing up by herself, evidently in better shape than Sophie.

Suddenly, Sophie heard a song coming from the tunnel. Harlan and Raffaella's heads quickly turned to the tunnel entrance, now about 200 metres away.

"Is it Anistula?" Sophie said, hope rising in her voice. She couldn't see.

The song grew louder. It was familiar. She knew where she had heard it before.

It was the song she had heard in Japan. It was a Japanese song; the workmen were singing.

Out of the tunnel stepped Tomoko.

She carried a big banner. She was followed by a range of Japanese people.

Sophie recognized them. Some were the forestry workers from the truck. There were people she didn't recognize. But most of them, surprisingly, she thought were from the bar.

They wore a variety of clothes. Some carried Japanese swords, some carried long naginata. Some of them carried the same sort of long bow, the curvy Japanese one, that Tomoko had.

Some of the forestry workers carried chain saws and axes. They were a motley bunch, of all ages, men, and women.

Harlan stared at Sophie perplexed. Sophie shrugged and shook her head. She didn't know what was going on. There were about...forty of these people, not really enough to make a difference here, and they appeared like a rag tag bunch. Some of them were old. But why were they here?

The singing stopped, and the whole field fell silent.

Tomoko silently took the group of Japanese people down the middle of the two lines between the two forces. They marched, singing their song, directly down the gap between the forces facing off.

Sophie felt a sense of relief, she had doubted Tomoko, felt disappointment with her, and even anger at leaving. But now here she was. She wondered what she was going to do. Was she going to try to stand between them between the two sides, in the middle, so they didn't fight each other? With a sudden pang of fear, Sophie realized that Tomoko was off on her own plan, without consulting them, Sophie had no idea what Tomoko was going to do.

Tomoko walked the group down between both lines. She didn't join the Fae but didn't join Adeline's group either. They continued walking down the middle between the two forces arrayed against each other, singing their song proudly, the longer weapons bounced on their shoulders as they marched in their rough column, the flags jostling in the air.

Raffaella just stared, shaking her head.

Harlan stared on with his mouth open. "Dang...what is she doing?"

Sophie shook her head slowly from side to side. "...I...have no idea."

Tomoko's group proceeded, still singing, off the battlefield, so they were no longer between the two forces, but to the side. Sophie observed the field, there were now three distinct forces, with two obviously facing each other.

Sophie realized they could now attack each other.

However, both sides were clearly not sure what to make of this new group. She was next to the edge of the Cervitaurs part of Adeline's army, which was on the right flank, and the Fae's left flank on the other.

Then Tomoko stepped forward out of her line, Sophie could see her hands fidgeting with her clothes, and she put them behind her back.

"I WILL SPEAK!"

Everyone turned to her. It wasn't like she had a huge commanding force, but it was peculiar, and the way they had marched between the two forces, had kept everyone silent.

She had the entire field's attention. Tomoko pointed to the Cervitaurs.

"You worship Adeline. Because she created you. But you are your own people. Adeline did create you, but you should not be her slaves. Cervitaurs aren't created to be slaves, you are free people, with free thought. Cervitaurs are their own people."

Tomoko, held her hands up, dramatically shaking them at the Cervitaurs.

"You should give thanks to Adeline for creating you, but you should be free to do what you want to do, to be what you want to be... To do what *you* want to do." She paused. "Er, that is my speech now, I rehearsed it three times. I was very nervous." She bowed to the Cervitaurs.

One of the Cervitaurs in the group, wearing a helmet, called out in response.

"Adeline created the Cervitaurs. We are loyal to her. We came here to fight the Fae, to fight the humans who oppress us."

Tomoko was quiet momentarily, but Sophie realized the question needed to be addressed, and quickly otherwise the momentum of the speech would be lost. She drew up a breath and called out loudly

"No one oppresses you." Sophie called out to the crowd of creatures before her. "Cervitaurs are free to live as they want."

Tomoko called out, "Adeline created you, but she didn't create all the Cervitaurs. There are other Cervitaurs who have been around as long as humans, living amongst them in peace."

Tomoko waved, and there was a ripple of motion amongst the   Japanese   people. Each one of them touched a part of their body. Some their shoulders, some their necks, some their chests.

Then Tomoko's motley group of Japanese people started changing.

There was a shimmer, and a flurry of blurred movement. Sophie gawked at the shimmering, fuzzy mass, the mass effect of individual spells, all morphed into one beautiful blur. Tens of spells all happening at once, flashing hypnotic shapes and beautiful flowing colours.

And then. Cervitaurs.

Tomoko's Japanese motley war band had revealed themselves as *Cervitaurs*.

They stood there holding their weapons. They became taller, somehow. Bigger. They still wore the same clothes. But they were Cervitaurs. Some female. Some huge males, with huge antlers.

Considerably more formidable than in their human form.

Adeline's Cervitaurs were shocked, they all took in a breath and immediately started talking to each other. Sophia peered over at Adeline. She was now standing up; she had regained energy. But she appeared confused, as her parents did, standing at either side of her.

"Wow, you turned up with forty Japanese Cervitaurs…well done. Tomoko…" Harlan's face beamed with admiration at the sight.

"Cat…amongst pigeons," Sophie said, almost chuckling at the audacity of it all. Raffaella glanced at her, and just nodded.

Now, Adeline's Cervitaurs were in disarray. Some of them turned to face each other. They were all talking intently. Adeline was calling out to them to stop talking, but they ignored her. Clearly, seeing these new Cervitaurs that weren't anything to do with Adeline, and apparently lived peacefully in human society, completely challenged them.

Suddenly, there was movement from the small ranks of Tomoko's Cervitaurs. Bravely, with his head held high, one of the Japanese Cervitaurs walked out of the ranks. He very obviously put his weapon down on the ground and held up his empty hands. He walked slowly towards Adeline's Cervitaurs. The odd arrow from the Goatkin fell near him, but they were far away.

He slowly, calmly, and defiantly walked up to the ranks of Cervitaurs in Adeline's army. He approached them, put his hand on one of their shoulders, and started talking to them. As he did, another of the Japanese Cervitaurs went over, and another. Adelines Cervitaurs broke ranks and meandered over to meet him. There was now a general conversation going on, and it looked like Adeline's Cervitaurs were eagerly asking questions.

The Cervitaur with the helmet on, had been talking to various Cervitaurs in his own ranks. The formed ranks of Adeline's Cervitaurs started to break up, as the Japanese Cervitaurs started wandering over and they started talking to each other.

Adeline was frustrated. Her parents to either side of her called, "Go back. GO BACK!"

The call was repeated in a guttural, almost braying voice from the odd angry Goatkin. But the Cervitaurs ignored Adeline's parents. They were clearly entranced by the appearance of their new Cervitaur kin.

Sophie smiled. Had Tomoko stopped a potentially huge battle here... without hurting a single person? Sophie shook her head, partially in disbelief, but mostly in admiration.

While the Goatkin and the Fae still faced-off against each other on their side of the field, the Cervitaur's lines were now all intertwined. The Cervitaurs all talked, like long lost cousins. Some of Adelines Cervitaurs stood there in awe, others eagerly asked questions. Some had put their weapons down.

Adeline's parents went over to the Cervitaurs to tell them to get back into line. The Cervitaurs started shouting at them, and some of the Japanese Cervitaurs now mixed into the group, started accusing her, in awkward English, of being a false god.

Sophie realized now was the time to act. She had regained enough of her energy, she realized if she personally challenged Adeline, she may be able to force her away without huge amounts of bloodshed.

Sophie took a deep breath. This was it. It was the chance to avoid an entire battle. She stood up, "Adeline. You must leave here. This is the home of the Fae. Possibly, the society of man has done harm to the Goatkin, and the Cervitaurs in the past, but *this* is the home of the Fae. They have done you no harm."

Adeline pushed forward through the ranks of the Goatkin, who parted to let her through. Sophie strode slowly through the ranks of the Fae towards her. They looked at her and opened their shields to let her get through.

"Soph!" Harlan quickly followed, with Raffaella, but Wystan and the army stopped him.

"Mages. Mage's combat between the two of them. Stay back. You'll get killed," Wystan screamed. The soldiers held him and Raffaella back, both struggling, but held firmly.

She looked around and couldn't see Tomoko in the chaos of all the Cervitaurs. She then walked towards Adeline. Adeline walked straight to meet her. All Sophie could think of doing was talking big, being confident, and bluffing. She realized now was not the time to show weakness. If she judged it wrong, she could see countless lives lost.

"Leave. Leave this place. Your Cervitaurs are not with you. You will not win." Sophie tried to sound brave, but she was full of doubt, and still fatigued.

Sophie had no idea if she would win. If the Fae could win the battle now. She just had to count on Adeline herself not knowing.

Adeline looked angry and focused. She was a little girl, but her presence was completely foreboding. Sophie realized she was angry enough that bluffs probably wouldn't work. Adeline was staring at Sophie, now just meters away. Sophie saw her lips twitch. She began to speak. She pointed directly at Sophie.

"Red Stripe," she said slowly. Ominously.

The words were spoken with power, with malevolence. Everyone went quiet. Sophie had never seen Adeline speak; she'd only seen her parents always speak for her. Those two words silenced everyone around her.

Sophie was shocked to hear such a frightening voice from a little girl. The crowd was quiet, even the unruly Goatkin stopped their braying. The whole field was eerily silent.

Then, lightning quick, Adeline drew a symbol in the air, then cast the spell with a flourish of a hand. Almost imperceptible to the eye, but Sophie had practiced watching symbols being drawn, and knew this one. She had seen it before. She knew what was coming.

The ground beneath them started to tremble, huge mounds of earth rose up.

Out of the ground, she could see the rising head and shoulders of a golem... made out of stone.

Chapter 41 - The Man of Stone.

Sophie shook her head, to clear her vision. Fatigue still made her eyes blurry, she tried to focus.

It was twice as big as the mud golems, standing in the array of Goatkin. In the mass of Goatkin, there was a wave of motion. As Goatkin panicked and scurried away from it, clearly worried about being trampled. A space in the crowd appeared around it. Many of them looked frightened and surprised by its sudden appearance.

The Golem was made of chunky blocks of grey stone. While the mud golems were skinnier, like men, the stone golem was thick and solid. It looked like it could crush cars, like it could batter down walls, and punch the rock sides of mountains, without a second thought. It was immensely heavy. It rose up out of the ground, its broad chest of solid rock. A solid square head of aged granite, with vertical lines running up the side and face of its granite like head.

Like the mud golem, it had slits for eyes and a mouth, seemingly too small for it to see out of. Soil and grass fell off its body as it finally finished rising.

Thinking fast, Sophie thought of the spell that had worked so far.

The stone Golem had risen quickly. It appeared disoriented for a second after its impressive birth from the ground.

Sophie quickly looked around her. The Fae were still behind her.

Sophie quickly drew the symbol for Sleep in the air. She focused all her energy and cast the symbol. She knew this was her one chance.

"Släfen," she commanded.

The spell hit the Golem with force. It had no effect. Sophie stepped back in shock, then quickly focused, thinking quickly of what spells she knew, what was likely to work on a giant monster made of stone. She quickly drew the symbol for mirror in the air, and conjured up two versions of herself, one on either side of her. Her doubles moved off to distract the monster, and as she guessed, it wasn't smart, it looked between the three of them, trying to work out which one to attack. It was the delay she needed.

The symbol for fire, a square with a little flame within it, appeared before her hand. She momentarily thought back to when she fought the clay golems. Their torsos were large and strong and soaked up damage, but she remembered their arms, which were thinner, could more easily be damaged. The bright orange flame spread from her hand, and she heard a gasp from some of the people behind her. The orange flame smashed into its shoulder, and blew the stone golem's arms clean off, bits of stone falling into the Cervitaurs, who jumped around in a sudden rush to escape the falling debris.

The stone Golem's arm detached from its body and momentarily slid against its side, before flipping over and crashing to the ground. But it kept coming. Sophie watched as the other arm closed its fist and it started moving towards her.

Sophie started stepping back. She needed another flame spell, but she was completely out of energy. She tried to bring energy into her hands to cast, but she had nothing, and trying to summon the energy made her head spin and her stomach nauseous. All she could do was step back and look up at the monolithic featureless face, as it strode towards her.

There was suddenly a bright light, and a lightning arc struck the golem. Sophie turned around to see Tomoko flying through the air. Midair, she transformed into a costume, it was a ridiculous showy white lace dress Sophie recognized from Tomoko's apartment.

The surrealness of Tomoko changing costume midflight momentarily jarred Sophie's concentration, but in some way, it fitted in with the surreal nature of what was happening.

Sophie knew Tomoko couldn't fly, but if she ran, and then cast the levitate spell, the energy carried her through the air so it looked like she could. A little gasp of admiration escaped Sophie, as Tomoko judged the natural fall in her levitation spell perfectly and landed next to her, taking a couple of footsteps to stop herself.

Adeline and her parents were completely taken aback. The stone golem stepped forward to attack Tomoko, but Tomoko instead drew a symbol in the air, and cast a spell, pushing it forward. Sophie couldn't recognize it, the symbols from the eastern path were the older Kanji letters of medieval Japan.

A crackling arc of lightning sprung from both hands of Tomoko and hit the golem in the head. It was bright, and furious. The blue light completely lit up Tomoko's face. Walking towards the Stone golem, she held her hands up, maintaining the electric arc, as the bolt grew stronger and stronger. Sophie could see Tomoko straining, her hands re-drawing the symbol again and again to boost the spell, the arc continuing to strike the golem in steady flashing pulses. Tomoko's whole body was completely bathed in the bright blue light of the lightning coming out of her hands.

Sophie looked around and could see it lit the faces of all around it. Half the people looked fearful, and half just looked on in awe. Tomoko's face strained as she concentrated. She raised her hands above her head and then cast them forward. She screamed at the top of her lungs.

The power of the lighting arc surged from her hands hitting with full force into the head of the golem. The surge of lighting smashed into its stone head. There was an awful cracking sound, like a short sharp explosion.

A split appeared in the Golem's head, it cracked and as it did, the golem started moving towards them. Then its stone head completely separated, splitting into two, the two parts shearing off and falling off the shoulders of the golem, toppling to the ground.

The towering, headless stone golem kept stepping forward, blindly lumbering towards Tomoko and Sophie. It slowed until it stood still, a grotesque, angular roughly hewn headless statue. It stood still at an obtuse angle, not able to support its weight.

For five seconds.

Then it slowly started to tilt, leaning to its right. The Goatkin saw it falling towards them, and quickly broke ranks, running in all directions.

It collapsed onto the ground.

Tomoko shoulders slumped; she shook her head to get her wits; Sophie could see the energy sapped out of her face. But seeing the crumbling stone figure, defeated, gave Sophie a last boost of energy. The feeling of a final triumph, satisfaction, and joy at seeing Tomoko do so well. She fought off the fatigue and raised her head and crossed her arms. Defiant.

Sophie scanned around her. The Fae behind her were smiling. The Cervitaurs from both sides looked on silently, still in shock at what they had seen.

The Goatkin however, were more fearful, and as a body, were starting to waiver, inching back from the stone golem, and from Sophie and Tomoko.

Adeline now appeared weak. She was a stronger, more practiced mage, than both Tomoko and Sophia. But evidently had been casting spells for longer before they got there. She was now exhausted. Sophie had no idea if she was going to continue the combat. Sophie put her hands in front of her but knew she wouldn't even have the energy to be able to even draw a symbol.

Adeline's parents came out of the line, still looking defiant, with a large Goatkin, it's great bulk and height rose a metre above the rest. It carried a great double headed axe, like the minotaur's on its shoulders.

The creature was clearly the largest of any of Adeline's little army,   except   for   the   golems. It strode, taking large steps with its big gait towards Sophie, and hissed at her, saliva dripping off its furry, wet muzzle. A long disgusting bedraggled beard hung off its chin, matted and wet with drool. Its twisted horns were majestic but added a demonic touch to its appearance. It growled at both Tomoko and Sophie.

Suddenly a black figure came out from the shield wall and appeared in front of them, slightly pushing Sophie out of the way. It was Raffaella. She stood in her practiced stance, with her longsword on her shoulder, very much between the goat creature and Sophie, protecting her.

"I have done little with this sword today. I very much desire to use it."

The Goatkin, substantially both wider and taller than Raffaella, looked at her, it's head askew, like it was trying to work out what she said, or if it should be concerned.

It sneered, opening its mouth, its long tongue hanging out over its wet muzzle. It circled around Raffaella, with its axe above its head. Raffaella circled around it, matching its steps, but kept herself between it and Sophie. It suddenly stepped forward, the huge goat creature feigned a low blow, sweeping along the ground with its axe, aiming at Raffaella's leg. As Raffaella went to block low, it changed its blow direction, bringing the axe back over its own head and then attacking her from the other side.

Raffaella called out, "Hah."

Sophie held her breath. Raffaella quickly brought her sword up and blocked the blow. The goat creature, angry that the trick blow hadn't worked, threw a flurry of furious blows, screaming all the time as it did.

Raffaella caught them all and then started her own flurry of blows back, faster, moving from side to side, and stepping with them, throwing them all around.

The goat creature blocked the blows with the hilt of his axe, and Sophie saw chunks of wood and rope come off the axe handle as Raffaella's sword chopped at it.

The large goatkin brayed loudly, a demonic beastly sound, then pushed Raffaella's sword back with its axe. It then deliberately stepped back from her, its long legs easily allowing it to step back to disengage. To Sophie, it looked like it was reconsidering fighting with Raffaella.

It then backed away, facing Raffaella, and keeping a tight grip on its axe. It kept its eyes on her the whole time, as Raffaella kept her eyes on it. It eventually turned and went back into the body of Goatkin.

Sophie realised she had been holding her breath all the time and exhaled.

As the Goatkin pulled back, Sophie could see Adeline standing there amongst them, facing her. Sophie was shocked at how she looked.

Fatigued, no, actually sick.

Clearly, she had probably cast *too* much magic, beyond what her body could take. It had taken its toll.

At that point, dramatically, Adeline's small body flopped to the ground.

Adeline's mother, Birgit, was standing next to her, and Sophie expected her to immediately drop to Adeline and help her.

But instead, strangely, Birgit held her head, like she was recovering. She shook her head, her fingers, running through her hair wildly for a few seconds, then appeared like she was coming out of a daze.

She spun around, as if to get her bearings. From the expression on her face, it was like she was seeing what was around, for the first time. Sophie looked on, partially in shock at this.

Then she saw Adeline's father.

She lunged at him, screaming. He was momentarily surprised, but he grabbed a knife from one of the Goatkin to defend himself. The Goatkin around them stepped back in confusion.

There was a struggle, and Sophie's mother had her hands around his neck. She screamed and fell to the ground.

There was a gasp from Tomoko next to her.

"He's killed her," Harlan said, the shock evident in his voice.

Sophie screamed, "Tomoko, someone, Shoot him!"

A Fae sprang forward, nocking an arrow, but too late. As they watched Adeline's father, he grinned, and with a quick hand motion, waved over his chest, and a blue blur, he changed his human form into a Cervitaur. Amid the press and moving crowd, he disappeared, now one of many Cervitaurs mixed with Goatkin, a mass of horns, fur and weapons, moving back to the tunnel.

The Goatkin picked up Adeline, who was now starting to murmur and wake up. The Goatkin formed up into rough lines, and quietly, with some talking, started shuffling back that way as well.

They slowly meandered off in a mob, the occasional bleating sound, the occasional curse.

The only thing remaining was Birgit's body. It lay on the ground, motionless. Four Fae strode forward, put it on a stretcher and took it away. She had been their enemy, but Sophie could only feel sad looking at her.

Sophie watched silently, slightly stunned. It was an unexpected end.

Most of Adeline's Cervitaurs, however, did not leave. They stayed talking to the Japanese Cervitaurs. Sophie noticed one of them smile, as they talked. The Cervitaurs were now friendly.

Sophie realized the enemy had largely left the field.

It was over.

Sophie's shoulders slumped and she flopped to the ground. Her three friends gathered around her. Harlan clapped her on the shoulder, rubbing her back, and she weakly smiled. He then gave both Tomoko and Raffaella a big hug. Tomoko was, as always, awkward in the grip of Harlan's big hug, she smiled anyway.

Harlan shook his head. "I didn't expect that to happen. I'm not quite sure..."

"I guess that man, the father was Mabuse, if he is somehow still alive. Or someone who knows Mabuse's techniques and methods. Someone controlling them." Sophie said.

"The mother. Somehow under hypnotism?" Tomoko asked.

"I think. Maybe..." Sophie paused, thinking. "Maybe... he controlled Adeline and used her magic for how he wanted. Including controlling Adeline's mother." Sophie said.

"What? Yeah, well, like controlling a puppet. Except the puppet can cast powerful spells." Harlan grimaced.

Sophie shivered; the whole thing was creepy. She realised having spells was powerful knowledge, but it attracted people that wanted that power. She thought that the same could have happened to her, or Tomoko.

Tomoko stood up as some Cervitaurs walked past. "Wait, I have to introduce you to someone." She quickly waved, and called out to one of the Cervitaurs, who came over. It was the Cervitaur with the helmet.

He removed the helmet, and Sophie realized it was Redbeard.

"Oh, well done!" Sophie called out, realizing what was going on.

"Thank you. It looks like we ended up working well together anyway."

"I instigated the groups coming together from inside the Cervitaurs, while Tomoko and Akshay worked from the other side, we snuck a few of our Bavarian Cervitaurs into the crowd to help." Sophie looked around, and Redbeard pointed. She hadn't previously seen Akshay amongst the crowd, but now spotted him. He was waving his hands around, diplomatically, completely in the thick of negotiations, and looked like he was enjoying it.

"Dang... good job Redbeard. You and Tomoko and Akshay saved a lot of lives here," Harlan said.

"Thank you...er, my name is actually John," Redbeard said.

Sophie grabbed Tomoko by the arm. "Tomoko, you ran off, and I was pretty disappointed, but then you returned, and it was probably what saved us. Thank you." Sophie noticed the people around them had stopped talking and were looking at them both.

"It wasn't just me, the four of us, as a team, and the Fae," Tomoko said. Sophie could see she was getting a little emotional, her voice was breaking. Tomoko had always been the least confident, so her throwing herself into the battle like she did had been nothing short of incredible.

"How did you get them to come from Japan?" Sophie asked.

"I had a hunch they were Cervitaurs, from some of the decorations in the Izakaya, but they clearly wouldn't admit it to outsiders. I went there and showed them." She pulled out her phone. "This." Tomoko pulled out her phone and played a little video clip she had taken of Adeline's Cervitaurs, just before they entered the gateway. "Sometimes words just aren't enough. I told them the rising was happening right now and we needed help. When they saw the video, they all just grabbed whatever they could use for weapons and came to help."

As they continued talking, Sophie looked over the field, and considered how lucky they had been. They had arrived and stopped a huge battle, which would have cost countless lives, and still driven Adeline and her army from the field and saved the home of the Fae. It was the most amazing thing she had ever seen in her life.

Chapter 42 - The first Saturday after a battle

It was Saturday.

Since the battle, there had been some conversations with the Fae, who were very grateful, and appeared to be taking a liking to their newly found kin, Harlan. They'd gone for coffee with Akshay and Redbeard, (also very grateful), and Sophie had even had a chat with Redbeard and found out he was a great admirer of one her favorite authors, Emily Bronte. Akshay was keen to keep in contact with them, and after a frank discussion, they both regretted their earlier conflict.

In the end, it was a relief that things had come together as they did, particularly Tomoko's timely appearance.

Apart from that, Sophie took the next two days to wind down, there had been so much going on, it was their first chance for a break. It was time to concentrate on homework. But… it was also time to get back to Johannes and focus more seriously on her next level of spells.

It had taken a few hours after the battle, until she fully got the energy back that had been sapped from spell casting. She felt fine.

Sophie picked up her smartphone. After some discussion, and a fair amount of pressure from the others, Sophie had told them she would call Rupert. She wasn't keen to, but officially they were acting for him on behalf of the queen, so it was important.

The phone rang through, and though Sophie knew it was her mother on her phone, she was talking in Rupert's voice, in Rupert's character. Sophie could hear other people around in the background, so her mother probably couldn't have changed. If she wanted to.

"Sophie old girl. Nice of you to call. You know, you could have reported in more often."

"Well, Mama, if you'd called me more often…"

"Soph, please can we move on about this, and talk about it, old girl?"

Sophie ignored the comment and adopted a serious voice. "We stopped the rising. Split the Cervitaurs from Adeline. Last we heard, Adeline was unconscious, a few Cervitaurs were loyal. The Goatkin still support her, but most of the Cervitaurs are with Akshay."

"Yes, I'd heard a smidgeon of what has happened, not all. Jolly good work old girl. I'll be sending a bonus payment through to Harlan, into the account. Anyway, a wee bit of news for you. Adeline's father is in hospital, I think there may be some hope for him."

"Hospital?

"Yes, blond man, you rescued him from the Unter Kathedrale."

"Oh." Sophie realised what had happened. She went silent. Lars, the man they had assumed was Adeline's father all along was someone else. And he had control of Adeline. He must have been something to do with Mabuse.

"We thought, another man with her was her father. Mom, do you know about some person called Mabuse?"

"Yes, old girl, I've had to look up about him. He's a mystery. Someone may have got hold of his manifesto. Bad show old girl. Please be careful," Rupert said. It sounded like he was thinking about something, as he said it. He said *careful* slowly for emphasis.

"You'll need to keep an eye out for this Doctor Mabuse fellow. Stay safe and call me more often. Will you?"

"Maybe, Mama. Maybe."

***

Ernst was around, puttering about. Sophie still wasn't happy with either of her parents. He had been trying to make overtures to her, but overwhelmingly, she had noticed that he wasn't happy. It was obvious to both that the house had been different since he had lost his temper. It just wasn't as happy a place as before.

Ernst looked at his watch. "Sophie, it's just coming up to four p.m. I want to talk to you."

"Why?" Sophie said, hearing a touch of anger in her own voice.

"Please just sit down."

"Is this about magic?" She checked his face for a sign of what was coming. He didn't look like he was going to get angry. She'd told her father nothing about what had happened, and she was pretty sure he wouldn't find out otherwise.

"Please..." He motioned to the chair. She sat down. He brought out some nice strudel, and a cappuccino he had made for her.

"Sophie, I want to talk to you about something. Sort of serious."

"Papa. I'm still angry with you about Hisako."

At that point there was a knock on the door. Ernst checked his watch. "Ah four p.m. Well, that's what I wanted to talk to you about. Come in!"

The door opened. It was Hisako. Sophie glanced over at her and Ernst.

Hisako strode in and plonked down next to Ernst. "Sophie! So good to see you."

"Oh, Papa! Hisako is coming back to work for us?"

Ernst shook his head, looking serious.

"No, she's not."

Sophie studied them both. They looked peculiar. Then she noticed Hisako's hand on Ernst's knee.

Ernst grinned. "Hisako is coming back to *live* with us. We're going out."

"What? How did you keep this secret from me?" Sophie sat back in her chair. Gobsmacked.

Ernst put his hand on Hisako's shoulder.

"Well, you've hardly been here much lately. I know I made a mess of it. But it was... well... the time Hisako was away from the house made me realise she was so important to me. I knew when she was out of our lives, how much I needed her. I split up with Annika, and well, caught up with Hisako recently...and we had a chat." Ernst beamed, staring at Hisako's face. Hisako's face was illuminated with happiness.

"I'm very fond of Ernst, Sophie... but we both want to know how you feel?"

Hisako's eyes met Sophie's earnestly. It was almost like they were asking her for her approval! Sophie felt tears well up in her eyes.

"I'm very happy for you both, and I think you both belong together!" She had to rub her eyes with her sleeve and felt embarrassed. She realised, for years, she had wanted them to be together. Now they finally were. The emotions started bubbling up inside her and she felt the urge to fight back tears. Ernst quickly rushed off to get some tissues from the kitchen.

"I'm really happy." Hisako whispered.

Ernst came back and plopped the box of tissues down on the table, Sophie took one and dabbed her eyes with it.

"Sophie, about magic. Hisako and I have spent a lot of time talking about it. I know it is no longer illegal here, I want you to be careful, but I'm not going to stop you if you are interested in it. I know I reacted strongly about it. There's a reason why. I will tell you why one day."

Sophie already had an inkling about why, but she decided not to raise it, the vibe was very happy, and she wasn't going to spoil the moment.

"Thanks, Papa. Hey, I'm sorry to spoil the moment, but the guys are coming over, is that okay?" Sophie asked permission, after it had been arranged.

Ernst nodded. "Sure."

"I think Harlan and the others will be happy to hear the news." Sophie nodded and picked up her cappuccino.

About an hour later, Tomoko, Raffaella and Harlan showed up at the door.

The four sat around the lounge at Sophie's house. Ernst put some drinks on the low table in front of them, and then puttered about in the background laughing with Hisako. The sound of Hisako's laughter sent a happy feeling through Sophie's body.

"Yeah, I am so relieved. It's over and we can chill," Harlan said.

"Yeah...except, I don't have a real excuse for not doing my Trigonometry homework anymore." Sophie grimaced as she thought of the major schoolwork that had built up lately. It would all need to be caught up.

"I'll have more time for scooters, I have two jobs I need to do for clients. I love the Vespa, but you know, this was very exciting..." Raffaella paused. "Magic, giant golems, defeating an invasion by giant deer men."

"Well technically, they are Stag men," Tomoko said.

"Cervitaurs. So, what do we do about Adeline?" Sophie said, raising an eyebrow.

"Well, according to Akshay, most of the Cervitaurs have joined his community and deserted her. He said she quickly fled the Fae's land after the battle," Tomoko said. "She has left her base and left Bamberg. Let's leave her be?"

"She still has those goat people as allies. From the Netherworld. She has that huge Minotaur with her."

"Is it still alive?" Raffaella asked.

"Yeah, I think so. The Fae said its body was gone from the battlefield," Harlan said.

"Adeline will reappear. With more demons. She is unbridled chaos, the demonic puppet child Queen of the dark," Raffaella said, in a particularly morbid tone.

"Raffy. *Demonic puppet child queen of the dark.* Always with the melodrama." Harlan rolled his eyes.

She stared at him. "Don't call me that."

Sophie ignored them. "If she reappears, we will deal with her. We'll improve our spells. We have two mages...and Circle 66 is just going to get better and better."

There was a knock on the door.

"Package delivery for Papa, I think."

Ernst went to the door, spoke to the delivery person, then came over and dumped a box on Sophie's lap, and ruffled up her hair.

"It is for you, *mein schatzi.*"

Sophie half grinned at him. He was in a good mood. She examined the box, slightly alarmed.

"Are you expecting something?" Harlan said.

Sophie tried to remember if she had ordered something. "Hmm... not that I can remember."

"Could be... something dangerous?" Tomoko eyed it off, suspiciously.

Sophie Turned the box around. "It's from Japan. I don't know anyone from Japan. well...apart from Tomoko's Cervitaurs."

"Did you order some Manga?" Raffaella asked.

"No," Sophie said, shaking it gently.

"Maybe it's a bomb," Rafaella said.

Sophie affixed Raffaella with an odd glance, grabbed the box and ripped it open. Tomoko yelped and Harlan shifted back from it, clearly concerned. In it were two dreamcast headsets.

"Dreamcast headsets." A broad smile appeared on her face. "I...er... wow." She picked up the card and read it aloud.

"To Sophie. All I can say is...thank you. P.S. Please make sure the other goes to Raffaella. Marcus."

Sophie turned the headsets around in her hand, examining them. They had little tags tied to them with wire. One said *Sophie. Starlight 1972.* She read the second one. "Raffaella... Jorge, The Hatmaker 1481. Oh!" Sophie glanced at Raffaella. "This is yours."

Raffaella took it, staring at it curiously for a minute or two. "Hatmaker?" she said simply.

It dawned on Sophie that the headset was a whole new talented ancestor to learn from, and deal with. But 1972? Part of her wanted to try it straight away, but she put aside the compulsion and put it down. She needed a break. Her body, her brain, her schoolwork needed a break. She needed a normal life for a while.

"Let's celebrate. I need to introduce you to something very important to me, and it's the perfect celebration thing. Japanese Ramen."

"There's no Japanese Restaurants in Bamberg." Harlan raised an eyebrow.

Tomoko grinned. "I said *Japanese* Ramen."

"Okay, I'll get my keys and helmet," Sophie said, smiling broadly.

***

Once they were out of the house, Sophie explained what Rupert had said about Adeline's father being the man they rescued from the Unter Kathedrale. There was a flurry of questions, only some of which Sophie could answer. Harlan, however, was happy they would be receiving a payment from Rupert for the completion of their work.

The blue haze shimmered around them as the gate carried them from the obelisk in Germany, to the obelisk in Japan. Sophie watched as the blur disappeared, and she could see around her. The four scooters were packed into a tight space. The obelisk translocation spell had a limited area it could transport, but she was sure it was bigger than the space their four scooters took up, squashed together so they were touching each other.

Sophie sat on top of a brand-new small scooter, blue, with a big exhaust sticking out, and glyphs of protection painted all over it. It was good to finally have her own.

Harlan glanced at them all. "Everyone got their passports?" They all nodded.

"International drivers' license," Sophie said, smiling. They all nodded.

"Okay!" Sophie took off from the Japanese stone circle, towards the road, and the others followed.

Chapter 43 - Talented Ancestors in Nihon

Marcus waited patiently at the street crossing for the walk sign to change, even though there was not a single car in sight. This was the custom in Japan; it was one of a few unusual Japanese customs he had gotten used to over his stay. There were a lot of other customs he still couldn't get used to, like not being able to walk and eat on the footpath.

He walked up to a Japanese lady standing outside a restaurant.

"Well, hello, my dear."

"Hello, Marcus... what's kept you?"

"You know... distractions." Marcus peered into the window of the restaurant. He had to peek between some signs stuck on the window, signs advertising the opening hours and some menus in (mostly correct) English and Japanese. It was hard to see who was in the restaurant, but mercifully, it had high booths they could hide behind.

"Always *the distractions*, Marcus san." Her face indicated disapproval for five seconds, but she then chuckled. "Okay, you will need these, if you want to be unrecognised."

She handed him a Japanese team baseball cap, and some sunglasses. He quickly put them on. He checked himself in the reflection in the glass window. The combination was preposterous, but it would hide him and wasn't bizarre enough that it would attract too much attention.

"Where are they? Are they in there already?" he asked as he put on the glasses, then fitted the hat over the top.

"Yes." They've been there for a while.

"And our friend?"

"He said he would meet us inside."

"Ahh…I see. All good then. Shall we go inside, Mein Frau?" He motioned for her to go through the doorway. He always felt charming when he called her that. She patted him on the shoulder.

They went into the restaurant and sat down. As they were sitting down, another man came in, with long hair and sunglasses. He came over to the seat where they were. Marcus nodded and gave him a grin.

"Oh, hello, Ken. Here, we saved you a seat."

The man greeted Marcus and his wife, sat down, taking his jacket off. He half smiled.

He appears serious today Marcus thought. Marcus noticed him playing with the ring on his finger but tried not to stare at it. One of the rarest and most valuable magic relics in the world, Marcus felt a pang of jealousy. But Ken needed it; the ring was keeping him alive. Keeping him young.

"Before you ask, here." Marcus pulled out his phone, flicked through some pictures, and then held it back at an angle so the three could all see the picture on the phone. "He's in England. Paramita, the child of Sun Wukong. He refers to himself as John Smith."

"John Smith?" Ken smiled, and Marcus felt relieved. Ken was tense, but now appeared relaxed to hear the news. "England. Well, it is better he is there than here. They can manage the trouble he creates."

"That's not why I got you to come here in a rush though. She is here," Marcus said.

"Omoshiroi… so…she is here?" Ken asked.

"Sitting over there. Tomoko. With the others. Three Gaijin," Marcus said.

Ken peeked over. "*She* is my descendant?"

"Yes. Kentaro san, will you go and talk with her?" Yoko said.

"Yes, I will, but not today. Today we just watch."

Marcus nodded. He realized the situation was probably strange for Kentaro. There was a familiar sound playing in the background, but it was out of place in Japan. Initially confused, his face lit up, beaming with recognition.

"Is that AC/DC? I love these guys!"

The End

www.ingramcontent.com/pod-product-compliance
Lightning Source LLC
Chambersburg PA
CBHW051938220626
47052CB00004B/699